2

"I'm Ramsey Sage. Tell me what I need to do."

♥ ♥ ♥

*H*e wore extremely faded blue jeans, slashed at both knees, and an equally faded denim work shirt whose sleeves appeared to have been ripped completely from their seams—she hated to think how. A tattoo of black barbed wire completely encircled one arm over—okay, admittedly very nice—biceps. With a hasty glance beyond him, she saw a motorcycle parked at the curb that was as disreputable-looking as he was.

"So I gathered," she replied as she automatically accepted his hand and shook it.

He had a sturdy, confident grip, his large fingers swallowing hers. She glanced down at their joined hands, and when she saw her perfectly pink polished nails folded over his dark knuckles abraded with wounds, a thrill of something sharp and frenetic shot through her. For some reason, seeing the contrast between their hands made Claire curious about the other differences between his body and hers.

"Won't you come in?" she invited. "We can all chat."

Books by
Elizabeth Bevarly

THE THING ABOUT MEN
THE RING ON HER FINGER
TAKE ME, I'M YOURS
HE COULD BE THE ONE
HOW TO TRAP A TYCOON
HER MAN FRIDAY
MY MAN PENDLETON

ELIZABETH BEVARLY

The Thing About MEN

AVON BOOKS
An Imprint of HarperCollins*Publishers*

This is a work of fiction. Names, characters, places, and incidents are products of the author's imagination or are used fictitiously and are not to be construed as real. Any resemblance to actual events, locales, organizations, or persons, living or dead, is entirely coincidental.

AVON BOOKS
An Imprint of HarperCollins*Publishers*
10 East 53rd Street
New York, New York 10022-5299

Copyright © 2004 by Elizabeth Bevarly
The Thing About Men copyright © 2004 by Elizabeth Bevarly; *Daisy's Back in Town* copyright © 2004 by Rachel Gibson; *A Wild Pursuit* copyright © 2004 by Eloisa James; *Your Wicked Ways* copyright © 2004 by Eloisa James
ISBN: 0-06-050946-5
www.avonromance.com

First Avon Books paperback printing: January 2004

Avon Trademark Reg. U.S. Pat. Off. and in Other Countries, Marca Registrada, Hecho en U.S.A.
HarperCollins® is a registered trademark of HarperCollins Publishers Inc.

Printed in the U.S.A.

10 9 8 7 6 5 4 3 2 1

Growing up, I was incredibly fortunate to have, almost literally, two moms: my mother, who was kind enough to give birth to me, and her twin sister, who shared the same DNA, thereby making her a more than reasonable facsimile of my mom. Better still, my aunt was kind enough to marry and produce four offspring of her own, thereby providing me with what felt very much like a second father and four extra siblings in addition to my two brothers. Best of all, she had the decency to make one of these offspring a girl, thereby giving me the equivalent of a sister, which I wouldn't have had otherwise.

So this book, which deals with second families, is dedicated to my second family, the Stuckers: Aunt Dot, Uncle Washie, Hal, Michael, Scott, and Lisa. Though you may be far-flung, you're never far away. (And Michael, Lisa, and I forgive you for the Barbie/bottle rocket/clothesline incident, even though Barbie was scarred for life after that.)

I love you guys.

Acknowledgments

A few thanks. First and foremost to everyone at Avon Books, for having so much patience with and enthusiasm for me. It is truly appreciated. Thanks also to the friends who keep me on solid ground (you know who you are, and so does anyone else who's ever read my acknowledgments pages). Thanks to Terri and Mike Medeiros and Jean Willett, for some very quick info. Thanks to David Cook and Carol Conaway, for more than I can ever repay you for. Thanks to Cherry Poppin' Daddies, whose album *Zoot Suit Riot* gave me just the right musical push to get this book moving and keep it on track. And thanks to Steve Earle, who makes music that gets me through the day (and through life, quite frankly).

Most of all, as always, thanks to David and Eli, for patience and enthusiasm of a different sort. I can't imagine what kind of lunatic I'd be without you guys. (Oh, wait—I just did. And it was a horrifying picture.) Thanks to you both for so many things. I love you.

One

"*W*hat do you mean the chicken is still alive?"

Claire Willoughby gaped at her producer in stark-staring terror, her mind racing with all the ramifications the live chicken brought with it. And there were plenty. "It can't still be alive," she said. "I have to cook it on camera in thirty minutes. How's it going to go from cage to frying pan, unless we . . ."

The rest of that statement didn't even bear thinking about, let alone speaking aloud. Especially not by a woman wearing beige Ann Taylor separates and ivory Bandolino pumps.

"Sorry, Claire, but there must have been a mix-up in the directions," her producer, Nina Ritchie, replied without a hint of apology as she lit a new cigarette with the still-burning butt of her last one.

The set for the show was supposed to be smoke-free, but the first time Claire had reminded Nina of that, Nina had set fire to a trash can in the women's room in what she *swore* was an accident that occurred while she was trying to put out the offending cigarette. So Claire didn't mention her producer's cigarette now. She didn't want to put the good people of the Nashville Fire Department through all that trouble again.

"For some reason," the tall, too-slim redhead continued, "they delivered a live chicken instead of a broiler/fryer." She stubbed out the butt on her clipboard, one marked by a variety of small black burn spots, and flicked it away heedlessly—beaning her production assistant in the side of the head in the process.

Then she inhaled deeply on the new cigarette, until its tip glowed bright orange. Everything about Nina was orangey today, Claire noted, from her hair to her Nehru jacket and sultan's trousers, to her amber beads and earrings, to her copper sandals. "And we're nowhere near a grocery store," she added, "so we don't have time to send someone out for another one. We either have to kill the chicken or kill the segment."

Oh, easy for her to say, Claire thought. Nina's last job had been as an assistant producer for one of those trash-talk day-time TV shows where things like Satanism and alien paternity and family fistfights had been daily staples. A chicken execution would be nothing to her.

Claire tucked a stray strand of pale blond hair back into the otherwise flawless chignon fixed at her nape as she pondered her dilemma. Aunt Halouise's "Red, White, and True Fried Chicken" was the centerpiece of their "Fourth of July Picnic Cookout" feature, and the "Fourth of July Picnic Cookout" feature was the centerpiece of today's show. And the irony was that the theme of Claire's nationally syndicated—and live—TV show, *Simple Pleasures*, like the theme of Claire's nationally distributed magazine, also called *Simple Pleasures*, was "Back to Basics." That was, in fact, pretty much the mission statement of her entire lifestyle business—to promote a return to the simpler ways of simpler times. Ways and times that had included, for example, raising livestock for the purpose of holiday cuisine.

Not that Claire thought the entire country should return to farming and animal husbandry as a way of life. But everyone at Simple Pleasures, Inc. *was* a big proponent of self-sustenance. They had to be if they wanted to remain employed. Still, Claire herself had always preferred to focus more on the gardening and sewing and baking sort of self-sustenance than she had the butchering-of-small-animals sort of self-sustenance. After all, there were some simple practices that weren't especially pleasurable. And those were the ones best glossed over and not featured on national daytime television. Especially during the summer, when children were out of school and very likely to be plastered to the family TV.

"No, wait, this could work," Ginny Lymon, Nina's recently beaned assistant, chimed in as she rubbed the side of her forehead. Claire wondered if she should tell the young woman that she'd missed a smudge of cigarette ash near her eye. Then again, Ginny wore so much liner and such dark shadow that an extra smudge of ash was negligible. And considering the fact that she dyed her hair jet-black, wore jet-black nail polish and lipstick, and dressed from head to toe in—surprise!—jet black, she'd probably welcome the added darkness. "If we cut the banjo bit," Ginny went on, "and push Dorcas Marcum's peony piece back 'til Monday, we could expand the chicken segment."

Claire eyed the production assistant with horror, worried that she and Ginny were on the same wavelength. Very cautiously, she asked, "And by 'expanding the chicken segment,' you would mean . . . ?"

Ginny shrugged. "We could kill and pluck it as part of the show."

Claire closed her eyes and willed herself not to pass out. Yep. She and Ginny were on the same wavelength, all right. But not one of those wavelengths that lapped lovingly at a tranquil beach in a soft, reaffirming way. No, this particular wavelength was more of a raging tsunami that threatened to wipe out all of Osaka.

"And after we've dealt with the thousands of letters and e-mails we receive from the ASPCA, PETA, and our animal-loving viewers," Claire said, "we can pack up the set, because the network will have canceled *Simple Pleasures*. Of course, that will be nothing compared to the angry, torch-bearing mob waiting for us outside the studio, something that will necessitate our running for our lives under cover of darkness."

"Oh, hell, Claire," Ginny said indignantly, her Southern twang more pronounced than usual, because of her irritation, "people who eat chicken know they're eatin' a dead animal. We'll just be showin' 'em how it got that way."

"Oh no, people don't know that," Claire countered vehemently. "All they know is that it's something edible, and quite possibly already marinated, and conveniently wrapped in plastic. People have a wonderful denial mechanism when it comes to the consumption of food. I mean, I know our mantra here at *Simple Pleasures* is 'Back to Basics,'" she added, "but, Ginny, when it comes to eviscerating small animals and cutting them up into little pieces, I don't think the average consumer wants to get any more *basic* than the meat case at Winn-Dixie."

"But—"

"Besides," Claire interjected, "who would kill and clean

the chicken on-air? Assuming we could get away with it, I mean, which I sincerely doubt we can, because I'm reasonably certain that the FCC has a rule against the slaughter of innocent animals on television, even if they are going to be lunch. *I'm* certainly not going to be the one to do it."

"I'd do it," Ginny said matter-of-factly. "I did it all the time back in Alabama. We did raise chickens on our farm, you know. For eatin'," she said pointedly.

And why did she make it sound as if she were going to follow up her chicken manifesto with a rousing rendition of "The Circle of Life"? Claire wondered. Not that she had any objection to the ingestion of meat. Au contraire. She was extremely fond of chicken Kiev in particular. But she was like the majority of the rest of the world in not wanting to actually *see* the chicken until it was fully Kieved. Because the only good chicken, as far as she was concerned, was a breaded one.

"We *cannot* kill a chicken on television," she said emphatically. Both Ginny and Nina opened their mouths to object, but Claire cut them off with a very decisive, "Nuh-uh. We'll just . . . We'll just . . . Hmmm . . ."

She tapped her foot anxiously as she thought for a moment. And after a moment, inspiration struck. "We'll expand the banjo and peony segments a few minutes each," she said. "Hey, everybody likes banjo music, right?"

"We-ell," Nina said, "I don't know about *that* . . ."

"Fine," Claire conceded. "*Most* people like banjo—" She halted when Nina rolled her eyes heavenward. "*Lots* of people like ban—" But again, she stopped when Nina began to rock lightly back and forth on her heels. "*Some* people like banjo music," she finally finished defiantly, "and it's as American as the Fourth of July, so it will fit in just fine with the rest of the show. And Dorcas can do both her red and white peonies," Claire continued, knowing their flower expert would be so thrilled, "and maybe she can throw in something blue, too."

"We still need something for the picnic cookout," Ginny reminded her. "And there's nothing more American than fried chicken." She sounded as if she were actually disappointed about not being able to wring a chicken's neck on live TV.

Scary, Claire thought.

Then, "Cheeseburgers are American," she said in a fit of inspiration. "They were invented here in the South, too, in Kentucky. It'll be perfect."

"Except that we don't have any ground beef," Nina pointed out. "And no time to send someone out to buy any. And we don't have a cow, either," she added with even more disappointment, as if she wouldn't mind seeing that butchered and ground up on live TV, too, because the slaughter of something warm and fuzzy with big brown eyes and long, long lashes would *really* spike the ratings.

"But Dorcas has some of those veggie burgers in the freezer in her dressing room," Claire countered, remembering the vegetarian practices of their flower expert, even though Claire always wondered how plant lovers could justify being vegetarians when it seemed that they would, by definition, be eating their best friends.

"*Veggie* burgers?" Ginny fairly spat. "Oh, now *that's* un-American."

"Well, we won't have to *tell* anyone they're veggie burgers," Claire said. "They *look* like ground beef. We'll just skip the prep that we would have done for the chicken and throw some spices onto the veggie burgers. Add a little ketchup and mayo after they're cooked, and nobody will know the difference. Look, where's Olive? She'll know what to do."

As if conjured by the question, Olive Tully, Claire's assistant and best friend in the whole, wide world, appeared at her side. Although with her short, brown hair, and whiskey-colored eyes framed by tiny, tortoiseshell glasses, and dressed in a brown linen jumper and sandals, she looked more like a pecan than an olive. Claire had known her since they had been thrown together as roommates at Vanderbilt thirteen years before and couldn't imagine how she would get along without her.

Back then, Claire had been embarking on a major in English, and Olive had been embarking on a major in self-discovery—meaning she had yet to declare a major and was only going to college because her mother had insisted, even though what she had really wanted was to marry and start a family right away, something that had been hindered by the fact that Olive had never been on a date in her entire life. But the two friends had clicked immediately, because Claire loved old things and Olive was old-fashioned.

Simple Pleasures, Inc. wouldn't, couldn't, exist without both women, but, really, Olive was the true driving force behind the company. It had been her idea originally, and she was the one who was knowledgeable about lifestyle trends and simple practices and all the things that made family life so familial and livable. Never mind that Olive had never had much of a family beyond her invalid—and now deceased—mother. Claire, who'd grown up in a state-sponsored group home, after all, had never had any family, either.

But because Olive Tully wasn't much of a people person—in fact, she was terrified of most people—she had balked, vehemently, at being in the foreground of the business. There were times when Claire suspected she wasn't all that crazy about being in the background of the business, either. Once it became apparent that the idea of Simple Pleasures might potentially become a reality, Olive had insisted that Claire should be the one everybody saw as the face of the business. Even when the business started to become a success, Olive had been adamant in her refusal to publicly accept any credit for it.

In fact, Olive's desire to remain anonymous was so strong that there were very few people even *inside* the company who knew she was, for all intents and purposes, the one really in charge. Even though the two women were equal partners in the business, Olive's name—and her person, for that matter—was omitted from any materials the company made public. Claire's name and likeness even appeared on the books that Olive really wrote, though the copyrights were owned by the company.

Claire had balked at the arrangement at first, thinking Olive's obsession with privacy was a tad extreme, but Olive had insisted. So even though, to the outside world, Claire Willoughby *was* Simple Pleasures, Inc., Claire knew she was actually little more than window dressing for the business. Truth be told, she was so organizationally challenged, she couldn't arrange her own underwear drawer, let alone tell people how to arrange their lives. But if Olive wanted to keep a low profile and content herself being the idea woman, Claire was willing to accommodate her by being the one who executed those ideas for their viewers and readers. Having never had the opportunity to be the center of attention in her own life, Claire certainly wasn't going to shy away from it now.

And the unconventional arrangement had worked very

well, because in barely ten years' time, the two women had built the business up from a too-many-margaritas-after-homecoming idea into a multimillion-dollar corporation that included, in addition to the television show and magazine, a limited chain of boutiques that sold "Simple Pleasures" housewares and linens, and entertainment and gardening supplies. In a few months, they'd be launching a new line of wedding essentials. And they'd just recently begun planning for a line of newborn and nursery accessories, not to mention a line for children. The business was flourishing at a rate they never could have imagined when they were in college.

So the last thing Claire needed now was to be linked with a chicken beheading. Bad lifestyle practices equaled bad press for a lifestyle expert. Even one whose expertise was channeled through her best friend/assistant. And bad press about a bad lifestyle could take down her entire business faster than Ginny Lymon could wring a chicken's neck.

"What's going on?" Olive asked as she joined the group.

Nina enjoyed another long drag on her cigarette, and said with no small amount of petulance, "Claire won't kill a chicken on her show."

Olive's eyes widened behind the frames of her glasses, until they were nearly as big as the frames of her glasses. "Well, I should certainly hope not. We don't need the health department here." She eyed Nina's cigarette meaningfully. "They might trip over the fire department."

Nina shot Olive a nasty glare. "Oh, does my smoking bother you? I'll just go into your office and put it out, why don't I?"

Now Olive narrowed her eyes behind her glasses. But she said nothing further, which surprised Claire not at all. Olive had, of course, been born with a backbone, but she didn't exercise it very often. As a result, she usually didn't get her way. Not that she seemed to mind. Or, if she did, she never showed it.

"Why would you even *suggest* that Claire murder a chicken on her show?" Olive asked the producer.

Quickly, the three women explained what was going on, then Olive nodded and pulled out her own ubiquitous clipboard and began rifling through the pages clipped there.

"It won't be a problem," she said. "We'll do the cheeseburgers, as Claire suggested, but we won't have to expand the peony or banjo segments."

"Oh, thank God," Nina said with much relief.

"I have a standby in the green room, a Betsy Ross reenactor I found out about just yesterday."

"You're kidding," Nina said, shaking her head. "Some woman actually goes around pretending to be Betsy Ross? That's the most pathetic thing I've ever heard. She needs to get a life."

"And I was trying to see if we could find room for her on today's show anyway," Olive continued, pretending the producer hadn't spoken. "This is serendipity."

"That's one word for it," Nina muttered. "Another would be—"

"And if we still have extra time," Olive interjected discreetly—*Yeah, work that backbone, Olive*, Claire thought—"we can add some banter."

"Banter?" Nina asked dubiously.

"Banter," Olive stated more decisively.

Whoa, you go, girlfriend, Claire thought. She wasn't sure what had gotten into her friend today, but Olive was acting like a wild woman.

"And just who is going to provide this banter?" Nina asked. "*Simple Pleasures* is pretty much a one-woman show. You want Claire should talk to herself? Or, wait, I know," she added in an evil voice, "why don't we put *you* on camera, Olive?"

Oh, now that was a low blow, Claire thought. Even though very few people at Simple Pleasures knew Olive was the driving force behind the business, *everybody* knew she suffered from profound stage fright. And, actually, *stage fright* was a pretty tame designation for what Olive had. *Mindnumbing, mouth-frothing terror of public speaking* was a more appropriate term. Claire was reasonably certain that Olive Tully held the world's record for walking-naked-in-public dreams.

And, sure enough, when Claire looked over at Olive, it was to see that her friend had gone pale at the mere suggestion of going on camera. "No," she said, "that won't be necessary. I was thinking Claire could talk American history with Betsy Ross or something."

"That's enough, Nina," Claire told her producer coolly, shouldering the prima donna mantle she only wore for occasions such as this one. "The show airs in less than thirty minutes, and I think we all have better things to do than bicker. Olive has things under control, *as usual*," she said resolutely. "So we can all go back to doing *our* jobs now."

Properly chastened—which meant she was sneering like a rabid Chihuahua—Nina enjoyed another long toke, expelling a stream of white smoke into Ginny's ear. "Twenty-one minutes," she said, correcting Claire's timing. "Better hop to it."

And having had the last word, as she always insisted, the producer spun on her heel and made her way toward her office. And all Claire could do was keep a watchful eye on the other woman's cigarette and hope Nina didn't make any stops along the way.

Surprisingly, the show went off without a hitch. Well, except for that one brief disturbance backstage that had sounded like a chicken squawking in fatal anguish, something that had made Claire flub a line and say, "chicken lynch" instead of "picnic bench." But she managed to recover—sort of—by telling a long-winded story about a local guano business she had recently read about, which, on second thought maybe wasn't such a good recovery after all, since it featured, well, guano. Still, at least it hadn't been a chicken decapitation, which—just a shot in the dark—probably would have been infinitely more offensive to her viewers.

In fact, just to make sure Ginny Lymon didn't execute the chicken out of spite or a desire for chicken salad, Claire brought the chicken and its cage into her dressing room for safekeeping. And she also named it Francesca. She had no idea why. Certainly the chicken didn't *look* like a Francesca. But it didn't look like Ginny Lymon's dinner entree, either. Still, by midafternoon, Claire had no idea what to do with the now homeless fowl.

She spent the rest of the day answering fan mail. *Simple Pleasures* received hundreds, sometimes thousands, of letters and e-mails each month, and the majority of them were answered by someone on Claire's staff. Some of those letters, however, were so charming that they were passed on to Claire for a personal response. There were even a handful of correspondents whom she had almost begun to think of as acquaintances, so frequent and sweet and revealing were their letters.

She smiled now as she read just such a letter from just such a viewer, a woman who always signed her letters, "Love, Eleanor, your #1 fan," along with a little hand-doodled heart. This one was dated nearly two weeks earlier, however, and Claire felt a pang of guilt that she had let Eleanor go so long without a reply. Really, she was going to have to learn to better organize her time. Maybe *she* should hire a lifestyle consultant . . .

Ah, well. Back to the fan mail, which Claire found infinitely more manageable than the mundane chore of life management. Eleanor Sage had begun writing nearly three years earlier, the week *Simple Pleasures* had premiered in only a handful of television markets. At first, the young woman's letters had simply proclaimed her love for the program. But eventually, they had begun to contain snippets of Eleanor's personal life, too. Most recently, those snippets had included anecdotes about the birth and ensuing adventures of Eleanor's daughter, now thirteen months old, whom Eleanor had named Anabel Claire Sage, after her deceased grandmother and her favorite celebrity.

When Claire had read Eleanor's letter about naming her daughter after her, she had been both deeply touched and slightly appalled. Naturally, she was flattered, but the thought that a television personality would hold a higher place in the woman's life than her family or her friends was just a trifle unnerving, even though Claire told herself it wasn't unusual for people to name their children after figures in popular culture. Nevertheless, Eleanor was a cheerful correspondent, and she never overstepped the bounds of propriety. She simply appeared to have adopted Claire's show and magazine, and even Claire herself, as a favorite pastime.

In today's letter, Eleanor had, as she frequently did, enclosed a photo of Anabel, a product of the Sears Portrait Studio that depicted a chubby, blue-eyed little munchkin dressed in a red gingham sunsuit, a matching floppy hat perched atop her pale blond curls. She had two more teeth than she'd had in her last professional photo—Claire had tacked it to the bulletin board over her computer—and was wearing tiny white sandals, because, according to Eleanor's letter, the little girl was now mobile.

"Oh, Claire, there you are," Olive said as she pushed open the door to Claire's dressing room. "I was afraid you'd gone home for the day, and we have a few things to go over for tomorrow's show before you leave."

Which made sense, because the two women lived in different parts of town. Olive's house was a quaint little cottage in Green Hills, even though, at this point, she could afford a sweeping estate home in one of the area's pricier neighborhoods. Claire's house, on the other hand *was* a sweeping estate home in one of the area's pricier neighborhoods, an old mansion in Belmont she had purchased a few years ago for half its value because it had been such a wreck. And also because Olive had thought an ensuing renovation of the place could contribute to a full season *Simple Pleasures*. All of the renovating and decorating ideas had been Olive's, but Claire had been the one to carry out the grunt work on camera. Not live, though, since a lot of that grunt work had consisted of unintentionally wrecking so many of Olive's good ideas, because Claire was lousy at things like renovation. Nevertheless, once the house was finished, Claire had been so delighted by the results—and dammit, she'd worked so hard to achieve them—that she'd decided to buy the place from Simple Pleasures, Inc. and call it home.

"Oh, can't it wait?" she asked now. "I'm exhausted. I just want to go home and take a bath and put on my pajamas and make some microwave popcorn and watch TV."

Olive smiled indulgently. "Wouldn't you rather go home and stencil a border around the perimeter of the kitchen? Or whip up a hearty stew from scratch? Or make soap from fennel?"

"Which, no doubt, is what you have planned for the evening," Claire said.

"Of course," her friend told her. "And if you ever want to adopt the lifestyle doyenne lifestyle yourself . . ."

Yeah, yeah, yeah, Claire thought. Honestly. Sometimes Olive really did take this Simple Pleasures stuff way too seriously. Like their viewers actually believed Claire lived what she preached, anyway. C'mon. Olive way underestimated the entertainment quotient for the show.

Nobody, Claire was sure, really went out after *Simple Pleasures* ended to light fires in their hearths and chop celery for homemade soup and weave trivets out of corn husks. They just liked to think someone else somewhere was doing that, because it seemed so civilized and organized and fantasized. But it would break Olive's heart for Claire to tell her that. Olive thought the twenty-first-century way of life was much too harsh, and she harbored a deep desire to have been born two centuries ago. Before sliced bread. Before moving pictures. Before computer solitaire. Before facials. Go figure.

"You know I'm not suited to those things," Claire said. "You know I don't have the knack for it that you do. *You're* the one who's into simple pleasures, Olive. You like all that old-fashioned stuff."

"Maybe I'm the old-fashioned one," Olive conceded, "but

you're the one who faces the contemporary public, the one everybody associates with *Simple Pleasures*. You really should at least try to live what you teach, Claire. Otherwise, everyone will think you're a big hypocrite."

"I am a big hypocrite," Claire reminded her friend. "*You're* the lifestyle expert. I'm just window dressing. But it's for the good of the business, so it's okay."

And it didn't bother Claire a bit to realize or admit that. Provided, of course, the general public didn't find out about the arrangement and get ticked off for feeling, oh, misled. Olive *was* the lifestyle expert. All Claire did was be charming on camera and in interviews, discussing her friend's ideas. And, you know, misleading the general public by letting them think she was the one who did all the research and came up with all the great ideas.

Details, details. Sheesh.

"You're a lot more than window dressing, and you know it," Olive corrected her. "The show is so popular because of you. The press and our viewers and readers can't get enough of you. We're *both* responsible for the success and achievements of *Simple Pleasures,*" she added emphatically. "And *together*, we're making Claire Willoughby the country's foremost lifestyle expert. But if your viewers and readers find out you don't really live the way you give the impression of living on TV, Claire, it could jeopardize the business. The tabloids would have a field day if they found out."

"Hmpf," Claire said eloquently in response. "I think you're overreacting."

"Hmpf," Olive replied in equally eloquent response. "People can be pretty bad-tempered when the world doesn't work the way they think it's supposed to work. Mark my words."

"Words marked," Claire replied dutifully.

But then she forgot all about them. Part of her, though, knew Olive was—at least partly—right. The more successful Simple Pleasures, Inc. had become, the bigger target Claire had become for the tabloids. So far, she'd avoided having anything much appear in print about her beyond the suggestion that she might, maybe, possibly, perhaps have given birth to Elvis's alien love child, but a call to the tabloid in question from her attorney had led to an immediate retraction. Claire didn't even know Elvis *was* an alien, nor had she spent any time with the man.

Olive must have noticed the photo of Anabel Sage Claire was holding then, because she suddenly cried, "Oh, is that a new picture of Anabel?" and plucked the photo out of Claire's hand. "Isn't she sweet?" she cooed further. "Look at that smile. Boy, I wouldn't mind having one or two of those of my own someday."

"Only one or two?" Claire teased.

Olive had said since college that she wanted to have a whole houseful of kids because she'd come from such a small family. But stage fright and mind-numbing, mouth-frothing terror of public speaking weren't her only fears. Olive Tully was scared to death of a host of things, not the least of which was the opposite sex, something Claire couldn't help thinking was bound to hinder her quest for that houseful of children. But the opposite sex—and its necessity for things like, oh, procreating—was something Claire had learned long ago not to mention around Olive, because it always made her look so sad.

So instead, she said, "What's going on with tomorrow's show that we need to talk about?"

"Oh. It's the goat lady," Olive said as she placed the photo of Anabel on Claire's desk with much care and reverence.

"What's wrong? Can't she make it? Is she feeling *baaaaaaad*?" Claire bleated, unable to stop herself.

"Ha-ha," Olive replied.

"Well, you said she's a goat lady."

"She *raises* goats," Olive replied testily. "And she makes stuff out of goat's milk. Soap, cheese, that sort of thing." She started to pull up a chair, clearly intending to get down to work, but she halted suddenly, and looked at Claire with a frown.

"What?" Claire asked. "What is it?"

Olive expelled a sigh of clear frustration. "I forgot. Chandler is here. He said he needs to talk to you."

Mention of Claire's attorney came as a surprise. Chandler Edison never came to the studio unless it was for what he termed "an urgent matter of utmost importance with potentially massive implications." He could be a bit redundant at times. Although Claire considered Chandler a friend, she always had an inexplicable impulse whenever he was around to suddenly start buttoning something up. Tight. But he *was* an excellent attorney, and he kept Simple Pleasures, Inc. honest. So she could tolerate, for the most part, that buttoning-up business.

Of course, Claire suspected Chandler wanted to make her honest, too. Or, rather, that he wanted to make an honest woman out of her. He'd stopped short of dropping down on one knee and popping the actual question, but he did drop the occasional remark about what a good team they made, then pop the observation about how, thanks to that great teamwork, their golden years together could be truly golden. "Golden," of course, being the operative word, since Chandler was pretty much motivated by dollar signs in just about every area of his life.

Not that Claire thought he was only interested in her for her money since he had scads of that himself. She was certain that Chandler was fond of her. And, really, she did like Chandler, too. She *did*. What woman wouldn't? He was handsome and successful, a member of one of Nashville's oldest and most prominent families. But she'd never felt anything more than a friendly sort of affection for him, and even that usually only came about after she'd consumed a good, dry Manhattan. Preferably during a two-for-one happy hour. At any rate, she'd never experienced for Chandler the kind of feeling a woman should have for a man she thought about marrying, that breathless kind of wanting, that aching sort of yearning, that endless, ferocious passion, that insistent, frenzied, needy demand, that hot, sweaty, wanton arousal that made a woman just want to rip off her clothes and wrap her naked body around a man and feed herself to him whole, that . . . that . . .

Ah, where was she? Oh, yes. At any rate, she'd never experienced that sort of, um, feeling for Chandler that a woman should have for a man with whom she intended to spend the rest of her life. So as often as Chandler might try to bring her around to his way of thinking, marriage-wise, Claire was confident that such an arrangement with him would be little more than, well, an arrangement. And, call her crazy, but when it came to arrangements, she'd much rather be talking in terms of furniture placement than in matters of the heart.

Her affirmations about Chandler were made even stronger when she left her dressing room to find him waiting for her in full attorney mode, even though it was approaching the end of the workday, and any other working stiff would have, by now, relaxed his attire a bit. But not Chandler Edison, oh no. Yes, he was stiff, but only in the nicest sense of the word.

He was dressed in a lightweight, fawn-colored suit only a few shades darker than his dusky blond hair, Italian oxfords that had probably cost him more than most people made in a week's time—they perfectly matched his Italian briefcase that had probably cost him more than most people made in a month's time—and a gold silk tie that complemented his brown eyes in a way that made them much less beady than usual.

"Claire," he said, reaching forward to take her hand in his without her having offered it, his voice oozing its usual charm. She battled the urge to lift her other hand to her jacket and button it. "I knew you'd still be here at work, which is why I didn't call before coming over. I hope you don't mind me taking such a liberty."

Only Chandler would think that coming to her workplace before calling was taking a liberty. Sometimes the man just had too much courtesy in him. Which, Claire supposed, could be another reason why she'd never felt that breathless, aching, ferocious, insistent, sweaty, wanton, ah . . . that feeling a woman should probably have for a man with whom she intended to spend the rest of her life. A woman—at least, a woman like Claire—rather looked forward to a man taking the initiative in some matters. Courtesy was a wonderful thing, naturally, but there were some activities to which courtesy didn't necessarily contribute in a positive manner. Like taking liberties, for example. Particularly those liberties that led to breathless, aching, ferocious, insistent, sweaty, wanton, ah . . . that feeling a woman should probably have for a man with whom she intended to spend the rest of her life.

Not that Claire thought it necessary to get sweaty with a man before consenting to marry him. But a little perspiration never hurt anyone. Especially *that* sort of perspiration. And *that* sort of perspiration was definitely one of life's simple pleasures. Well, maybe that sort of perspiration wasn't so simple, she conceded. But it certainly had been pleasurable when Claire experienced it. At least, she thought it had been pleasurable. It had been a while since she had experienced it, unfortunately, and her memory was a bit hazy on the matter, though she did recall bits and pieces of images that involved naked bodies, and the press of a man's mouth on her skin, and the glide of her fingers over sinuous muscles, and . . . a turkey baster?

Oh, no, wait. That had been last Thanksgiving. And it had been longer ago than last Thanksgiving that she'd experienced the perspiration thing. A quick tally told her just how long, and she suddenly realized why she was suddenly so preoccupied with breathless, aching, ferocious, insistent, sweaty, wanton, ah . . . that feeling a woman should probably have for a man with whom she intended to spend the rest of her life.

"Hello, Chandler," she said, pushing the thought away— which wasn't hard to do since, when she withdrew her hand from his, she had to fight the urge to wipe it on her skirt . . . and then button up her jacket for good measure. Honestly, for such an attractive man, Chandler sure did have some clammy hands. "What brings you out this way?"

He didn't reply at first, only studied Claire with much consideration, as if he wasn't quite sure how to answer such an easy question. Finally, though, he told her, "It's a legal matter."

Somehow, Claire refrained from replying with the observation, "Duh." That would have been in no way appropriate for someone whose name appeared on the cover of a book about good manners, even if she wasn't the one who'd written it. "I see," she said instead. "What kind of legal matter?"

"Can we go into your office?" he asked, sidestepping her question for now. "It's something of a, um . . . an unusual development."

Claire narrowed her eyes at him. Something was wrong. It wasn't like Chandler to dodge a matter, especially a legal matter, even it if was an um-unusual development. It was also unusual for him to say "Um." He was one of the most straightforward people Claire knew. Well, except for the marriage proposal thing. And now this thing—whatever it was.

"What kind of unusual development?" she asked.

"Let's go into your office," he said again, evading her once more. He took a step forward and curled the fingers of his free hand lightly around her upper arm, then gently steered her toward her office door. Vaguely, Claire noted that Chandler was, for once, taking the initiative in some matter, but she didn't much like him doing it. So, as benignly as she could, she stepped to the side, freeing her arm from his grip, halting before entering her office.

"Chandler, what is going on?" she demanded.

"I'll tell you inside," he said, striding into her office without her, thereby taking the initiative in some matter for a second time. And, for a second time, Claire didn't like it. He halted, however, when he saw Olive. "Oh," he said blandly. "Olive. Hello."

Olive must have sensed by Chandler's demeanor that he needed to speak to Claire alone, because she stood and gazed at the clock on Claire's desk. "Gosh, is that the time?" she asked. "I had no idea." She gathered up her clipboard and strode toward the door. "I really have to go," she said as she passed Claire. "I'll call you at home tonight, Claire. We can talk about tomorrow's show then."

Olive closed the office door behind herself, and Chandler moved to take the seat she had vacated. Claire returned to her own and waited, a sick feeling roiling through her stomach that something was terribly wrong, possibly with someone close to her.

But then she reminded herself that, other than Olive, and, perhaps, to a lesser extent, Chandler, there was no one close to her. And since they were obviously both fine, whatever was wrong couldn't have anything to do with them. Claire told herself that she should be reassured by the realization, but somehow, realizing that Olive and Chandler were the only people close to her just made her feel worse. Still, she told herself not to panic. Hey, it wasn't like someone she knew had died.

"So what's up?" she asked her attorney, starting to feel a little calmer now.

"Well, there's just no way to soften this, Claire," Chandler said. "I'm afraid someone you know has died."

Two

"*Someone* I know has *died*?" Claire echoed incredulously. "Who?"

In response to her frantic demand, Chandler settled his expensive briefcase on his knees to snap open first one latch, then the other. Unfortunately, the second one got caught and wouldn't unfasten, so he had to go to work on the combination wheel between the two, thumbing each of the three numbered tumblers, one by meticulous one, in an effort to make the latch come free, something that only left Claire feeling more agitated about the identity of the deceased.

That was the thing about men, she thought with much exasperation. Even their accessories had to be mechanized.

"Chandler," she said with as much patience as she could muster, "who died?"

"Hold on a minute," he said as he finally opened the briefcase and pulled out a sheaf of papers . . . one by meticulous one . . . checking their page numbers . . . one by meticulous one . . . then turning them right side up . . . one by meticulous one. "Ah, yes, here it is," he finally said, shaking out the last paper he picked up. "Eleanor Sage," he announced as he perused it.

"Not Eleanor Sage, my number one fan?" Claire said, distressed.

"Does Eleanor Sage, your number one fan, have a daughter named Anabel?" Chandler asked.

Claire nodded.

"Then it's Eleanor Sage your number one fan who has died," he confirmed.

"But . . . but she's my number one fan," Claire objected, as if such a distinction might somehow protect the woman from harm.

"Yes, well," Chandler said, "now whoever is your number two fan will step into that position."

"How did it happen?" Claire asked. "She was young, wasn't she?"

Chandler inspected his information again. "Twenty-four," he confirmed.

"What happened to her?"

Chandler glanced down to read over the material again. "Ah. Well. It's one of those things you hear about all the time, but I've never actually known it to happen to someone until now."

"What?" Claire asked.

Chandler glanced up. "She got hit by a bus."

Claire didn't know what to say. So she said the first thing that came to mind. "Poor Anabel. Left without a mother. I hope she and her father do all right."

Two things occurred to Claire as she voiced the remark. First, that Chandler was still fidgeting, and he wasn't normally a fidgeter. Second, that it was odd for her to be hearing about Eleanor's death from her attorney. In fact, it was odd for her to be hearing about Eleanor's death at all. In spite of their correspondence over the years, they were little more than long-distance acquaintances. Why would anyone think it necessary to alert Claire to this development?

"Chandler?" she asked softly. "What's going on?"

But he was busily rearranging the papers in his lap again, and he kept doing it as he replied. "Interesting you should mention Anabel's father that way," he said.

"Why is that interesting?" she asked, thinking she didn't find it interesting at all that she'd mentioned it. What she found it was troubling. Even more troubling was the fact that Chandler found it interesting.

"Because Anabel," he said, "appears not to have a father."

"Everyone has a father, Chandler," Claire told him. "It takes two sets of chromosomes to make a baby."

"But Anabel's mother didn't name that second set of chromosomes on her daughter's birth certificate."

Oh, yeah, Claire thought. They had definitely entered the troubling zone now. All persons still harboring the hope of a good outcome, please exit the train here.

"But if Anabel doesn't have a father," Claire said, "and now she doesn't have a mother, then who's going to . . . ?" For some reason, her brain refused to process any further than that whatever question it had been about to form.

"Funny you should say that," Chandler said.

Oh, Claire didn't think it was funny at all. Especially since she hadn't actually finished what she was about to say. "What do you mean?" she asked.

Chandler crossed one leg over the other and avoided her gaze. "Well, let's just say that when Eleanor Sage told you she's your number one fan, she really wasn't kidding. In fact, she thought so much of you that she named you in her will to be Anabel's legal guardian, should anything happen to her."

"Eleanor Sage expects *me* to raise her child?" Claire asked incredulously.

"I'm afraid so," Chandler told her.

"But I can't raise Anabel," she said. "I don't even know her. And not only do I not know the first thing about children, I have a business to run. A business that already consumes my entire life. Besides, I don't know the first thing about children."

Chandler, she noted, looked completely unmoved by her assurances. Probably, Claire thought, because she wasn't telling him anything that he didn't already know. So what could she do but tell him more things he already knew.

"I never even met Eleanor," she pointed out. "How could she expect a total stranger to raise her child? Did I mention I don't know the first thing about children?"

"You did actually mention that, yes," Chandler said.

"They can't make me be Anabel's guardian, can they?" she asked as desperation began to pound in her stomach and clutch at her throat.

"Well, under the circumstances," Chandler said, "you being a celebrity and Eleanor being a clearly delusional fan, no. I don't think we'd have a problem contesting Eleanor's will. There will still be some legal tap-dancing I'll need to do, but don't worry. I'll take care of it."

Claire nodded, but somehow she wasn't very comforted by his assurance. "Surely there's some other family member who could raise her," she said hopefully. "She must have

grandparents, right? And grandparents are notorious for dot-
ing on grandchildren. Because me, I don't know the first
thing about children."

"I'm afraid there are no grandparents," Chandler said.
"But Eleanor did have a brother, a Ramsey Sage, who
would, of course, be Anabel's uncle. He could potentially be
named guardian of the child."

"Oh, thank God," Claire said as she expelled a long sigh
of relief. "So then, what? I sign some papers turning legal
guardianship over to Uncle Ramsey? That shouldn't be so
hard, right?"

"Well, technically, no," Chandler said. "But there is one
small problem with regard to the man."

"What's that?" she asked warily.

"No one knows where he is."

As small problems went, Claire thought, that one was actually sort of gargantuan. "What do you mean no one knows
where he is? Human beings don't just disappear. Not unless
they've been abducted by aliens, but even then, isn't there
some kind of crop circle left behind or something? Does this
Ramsey Sage not have a crop circle? Because if he doesn't,
then he's probably not been abducted by aliens, in which
case, we'd have a good chance of finding him, I'd think."

She knew she was beginning to sound hysterical, but there
was a good reason for that. She was beginning to *feel* hysterical. Chandler, though, seemed not to notice anything out of
the ordinary in her behavior, something she decided not to
dwell on right now.

"No, no crop circle," he said. "No nothing. Not a trace of
him. According to Eleanor's attorney, her brother estranged
himself from the family quite some time ago. He left home
when she was a young child, and never returned."

Gee, Claire thought. Call her crazy, but not speaking to one's family for years, then falling off the face of the planet without leaving so much as a crop circle behind probably didn't bode well for any potential guardianship of a young child.

"It could take some time to locate him," Chandler added. "I'll have to hire a private investigator."

"Then do it," she said.

He nodded, jotting a note to himself. "In the meantime," he said, "how do you want to handle this? Do you want to assume guardianship of Anabel until her brother is found?"

"Of course not!" she insisted. "I don't know the first thing about children."

"So you've said."

"I mean, you said they can't make me be her guardian, right?"

"No, not under the circumstances," Chandler told her. Claire started to breathe a sigh of relief, until he added, "I'm sure the girl will be perfectly fine in the state's care."

Well, that got Claire's attention. She knew about state care. Her parents had both died in a house fire when Claire was only three—evidently one of them, or perhaps both, had passed out with a cigarette still burning in hand and hadn't bothered to inform anyone, including their sleeping daughter, about it. Fortunately for Claire, the fire department had entered the house through *her* window. Unfortunately for her parents, the firefighters weren't able to make it any farther into the house than her bedroom.

It was arguable, however, whether it was fortunate or unfortunate for Claire that neither of her parents had left behind any relatives suitable for raising her—all had either been too dilapidated, too debilitated, too disinterested, or too dysfunctional. Or worse, all of the above. So she had been made a ward of the state of Tennessee, and had done the rest of her growing up in what had been termed "a children's group home"—but which had in fact been an orphanage—continuously overlooked by potential adoptive families because of her age.

Claire had faced every birthday with dread, knowing the added year made her that much less desirable to people who wanted to begin their families from scratch. It had all culminated in her eighteenth birthday, the worst by far, because she had been booted out of the institution completely, having ceased to be a ward of the state and deemed able to take care of herself from there on out. Never mind that she was totally unprepared for life on the outside. Never mind that she had no one to greet her when she took those last steps out the front door of the home. Never mind that there hadn't been a soul on the planet to guide or welcome her anywhere, save the social worker most recently assigned to her case, who had assured Claire she could always call if she needed anything, then was never around to take Claire's calls.

In spite of her situation at eighteen, though, she had been accepted to Vanderbilt on a partial academic scholarship and had worked two jobs on campus to cover the rest of her expenses. The year she started at college was also the year she had met Olive, who, like Claire, hadn't had much in the way of relations save her ailing mother. They had bonded immediately. And they had taken care of each other. Little by little, each had become for the other the family neither had ever had. Were it not for Olive, Claire honestly wasn't sure where she would be.

"The state's care?" she asked softly, pushing unpleasant

thoughts of the past to the back of her brain, where they belonged.

Chandler nodded. "That's where Anabel is now, with the child welfare authorities in North Carolina, where Eleanor lived. The child can be put into foster care until her uncle is located."

Claire swallowed what felt very much like guilt, and asked, "And what if her uncle isn't located?"

"Then she'll be fine in foster care. Or she'll be placed in a children's group home."

That was what Claire was afraid of. In spite of her own benign experiences, every terrible cliché about the state welfare system roared up in her head. She tried to reassure herself that the vast majority of children in the system fared perfectly well, as she had—for the most part—and that many probably even flourished. Anabel, she told herself, would be perfectly all right there, awaiting the arrival of her uncle.

But what if her uncle never arrived? Or worse, what if he arrived, and he was a despicable human being? What if little Anabel ended up in a worse place with her uncle?

"I can't be Anabel's guardian, Chandler," Claire said again, more forcefully this time, because she truly knew she couldn't do it.

"I'll take care of it, Claire," he promised.

As he opened his mouth to explain exactly how he would do that, she interrupted him with a carefully uttered, "But."

Chandler glanced up from the papers he had begun sifting through again, looking concerned for the first time since his arrival. "But?"

Claire inhaled a deep breath and released it slowly and

hoped she wasn't making a terrible mistake. "But until you can locate Ramsey Sage, and until we know for sure that he'll be an appropriate guardian, Anabel can come and stay with me."

Now Chandler looked vaguely alarmed. "Claire, if you don't mind my saying so, I think you'd be making a terrible mistake. You don't know the first thing about children."

She couldn't disagree with him. Already, she was regretting the decision. But she couldn't let little Anabel go into foster care. The least Claire could do was make sure her number one fan's little girl was well cared for. She just hoped that said care ultimately fell into someone else's hands. Someone who would be devoted to Anabel and give her all the best. Someone who knew at least the first thing about children.

If—*when*—they found Ramsey Sage, she thought, he had damned well better be a good guy. Otherwise . . .

Well, *otherwise* didn't bear thinking about.

It occurred to Ramsey Sage as a beefy fist made contact with his lower lip and split it open that there must be a better way to live. That observation was really hammered home— literally—when his head connected with the tequila-soaked floor beneath him, slamming him to near unconsciousness. He lay there motionless for a moment, pretending to be dead— hey, it had worked before . . . just, you know, not today— letting the stale liquor seep into his already rank blue jeans and dingy T-shirt. Then he felt that same beefy fist and its mate clamp on to his shoulders and haul him to standing— sort of—again. And then a kind of slow-motion replay happened, and he found himself down on the floor once again.

Dope smugglers and murderers, he thought as he struggled to push himself up this time, were *such* a paranoid bunch.

Once he was standing—sort of—again, Ramsey raked both hands through his ink black, shoulder-length hair and decided to try and be reasonable. What the hell? Desperate times called for desperate measures. "Look, Valdez," he told the man to whose fist he had just introduced his lower lip—though not with the most courteous of responses, granted—"I know what you're thinking. And I can explain. Really."

Valdez muttered the equivalent of *The hell you can, you stupid sonofabitch* in his native tongue, then doubled up his fist again, presumably because he wanted it to meet another one of Ramsey's body parts, perhaps even more intimately this time than before, something Ramsey really didn't want to think about. So he took a step backward and held up both hands before him, palm out, knowing that, even in Spanish, that meant "Please don't hit me again. I've had enough, thank you." But Valdez's native tongue must have been Portuguese—or maybe he just wasn't a nice guy—because he hit Ramsey again anyway. Hard.

Hoo-kay, Ramsey thought as he pushed himself up this time, not bothering to stand—sort of—again, settling for a semirhythmic swaying instead. Obviously Valdez wasn't into verbal communication. Obviously he was more into that body language thing. So they'd just have to do this the hard way. Ramsey's fists might not be as beefy as the other man's were, but he'd bet they were every bit as well-versed in the etiquette of physical combat. With a quiet sigh of resignation—followed by a ferocious groan of animal intent—Ramsey launched himself at Valdez . . .

. . . and into a barroom brawl that exceeded even his usual standards for barroom brawling.

By the time it was over, even the waitress at Manny's Seaside Cantina—which was nowhere near the sea and which was less cantina than it was corrugated tin shack, though the original owner *was* named Manolo, even if he was now dead—had gotten in on the action. But then, Placida had never been one to shy away from a good bar fight, as evidenced by the fact that only three of her teeth were her own. Then again, at eighty-three years of age, and as a native of this part of Nicaragua, that was a pretty major accomplishment. Fortunately, Placida had always liked Ramsey, so she sided with him.

When the dust finally settled—and there was a lot of dust in this part of Nicaragua, especially of the figurative variety—Valdez and his boys had split. That is, they had left. They had also, of course, split Ramsey's lip—twice—but that was nothing new. If he had a centavo for every barroom bloodletting he'd endured over the past fifteen years, he wouldn't have to hang out with drug smugglers and murderers for a living, would he?

He helped Placida tidy up in the wake of the fight, then smiled—well, *grimaced* was probably more what he did, though he intended it for a smile—when she brought him a shot of tequila for his trouble.

The liquor burned his lips, his mouth, his throat, and his belly, though he suspected that was due to the quality—or lack thereof—of the spirits, and not his current state of disrepair. Still, he was well on the downhill side of thirty-five, he reminded himself. He really was getting too old for bar fights. Most of the guys he'd gone to high school with were probably CPAs and engineers and marketing analysts and such, all firmly footed on the corporate ladder somewhere, making their livings in traditional—and profitable—ways.

And what was Ramsey doing to earn his daily bread? Bleeding.

His classmates had all probably married by now, too, he thought further, and had doubtless started families long ago. They probably all drove SUVs, telling themselves it was in case they needed to do a little emergency off-roading on the way home from the grocery store, when in fact it was because they needed the extra hauling space for soccer nets and hockey sticks. They all probably had demure, dainty wives waiting for them when they got home, too, women who held a chilled martini in one hand and the evening news in the other. Or they'd married other corporate types like themselves and lived in child-free conspicuous consumption, with his 'n' hers BMWs in the garage and regular trips to the Caribbean.

But hey, Ramsey thought, trying to reassure himself, he already lived in the Caribbean. Kind of. It was over there somewhere. And he was certainly child-free. As for the conspicuous consumption, he thought as he conspicuously consumed what was left of his tequila, well . . . He'd never been the materialistic type, anyway. As evidenced by the fact that, currently, he slept in a tent and drove a mustang. The real kind of mustang, lower case, and not the upper-case car manufactured by the Ford Motor Company. Still, his mustang was the most reliable vehicle he'd ever owned. Provided he didn't feed it anything that gave it gas. And it hardly ever bit him anymore. Who needed a corporate ladder to climb and a martini-wielding wife when you had simple pleasures like that, right?

He expelled what he told himself was a sigh of contentment—and *not* a grumble of irritation—as he lowered the shot glass to the bar, then stopped breathing completely when he looked over to see Placida talking to a man in rumpled khaki shorts and an even more rumpled yellow Guayabera shirt. *Turista*, was Ramsey's first thought when he saw the man, so addled was his brain by a bad beating and even worse tequila. Then he remembered where he was and that the only *turistas* who came here were the ones who were taking home souvenirs of the illegal—and narcotic— variety. And he was glad he had located his .32 after the brawl had ended and tucked it back into the waistband of his blue jeans.

That gratification was made stronger when Ramsey saw Placida point at him, and the man's gaze follow her finger's direction.

American or European, Ramsey decided as the man made his way across the cantina to the end of the bar where he sat. His hair was mostly white, his eyes the faded blue of a man who was tired of seeing as much of the world as he had. And he was obviously uncomfortable in his wardrobe, another indication that he wasn't Hispanic. Any Latino man his age would have opted for a Guayabera shirt first thing in the morning. This man was obviously trying to fit in where he clearly felt he didn't fit in.

"Ramsey Sage?" he asked as he seated himself on the barstool next to Ramsey's.

"Who's asking?" Ramsey said by way of a reply.

The man reached into the pocket of his shorts and withdrew a wallet, flicked it open, tugged out some ID, and dropped it onto the bar. "Name's Gordon Stantler. I'm a private investigator from Nashville, Tennessee. I was hired to find you."

Although Ramsey did notice a definite Southern accent in the man's speech, he didn't know anyone in Nashville. And he couldn't imagine why anyone *anywhere* would want to find him. Not unless it was to do him harm. There were quite a few people who wanted to find him to do that. Which was all the more reason to be suspicious of Gordon Stantler.

"Can't help you," Ramsey said, leaving the man to make of that whatever he would.

"You're not Ramsey Sage?" Mr. Stantler asked, his tone of voice indicating that he didn't believe that for a second.

Ramsey shook his head.

"The waitress said you are."

"She's also been known to channel the ghost of Carmen Miranda from time to time," Ramsey said. "I wouldn't swear by anything she says. Not that I'm suggesting for a moment that Carmen Miranda was dishonest or anything like that," he qualified quickly, on the outside chance that this guy repped the Miranda estate.

"Gee, that's too bad that you're not him," Stantler said in a tone of voice that indicated he still didn't believe that for a second. Probably not about him not being Ramsey Sage, either. " 'Cause I have some pretty important news I have to give the guy when I find him."

Ramsey told himself not to fall for it. It was the oldest trick in the book. "Well, if I run into Ramsey Sage," he said, "I'll tell him you're looking for him."

"Tell him his sister is dead, too."

That, if nothing else the man said, made Ramsey think twice. And then three times. And then four. Because Ramsey did have a sister. But she'd been alive the last time he saw her. She'd also been only four years old the last time he saw her. Still, he'd spoken to her on the phone—even if she hadn't much spoken back—about two years ago, and she'd been alive then, too. Of course, anything could happen in two years. Hell, anything could happen in two minutes, as far as Ramsey was concerned. Even two seconds could mean the difference between life and death.

"Really," he said, telling himself the other man was at worst lying, and at best, mistaken. In an effort to trip him up, he added, "Which sister would that be?"

"From what I've been told," Stantler said, "the man only has one sister. Eleanor. Age twenty-four at the time of her death."

Ramsey swallowed hard. His sister's name was indeed Eleanor, and she would be twenty-four years old now. Still, there was no reason why he had to believe this guy. Eleanor was perfectly healthy and perfectly capable of taking care of herself. It wouldn't take much digging for anyone to find out about her and make up some story to lure Ramsey into a trap. It also, he realized then, wouldn't take much trouble for anyone to find her—or hurt her?—in an attempt to retaliate for some of the things Ramsey had done to those anyones in the past.

"If she's dead," he said, surprised at how unconcerned he was able to make himself sound, "then how'd it happen?"

"Traffic accident," Stantler told him.

And for some strange reason, Ramsey found himself on the verge of believing it. He also felt himself growing sick.

"She left behind a daughter," Gordon Stantler said further. And as the man completed the sentence, Ramsey felt the floor fall away beneath him. The rest of the PI's announcement seemed to be filtering through thick gauze as he spoke, because Ramsey had trouble hearing the rest of it. "She's thirteen months old," Stantler continued. "Anabel Claire Sage is her name. No father listed on the birth certificate. No other surviving relatives. Looks like she'll end up a ward of the state of North Carolina if we can't find her uncle."

Anabel Claire Sage, Ramsey repeated to himself. His grandmother had been named Anabel. Had Eleanor really had a daughter? And had she really died?

As Gordon Stantler continued to speak, Ramsey felt himself being hurtled backward in time twenty years. He had left home at the age of eighteen for what he'd considered then to be very good reasons, and he hadn't looked back once. Now, for the first time in almost two decades, he was looking back. And he didn't much like what he saw, especially of himself.

His parents were both dead, both planted in the ground before he'd even known they were gone. No one had been able to find him on either occasion to let him know what had happened, because the first time he'd been drunk in a seedy bar in an obscure village in Central America, and the second time he'd been drunk in a seedy bar in an obscure village in Central America. And now his sister Eleanor, who had only been four years old when he left home, was dead, too—and here he was, drunk in a seedy bar in an obscure village in Central America—and she had left behind a little girl who had no father.

He wondered what had led up to his sister's giving birth to a baby alone, without knowing—or perhaps without caring—who the father was. Probably, Eleanor could have used someone stable in her life after the death of their parents, he thought. Probably, she had needed a family member to help her through a rough patch, a family member who wasn't there because he was drunk in a seedy bar in an obscure village in Central America. Probably, Ramsey had let her down. But then, he'd let down everyone else in his life, too.

Anabel Claire Sage, he repeated to himself as his head gradually began to clear. A thirteen-month-old girl was the only blood relative he had left alive in the world. Where was he going to be when she needed him? he asked himself. Drunk in a seedy bar in an obscure village in Central America?

As quickly as he had fallen into the past, Ramsey jerked himself back into the present, turning on his barstool to look at Gordon Stantler. And finally, he told the man, "I'm Ramsey Sage. Tell me what I need to do."

Three

$\mathcal{A}$s she studied the man framed by her open front door, it took only one, very quick, perusal of Ramsey Sage for Claire to know everything she needed to know about him. He was completely unfit to be anyone's mother. Or father. Or guardian. No, this man, she was convinced after that one, very quick, perusal wasn't suited to care for a pet tick, let alone a thirteen-month-old child.

He wore extremely faded blue jeans, slashed at both knees, and an equally faded denim work shirt whose sleeves appeared to have been ripped completely from their seams—she hated to think how. A tattoo of black barbed wire completely encircled one arm over—okay, admittedly very nice—biceps, and a diamond stud earring—a half carat, if she knew her jewelry, and it went without saying that she did—winked in his right earlobe. His scruffy motorcycle boots clinked when he shifted his not inconsiderable weight from one foot to the other, thanks to their numerous chains, which she couldn't help thinking were all that was holding the footwear together. With a hasty glance beyond him, she saw a motorcycle parked at the curb that was as disreputable-looking as he was and realized the boots were as appropriate as they were appalling.

Yet as remarkable as his wardrobe was, it was Mr. Sage's face that commanded Claire's attention. He obviously hadn't had a haircut for some time, because his straight black tresses, shoved back from his tanned forehead by careless hands, hung nearly to his shoulders. And he obviously hadn't had a shave for some time, either, because the lower half of his face was shadowed and craggy with several days' growth of beard. What he *had* obviously had recently was a good beating, because his lip was cut in two places, his left cheek bore a ragged abrasion, his nose seemed a tad off-kilter, and his eyes . . .

She bit back a reluctant and all-too-wistful sigh that formed deep inside her as she considered those eyes. Well then. For such a rowdy, uncivil-looking man, Ramsey Sage, Claire had to concede, had the loveliest green eyes she had ever seen in her life. Even if one of them was discolored by a spectacular bruise at the moment. On any other man, those eyes would have even been feminine—well, except for the shiner—so long and sooty were the lashes framing them. On this man, however . . .

Okay, so even beaten up, Ramsey Sage was kind of attractive, she thought, perhaps even sexy, in a rough-around-the-edges, is-that-a-banana-in-your-pocket, he-man kind of way that most self-respecting women would *never* admit to finding attractive or sexy. What he clearly *wasn't* was cut out to be a daddy.

And with that, Claire realized she wouldn't *dare* turn Anabel over to her uncle, no questions asked. In fact, she had quite a few questions she intended to ask Mr. Ramsey Sage, starting with "How do you expect to transport a toddler on a Harley-Davidson?" and ending with "Are you *sure* you don't have a criminal record?" Because Mr. Ramsey Sage was one unsavory-looking character, silky inky locks and radiant emerald eyes notwithstanding.

"Miss Willoughby?" he said, his tone of voice surprisingly courteous in light of his coarse appearance. What was also surprising was the smile that punctuated his question. It was actually kind of charming. In a rakish, rascally, reprobate sort of way.

"Yes, I'm Claire Willoughby," she told him.

"Ramsey Sage," he said. Then he stuck out his hand cordially, another polite gesture she wouldn't have expected of him.

He was a fascinating mix of puzzles, his appearance marking him as a troublemaker and borderline felon, his demeanor perfectly polite. Had Claire seen him walking down the street toward her, she would have crossed to the other side. But had she been speaking to him on the phone, she would have been charmed by his voice and manners. Just what kind of man was Ramsey Sage?

"So I gathered," she replied as she automatically accepted his hand and shook it.

He had a sturdy, confident grip, his large fingers virtually swallowing hers. She glanced down at their joined hands, and when she saw her perfectly pink polished nails folded over his dark knuckles abraded with wounds, a thrill of something sharp and frenetic shot through her. Though that wasn't just because she realized Mr. Sage had given as good as he had gotten in the brawl that had left him so battered. No, it was the simple sight of her well-groomed hand against his big, brawny mitt that did it. Because for some reason, seeing the contrast between their hands made Claire curious about all the other differences between his body and hers. He pumped her hand three times—although she really wished she'd thought of another word besides *pumped* for the gesture—then released it, and for some reason, she felt oddly bereft when he did.

"I'm Anabel's uncle," he added unnecessarily. "Eleanor's brother? I spoke with your attorney."

"Won't you come in?" she invited. "Chandler is here now. We can all chat."

And they were going to have a lot more to chat about than Claire had initially thought, too. Like how his arrival had made this temporary arrangement with Anabel suddenly seem much less temporary.

"Is Anabel here?" Mr. Sage asked before making a move to enter.

"Not yet," Claire told him. "It's taken nearly a week to get everything worked out with the authorities in North Carolina. But I spoke with the social worker assigned to the case yesterday, and he said he'd be here with her this afternoon. I'm actually expecting them anytime now. It was rather fortuitous that you were located as quickly as you were."

And also rather amazing, especially since no one seemed to know *why* Ramsey Sage had been drunk in a seedy bar in an obscure village in Central America when they found him. Nor did anyone seem to know how he had gotten there. Even Chandler's private detective still had a lot of pieces missing from the puzzle that was Ramsey Sage, because Ramsey Sage himself had evidently been no help at all providing any answers. It was something Claire decided not to think about, mostly because it didn't bode well for his being named Anabel's permanent guardian.

"Please come in," she invited him again, stepping aside to offer a physical punctuation mark to the invitation.

But he hesitated for a moment, as if he were reluctant to enter. He surveyed what he could see of the big house from his place on the front porch, and when his gaze returned to hers, Claire could see from his expression that he didn't approve. Why he wouldn't approve, she couldn't imagine. It was certainly a vast improvement over the crowded, spartan institution where she'd grown up, and the tiny, spartan apartment she and Olive had shared in college. She'd made the place as warm and inviting as she could, especially on the inside, and she couldn't imagine why anyone—especially a harsh, raggedy, beaten-up man like Ramsey Sage—would disapprove.

Although he smiled at her again as he took a step forward, the naturally breezy grin he had displayed a moment ago was gone, and the one he wore now was decidedly more manufactured. Claire tried not to notice how the air around her seemed to come alive as he passed. She couldn't help noticing, though, how he smelled of heavy machinery and raucous man and endless summer nights, a combination she found strangely appealing since she'd never been drawn to any of those things before. Oh, certainly she enjoyed a summer evening as much as the next person, but she couldn't imagine anything that might make one seem endless.

Then Ramsey Sage looked at her again with his smoldering green gaze, and she suddenly had a very good idea indeed what might make a summer night seem to go on forever, an especially graphic, surprisingly explicit idea, in fact, one that had her squirming on her flowered chintz sofa beneath Ramsey Sage, her blouse gaping open, her skirt hiked up over her hips, her brassiere pushed high, her pearl necklace clenched in his teeth as he tore it from her neck and sent the perfect little beads scattering across the Oriental rug and hardwood floors before dragging his hot mouth across her collarbone and down between her breasts, moving over to close his lips over one nipple, tugging her inside, laving her, licking her, tasting her deeply, and then . . . and then . . . and then . . .

And, good *heavens*, where had such a thought come from? Claire wondered as she shook the image out of her brain. Heat flooded her cheeks, and her lips parted in shock, and she hoped Ramsey Sage couldn't tell what she was thinking about. Because not only did Claire normally not think about such things in such detail, she didn't think about them in mixed company. And she certainly didn't think about them with men like Ramsey Sage cast in the role of seducer.

Seducer nothing, she thought as she closed the door behind him, wishing she could close the door on her rampant thoughts as easily. Ramsey Sage looked like the kind of man who would take whatever he wanted, whoever he wanted, whenever he wanted, the rest of the world be damned. And the wantee, Claire was certain, would go along quite willingly, and when it was over, be left feeling as if she had just experienced the highest summit of joy.

She followed Mr. Sage into the living room, but following him left her gazing, however involuntarily, at his backside— all right, so maybe it wasn't all *that* involuntary—and she couldn't help noting that his backside was every bit as noteworthy as his front side had been. Because his faded jeans hugged his taut hindquarters and strong thighs with much affection, and his denim work shirt strained against the muscles of his broad back. His arms were nicely bulked with sinew without being overblown, his biceps and forearms curving appreciably with muscle, his skin bronzed and powerful beneath that oddly erotic, barbed-wire tattoo.

And, strangely, Claire found herself wanting to trace the circumference of that tattoo with her fingertips, and oh, my, but that endless-summer-night thing was starting up again, growing more and more graphic and explicit in her mind—and on her body, too, she had to admit—with every passing moment.

Clink, clink, clink went the chains on his boots as he walked.

And *zing* went the strings of her heart.

"Won't you sit down, Mr. Sage?" she said as he continued across the living room to where Chandler stood to greet him upon his arrival. And also as she continued to ogle his backside. "This is Handler, ah, I mean *Chandler*. Chandler Edison. He's my, um . . . my attorney."

Boy, she was really going to have to be careful. Because in addition to misintroducing Chandler by a moniker that had been what Claire was thinking about doing to Mr. Sage's backside, she had almost called Chandler her "buttorney." That would have really been embarrassing.

"Mr. Edison, good to finally meet you," Ramsey Sage said as he approached Chandler, politely extending his hand again, and surprising Claire once more with his manners.

"Mr. Sage," Chandler replied as he shook the proffered hand, though with none of the easiness Ramsey Sage exhibited, and with all of the reluctance one might expect of Chandler, seeing as how he had a nasty aversion to denim.

"Call me Ramsey," Ramsey told Chandler. Then he turned to Claire and added, "You, too, Miss Willoughby."

Claire told herself to extend the same courtesy to him, but

something prohibited her. She wasn't sure she could be responsible for her actions if she heard her given name spoken in that dark, velvety baritone of his. So she only nodded her acknowledgment of his comment and decided to skirt the issue as best she could by calling him nothing at all. The last thing she needed to do anyway was slip up and address him as Mr. Hunka Hunka Burnin' Love.

And just what had gotten into her anyway? she demanded of herself. This was getting silly. Ramsey Sage was a walking, talking warning label for decent women everywhere. He was unkempt, unclean, and uncompromising. Not to mention potentially dangerous. She was probably crazy to even invite him into her home, whether he approved of it or not. And she was even crazier to think there was any chance he would be able to care for Anabel. She bit back the panic that began to rise in her throat and wondered what she was supposed to do. If Ramsey Sage couldn't take on the care and feeding of his niece, then who could? Claire certainly didn't want to be responsible for the little girl any longer than she had to be. She didn't know the first thing about children.

How had she gotten into this mess? And more to the point, what was she going to do to get out of it?

"So Anabel will be here in just a little while?" Ramsey asked. But there was something in his voice when he posed the question that went beyond mere curiosity. As odd as it seemed coming from a man like him, he sounded almost wistful when he spoke.

"Mr. Webster said he'd be here with her by three at the latest," Chandler replied. "That's the social worker Anabel has been assigned to here in Nashville," he added by way of an explanation. "Davis Webster."

"There's a social worker involved?" Ramsey asked, his voice filled with obvious concern. "Why? Is Anabel okay?"

"Oh, she's fine," Claire hastened to assure him. "At least, according to Mr. Webster, she is. But evidently it's customary for a social worker to be assigned to situations like this, when a child is about to be placed in a new situation. He'll be making regular visits for the first few months, to make sure everything's running smoothly and to see if we need additional counseling or anything."

"Why would anyone need counseling?" Ramsey asked, still sounding concerned.

"I can't imagine," Claire lied effortlessly. "But don't worry. Mr. Webster has been very courteous on the phone. I'm sure he'll be nice in person. While we're waiting for him, though, I was hoping you and Chandler and I could chat a bit."

"Fine," Ramsey said. "What is it you want to talk about?"

Well, let's start with the length of your criminal record, Claire thought. *Is it longer than, say, the coastal boundary of Alaska? And is that including or excluding the Aleutians?* Aloud, however, she said, "Oh, this and that. Iced tea?" she added before he had a chance to object to her vagueness.

Hastily, she headed across the room to seat herself in the center of the loveseat, telling herself it was because she wanted to be near the silver tray holding iced tea accoutrements and not because it dictated that Mr. Sage—and Chandler, for that matter—would have to take their own seats in the matching Queen Anne chairs that flanked the loveseat on the other side of the coffee table.

Chandler, however, seemed not to realize that, because instead of seating himself in one of the floral chintz-covered chairs, he squeezed himself in on Claire's right side, much too close for her comfort. But she was only uncomfortable because she wasn't able to properly pour iced tea, of course. Not because she suddenly wanted to check her blouse to make sure she was all buttoned up good and tight.

"Chandler," she said softly, nudging him as unobtrusively as she could, hoping he would take the hint.

But he only gazed back at her, his dark blond eyebrows arched in question, as if he had no idea what she was telling him.

"Do you mind?" she said less softly, nudging him a bit more obtrusively. Provided, of course, that *obtrusively* was in fact a word. "I need to pour the tea," she elaborated.

"Oh, yes, by all means do," he told her enthusiastically, dropping his own voice, though she couldn't imagine why. He seemed to think they were playing *I've Got a Secret*. Except that they were using totally different rules than one was supposed to use when playing that game. Even so, Claire could already tell, after only one clue, that Chandler's secret was, "I'm a bit thickheaded."

Clearly he wasn't going to take the hint. Not when he wasn't even getting the hint. So Claire gave in to his nearness and tried not to squirm. She also tried to not make a big mess as she poured three tall, cool glasses of tea. And she tried not to check her buttons again, either.

Ramsey, she was pleased to see, did understand where he was supposed to sit, and he loped over to the Queen Anne chair on her left and dropped into it—all right, he knew where he was supposed to *slouch*, she amended. But he smiled knowingly at Chandler as he did so, and Claire felt a momentary pang of envy that he seemed to understand the attorney's actions when she didn't. Ah, well. One of those "guy things" she'd read so much about, she supposed. It was nice to see the two men bonding. Or something.

That was the thing about men. They had a language all their own. Unfortunately, it was about as intelligible to most women as baseball statistics were.

"Here you are," she said as she extended a glass to Ramsey. Since Chandler was sitting so close, she thought, he could just get his own.

With a heartfelt sigh, she leaned back on the loveseat and tried to relax a little. Then she looked at Ramsey again, who was looking back at her in a way that started up all that heartstrings-zinging again, and Claire decided there was no way she'd be able to relax as long as he was anywhere within her zip code. Area code. Hemisphere. Solar system.

Whatever.

Ramsey Sage sipped his iced tea slowly—wow, was it sweet—and eyed his hostess and her trained attorney with much interest. Never in his life had he seen two more courteous, more refined, better-dressed people. Which naturally made him extremely suspicious. Not that he didn't believe people like them existed in the world—somewhere—but he sure as hell had never encountered any up close like this before. Until now, he'd always been under the impression that people like this only existed in glossy publications with names like *Affluence Annual, Money Monthly, Wealth Weekly,* and *Dinero Daily.* He'd wouldn't have thought he could coexist with such folks on the same plane of reality without there being some kind of major shift of the earth's axis that caused, at the very least, killer tidal waves. But here he sat with them, plain as day, and he felt nary a tremor of plate tectonics.

He couldn't remember the last time he'd been in surroundings like these, so extravagant and expensive and excessive. For the last three years, he'd lived his life in the most primitive, most crude, most dangerous environment a person could imagine, a place populated by killers and criminals and crooks. Now, less than twenty-four hours after leaving that world, he had entered its utter antithesis.

Claire Willoughby's furnishings were old and yet elegant, leftovers from an era of culture and finery the world would never see again. Behind the loveseat where she had perched herself like a fragile finch waiting to take flight was a fireplace framed by an ornate mahogany mantelpiece, and built-in bookcases—likewise mahogany—crammed full of leather-bound tomes from floor to ceiling on each side. Right now, the massive fireplace was filled with a floral arrangement of dizzying, variegated hues, but Ramsey could easily imagine a roaring fire there during the cold heart of winter, and how much warmer the room would be because of it.

Not that it didn't seem warm now, he reflected as he let his gaze travel over the rest of the furnishings and became even more impressed—however reluctantly—with their opulence. He told himself it was a crime that there were people enjoying such luxury when folks in other places were literally living in the dirt. He told himself Claire Willoughby should be ashamed of herself for being so conspicuously consumptive. Hell, there were rooms in the Smithsonian that weren't this well furnished.

But Ramsey couldn't quite bring himself to feel as resentful as he told himself he should feel. As uncomfortable as he was here, there was something about the place that still made him feel welcome. Sort of. And there was something that kept the house from feeling like a museum. Inescapably, his gaze returned to Claire Willoughby, and he knew what that something was. As cultured and refined as she looked in her sleeveless lavender blouse and beige skirt, he suspected she wasn't born to this lifestyle. Maybe it was because she tried so hard to appear to fit in, he thought.

He shrugged off the observation. No sense getting maudlin. He was only going to be in this world long enough to claim what was left of his family. Then he'd never see Claire Willoughby again.

And why did that realization bother him? he wondered. Jeez, he'd just met the woman. And God knew neither one of them had the first thing in common. Even if he'd been looking to get involved with someone—which he most certainly was *not*, especially with impending fatherhood looming on the horizon—Claire Willoughby was the last sort of woman he should be trying to make time with.

Not that she would welcome him wanting to make time with her, anyway, he thought further. Even if she wasn't born to the high life, she was certainly firmly entrenched there now. And even if he didn't feel entirely uncomfortable in her house, she hadn't exactly gone out of her way to make Ramsey feel welcome. On the contrary, she had invisible walls all around her, ten feet high and three feet thick, that declared her totally unattainable. Ramsey would do well to keep his distance. Not that he had much choice in the matter.

Still, he had to admit, she was very attractive, in a martini-dry-please-Jeeves, ivory-tower, do-wash-your-hands-before-dinner kind of way, with her dark blond hair swept back from her face in some sort of Grace Kelly 'do, and her creamy complexion flawless, and a sedate strand of pearls encircling her throat that he would just love to see her wearing with nothing else.

Oops. Getting a little ahead of himself there. Especially since, judging by the way Mr. Chandler Keep-Your-Mitts-to-Yourself Edison had seated himself so close to her, Claire Willoughby was already taken. If anybody was going to be seeing her in pearls and nothing else, it was the smarmy attorney.

There was just no accounting for taste.

"So, Mr. Sage," Claire began, bringing Ramsey's attention back to the here and now, "just what is it you do for a living?"

Oh, boy. Here it came. The last thing he wanted to discuss with these people was the way he made his living. If they found out how he'd spent the last few years, they'd not only run screaming in horror in the other direction, but they'd never turn over Anabel to his safekeeping. And he did intend to keep Anabel safe, no matter what these two concluded about him. He was done living life on the edge. He knew that much. He just wished he also knew what he would be doing now to earn an income, since he had stepped back from the precipice. Because the thing he was trained to do wasn't exactly the most stable business in the world. Nor was it the most scrupulous. And it certainly didn't put him in an environment that was suitable for raising a child. Not unless he wanted that child to grow up to become a menace to society.

So he only lifted one shoulder and let it drop in what he hoped Miss Claire Willoughby would interpret as a half-hearted sort of shrug. Somehow, though, the gesture felt in no way careless. "Oh, this and that," he said evasively.

She nodded, but it obviously wasn't with approval. "I see," she said. But he could tell she really didn't. "And where is it that you do this and that?"

He performed that not-careless little shrug again, and said, "Oh, here and there."

"I see," she said again. But Ramsey could pretty much tell she was lying. "And how long have you been doing this and that here and there? Is it a full-time position?"

"It's actually kind of now and then," he told her. Because his was the kind of job that didn't have regular hours. You took advantage of the situation when you could and hoped for the best. Or rather, you looked for a break in the action where you could find one and hoped you didn't get gunned down. Details, details.

"So you've been doing this and that, here and there, now and then, is that right?" she asked.

He nodded. "That's it."

"Sounds like quite the desirable position."

Ramsey wasn't positive, but he was pretty sure she was being sarcastic. Boy, some role model she was. Lying and sarcastic. This was the last sort of environment he wanted to have his niece raised in.

"Miss Willoughby," he began.

"Mr. Sage," she said at the same time.

"Ramsey," he quickly corrected her. "I told you to call me Ramsey."

She dipped her head forward in silent acknowledgment, and he waited for her to extend the same courtesy to him. But it never came. Instead, she said, "I understand that when the private investigator Chandler hired to find you finally located you, you had just concluded a, ah, tussle, in a, ah, tavern. Is that correct?"

Wow, Ramsey thought. She really was polite. Because what he had been doing down in Central America had been a far cry from tussling in a tavern. But if that was how she wanted to refer to it, then, by golly, he wasn't going to stop her. In fact, the way she described it—tussling in a tavern, who woulda thunk it?—actually made it sound kind of fun. And really, when he thought about it now, he realized that, in a bizarre kind of way, it had been kind of fun. In spite of being beaten nearly senseless sometimes, Ramsey always felt better after a good fight, as if he'd purged his system of something toxic and unpleasant. Bar brawling was a primitive sort of communication, to be sure, but it had been around for a few millennia and was spoken universally by men. Things got settled in a good bar brawl. Or even in a good tavern tussle. Maybe not always the way you wanted them to get settled, but the answers you got always had a definite punctuation mark to them.

But then, he reminded himself, Claire Willoughby probably thought what he'd been doing was *bad*. And she probably thought it wouldn't be appropriate behavior for someone who wanted to raise a child. And, probably, it wasn't appropriate behavior for someone who wanted to raise a child. So Ramsey was probably going to have to find a different way to communicate with men with whom he'd taken exception, one that *didn't* involve whupping them upside the head.

Boy. This parenting stuff was really going to be hard.

So instead of agreeing with Claire that he had indeed been tussling in a tavern when the PI found him, he told her, "Actually, I was conducting business." And, really, that was true. He just neglected to mention that his business on that particular day had been not getting the shit kicked out of him.

"Business," she echoed dubiously. "And did your business that day involve 'this' or 'that'?" she wanted to know.

"If memory serves, that was more of a 'this' day," he told her.

She nodded. But she didn't look like she was buying any of it.

So he added, "I had made a transaction with that particular client earlier in the week, and he thought I tried to rip him off, that's all."

"And did you?" she ask. "Rip him off, I mean?"

"Of course not," Ramsey said, stung. Just because the cocaine he'd passed to Valdez had been low-grade, that was no reason for the guy to beat him senseless. As effective as the tussle had been in settling things, they could have talked. That was the problem with the drug trade these days. Everyone jumped to conclusions.

"And what did the transaction involve exactly?" Claire asked.

Ramsey thought for a moment. He certainly wasn't going to tell her he'd been peddling drugs to the guy. But *dealing in pharmaceuticals* didn't seem like the most prudent answer to give, either, and she'd probably be suspicious if he said *selling mood enhancers*. So he settled on, "I was helping the guy plan a little vacation." *From reality*, he added to himself.

"A vacation," she repeated even more dubiously. "So you're like . . . a travel agent?"

"You could say that." Even though Ramsey probably wouldn't.

"How fascinating."

"It has its moments." Hoo boy, that was the truth.

Claire eyed him thoughtfully for a moment. "Then do you travel often? I mean, often enough that a young child might be a liability?"

"Oh, I'm not planning on staying in my current line of work," he told her, thinking that would make her feel better.

"So then you'll be unemployed?"

Until she said that. "No, no," he told her. "I'll find something."

"Do you have any prospects?"

"One or two," he lied. But it wasn't a big lie. *One or two* was only one or two away from his actual number, which was zero.

"Doing this and that, here and there, now and then?" she asked.

"Well, I hope it'll be more doing this, here, now. But, yeah, sorta like that."

"I see," she said again. And he could tell she was lying again.

"Look, Miss Willoughby," he began. He hoped she might interject that he should please call her Claire, but she only raised one delicate blond eyebrow in silent question. Fine. "Once Anabel is here," he continued, "then I'm sure we'll be able to—"

"It's just, Mr. Sage," the attorney interrupted, and until that moment, Ramsey had almost been able to forget about the guy's presence—or lack thereof—"Claire is concerned, and I am, too," he hastened to add, "that perhaps you're not equipped to take on the burden of a very young child. She— I mean, we—just want to make sure Anabel will be well cared for, that's all. Mr. Webster, the social worker, shares our concern. All we ask is that you assuage our fears by letting us know you can provide a safe, stable environment for the little girl."

His words and tone of voice were courteous enough, but there was something in the attorney's expression—probably the way he had his lip curled with distaste back from his slightly pointed teeth—that made Ramsey think the guy disapproved of him. Gee, he would have sworn the two of them didn't have anything in common. But Ramsey didn't approve of the attorney, either. What a coincidence.

Still, Ramsey wished he could assuage their fears about his taking on the care and feeding of his niece. Hell, he wished he could assuage his own fears about that. But there was one, very important thing he did know, one, very important thing about Ramsey that superseded everything about Claire. He was Anabel's family. And she was his. They were all each other had left of the Sage name and heritage, not that that heritage had all that much to recommend it. Nevertheless, family ties would count for more than anything Claire had to offer his niece.

Except maybe for her obvious millions of dollars.

And her big, beautiful house.

And her clearly well paying job, whatever it was.

And her tie to a nice community.

Okay, okay, so Claire Willoughby could give Anabel lots of things that Ramsey couldn't. But they were unimportant things. Tangible things. Things that applied to the exterior. What Ramsey had to offer his niece went straight to the heart. Anabel belonged with him. They were family. And that was the only thing that really mattered.

Yeah, he'd spent the last part of his life in a questionable environment. But he'd managed to keep himself tolerably safe and reasonably well cared for, even while living among some of the most heinous people who walked the planet. And now that he was back among polite society—well, except for attorney boy over there—staying safe should be a piece of cake. He *could* take care of Anabel. And he *would*. Somehow. He just wished he could make Claire and her trained attorney understand that.

Ramsey met Edison's gaze long enough to let the other man know he didn't like him any more than Edison liked Ramsey, then shifted his attention to Claire. He figured it was more important to impress her, though, deep down, he had to wonder what his real reasons might be for wanting to impress her. And he did everything he could to hold her cool blue gaze hostage when he spoke to her.

"Miss Willoughby," he began. Then, the hell with it, "Claire," he amended. Oh, yeah. It felt much more natural to call her that. She seemed momentarily irritated by the familiarity, then she relaxed, meeting his gaze unflinchingly. "I know you're concerned for Anabel," he continued. "And I appreciate the fact that you're not willing to turn her over to the first person who comes looking for her. I know I don't look like much of a provider. But looks can be deceiving. I promise you, I will take good care of her. She's my niece. We're family. A small family, granted, but a family nonetheless. She doesn't have anyone but me, and I don't have anyone but her. It wouldn't be fair to separate us. She and I belong together. We're . . . we're all we have left, you know? We . . . we . . ."

The weirdest thing happened as Ramsey was talking to Claire, and that was why his voice drifted off the way it did. Because as he spoke to her about what was left of his family, tears began to form in her eyes. And then suddenly, those tears welled up until one went tumbling over the brim, gliding slowly, silently, down her cheek. He couldn't believe it. He didn't think he was speaking especially poignantly. On the contrary, he was just stating the facts as he saw them. But Claire Willoughby had been moved to tears by his words. Literally. She was actually crying.

Without thinking, he stood and moved to sit beside her on

the loveseat, squeezing himself in between her and the over-stuffed arm, a not-unpleasant place to be, he had to admit. Then he lifted a hand to gently thumb away the solitary tear that held him entranced. As soon as he completed the gesture, though, he realized his behavior might be misconstrued as overstepping his bounds—not to mention his social rank. But he didn't mean to be ill-mannered and forward. He just wanted her to stop crying.

Claire, though, evidently didn't think he had behaved badly, because she only continued to look at him as if she understood completely what he was talking about. In fact, she kind of looked like she wanted to say something, too. She even opened her mouth as if she intended to speak, but no words ever came out. Instead, another tear fell from her other eye, and, instinctively, Ramsey lifted his other hand to brush that one away, too.

Now he had her face framed with both hands, and her eyes were fixed on his, and her mouth was partially open, and at some point, his heart had begun to hammer hard in his chest, and the moment was just really, really weird, because the way they were looking at each other was the way people looked at each other before they kissed each other, and then Ramsey found himself *wanting* to kiss her—deeply, madly, relentlessly—and it was all he could do not to dip his head what few inches remained between them and cover her mouth with his own.

Well, it was all he could do not to do that with the help of attorney boy. Because unlike Claire, Edison did evidently take offense at Ramsey's behavior. Big-time. He shot to his feet and moved to stand between Ramsey and Claire, no easy feat since a marble-topped coffee table took up most of the space there. But somehow he managed to wedge himself between Ramsey's knees and Claire's, then he squished himself down on the sofa between the two of them, something that very effectively pushed Ramsey's hands back into his lap, even though he was tempted to push them into Edison's face.

Oh, no, wait. He couldn't do that. Because fighting was wrong for guys who were trying to set a good example so that they could raise what little family they had left. Ramsey had to start making these moral distinctions if he was going to be an appropriate father to Anabel.

Okay, so he got the message. Obviously Claire and Edison *were* an item, and the latter half of that item didn't much care for the former half being touched by anyone other than himself. More was the pity. Because it had been a long time since Ramsey had touched a woman without having to pay for the privilege in one way or another. And even that one scant caress of Claire's face had made him want more. Lots more. She was soft in a way he'd never imagined a woman could be. And warm. And sweet-smelling. And fine. He'd never known a woman could feel so good.

Hell, he thought then, it wasn't that it had been a long time since he'd touched a woman without having to pay for the privilege in one way or another. It was that he'd *never* touched a woman like Claire. Not one who was all cool culture and calm comportment and classy custom. And boy, was she beautiful. Looking at her made him want to break into song. One of those foreign language songs, too, the kind that went on forever. And no, he wasn't talking about the "Macarena."

But Ramsey wasn't a man of elegance and beauty and refinement. Nor was he normally attracted to women of that ilk. He'd lost his virginity when he was fifteen, to the "fast" girl at his high school, the one with the too-short skirts and the too-long legs, all mascara and lipstick and Sweet Honesty perfume. And he'd had such a good time with her that he'd always looked for bad girls after that, women who enjoyed sex as much as he did, often more. Which, as far as he was concerned, made them good girls. Really good girls, some of them. One had even been exceptional, but that had probably been because she was double-jointed.

But none of them had been like Claire. And Ramsey honestly wasn't sure he'd know what to do with a woman like her. Other than wipe away her tears, anyway. And something told him that if he got involved with a woman like her, there would most definitely be tears. So, really, she was better off with Edison. They were two of a kind.

And as if Claire wanted to remind Ramsey of that very thing—and maybe remind herself, too—she suddenly stood, snapping herself to attention until her back was ramrod straight. With one quick, but very graceful, swipe of her hand across her eyes, both her tears and the lost look she'd had about her were gone. Once again, she was in total control. Once again, she was cool and crisp and cultivated. Once again, she was completely unattainable. Especially since, the minute she saw Ramsey looking at her, she turned her back on him and, without a word, began to walk away, hastening her stride with every step. But as she beat her hasty retreat, she lifted a hand to her eyes again, and if Ramsey hadn't known better, if he hadn't known she and Edison were two of a kind, he would have thought she was wiping away another tear.

Four

The doorbell rang for the third time in less than an hour just as Claire was blowing her nose for the third time in less than a minute. The first time had been because of Chandler's arrival—the doorbell, not the nose-blowing, naturally. The second time had been because of Ramsey Sage's arrival—the doorbell *and* the nose-blowing, since his eloquent little appeal to her about family had really struck a nerve. The third time, she was reasonably sure, would be the social worker, Davis Webster, ringing, with Anabel in tow.

Which meant that Claire had to get a hold of herself. Honestly, there was no reason for her to be crying. Just because Ramsey had spoken so poignantly about his nonexistent relations and the dissolution of his family? Just because his voice had sounded so strangely melancholy when he did? Just because what he had said of his empty clan brought to the surface her own feelings of emptiness in knowing she had no clan to begin with? Just because a family was the one thing she had always wanted and had never had, and probably never would have, even though she celebrated family every damned day in her work? Just because she felt like such an outcast from society because she'd never in her life had the very thing that defined the culture in which she'd grown up? Was that any reason to cry? Of course not.

By the time Claire made her way back to the sitting room, she had collected herself reasonably well, and she saw that Chandler had kept things under control during her absence. If one defined the term "under control" to mean that he and Ramsey were both on their feet, glaring at each other in uncomfortable silence. She was about to say something to them—something along the lines of "Oh, please, just get over yourselves already"—when the door-bell sounded again, alerting her to a much more pressing development.

Anabel Sage had arrived.

Inhaling deeply, Claire covered what little distance re-mained between her and the front door, and opened it. How-ever, surprisingly, her gaze didn't fall immediately on the little girl who was to be her temporary—Claire hoped—ward, even though Anabel's imminent arrival and all its re-sultant anxiety had been at the forefront of Claire's brain for the past week. No, it was the person carrying little Anabel who drew her eye.

The words *boyishly handsome* came to mind when she saw the man, but then she decided they really would have done him a disservice. Because the phrase suggested he had youthful and conventional good looks, and that wasn't the case at all. Even though he looked to be in his early thirties, there was an air about him of being much older. His features might have been ordinary enough when taken individually—though his nose was a bit too thin, perhaps, and his lips a touch too full—but they were arranged on a face that looked as if it had been hewn by gods, all sharp planes and fierce angles. He was tall and lean and rangy, and in addition to tumultuous, overly long, pale blond curls, he claimed tumultuous, overly large, pale blue eyes, eyes that seemed to be almost vacant somehow. Claire could think of no other way to describe them. They offered no clue as to what the man was like, or what he might be thinking or feeling.

But as extraordinary as all that was, it wasn't the most remarkable part about him. The most remarkable part was in the man's wardrobe selection. Specifically, it was in *why* he had selected that particular wardrobe. Because he was wearing the ugliest, most obnoxious Hawaiian shirt Claire had ever seen, one decorated with a pattern that could have only been inspired by an LSD trip gone horribly wrong: purple and red and orange Tiki faces interposed over chartreuse coconut shell umbrella drinks. Add to the shirt his excessively baggy khakis, not to mention his ragged, red high-top sneakers, and arm him with a battered leather satchel that was slung over one shoulder and banged against the opposite hip, and Davis Webster looked more like a man who had been living on the streets for some time than he did a social worker.

And all Claire could think when she saw him was that those state budget cuts must have been a lot worse than the newspapers let on.

"Hey," he said by way of a greeting.

He also smiled, but there was nothing in the gesture that put Claire at ease, because the smile felt all wrong. Yes, he was smiling, but he was obviously not happy about it. In fact, he didn't seem as if he were happy about anything.

"I'm Davis Webster, the social worker assigned to Anabel's case," he added unnecessarily, extending his free hand toward Claire. "You must be Ms. Willoughby."

She nodded as she automatically took his hand, but he released her after one quick jerk, as if he were no more interested in shaking her hand than he was in smiling at her. When he released her, he reached down to collect a weathered weekender bag, then proceeded to enter the house, clearly feeling welcome enough there that he didn't see the need to wait for a formal invitation. Nor did he evidently see any need to introduce Claire to Anabel.

Claire tried to reassure herself that it might just be a common practice for Davis Webster not to wait around for a formal invitation, but somehow, that didn't really reassure her very much. It didn't help, either, that she was obligated to step aside to let him pass not because she was a good hostess, but because she risked getting run over if she didn't, since he obviously felt so welcome that he wasn't going to let a little thing like the owner of the house get in his way. Literally. Claire wasn't sure if his forwardness was because it was just his way as a human being to be forward, or if maybe it was a customary tactic of social workers everywhere, to go ahead and enter the premises without waiting for a formal invitation, just in case you caught someone off guard, doing something they shouldn't, because then it would make them unfit as parents and you could nail their ass to the wall.

Because, somehow, Claire did get the feeling that Davis Webster was the kind of man who would look for the worst in people, if for no other reason than that the worst was what he expected of them. And it wasn't just his false smile and his exhausted-looking accoutrements that made her think that, either. There was a sort of flatness and fatigue in his voice—in fact, there was a flatness and fatigue all about him—that suggested he just didn't give a damn about anything or anybody.

"My goodness, won't you come in?" she invited formally, even though he was already making his way into the sitting room.

He spun around at the question, looking faintly surprised by it, almost as if he hadn't even realized what he was doing. But then that impression, too, was gone, and he regrouped enough that Claire was left looking at another blank smile from him that meant absolutely nothing.

"Thanks, don't mind if I do," he said in that same lifeless voice.

Then he turned around again and crossed the sitting room to where Chandler and Ramsey were still standing with their hands hooked on their hips glaring at each other, as if they were challenging each other to . . . something. Some guy thing that Claire couldn't hope to understand because, thankfully, her body produced too much estrogen. Davis came to a halt between the two men, looked first at one, then the other, then set down the weekender bag on the floor. And then he fisted the hand that wasn't holding Anabel onto his free hip and began glaring, too. Were she a painter recording the scene on canvas, Claire would have titled her creation *Early Man Invents the Greeting*.

That was the thing about men. They really knew how to keep conversation to a minimum.

Ah, well, she thought. At least they were all on speaking terms.

As if to illustrate that, both men turned to look at Davis Webster, then nodded silently in reception and relaxed their stances some. And Claire thanked every god she could think of that she had been born the estrogen producer she was. Because testosterone clearly did something to the human brain she didn't want done to hers.

" 'Hello,' I think, is the word you're all looking for," she told the men as she made her way toward the group. "It's a traditional word of salutation that we use in this culture." Then, before any of the men had a chance to comment—not that any of them seemed inclined to comment, because they were all too busy looking at her as if she were an idiot—she added, "Mr. Webster, this is my attorney, Chandler Edison, and this is Anabel's uncle, Ramsey Sage."

"I'm Chandler Edison," Chandler was quick to say, lest the social worker think Ramsey was the attorney instead. Which, of course, would have been easy to do, since so many attorneys these days had those barbed-wire tattoos encircling their bulging biceps beneath the ripped-out sleeves of their denim work shirts. It was a natural mistake to make.

"Pleasure," Davis Webster said as he shook Chandler's hand with another one of those quick shake-and-release things he'd used on Claire. And funny how he used the word *pleasure*, when he acted as if meeting Chandler was more of an ordeal than anything else. Then again, it probably wouldn't be polite to reply "Ordeal" when meeting someone, even if that was the case. Then again—again—meeting Chandler could be an ordeal, Claire knew. Especially during allergy season.

"Ramsey Sage," Ramsey added, stepping forward to elbow Chandler out of the way, lest the social worker think Chandler was Anabel's uncle. Which, of course, would have been easy to do since so many uncles these days sneered at the little girls who were supposed to be their nieces, which was precisely what Chandler was doing at the moment, Claire observed with a frown.

Well, she knew he wasn't fond of children, but he didn't have to be so obvious about it. The least he could do was pretend he was delighted by the child's arrival, just as Claire intended to do.

Anabel, however, took matters into her own hands then, and she seemed no more impressed to make the two men's acquaintances than Davis was, nor did she clearly intend to pretend anything. Because she suddenly began to howl. Loudly. Lustily. Lengthily. And only then did Claire really begin to process the reason why all of them had come together today—that, according to authorities in two states, she was utterly and completely responsible, however temporarily, for a young child. Because it finally hit her then—hit her like a brick upside the head, in fact—just exactly what she'd done by conceding to Eleanor Sage's final wishes, however temporarily. Claire was Anabel's legal guardian. At least until a judge decided that it would be okay for Ramsey Sage to take over that task himself.

If a judge decided that. And if Claire decided that, too.

Because looking again at Ramsey Sage, and noting his bedraggled clothes and overly long hair and diamond earring and barbed-wire tattoo, and recalling again his invisible means of support, it occurred to Claire that maybe, just maybe, a judge would have to be crazy to name the man anyone's guardian. And maybe, just maybe, Claire would have to be crazy to even let things go that far. And if that were the case, then she was going to be responsible for raising Anabel to adulthood, all by herself.

A wave of dizziness overcame her, and it was only with a very focused effort that she managed to make her way to the sofa to sit down. Making matters worse, Anabel continued to howl, her bellows growing louder with every breath she inhaled. Worst of all, though, the three men surrounding the baby launched into activity in an effort to make her stop, their attempts louder and more irritating even than the squalling child. And when none seemed able to soothe the distraught toddler, they all turned on each other.

"What did you do to her, Edison?" That from Ramsey Sage in a very accusatory tone. "I wouldn't put it past you, pinching a kid."

"I didn't do anything. You scared her, you big . . . big . . . biker dude." That from Chandler in a very wimpy tone. "I don't blame her for being terrified."

"Oh, you scared of me?" That from Ramsey in a very proud tone.

"How dare you! Of course I'm not scared of you." That from Chandler in a very scared tone.

"Both of you knock it off." That from Davis Webster in a very second grade teacher tone. "This is getting us nowhere."

And through it all, Anabel kept howling in a very exasperated tone.

Since the baby was the only one acting her age at the moment, she was the one to whom Claire turned her attention. And she saw immediately that Anabel Claire Sage looked exactly like her photographs. Well, except for the red face and wide-open mouth. But even at that, Claire would have easily recognized her. She was little and soft and round and blond, and her eyes, filled with tears as they were, were enormous and blue. And when she saw that Claire was staring at her, the little girl fixed her gaze intently on Claire's face, and, for a moment, she stopped crying.

And in that moment, Claire felt an instantaneous and odd sort of connection to the child. Anabel Sage was completely alone in the world. Claire hadn't been much older than Anabel when she'd lost her own mother and father and, like Anabel, had been turned over to the care of the state. Had things gone differently, Anabel might have been carted off to an institution to be raised by strangers, just as Claire had been. Had things gone differently, Claire might have been cared for by someone who took at least some small interest in her welfare, someone with whom she might have established some semblance of a family, regardless of how small and unconventional.

Chance. It was a strange thing. And best not thought upon for any length of time.

So Claire didn't think about it. Instead, she marveled at the little girl Davis Webster held with such astonishing ease, as if he didn't feel at all uncomfortable handling a child, even one who was screaming like a banshee on a wicked whiskey drunk. Maybe he didn't seem like a happy man, she thought, and maybe he was a horrible, horrible dresser, but at least he was comfortable in the presence of children. That had to count for something.

"Gentlemen, please," Claire interjected when the three men showed no signs of slowing down anytime soon. "You're *all* upsetting the baby." And then she surprised herself by standing and taking a few steps toward Davis Webster, and reaching for Anabel herself.

But before she could make contact, Davis Webster, obviously sensing her intentions, took a step away, pulling Anabel closer to himself as if trying to shield her. His action took Claire by surprise. Of course, she knew this interview was, technically, conditional, and that if the social worker found any reason to think she was incapable of caring for the girl, he could keep Anabel in state's care. But surely he could see that wasn't the case. Couldn't he?

Then she realized that Chandler and Ramsey were standing toe to toe, each accusing the other of being everything from a "ragged vagabond pettifogger"—one guess as to which of them that particular epithet had come from—to a "bogus candyass jerk." Okay, so maybe, under the circumstances, she could see where Davis Webster might have one or two—hundred—concerns. All she had to do was show him he was wrong about this being an unfit environment for a child.

She just hoped that he *was* wrong.

Chandler and Ramsey did have the decency to quiet themselves at Claire's stern look, though the glaring thing kept on in full force. So she decided to ignore them both and instead smiled softly at Davis Webster, gesturing toward the loveseat in a silent invitation that he and Anabel should sit down. Then she folded herself onto it, too, and smiled some more.

Surprisingly, she didn't have to force the smile, either. Because there was something in the way that Anabel returned her scrutiny that made a bubble of pure delight ascend inside her. The little girl was dressed in a poofy little playsuit of purple-and-yellow plaid, her pudgy feet encased in sandals the color of fresh butter. With the blond curls framing her round face, and with her facial features twisted tight in intensity as she focused her attention on Claire, Anabel vaguely resembled a pansy. The fanciful notion was unlike Claire, and she was strangely delighted by her own whimsy.

"So this is Anabel," she said to start them off. She dipped her head toward the little girl, bringing their faces closer, grateful to note that the baby's howling had ebbed to a few soft hiccuping sobs. Better than that, when Claire's face was within reach, Anabel lifted a pudgy little hand and, after only a moment's hesitation, settled it open-palmed against

Claire's cheek. The touch was so unexpected, so gentle, so sweet, that something inside Claire felt as if it were melting. Really, in spite of everything, Anabel was pretty adorable.

"This is Anabel," Davis confirmed, even though that really wasn't necessary for him to do. What was also unnecessary was for him to turn his knees to the side, so that Anabel was pulled farther away from Claire, something that removed the toddler's hand from her face. Claire wasn't sure what Davis Webster's problem was, but she wished he'd get over it. Even if he'd never met her before, how could he possibly think—how could he simply *assume*—that she was a threat to the little girl?

Straightening again, Claire met the social worker's gaze. She smiled again, but this time the expression was forced. The man didn't exactly generate a feeling of warmth and goodwill.

"Guess we have a lot to talk about, don't we?" she asked softly. And although the question was meant for Davis, somehow she seemed to be posing it to Anabel instead.

"Yes, we do," Davis told her in reply.

But it was Anabel who smiled, and somehow, amid the chaos, that made Claire think that, somehow, everything was going to be all right.

Probably.

Eventually.

She hoped.

As much as Ramsey would have liked to continue his glaring match with Edison—hey, he was winning, after all— he knew there were infinitely larger matters to consider right now. Of course, the largest matter was actually pretty small, he noted as he stole another glance at the little girl perched on Davis Webster's knee. But she sure was cute, his niece.

His niece.

Only now was he beginning to understand just how much his life was going to change, once he assumed responsibility for his sister's child. Until now, he'd pretty much taken his entire life day by day, sometimes hour by hour, and had never made plans beyond the end of the week. And even then, his plans had, for the most part, involved only a couple of things: one, get the job done, and two, stay alive. Which was probably why he'd never made plans beyond the end of the week, now that he thought about it. Oh, he was good at what he did for a living, and he was careful, but even the best guys in the business could come to a bad end. They didn't take care of business, so they didn't stay alive.

Yeah, times had been a lot simpler then.

Now, though, with a baby on board, Ramsey had a whole host of plans to make, and he had to make them way beyond the end of the week. At the moment, however, the most important thing was getting to know Anabel and making a good impression on the social worker. Which, all modesty aside, should be a piece of cake. Because he'd certainly never had trouble getting to know the feminine half of the world before—au contraire—and he'd never had trouble misleading, ah . . . that was, *impressing* . . . government officials.

Yeah, he and Anabel ought to be making their way home anytime now. Ramsey just wished "home" at this point was a house more like Claire's, well anchored in a good neighborhood and decorated in Early Conspicuous Consumption, and less like a room at the Budget Motor-on-Inn decorated in Early Eisenhower Era—though not because it had any sort of retrofashionable thing going on, that was for sure. But thinking about taking Anabel home—to a *home* home, one rooted in suburbia with three bedrooms and one and a half baths, on a plot of land he'd be responsible for tending and paying for himself—made a shudder of fear wind through him.

Ramsey wasn't used to being responsible for anyone but himself. And he sure as hell hadn't ever planned to put down roots anywhere. The thought of tying himself to one area for any length of time didn't sit well with him. The thought of tying himself to one area *and* another human being sat even worse. As did thoughts of a mortgage and crabgrass and clogged drains and termites and three square meals a day. God, he was going to have to learn to cook. He'd have to familiarize himself with that food pyramid thing. Couldn't feed a baby on the diet he'd been living on lately—tequila and burritos and Ho-Ho's. And someday Anabel would go to school. He'd have to join the PTA. Be a room parent. Go to soccer practice and gymnastics. Sit with all the moms in the bleachers, who were reading romance novels and trading recipes and talking about their husbands' 401(K)s. He'd have to help Anabel with her homework. Make science projects out of pipe cleaners and Styrofoam balls . . .

A sudden image popped into his head of himself in fifteen years: his hair thinning, his gut expanding, standing in front of a propane grill, wearing plaid Bermuda shorts and a polo shirt, with a lobster claw oven mitt on one hand and an apron that said "Who Invited All These Tacky People?" slung around his neck.

Oh, God . . . What was he getting himself into? Facing down Valdez in a tavern tussle was a piece of cake compared to fatherhood.

Shaking off the fears of what lay ahead, not to mention the realization that he had absolutely nothing to offer in the way of child-rearing qualities—hey, he'd bluffed his way

out of worse situations than this one, by God . . . probably—
Ramsey eyed his companions and tried to figure out where
he was supposed to sit. Edison, he noticed, had parked himself back on the loveseat way closer to Claire than was socially acceptable, in Ramsey's opinion. And there wasn't
much room between Claire and the social worker and Anabel, either. Which left Ramsey with no alternative but to
seat himself in the chair he had occupied earlier, farther
away from his niece than anyone else in the room.

And he tried not to think about how significant that was,
seeing as how he'd always distanced himself from his family. Those days were over, dammit. From here on out, he was
going to do whatever he had to do to keep the Sages together.

But try as he might to think of an opening that would
work in his favor, all Ramsey could do was watch the way
Claire was looking at Anabel, as if she were both drawn to
and repelled by the little girl. She looked nervous, but curious, fearful, but hopeful, overwhelmed, but undeterred. If he
didn't know better, he'd think she was halfway entertaining
the idea that maybe *she* should be the one to—

Nah, he immediately reassured himself. Edison had made
it clear on the phone that the last thing Claire wanted or
needed in her life was a child to look after. She had a huge
business to run, and a million professional obligations to
meet, which left no time for anything so mundane as "family." Plus, according to the attorney, she didn't know the first
thing about children. Likewise, according to the attorney,
she was as eager for things to work out between Anabel and
Ramsey as Ramsey was. And although Edison hadn't said it
in so many words, he'd pretty much made it clear that Claire
would then be delighted to wash her hands of both Sages.

Which was just fine with Ramsey. Because he'd be delighted to wash his hands of her—and her Grace Kelly 'do, and her creamy, flawless complexion, and her sedate strand of pearls encircling her throat that he would just love to see her wearing with nothing else. So there. Then he could get on with his life. His new life. As a father. With his sister's daughter to raise to adulthood. And a lobster claw oven mitt to don.

Another wave of terror rose inside him then, and Ramsey had to battle all the doubts that had plagued him since his return to the States to claim his niece. He could do this, he told himself. He could take care of Anabel and be a good provider. He owed it to his niece to see that she wasn't raised among strangers. And he owed that to Eleanor, too, because he'd left her to fend for herself when he'd selfishly left home. And he also owed it to himself, he thought further, because he needed to know he still had a few decent bones left in his body. He finally had a chance to make right in the present a few things he'd done wrong in the past. He couldn't bring back his family and fix everything that had needed fixing there, but he could sure as hell see to it that his niece didn't end up in a broken environment, too.

Still, Claire *was* looking at Anabel in a way that made Ramsey think she was more interested in the little girl than Edison had led him to think. Surely, though, that was only his imagination.

"So, Webster," Ramsey said to the social worker, still not sure how to insinuate himself favorably into the situation, but knowing it was imperative that he do just that. "How was the trip from North Carolina?"

Davis Webster glanced up at him, and judging by his expression, he'd completely forgotten Ramsey was there until now. Gee, that probably wasn't good. "Actually, Mr. Sage,"

he said, "I live here in Nashville. Anabel's case was transferred over from Raleigh. She was brought here by another
social worker."

Ramsey nodded. "Oh. Yeah. Okay. I guess that makes
sense."

Boy, he was scorin' some points now. Webster was sure to
be making a mental note of Ramsey's keen reasoning, not to
mention his vast and sophisticated vocabulary.

"So," he tried again, still scrambling for something to say
that might win the social worker over to his side, "how 'bout
them Titans, huh?" And he congratulated himself for remembering that there was a professional football team in
Tennessee. Had he not seen the headlines in the paper he'd
perused over lunch earlier about the upcoming season,
though, he would have forgotten all about that, because it
had been so long since he'd followed American sports. Or
any sports, really. Except *fútbol*, and only because he'd had
no choice there, seeing as how that was the second biggest
religion in Latin America, right after Catholicism.

"I'm not much of a sports fan," Webster replied. "So I
have no opinion on the Titans one way or another."

Ramsey nodded again. "Gotcha." He was about to take
another stab at manly pursuits, but Webster turned his attention to Claire. Almost, Ramsey thought, as if he were trying
to avoid Ramsey.

In a word, Hmmm . . .

"Did you get the list of Anabel's requirements that I faxed
you?" Davis asked Claire.

She nodded. "I think we were able to take care of everything."

List of requirements? Ramsey echoed to himself. How
come nobody had faxed *him* a list of requirements? Okay, so

maybe because he didn't have a fax machine—but that was no excuse. Someone could have at least *offered*.

"We've fixed up the guest bedroom next to mine," Claire continued. "I think Anabel will be very comfortable in there."

"Excellent," Webster replied. "You won't mind showing it to me."

Ramsey noted that what the social worker said was a statement, not a question, thereby indicating he was giving an order, not making a request, even though the latter would have been much more polite than the former. Obviously, this guy didn't mess around. Obviously, this guy was used to giving orders and having them followed without hesitation or question. Obviously, Ramsey was going to have some problems here.

"Of course," Claire immediately—obediently—replied. "I'll be happy to show you the room. Olive is in there now, seeing to the finishing touches."

"And Olive is . . ."

Wow, even that didn't come off sounding like a question, Ramsey noted. This guy really did insist on being answered.

"My best friend?" Claire said quickly, suddenly sounding ten years younger than she was, and suddenly speaking in the inquisitive tense, even though she was the one offering answers. "She's also my assistant? Olive will be taking care of Anabel occasionally? When I have to work? Surely Chandler told you that?"

Webster looked past Claire, at the attorney. "Actually, Mr. Edison never mentioned your friend-slash-assistant," he said in a voice of unmistakable disapproval.

Ramsey hadn't known what the word *chagrined* meant until that moment. But that had to be the way Edison was look-

ing. Ramsey smiled. Gee, maybe it wouldn't be so bad to
bow out of the conversation for a few minutes. At least long
enough to see Edison get embarrassed. If Ramsey waited
long enough, the attorney might even reach the humiliated
stage, and that was definitely something worth seeing.

"Chandler?" Claire said, turning around to look at the attorney full on. "Is this true?"

"Well, I meant to tell Mr. Webster about Olive," Edison
said. "I just forgot, that was all. There were so many other
things to cover. And Olive isn't exactly the most memorable
person, you know."

Ooo, bad move, Edison, Ramsey thought. Even he knew
better than to dis' Claire's friend-slash-assistant, and he
didn't even know who the hell this Olive was. Because
Claire obviously didn't think her friend-slash-assistant was
as unmemorable as Edison did.

"Olive and I have known each other since college, Chandler," she reminded the attorney in a *very* frosty tone. Oh,
yeah, Ramsey thought, humiliation would be coming anytime now. "Which I don't think I need to point out," she
added, "is a lot longer than I've known you."

Ooo, score one for the lady.

"*And* she's my best friend," Claire repeated.

Ooo, score two for the lady.

"Of course," the attorney agreed. "I'm sorry," he further
apologized. "As I said, Mr. Webster and I had much to cover
in our conversation, and Olive's name just never came up,
that's all."

In response to his assertions, Claire arched that elegant
blond eyebrow of hers again, then turned her back on the attorney to address the social worker instead.

Game to the lady. Hoo-wah.

"Olive is wonderful?" Claire assured Webster, returning to her uncertain voice and posture again. "And between the two of us? Anabel will never have to be left with a sitter?"

Something about the way she said that made Ramsey think she was punctuating the comment with a fervent, but silent, *I hope?*

"Naturally, I'll be interviewing this Olive," Webster said.

"That won't be a problem?" Claire told him, sounding as if she were shaving another ten years off her life. "As I said, she's here at the house now? You can talk to her this afternoon?"

"I will."

"O-o-okay?"

Wow, Ramsey could almost hear the vertebrae crack in her back when she snapped to attention the way she did. Then again, Webster definitely had a way about him of making people feel like they were children and he was . . . well, Hitler.

But Ramsey didn't let that deter him. Everyone was talking like Anabel would be staying with Claire indefinitely, and he needed to make clear his intention that his niece would be leaving with him. Today. Because when he'd spoken to Edison on the phone, the attorney had made clear *his* intention that Anabel leave with Ramsey. Today. In fact, the attorney had made it sound like it was a done deal, that Ramsey need do little other than sign on the dotted line, and he'd have his family back together again.

"Look, Mr. Webster," Ramsey began, making sure he used the proper form of address this time. Probably, it hadn't been a good idea to just call him Webster a minute ago. He just wasn't used to interacting with decent human beings, that was all. It had been too long since he'd had to worry about another person's feelings, because he'd been living so long with people who didn't have any feelings. "Mr. Webster," he started again, "I don't mean to presume, but all of you seem to be working under the idea that Anabel will be staying here with Claire."

Webster gazed back at him with an expression that might have been faintly amused, had the man been the type to let other people know what he was thinking—and had the man been the type to get amused. "That could be," he told Ramsey, "because Anabel *will* be staying here with Ms. Willoughby."

Whoa, whoa, whoa, Ramsey thought. That wasn't what he'd had in mind at all. "But—" he began.

"Provided, of course, I find everything in order," the social worker added.

"But—"

"And so far, everything seems to be in order."

"But—"

"Of course, I still have this Olive to interview."

"But—"

"However, Ms. Willoughby's assurances have made an impression, so I don't think I'll have any objection to this arrangement."

"But—"

"Which the courts ordered."

"But—"

"And which your sister wanted."

"But—"

"But what, Mr. Sage?"

"But . . . I'm Anabel's uncle," he finally got out, thinking that argument must hold a hell of a lot more weight than placing the child with a complete stranger. Of course, Ramsey was no more familiar with the child than Claire was, having made Anabel's acquaintance at exactly the same time, but a blood tie had to be worth something, didn't it? It had to be worth more than a big house and millions of dollars and a good job and staunch ties to a community. Blood ties— family ties—were the most valuable thing in the world, right?

Oh, sure, he taunted himself. Look how much *he'd* always valued family ties. He'd walked out on his family almost two decades ago and never looked back once. That was how much *he'd* cherished them.

"Yes, you are Anabel's uncle," Webster agreed. "But Ms. Willoughby is the person Eleanor Sage indicated should raise her child."

"But, I'm Eleanor's brother," he pointed out, even though he was reasonably certain that such an argument would hold no more weight with anyone than the fact that he was Anabel's uncle did.

"That may be," Webster conceded, clearly striving to be diplomatic, "but Eleanor evidently didn't think you would be the best provider for her daughter." He drove his gaze up and down Ramsey's person before adding, "I can't imagine why not. After all, you're unshaven, you're untidy, and, quite frankly, you don't smell all that good. And I'm assuming that rattletrap bike out there is yours. I'd think any woman would be delighted to have you raising her child."

Okay, so maybe *striving to be diplomatic* had been the wrong impression, Ramsey thought. Clearly this guy didn't care who he offended. He gaped at Webster in disbelief for a moment, then opened his mouth to let loose with both barrels. But something prohibited him from firing.

That something being that he realized Davis Webster was absolutely right.

Ramsey looked down at his attire then, at the ragged jeans and the ripped shirt and the dusty, beat-up boots. Then he lifted a hand to scrub it over the days-old growth of beard on his jaw, and recalled that his face bore obvious evidence of having been used as a punching bag not long ago. Then he remembered that he'd roared up to the palatial Willoughby estate on a Harley hog he'd bought off a guy named Snake in Brownsville, Texas, for two hundred bucks and a case of tequila.

And then he thought, *Oh, hell*.

What had be been thinking, coming here today looking like this? *Of course* no one was going to let him come near Anabel. Who in their right mind *would* let a man who looked like he did come near a small child? Man, he'd been hanging out with thugs and criminals for so long, he really had forgotten that there was a whole 'nother world out there, one that *wasn't* populated by thugs and criminals, and one where there *were* rules and regulations. At the very least, there were traditions and customs that governed polite behavior. Of course, they were traditions and customs that Ramsey had once found so restrictive they'd nearly strangled him, but that was beside the point.

He wasn't a wild, unfocused eighteen-year-old kid anymore. And he wasn't a twentysomething loose cannon who'd immersed himself in a world most people—people who lived normal, productive, decent lives—never even thought about. He was a man of thirty-eight who had a child's welfare to consider. At least, he *hoped* he'd have a child's welfare to consider. He may have already mucked it up beyond repair by coming here today without thinking first.

But it honestly hadn't occurred to him to clean himself up and dress like a normal, productive member of society. He'd been so eager and anxious to get to his niece that he hadn't wanted to add any more time to the trip than he already had by doing something so mundane as, say . . . shaving and showering. The only reason he'd stopped long enough to get a motel room was so that he'd know he had someplace to take Anabel once he claimed her.

"But I'm Anabel's uncle," he said again. Unfortunately he spoke with much less conviction this time. Probably because he was feeling much less conviction this time.

"And I'm sure Ms. Willoughby won't mind if you come to visit your niece on occasion," Webster told him.

Ramsey's gaze flew to Claire's then, and his worst fears were confirmed. She really was thinking maybe she should be the one to raise Anabel, he realized then. Maybe not in her conscious mind, but the idea was rooted in her subconscious, even if it hadn't yet come to fruition. He could tell by the way she had been looking at Anabel and by the way she had been reassuring Webster. She'd fixed up a room, he reminded himself. Had bought all of Anabel's *requirements*. Maybe she was only planning on a temporary arrangement at this point, but it was an arrangement nonetheless. And temporary could still last a long time.

He knew then that he was going to have a fight on his hands, winning custody of his niece from Claire Willoughby. A worse fight than the garden-variety tavern tussle he was accustomed to, too. And where he usually fared pretty well with physical altercations, often with men twice his size, he could very well be beaten this time, by a wispy blond beauty no bigger than a good-sized golden retriever. Though that probably wasn't an analogy he should use aloud in her presence. But to any court in the country, Claire was clearly better suited than he to raise a child. She was rich, she had strong ties to the community, she had a stable job, and she was a woman. That last fact, in particular, had not escaped Ramsey's notice.

But she didn't trust him any farther than she could throw him, and a little thing like her would barely be able to get him off the ground. And if that was how she was reacting after an exchange of simple conversation and sweet tea, then how was she going to react when she found out what he did for a living? Then again, if what he did for a living ever came out, it could cost him the guardianship of Anabel. What judge in his right mind would turn over a thirteen-month-old girl to a guy who spent ninety percent of his time with drug dealers and murderers? Despite what he'd told Claire about finding "something else" to do for a living, Ramsey wasn't sure he knew how to do anything else. On the other hand, considering the danger and insanity of his profession, how much longer did he think he could keep it up?

Maybe this whole thing with Anabel was a sign from the Great Beyond telling him to get out while the getting was good—i.e., while he was still alive. Because one thing Ramsey had learned during his years of being surrounded by drug dealers and murderers was that the life span for guys like him wasn't exactly spanned. He was just grateful he'd been able to take a sabbatical—so to speak—for a while, to figure things out.

"Edison led me to believe I'd be named Anabel's guardian," Ramsey told the social worker plainly, in spite of his misgivings. "Today. I mean, I know I don't look like much, but I'm still her family. And Edison said—"

"Chandler and I thought perhaps you might be better

equipped to care for Anabel than I am," Claire interjected. And she *was* being diplomatic, Ramsey thought. "But that was before . . ."

And because she was being so damned diplomatic, her voice trailed off, and she didn't finish her statement by pointing out that that was before Ramsey had shown up looking like the wretched refuse of society.

Wow. The game really was going to go to the lady, he thought. As was his niece, if he didn't do something quick.

"I can take care of Anabel," he said emphatically.

And because she was so goddamned diplomatic, Claire didn't say anything in response to that.

"I can," he insisted.

But it was Davis Webster who finally spoke. "The fact is, Mr. Sage, your sister designated in her will that Ms. Willoughby should be your niece's guardian. And unless Ms. Willoughby takes exception and a judge orders otherwise, that's the only arrangement I can consider."

Unless Ms. Willoughby takes exception and a judge orders otherwise, Ramsey repeated to himself. Not *until* Ms. Willoughby takes exception and a judge orders otherwise. Meaning there was no chance he'd be leaving the Willoughby place with his niece today, and little chance he'd be leaving the Willoughby place with his niece any other day. Because obviously the Willoughby place was where his niece belonged.

No, he immediately told himself. Not. Bloody. Likely.

Anabel didn't belong here. She didn't belong with strangers. She belonged with her family. Even if that family only numbered one. Even if that family hadn't been around much lately. That family was here now. And that family wasn't going anywhere. Not until it was united again.

"Then I'll find a judge to order otherwise," Ramsey said, understanding, for the first time that day—maybe for the first time in his life—just how big a fight he had on his hands. He didn't worry about the Ms. Willoughby taking exception part. Because at the moment, he didn't give a damn about that.

"Mr. Sage," Claire began.

But when Ramsey turned to look at her, whatever words she had intended to say dried up completely. Even when she lifted a hand to her throat, ostensibly in an effort to help those words along, nothing more emerged. Probably, he thought, because he was glaring at her with a lot more wattage than he'd used on Edison. So she only swallowed with some difficulty and closed her mouth again.

"As I said, we have a lot to talk about," Webster reiterated, turning toward Claire, dismissing Ramsey. "So we might as well get started."

"You talk," Ramsey told them all, standing. "I have a few things I need to do. And then I'll be back for Anabel."

And without waiting to see how anyone would react to his vow—because, dammit, he didn't care how anyone reacted—he stood and strode across the big living room, to the front door. Then he opened it, passed through it, and began to make some decisions.

For the first time in his life, Ramsey was going to do some thinking before he acted.

Five

$\mathcal{O}$live was horrified when the door to Anabel's room opened and a small group of people came in, not only because she hadn't been expecting a group of people, small or otherwise, but because Olive really didn't like groups of people. She'd always felt infinitely more comfortable when she was alone. Claire was just about the only other human being, besides her parents, that Olive Tully had allowed to get close. It had helped back in college that Claire had felt as alienated and uneasy in social settings as Olive did. That, as much as anything, had cemented their friendship.

Claire, however, had eventually climbed over the walls she'd erected around herself, and these days, she moved about freely in most social circles. But then, Claire's walls hadn't had their foundations laid deep in fear, and Claire had never had to worry about self-preservation the way Olive had.

And it was those preservative instincts that jumped to the fore now, since Olive saw that the small group of people included, in addition to Claire and Chandler—who, these days, anyway, didn't bother Olive so much, because he couldn't instill fear in a garden slug—a total stranger, as well. And when she noted the presence of that total stranger, Olive did what she always did in such situations. She automatically began to back away from the group, hoping maybe they hadn't noticed her yet, and she'd be able to duck out without being seen.

But after only two steps, she stopped dead in her tracks, which just went to show how very startled she was. Normally, once Olive started retreating, she didn't stop until she had completely escaped from whatever had made her retreat. But this time she did, when she got a better look at the . . . creature . . . accompanying Claire and Chandler. Because it was the most heinous sort of monster she could imagine, the kind of beast that had haunted her dreams since she was old enough to understand such menaces. And it was more dangerous than anything she could encounter, living, dead, or undead.

The man was *gorgeous*.

But worse than that, he was *flamboyant*. From the collar of his garishly colored Hawaiian shirt right down to the tips of his red high-top sneakers. The man would, to put it mildly, stand out in a crowd. Of circus freaks. Dressed like flamingos. Dancing the merengue.

Oh, this was *terrible*. This was the last thing she needed, to meet a gorgeous man who was flamboyant.

Fortunately, when the man's gaze began to travel around the room, it coasted right over Olive. He surveyed the furnishings, the rugs, the curtains on the windows, everything. Everything except her. He didn't notice her at all, which, she reminded herself, was the whole point, so why did she feel so slighted? He wasn't *supposed* to notice her. No one was. That was why she dressed as she did, in a completely nondescript way. She was wearing a plain, beige linen sheath and plain, beige sandals, and little else, save her plain, beige underthings. She didn't even wear jewelry, had never even had her ears pierced. Once, for Christmas, Claire had given her a pair of gold clip earrings fashioned into tiny, modest knots and a beautiful gold chain, simple in design, expensive in nature. But as touched as Olive had been by the gesture, and as much as she loved the set, she never wore them. Someone might notice them. Someone might notice *her*. And she couldn't have that.

So why did it bother her now, when this gorgeous, flamboyant man hadn't even seen her standing there?

"The room is fine," the man told Claire, turning back to face her. "Better than fine, actually," he added, sounding as if he resented having to make such a concession. "Anabel should be very comfortable here. Now, about this Olive person you mentioned. Where is she?"

Claire's gaze flew to Olive, and she was clearly embarrassed on Olive's behalf by the man's question. "She's, um . . . she's standing right there," she told the gorgeous, flamboyant—but obviously oblivious—man, opening her hand in Olive's direction.

Immediately, the man turned toward Olive, looking genuinely shocked to see her standing there. Uneasily, she lifted a hand waist high in a hasty greeting, then dropped it back to her side, twisting her fingers nervously in the fabric of her dress.

"Hello," she said softly, her voice sounding hoarse and strained, her stomach knotted with nerves. She cleared her throat a bit before continuing, "I'm Olive. Olive Tully."

"I . . . I'm sorry," the man apologized. And he did have the decency to look honestly embarrassed. "I didn't see you there."

"That's okay," she told him. And it really was okay, because no one was ever supposed to.

Still feeling anxious, she lifted her hand to her glasses, adjusting the frames on her nose even though they had no need to be adjusted. Then she ran her hand back over her straight, brown hair, knowing the gesture was unnecessary, because her hair was too short to ever get messed up, but feeling, for some reason, like she needed to do it anyway.

"This is Davis Webster, Olive," Claire said. "He's the social worker assigned to Anabel's case. He needs to talk to you."

A wild panic ripped through Olive at the announcement. As far as she was concerned, the only thing worse than being noticed by a total stranger was being spoken to by a total stranger. Bad enough she'd had to come up with a proper greeting. No way would she actually be able to converse with the man. Even if he hadn't been gorgeous, she would have had trouble chatting with him. Add to that the fact that he was flamboyant, and someone might notice her talking to him, and she didn't stand a chance.

"*Me?*" she said, her voice sounding like a squeak. "Why does he need to talk to *me?*"

"Because I told him you would be caring for Anabel sometimes."

Putting aside, for now, the fact that she and Claire weren't supposed to be caring for Anabel because the girl's uncle was supposed to be doing that—What was up with that, anyway?—Olive swallowed the terror that rose in her throat at hearing that she had to talk to Gorgeous Davis Webster.

"Is that true?" Gorgeous Davis Webster asked her. Asked her point-blank, too, which meant she was going to have to come up with an answer for him. Immediately.

"Uh-huh," she said, congratulating herself for not only coming up with an answer, but coming up with the right answer, even if it wasn't uttered in the most convincing voice. Or in real words, for that matter. She cleared her throat indelicately and tried again. "I mean, yes. Yes, I'll be taking care of Anabel when Claire has to work."

"I thought you worked as Ms. Willoughby's assistant."

Olive nodded. "Yes," she said. "I do." *Oh, bravo, Olive!* she applauded herself. *That's* two *right answers! With real words, no less!*

Gorgeous Davis Webster eyed her thoughtfully for a moment. "And seeing as how Ms. Willoughby's job is demanding enough for her to require an assistant," he said, "you must be a very busy lady, too."

Olive opened her mouth to agree, then realized she was walking into a trap. "I'd never be too busy for Anabel," she said, amazed not at her quick thinking—she was always quick in that—but her quick talking. Usually, it took a moment or two—or ten—for her to get her quick thoughts out of her mouth, especially when she was talking to someone she wasn't used to talking to. Sometimes it took days for her to do that. Something about Davis Webster, though, generated a feeling of urgency, and it felt strangely normal to reply so quickly to him.

She tried to tell herself that the urgency was a result of her concern about Anabel, but somehow she suspected it was the result of something much more elemental. Something much more . . . sexual. Something that Davis Webster as a man made her feel as a woman. And Olive didn't allow herself to have such thoughts, thoughts about men and what they could provide for a woman, and how badly some women—especially one woman—needed what they could provide. She'd realized a long time ago that she would never have a relationship like that with anyone, and, as a result, she'd made the decision a long time ago not to have feelings like that for anyone. Now, though, she couldn't help thinking maybe those feelings had found her anyway. It was just too bad there wouldn't be a relationship to accompany them.

She looked at Davis Webster again, at the unruly blond curls that she found herself wanting to brush back from his forehead with careless fingers, at the chiseled cheekbones and resolute jaw she would love to trace with curious fingertips. Although he was slim, his shoulders were broad and his bare forearms were muscular, attributes that only made him seem even taller than he already was. Really, if he wanted to, the man could have lifted her with one arm and hauled her easily away, to do with her whatever he wanted. But then she observed the way he held Anabel so easily, so carefully, as if he were trying to protect her from all the world's dangers, and Olive knew this man would never carry any woman away against her will. Would that her will were that strong.

Such an alluring mix of ripe sexuality and open tenderness, she thought as she concluded her survey of the man. And try as she did to quell them, a host of unfamiliar, unwelcome—though not especially unpleasant—sensations began to wind through her.

Davis Webster dipped his head in silent acknowledgment of her remark—and as the heat of embarrassment spread through her, she realized he was acknowledging her frank study of him, too—then he almost smiled. "Ms. Willoughby," he said to Claire, "would you mind taking

Anabel for a little while? She can explore her new room. Ms. Tully and I need to chat. Where would a good place for that be?"

Olive swallowed hard. Oh, God. He wanted to be alone with her. To talk. She really was a goner.

"You can use my office, on the other side of my bedroom, two doors down," she heard Claire say. But Olive's eyes never left Davis Webster's. Worse than that, his never left hers.

"Good," he said. "Ms. Tully?"

And then he swept an open hand toward the door.

Oh, yeah, Olive thought. She was a goner for sure.

Normally, Olive felt right at home in Claire's office, because she was in it almost as often as she was in her own office, and the decor for the two rooms was so similar. A hand-hooked floral rug spanned much of the cherry hardwood floors, and floor-to-ceiling cherry bookcases lined two walls opposite each other, all of them crammed full of books on cooking, decorating, and lifestyle topics. Though that was really for show, since Olive consulted them with far more frequency than Claire did. A third wall consisted almost entirely of windows, beveled along their panes, their lace curtains thrown open wide to reveal the lush green trees of the rambling garden in back. The sky above those trees today was blue and limitless, with patches of wispy white clouds stretched across it. Normally, the view would have made Olive feel peaceful, as if there were nothing in the world that could touch her. But normally, she wasn't sharing the view with someone like Davis Webster.

Having preceded him into the office, she turned to face

him, and was troubled to see him closing the door behind him. Even worse, once it was closed, he leaned his big body back against it, crossing his arms over his ample chest in a deceptively careless way, effectively barring any effort she might make to escape. What was really disturbing, though, was that he seemed to have placed himself in such a way precisely because he knew the first thing she would do upon entering the room—what she did every time she entered a room—would be to plan her escape route, should escape become necessary.

Not that she wanted to escape, necessarily. She just wanted to have that avenue open, should she be, say, overcome with the urge to flee in panic. Escape, flee in panic, it was all a matter of semantics. But she had always known where the closest exit lay in any situation, and had known how to get to it—and through it—no matter what.

Unless, of course, someone like Mr. Webster happened to position himself in such a way that she would have to wrestle him to the ground in order to get through it. Not that wrestling Mr. Webster to the ground was necessarily such an off-putting idea . . .

Olive closed her eyes for a moment and rejected the idea. There would be no wrestling of Mr. Webster, she told herself firmly. Not just because she honestly wouldn't know how to go about such a thing, and not just because he would be far too formidable a person to wrestle. But also because such an idea would assume that he was open to the possibility of being wrestled by her, and that, she was certain, wouldn't be the case at all. Not that he didn't look like he'd be very good at wrestling, mind you. She just didn't think he'd want to wrestle with the likes of her. No, Mr. Webster was probably more inclined to wrestle someone of his own stature, some-one tall and blond and showy, someone with an ample chest—though ample in ways other than the muscular—and not someone small and negligible and beige.

That made her feel a little better about the situation for some reason, so Olive opened her eyes and met his gaze lev-elly, feeling uncharacteristically brave when she did it. *Fine*, she thought. *Go ahead and ask your questions, Mr. Webster. Do your worst.*

She could handle this, she thought. She could talk to him and remain unruffled. She could take whatever questions he dished out.

Bring 'em on.

But instead of bringing on the questions, what Mr. Web-ster brought on was himself, and that wasn't what she had meant at all. Pushing himself away from the door—but keeping himself directly in front of it—he took a few delib-erate steps forward. Toward Olive. And it was all she could do not to take a few, less deliberate, steps backward. In re-treat. But when he continued to walk toward her, still keep-ing his body firmly between her and the door, she surrendered to the apprehension rising inside her, and, as he came to a stop, she completed one step back. So Mr. Webster took another step forward. And Olive took another step back. Mr. Webster completed another forward. So Olive completed another back. Narrowing his eyes at her, he took one more. Her heart began to pound heavily in her chest at his obvious attempt to intimidate her—at least, she thought he was trying to intimidate her—but, valiantly, she took one more step in retreat.

Or, rather, she tried to take one more step in retreat. Un-fortunately, by then, she had moved back so much that, in-

stead of completing a step backward, she bumped her fanny
into the edge of Claire's desk.

"Uh-oh," Davis said when he noted her collision with the
oversize antique writing table.

"Ah, actually," she stammered, "I was thinking more
along the lines of, um, 'Oops.'" Because, gosh, *Oops* was
just so much more articulate than *Uh-oh*, wasn't it?

He smiled at her, but the gesture was lacking in anything
remotely resembling happiness or joy. No, his smile was
more of the predatory variety, which did nothing to soothe
Olive's already frazzled nerves.

"Do I make you nervous, Ms. Tully?" he asked softly.

She swallowed hard. "A little," she lied. Because actually,
he made her nervous a lot.

He hesitated only a moment before asking, "Why?"

"It's nothing personal," she assured him, battling the almost overwhelming urge to bend down and scramble beneath Claire's desk. "Everyone makes me nervous."

"Really," he said. Said, not asked, as if her reply, though
interesting, wasn't a surprise to him at all. "And why is that,
I wonder?"

She managed a sort of halfhearted shrug, then reached behind herself to clutch the edge of Claire's desk. Although
Olive had won the battle not to crawl under it, her knees still
felt watery, and she needed to cling to something to keep
them from buckling beneath her completely.

And then, seemingly without even moving, Davis was
suddenly standing right beside her, leaning back against
Claire's desk, and turning his body to face her. And even
though he didn't quite touch her, he was *awfully* close. But
he crossed his arms over his chest, hooked one ankle over
the other, and gazed down at Olive with faint amusement.

"I only want to ask you a few mundane questions," he told her, "to reassure myself that you'll be an appropriate caretaker for Anabel."

"Then ask them," Olive said. With no small effort, she forced herself to straighten up, then pushed herself away from the desk and strode to the center of the room. That put her in direct line with the door, and that made her feel much better about things. "And stop trying to make me feel uncomfortable," she added.

He turned his body again to face her, looking even more amused. "What makes you think I'm trying to make you feel uncomfortable?"

"I don't know," she confessed, crossing her arms over her chest now. And then she realized what a defensive gesture that was on her part. So maybe the fact that Davis had done the same thing was because he was feeling defensive, too. "Maybe I think you're doing it," she said, "because you feel uncomfortable, too." And only then did she realize that that was indeed how he felt, and that his way of combatting his discomfort was to turn it on someone else.

For one split second, he let his arrogant expression slip enough that Olive saw the truth in what she had said. Then, just as quickly, his self-possession was back. But he didn't belabor her remark. Instead, he went straight into his interrogation.

"So, Ms. Tully, are you a native of Tennessee?" he asked her.

Ooo, he was going to start off with the tough ones. But that was okay. She was up for it. She shook her head. "No, I was born in New Jersey." *I think*, she added to herself. It had been so long since she'd had to answer that question that she honestly couldn't remember for sure what answer she was supposed to give. Then she gave herself a quick mental nod. Yeah, New Jersey. That was right. That much of their past they had agreed to stay with. "Newark," she elaborated further, thinking, Why the hell not? She did have a few vague memories of the place she could pull up if he wanted specifics. And it had been years since she'd actually lived there. Her trail since then was cluttered and nearly impossible to follow.

"Is that where you grew up?" he asked.

She shook her head again. "No, we left before I started school. I moved around a lot as a child. I lived in quite a few places before settling here when I went to college."

"Father in the military?" he asked.

"Mother," she corrected him.

"I see."

Oh, Olive sincerely doubted that. But she'd let him think he understood if it made him feel better.

He grinned, and somehow she knew he had been hoping to trip her up. She didn't know how she knew that, but she did. He wanted her to reveal herself as inappropriate in some way. He was looking for the worst in her, not the best. Maybe because he didn't think there was any best. For some reason, though, she didn't take it personally.

As Davis Webster eyed with much interest Claire Willoughby's assistant, he realized he had at least a couple dozen questions he wanted to ask her. Unfortunately, most of them weren't included in the social worker's handbook of questions to ask prospective guardians. No, these were all questions that appeared in his own handbook, in the chapter headed, "None of Your Damned Business." And question number one was Why does Olive Tully go out of her way to make people overlook her?

Because she did go out of her way to make people overlook her. That could be the only reason why Davis had overlooked her when he'd made his initial inventory of Anabel Sage's new bedroom. Although she wasn't what might be termed beautiful, she was attractive, in a quiet, subdued sort of way, and Davis did generally notice attractive women—especially the quiet, subdued sort, more was the pity—even if he didn't respond to them with the enthusiasm he once had. Her loose-fitting dress didn't fit loosely enough to hide some decent curves, and her little brown glasses, instead of hiding her dark eyes, only served to make them seem even larger. She wore absolutely no makeup, but that just made her seem more vulnerable somehow, and roused in him a desire to . . .

Something. Davis wasn't sure what. He only knew that Olive Tully made him feel a way he hadn't felt in a very long time, maybe a way he'd never felt before. She seemed to need protection for some reason. Yet at the same time, she seemed perfectly capable of taking care of herself.

Even more than why she tried to make people overlook her, though, Davis wanted to ask her what, precisely, she was trying to hide. Besides herself, he meant. Because she clearly was trying to hide something. Including herself, he meant.

"How long have you been working for Ms. Willoughby?" he asked. Even though what he found himself really wondering about was what she was wearing under her plain, unadorned dress. Were her underthings plain and unadorned, as well? Or was she one of those women who liked to save the present for after it was unwrapped and surprise a man with something daring and delicious and debauched underneath.

Because Davis knew there were an awful lot of people

who hid their debauchery beneath plain, even pleasant, packages. Worse, there were a lot of people who hid their depravity. And in his line of work, he'd met way more than his fair share of them. There were times when he wondered what kept him from chucking it all and moving to some out-of-the-way Tibetan mountaintop, where he could finish his days—hopefully blessedly few of them—in solitude and peace. Well, as much peace as a man could expect in this world.

Then he reminded himself he had been thinking not about the sad state of the world, but about Olive Tully's underthings, a much nicer thought to have occupying his mind. Then he reminded himself that it was also an inappropriate thought to have occupying his mind. Not only had she posted NO TRESPASSING signs all over herself, but the last thing he needed was to get mixed up personally in one of his cases. He'd learned a long time ago that it was a bad idea to start caring about the kids you were assigned to take care of. It was an even worse idea to start caring about their mothers.

Not that Olive Tully was anyone's mother. But she was a woman. And she was attractive. And she was vulnerable. As far as Davis was concerned, that in itself wasn't a good combination. Add to it the fact that she was associated with one of his cases, and it really made for a bad mix.

"Claire and I have known each other since college," she told him now, jerking him out of his ruminations, something for which he was profoundly grateful.

"I didn't ask how long you'd known her," he said, noting how she had sidestepped his question. "I asked how long you've worked for her."

"I've been employed by Simple Pleasures for as long as Claire has."

Davis expelled an impatient sound. She was good at eva-
sion, he'd grant her that. He wondered how long she'd been
practicing it. "And that would be how long?" he asked.

"We started the business about ten years ago."

Gee, Davis thought, now they were getting somewhere.
Sort of. "And how many hours a week do you work?"

"It depends on what's going on," she said. "The show
goes into hiatus in August, then comes back in November
for the holidays. Then we go on hiatus again at the end of
February, after Valentine's Day, until May, when we start up
again for the bridal season and summertime. So those are
slower times for us."

"But there's a magazine for the business, as well, isn't
there?" Davis asked.

Olive nodded. "But really, Claire's more of a figurehead
on that. She's listed as executive editor, but mostly she just
oversees the content, writes one monthly column, and gives
the issue final approval. Others write and edit the bulk of it."

There was no reason for Davis to think she might be lying
to him. For some reason, though, he couldn't shake the impression that she was lying to him. Or that she was at least
misleading him. And not just about her position at Simple
Pleasures, either. But what could a woman like her have to
lie about? he asked himself. She didn't seem the notorious
type. On the contrary, she seemed much more the hide-and-
whatever-you-do-don't-seek-me type.

All in all, it made her much too interesting to him. Which
meant he would be best served if he just hurried up and finished this interview and left Anabel Sage in the capable
hands of Claire Willoughby. He just wished he could convince himself that her hands were, in fact, capable.

And really, he did think Claire was a good candidate for

guardianship. Davis had good instincts about people—well, *now* he did, even if that hadn't always been the case. And nothing had sounded any alarm bells since he'd entered the Willoughby home. He only wished he could shake his uneasiness that Olive Tully was hiding something. Her hands just didn't seem quite as capable—quite as clean?—as Claire's did. No, her hands . . .

Well. He probably shouldn't think too much about Olive's hands. Not when he found the rest of her so intriguing.

So Davis continued as quickly as he could with his interview, until he was satisfied—at least as satisfied as he could be—that Olive Tully, like Claire Willoughby, was a responsible, caring individual who would put Anabel Sage's welfare ahead of everything else.

Not that he believed for a moment that the two women *would* put Anabel Sage's welfare ahead of everything else. Nobody did that for kids anymore. Everyone was too caught up in the I-got-mine desperation of the new millennium to put something so mundane as a child's welfare ahead of their own interests. But he was reasonably confident that the two women would be adequate caretakers for Anabel and see to her basic needs. They wouldn't mistreat her. As far as Davis was concerned, that was about as good as it got in his line of work.

After a few last perfunctory questions, he concluded his interview with Ms. Tully, even though there were a host of nonperfunctory questions he would have liked to throw into the mix.

Who are you, really?

Where do you come from?

Why are you trying to hide?

When will you tell me the truth about yourself?

How can you look so plain but be so fascinating?
What are you wearing under that dress?

And then Davis shoved himself away from the desk and began to make his way toward the office door. But he couldn't help noticing that Olive Tully flinched the moment he took a step in her direction, nor did he miss the fact that she immediately turned and raced him to the door, passing through it before he even arrived. As he stepped out into the hallway, he was just in time to see her escape into the room they had left earlier, the one designated as Anabel Sage's newly redone bedroom. And hearing a cacophonous chorus of chaos coming from inside, he hastened his step, to see what was causing the ruckus.

Even forewarned, however, he was in no way prepared for the sight that greeted him upon entering what had been, only moments ago, a peaceful, welcoming refuge. During the short time he had been leering at—or, rather, questioning— Olive Tully, Anabel's bedroom had become Bedlam. The embroidered quilt that had been spread so carefully in the crib before was now hanging half-in and half-out of it. Toys—what were left of them, anyway—were scattered everywhere. A wooden puzzle that was supposed to contain all fifty states now seemed to be at war with itself, though, strangely, Canada appeared to be winning. A beheaded Raggedy Ann lay dead near the door, and a rubber duck had been lynched from the overhead light fixture. And an over-size Winnie-the-Pooh, Davis saw, had been completely eviscerated.

A lamp had been overturned and was sputtering ominously, and Claire Willoughby had her hands full—literally—trying to keep little Anabel from electrocuting herself with it. And where Claire had been so well put-together earlier, now her sleekly arranged hair hung down around her shoulders in knotted clumps, her cool lavender blouse bore a smear of what Davis assured himself couldn't possibly be blood, and her skirt was ripped up the side from knee to midthigh. Chandler Edison, Davis saw, wasn't far away from her, down on his knees, collecting what appeared to be the remnants of her broken pearl necklace. His jacket was gone, his necktie was askew, and one of his shoes was missing.

When Claire glanced up and saw Davis evaluating the scene, she struggled to stand up, with Anabel in her arms. No sooner had she risen to her knees, however, than Anabel twisted and jerked, pushing her back down onto her fanny. Hard.

"I, ah . . . I think maybe we should, um, move that lamp out of here," she said as she valiantly reined in the toddler again. "The overhead fixture should provide plenty of light." She glanced up and saw the rubber duck twisting in the wind above them. "Well, once we free the duckie, I mean."

Davis said nothing in response, only strode over to the lamp in question and jerked the plug out of the wall, something that put an end to both the *bzzt*ing sound and the faint scent of something about to catch fire. Just in time, too, he couldn't help noting, because right as he defused the lamp, little Anabel freed herself from Claire's clutches and went stampeding toward it. Fortunately, Davis snatched it out of reach before the little girl got to it, something that made Anabel fall down onto her bottom and begin to howl like a rabid dog.

Wow. Davis had never heard a sound like that before in his life. It gave him goose bumps. And a migraine. And also chest pains.

He lifted a hand to his forehead and rubbed hard at the

migraine—to no avail, unfortunately. "You know," he said, "I'm only required to make weekly visits, but under the circumstances, maybe it would be better if I came more often."

Like every five minutes, he couldn't help thinking. Involuntarily, he cast a glance at Olive Tully, at the way she was bent over picking up toys, and how her loose dress draped just so beautifully over a very nicely rounded derriere. He remembered her pleasant face and startled eyes, and he wondered again what she was hiding. And then he thought about what it would do to him to have contact more than once a week with an attractive, enigmatic mystery woman who made him feel more curious—and more interested—than he'd felt about anything for a very long time.

He didn't have time for this, he thought. He did not have even a single extra moment to spend on Anabel Sage's case. He had fifty other cases on his desk right now, and none of them looked especially promising. Anabel Sage was almost certainly in a better position than any other child assigned to him. But her situation was the one he wanted to come back and check on most frequently.

Only that wasn't necessarily because of Anabel, he had to admit. No, it was just as much because of Olive. And that was the last reason in the world Davis needed to have driving him.

Man, oh, man. It was going to be a long, hot summer for sure.

Six

$\mathcal{C}$laire wasn't especially surprised when Ramsey Sage arrived at her front door again a week after slamming it on his way out. What did surprise her was that he wasn't accompanied by an attorney and sheaves of legal documents. And although she wasn't surprised, either, to see that he had cleaned himself up—kind of—she was surprised that he hadn't tried any harder than he had to improve his image.

Although he had shaved, something that had only made more prominent all his intriguing features, his black hair still hung down to nearly his shoulders, and was still pushed carelessly back from his face. If he'd had it trimmed, it wasn't by much. A small, more sedate, gold hoop winked in his earlobe this time, and although he was still clad in denim, his jeans were a bit less deteriorated, and his black T-shirt, though well worn enough to mold itself to his muscular torso, was only marginally faded and still sported two sleeves. But they were rolled up to expose his barbed-wire tattoo, not to mention those salient biceps, which Claire really didn't notice anyway. Well, not *too* much. Only for a few seconds. Okay, a full minute, but no more than that, honest. Because after the passage of a full minute, when Claire had yet to utter a single word of greeting—well, how was she supposed to think, when his biceps were so salient?—Ramsey spoke a few himself.

"Hi, Claire," he greeted her, his voice edged with sarcasm. "Didja miss me?"

Okay, so probably she shouldn't be surprised by his irreverence, either, she thought. But that did surprise her for some reason. Even though his antagonism last week when he'd left had been nearly palpable, and even though the two of them were pretty much adversaries, she had thought when she saw him again, they might be able to speak to each other as civil human beings. Then again, no one could accuse Ramsey Sage of being civilized, she reminded herself. No, he was as far from being domesticated as they came.

Not that she was one to talk at the moment, she thought, considering her own appearance. She ran a hand anxiously down the front of her pink sleeveless blouse and made a quick survey of her long khaki shorts, just to be sure there was nothing on them, like, say . . . baby stuff. Because she had been covered with things like . . . baby stuff . . . quite a few times this week. So many times, in fact, that she was amazed to find she was currently baby-stuff-free.

But because of the baby who made the stuff, she had stopped bothering to do anything much with her wardrobe, or her hair, or herself while she was at home. Anabel did so delight in conducting mass chaos whenever she was around, particularly on Claire's wardrobe and Claire's hair and Claire's self. Usually by getting stuff all over Claire's wardrobe, and yanking Claire's hair hard enough to free it from her tidy hairdo—and often her scalp—and drooling all over Claire's self. The little angel. So today, as had become her habit, she wore her hair loosely plaited in a long, fat braid that fell to nearly the center of her back. And because Olive had taken the brunt of Anabel's care today—or, rather, because Olive had delighted in caring for the little seraph today, Claire hastily corrected herself—her braid was still reasonably intact.

In spite of her less-than-cordial appearance, she replied as cordially as she could, "Mr. Sage. How nice to see you again."

"Yeah, I bet it is," he fairly growled.

"Truly," she assured him. And in a way, it was nice to see him again. For all his incivility, he was certainly not difficult to look at. One might even go so far as to say that, especially cleaned up a bit, Ramsey Sage was easy on the eye. In an insolent, defiant, indecent sort of way. "In fact," she added, "I was rather expecting you before now."

"Were you *rather*?" he echoed caustically, *aahing* over the first vowel in that last word a little longer than was necessary, mocking her. Then, as if to hammer it home, he added, still mockingly, "Truly?"

Claire refrained from commenting. Obviously nothing she was going to say to him would be met with courtesy. She supposed she couldn't blame him, all things considered. But he might do well to realize that he would be more successful in continuing any dialogue he wanted to have with her if he softened his stance instead of hardening it.

"Aren't you going to invite me in?" he asked.

"I haven't decided yet," she told him. "So far, I'm not inclined to. Not when your behavior has been less than inviting."

He narrowed his eyes at her, his lips parting fractionally, as if he hadn't expected her to reply in such a way. Obviously, Mr. Sage had assumed she would be polite and let him steamroller right over her. Obviously, he thought being courteous and lacking resolve were identical conditions. Obviously, he was a big ignoramus. Because having read the book Olive authored under her name about manners, Claire knew the most successful strong-arm tactics were rooted in politeness. Diplomacy, after all, had kept the world a reasonably peaceful place, in spite of its being ruled by men.

Because that was the thing about men. They could be well behaved if they put their minds to it. She just wished Ramsey Sage's mind would put out more. Or something like that.

"I see," he said, his voice touched now with . . . My goodness. Was that politeness she heard? "My apologies," he added, sounding almost apologetic when he did. "I'll do my best to be more inviting in the future."

Something about the way he said the word *inviting* made Claire think of something other than good manners. Because the way he said it made her think of naughtiness instead. Probably because the way he looked at her when he said it was rather naughty. But not in the way a child is naughty—heaven knew Claire had had enough experience with that this week to know it when she saw it. And there was nothing childlike in Ramsey's look at all. Feral, wanton, and salacious, yes. Childlike? Nuh-uh.

In spite of that, "Maybe you should come in," she said.

She battled immediate misgivings even as she extended the invitation. She still wasn't sure about his motives. Or his intentions. Or his character, for that matter. But Chandler and Olive were both at the house, and one bloodcurdling scream from Claire would have them both running. For some reason, though, the thought brought her little comfort. And the way Ramsey sauntered into her house brought her even less comfort. Because there was something about the way the man moved that made Claire want to shiver all over. Not that watching him move made her cold. Au contraire. There was just such an assuredness, such a confidence, such an out-and-out arrogance to his swagger, he was very nearly overwhelming in his masculinity. She wouldn't have thought herself the kind of woman who would respond to such manly manliness in a man. But in Ramsey's case, she responded. Really, really well.

As soon as she closed the door behind him, he spun around to look at her again, almost as if he were reluctant to turn his back on her. What a coincidence. She was afraid to turn her back on him, too. Unless maybe it involved . . . um, never mind. The main thing was, they were both on the same wavelength at the moment—sort of—which meant cooperation couldn't be too far behind. Or, rather, too far in the rear. Or, better still, at hand. Oh, dammit, why did cooperation always have to come with a body part? And why couldn't Claire think of anything besides body parts anyway?

Probably because the body parts of the person to whom she was currently speaking were just the kind of body parts one couldn't help thinking about. Fortunately, Ramsey's mouth—another nice body part, incidentally—opened then, and he began to speak, something that helped to take Claire's mind off of all his other body parts. For now.

"You know," he said, "I halfway thought about cutting my hair and buying a suit before I came back here. And I also thought about carting a briefcase with me and throwing around words like *habeas corpus* and *ab initio* and *certiorari* and—"

"*Non compos mentis*?" Claire added helpfully.

"*Quid pro quo*," Ramsey deftly countered, his expression altering not at all. "But something stopped me."

"The fact that you don't understand Latin?" she asked benignly.

He smiled, but there was something smug and knowing in the gesture. "No," he said. "I realized if I did that, I'd be just like Edison, and that frankly scared the hell outta me."

"Ah."

"I'm not going to change who I am to appease you and your attorney. I'm fine just the way I am."

Somehow, she refrained from expelling a robust, "Oh, yeah, baby!" Instead, she only offered him a polite nod.

"This is me, Claire," he told her. "Take me or leave me."

For some reason, she didn't want to do either of those things. Not yet. She wasn't sure what she *did* want to do with Ramsey Sage at this point, mind you—other than enjoy the visual feast that was his body parts—but she was fair-minded enough to give the man a chance.

"I never asked you to change who you are, Mr. Sage," she said.

"But you won't consider me a suitable caretaker for Anabel the way I am now," he countered.

Claire thought it best to keep her mouth shut on that one.

Obviously understanding her response, Ramsey was the one to nod politely this time. "It's not that I need to change," he reiterated, "nor do I need to mislead you into thinking I'm something I'm not."

"No?"

"No. What I need to do is convince you that I'm perfectly capable of raising Anabel being the man I am right now."

"And how do you intend to convince me of that?" Claire asked.

She had barely finished voicing the question when Ramsey began to stride toward her, taking slow, measured steps until he stood nearly toe-to-toe with her. Until that moment, there had always been a good bit of distance between the two of them. Until that moment, she hadn't really been aware of just how tall he was, or how broad, or how hard. Until that moment, she hadn't realized how the heat of his body could mingle with her own, or how his scent, so potent, so robust, could combine with her sweeter one to produce another that was an intriguing mix of both. Until that moment, she hadn't appreciated just how positively handsome he was, how his mouth curved just so perfectly, and how his eyes were so clear and so green and so deep, a woman gazing into them, if she wasn't careful, might drown.

And until that moment, she hadn't remembered how good it could feel to simply be close to a man.

"That's why I came here today, Claire," Ramsey said softly. "To prove it to you."

And, honestly, for one scant, delirious moment, Claire thought he was talking about proving something else entirely to her, and her stomach pitched, and her chest tightened, and her flesh grew hot, and her mouth went dry, and she began to think, *Yes, oh, yes, please do prove it to me, prove it all night, like in the song, and then we can do it again in the morning.* But then she remembered he was talking about Anabel and how he wanted to take care of her, not Claire. Because Claire was his adversary, not his ally. And she certainly wasn't his lover.

She swallowed hard in an effort to alleviate the dryness in her mouth and the knot in her throat. And finally, she managed to say, fairly evenly, she was proud to note, "It's going to take more than one day for you to do that, Mr. Sage."

Impossibly, he took another step toward her, bringing his body even closer to hers, almost touching her. "I don't have a problem with that," he murmured. He dipped his head to hers, his hair falling forward, and she could almost swear she felt a silky, inky lock of it whisper over her temple. "Do you?" he asked softly.

Claire shook her head. But for the life of her, she couldn't utter a single word in response. Probably because, by then, her heart had leapt into her throat, cutting off any potential for speech. Or breath. Or coherent thought.

"Fine," he said, the single word skittering warmly over her cheek as he said it. "Then just tell me what to do, Claire. Tell me, and I'll do it. I'll do anything to prove to you that I'm a decent guy."

Oh, she sincerely doubted that. Because everything about Ramsey Sage screamed indecent.

Her lips parted for her to speak—because, surely, that could be the only reason why they would part—but anything she might have said was thankfully cut short. Because Chandler suddenly appeared on the stairway behind them, fairly shouting, "Claire, for God's sake, you have got to do something about that—" But his complaint was cut short when he saw Ramsey standing with her in the foyer, closer than was socially responsible. "Oh. Mr. Sage," he said. "How nice to see you again."

But Chandler was clearly no more happy to see Ramsey now than he would be to see a big glob of sun-warmed Double Bubble stuck to his shoe. Because the way he stepped forward and shook Ramsey's hand now was pretty much the same way he'd stepped backward and shaken off the baby doody that had gotten on his fingers after that unfortunate episode with Anabel earlier in the week.

Of course, there had been many unfortunate episodes with Anabel in the past week. The infamous baby doody incident had just been the beginning. The little darling had proven to be quite a challenge for all of them. Of course, Claire didn't know the first thing about children—had she mentioned that?—especially such young children. It could very well be commonplace for them to frequently get into things they weren't supposed to. And it could be that none of them responded to the word *No*. Or the exclamation *No!* Or the outcry *NO!* Or the convulsion *NOOOO!!!* Even Olive, cool, calm, collected Olive, had been thrown into a bona fide tizzy once or twice.

And how was Claire supposed to know that diapers came in different sizes, and that if you put the wrong size on the baby, then baby doody came shooting up the back and all over one's attorney's hand? It had been an honest mistake. It could have happened to anyone.

Live and learn.

"I assume you've come to discuss Anabel," Chandler said.

Ramsey nodded. "Yeah, I've—"

"Decided to sue for custody," Chandler finished for him, sounding imminently relieved by the news, even though that wasn't the news Ramsey had come to deliver.

Before Claire could explain, though, Ramsey told Chandler, "No, I've decided *not* to begin legal proceedings to have her guardianship transferred over to me."

But instead of making her feel better, hearing him spell it out that way made Claire feel almost panicky, and she realized that, deep down, she had kind of been hoping Ramsey *would* sue her. In spite of everything, she really wasn't prepared or equipped to raise a small child to adulthood, especially a child who, technically, wasn't her responsibility. Truth be told, she wished she *could* find some reason to turn over

Anabel's guardianship to Ramsey. The little girl belonged with her family, not strangers—even if those strangers were kind of taking a liking to her, in spite of her baby stuff and her chaos and her doody. But until Ramsey could prove he would be a good caretaker—which, frankly, didn't seem likely—Claire couldn't possibly turn her back on Anabel.

"You're *not* going to sue for custody?" Chandler asked.

"No," Ramsey told the other man. "Right now, I'd like to see if we could reach some other kind of arrangement."

"What kind of arrangement?" Chandler asked.

But Ramsey responded to Claire when he said, "I'd like to visit my niece on a regular basis, and, if all goes well, I'd like for Claire to voluntarily relinquish custody."

Claire studied Ramsey thoughtfully before replying. What he was proposing, was, of course, utterly understandable and altogether acceptable. Except that it would necessitate *her* seeing him on a regular basis, too, and that would necessitate her wondering about—and, inescapably, thinking about—his tattoo and his biceps and his torso and his eyes and his hindquarters and . . . Well, anyway, that would necessitate her seeing *him* and wondering about *him* and thinking about *him* on a regular basis.

Not that she wasn't already doing that anyway, because she *had* thought about his tattoo and his biceps and his torso and his eyes and his hind quarters and . . . Well, she had thought about *him* more than once over the past week. Which was the problem. Because in addition to being un-equipped and unprepared for Anabel's appearance in her life, Claire was also unequipped and unprepared for a raging tower of manhood like Ramsey Sage in her life.

Not only did Claire not have time for a family, she didn't have time for an attraction, either. Especially to a man who considered her an enemy of the first quarter. And what she felt whenever Ramsey Sage was around, she was afraid, was bordering on an attraction. And it had the potential to go way beyond attraction and enter into territory she'd probably be better off not trying to find a word for, because it could only lead to trouble. And also to a tingling in body parts that were better left untingled by a man like him.

"Mr. Sage, I—"

"Can I see her? Please?" he asked, before Claire had a chance to reply to his suggestion. And although he spoke in the same casual fashion he had been speaking in since she'd opened her door to him, his eyes held a pleading sort of hunger that nearly broke her heart.

"Of course," she said, relenting. "Anabel is in her room with Olive. I'll show you the way."

And, oh, thank God that Anabel was in her room with Olive, and not elsewhere in the house with Claire. Because had Ramsey witnessed for himself the way Claire had absolutely no control over the child, he would have had grounds for a custody suit and would have changed his mind in a heartbeat and would have fled the scene to file one forthwith. Stable, solid grounds, too. Like frozen arctic tundra grounds. Olive, on the other hand, had done surprisingly well with the little girl, had been so much more patient and calming and playful than Claire had been able to be. Not that Claire disliked the little sweetheart, but Anabel Claire Sage was a handful of . . . something . . . that was for sure.

The little love.

And Anabel was also a night person, which meant that around eleven o'clock every night, which was *way* past Claire's bedtime, even when she didn't have to be at the studio at six A.M. every morning, Anabel wanted to play games like

"Find the Diaper I Just Took Off That May or May Not Have Doody in It" and "Chase Me through the Entire House" and "Where's the Priceless Baccarat Vase that Used to Be on that Side Table?" Claire, on the other hand, wanted to sleep. A lot. She also still hoped to someday find that vase.

Such a darling.

"Chandler," Claire began. But she halted when she took her first good look at him since he'd entered, because she immediately realized he had just come from Anabel's room himself. She knew that because his tawny suit jacket was unbuttoned—in fact, it seemed to be *missing* all of its buttons—his pale blond hair was sticking up in tufts all over his head, even though he'd obviously made no small effort to smooth it down again, and one side of his collar was flipped up over a tie that was stained with something Claire assured herself couldn't possibly be blood.

"What happened?" she asked the attorney, even though she was pretty sure she knew the answer to that question, too.

"The usual," Chandler replied.

"The usual?" Ramsey echoed.

Oops, Claire thought, trying to come up with a rational explanation for why Chandler looked the way he did. After all, there was no reason to give Ramsey more fuel to fire up his legal matter that didn't seem to be much of a legal matter—yet. There was no reason to tell him that every time Anabel entered a room, she did what the child psychologists in the books Claire had been reading called "taking control of the situation" . . . and then toppling the situation and all of its occupants into a ruin that rivaled the fall of the Roman Empire.

Not that she wanted to keep Ramsey from winning his legal matter, either, and leave her in charge of Anabel—oh, dear heavenly God—but she still wasn't convinced he was the right candidate for the job. What Claire wanted was what would be best for Anabel. Before last week, she had hoped that the best thing for Anabel would be her uncle. Right now, however, the closest thing to the best for Anabel was keeping the child right where she was. Until Claire could be certain Ramsey Sage was a solid, stable, decent sort, she would battle with him for the right to care for the little girl.

Hence, she couldn't let him find out just what a bad caregiver she was herself.

"What Chandler meant by 'the usual,'" she said quickly, "was that he and Anabel were playing a little game the two of them love to play together." She turned to look at Chandler, deliberately giving Ramsey her back, then winked as obviously as she could. "Isn't that right, Chandler?" Wink, wink. "You and Anabel love to play that game?" Wink, wink.

But Chandler only gazed at her as if the lights had suddenly gone dim. "Game?" he said. "What game?"

"*That* game," Claire told him emphatically. *Wink, wink.* "You know . . ." *Wink, wink.* "The one Anabel just loves to play with you." Wink, wink, wink, wink . . . *wiiiiink.*

Finally, Chandler seemed to get it, because he drew his head back and said, "Oh, *that* game. Yes, Anabel does so love it."

"And what game is that?" Ramsey asked suspiciously.

Chandler turned now to the other man. "It's called 'Rip All the Buttons off Mr. Edison's Coat and Stuff Them into My Mouth,'" he said.

Now Ramsey was the one looking at them as if the lights had suddenly gone dim. "I didn't think children that age were supposed to be allowed to put small objects into their mouths," he said.

Wow, Ramsey had been doing some reading, too, Claire

thought. She turned her back on him again to glare at Chandler. "Not *that* game," she said. Wink, *dammit*, wink. "You know we don't let her play *that* game anymore. The other game." Wink, *you big jerk*, wink.

"Oh, yes, of course," Chandler replied obediently. "The other game."

"The other game?" Ramsey asked, even more suspiciously, if Claire wasn't mistaken.

Chandler nodded. Speaking to Ramsey, but still eyeing Claire, he said, "Yes, that one is called 'Spit the Buttons into Mr. Chandler's Hand, Thereby Making a Disgusting Mess, and Then, When He's Not Looking, Push Him Down from Behind and Turn Him into a Horsy.'"

Claire turned back to Ramsey "Or just 'Horsy' for short," she said, smiling. "His necktie makes for a wonderful set of reins."

"Mm," Chandler said noncommittally, tugging uncomfortably at the accessory in question, which, Claire noticed, had an awful lot of baby stuff on it.

"Are you sure I can't get you some iced tea?" Claire asked.

Ramsey shook his head. "Just Anabel."

That's what she had been afraid of. "Fine," she conceded helplessly. "Follow me."

Claire found Olive and Anabel right where she'd left them, in the big guest room they had converted into a nursery. Claire hesitated to refer to it as "Anabel's room," because she was still convinced—or maybe just still mired in denial— that the arrangement was only temporary and that "Anabel's room" would eventually go back to being "the big guest room." And she decided not to think about why that thought kind of bothered her.

At the time, the room had seemed the perfect place for the little girl. Well, except for the fact that the bed was queen-sized and there hadn't been a single appropriate thing in it for a child to play with. But Claire and Olive had bought a crib to match the furniture, and then they'd pretty much emptied out the toddler section at Toys "R" Us—though nothing had enchanted Anabel like that priceless Baccarat vase, the little precious—so now the room really was perfect.

At the center of it sat Olive, on the floor with Anabel. And where Olive was dressed in her usual color-free, nondescript way, with beige trousers and a loose-fitting, raw silk T-shirt the color of sand, Anabel shone like a bright beacon. Her blond hair was wispy and fine, her two stubby ponytails lopsided and tied with bright red ribbons to match the cherry red romper she wore. She sported only one tiny white sandal—heaven only knew where the other was, the little darling—and her bare foot appeared to have been drawn on extensively with six or seven different colors of marker. The little love.

She really was very cute, Claire had to concede, in spite of everything. And she had brought some excitement into their lives unlike any they had experienced before. To put it mildly. And she did rather melt one's heart with that little four-toothed smile of hers, she further relented when Anabel turned and treated Claire to just such a gesture.

Still, Claire's life wasn't conducive to raising a family. Or even a child. Now if she could just convince herself that Ramsey Sage's life *was* conducive to that . . .

She inhaled a deep breath, and before she even realized she had meant to speak, she told Olive, "Ramsey Sage is back."

Claire had thought Olive would be relieved by the news, since it was sort of a step in the right direction, but when Olive glanced up, she looked vaguely alarmed.

"I was kind of hoping he wouldn't come back," she said softly.

That surprised Claire. "Why?"

Her friend shrugged and said nothing.

"He's outside," Claire said. "You can meet him."

Immediately, Olive's face went pale, and, abruptly, she stood. "Oh, no. I don't want to meet him."

"But—" Claire began

"I don't want to meet him," Olive reiterated more adamantly. "Just tell me when he's gone." She spoke those last words over her shoulder, as she'd already begun to make tracks toward the door that connected Anabel's room—or, rather, the big guest room—to Claire's bedroom.

"But—" Claire tried again.

To no avail. Olive fled through the door without so much as a good-bye. Sighing, Claire opened the door that led to the hallway and looked out to find Ramsey Sage leaning against the opposite wall. He strode forward casually at her unspoken invitation, but halted when he was scarcely a few feet inside the room, his gaze lighting on Anabel. The little girl seemed to feel the heat of that gaze the moment he leveled it on her—Claire supposed no one of the female persuasion could possibly be immune—because she spun quickly around to gaze back at him. Her blue eyes went wide, and her mouth fell partially open, and for the first time in a week, she stood absolutely still.

For the briefest of moments, time seemed to come to a complete stop. Claire could almost hear a zap of connection resonate between uncle and niece, could almost feel the room shiver with a sort of combining consciousness that ran between the two. Then Anabel took one tentative step forward, halted, and smiled. Smiled the kind of smile that indicates absolute and unequivocal joy.

Then she lifted her arms high into the air, let out another squeal of delight, and shouted out, "Dada!"

Ramsey stopped dead in his tracks when he saw his niece, because his entire world skated out from beneath him the minute she turned around. Last week, he hadn't gotten a good look at Anabel, thanks to the social worker's efforts to keep him at a distance and his niece's preoccupation with Claire Willoughby. But now he saw her full on and had her undivided attention. Until now, he hadn't been able to recall a lot about Eleanor, as hard as he'd tried since learning of her death. She'd only been four when he left home, and he hadn't thought much about her over the years, because he'd done his best not to think about anything that had happened during the unhappy period of his childhood and youth. But seeing Anabel now, it was as if a door in his brain he'd locked tight two decades ago was suddenly flung open wide, and it spilled out all the dusty, dirty clutter of his early life. A life he would just as soon have never thought about again.

Anabel looked *exactly* like her mother. Ramsey knew that because, suddenly, he remembered Eleanor all too well.

He'd been fourteen when she was born, a late-life surprise to his parents, just as he had been an early-life surprise to them. He remembered when they had brought her home from the hospital, how small and pink and fragile she'd been, and how his first thought upon seeing her was that she would have been better off had she not been born at all.

The Sage house had been a war zone the entire time Ramsey had grown up. He could think of no other way to describe it. He couldn't recall a single day when his parents hadn't fought bitterly about something, unless he counted the days when his parents were too drunk to even get out of bed. Ramsey had been forced to be responsible for himself the whole time he was growing up, had begun making his way in the world before he even knew how the world worked. And he'd known when his parents brought Eleanor home that she was in for the same fate.

He'd cared for her as much as he could, had tried to give her the affection his parents denied them both. But because he'd never been shown love himself, Ramsey had never felt like he was any good at giving it. In many ways, trying to take care of his sister had only reinforced what a failure he was at the whole human experience. He'd never felt as if he could do anything right, because he'd had no idea how things should be done. And a part of him had wondered at times if he was doing his sister more harm than good, trying to make things easier for her. The world wasn't exactly a hospitable place, and trying to pillow Eleanor's experiences would only make it harder for her later.

But by the time he turned eighteen, the June after he graduated from high school, Ramsey had become so unhappy that he decided to strike out on his own. And as he closed the door to his parents' house on his way out, he promised himself he would never look back. He'd figured if he had to take care of himself, he could at least do it in surroundings he chose for himself. And if he was going to be deprived of love and consideration, at least he'd be alone during that deprivation. Then he might at least have a reason for why he felt so alone and unhappy all the time.

He'd felt terrible about leaving Eleanor, but he'd known she would learn to take care of herself, just as he had. And although there had been times when he'd been tempted to return to check on her, or even to take her away from their parents and care for her himself, he'd had to be realistic. Hell, he was a young, unfocused kid who was totally clueless about so many things, and he'd begun working two jobs and taking college courses at night. Had he tried to tend to Eleanor under such conditions, he would have been worse at parenting than his parents had been.

And, truth be told, at that point, he really had wanted to just forget about everything he'd left behind. He'd wanted to start over, pretend he was just like everyone else, create a life for himself that at least felt like it had some purpose. Instead, he'd only found more loneliness, more isolation. There had a been a brief bright spot in his early twenties, when he had met someone who showed him what it was like to genuinely care about someone and be cared for in return. But that bright spot had burned too hot, too fast, and it had fizzled out too quickly. Still, it had gone a long way toward preventing him from becoming the same kind of person his parents had been, people who had been incapable of giving love at all. And now . . .

He looked at Anabel again, at the way she was staring back at him, almost as if she recognized him. Now, he thought, he had a chance to make up for abandoning Eleanor. He hadn't been able to take care of his sister, hadn't been able to show her any happiness in her life. But by God, he could take care of Anabel, make sure she was happy. Even if it meant going toe-to-toe with Claire Willoughby. Hell, he could take her. He'd do whatever he had to do to reunite his family.

Almost as if Anabel understood what he was thinking, she suddenly shot her hands straight up into the air, grinning just about the biggest grin Ramsey had ever seen. He couldn't help the smile he felt curling his own lips in response. But then she shouted out "Dada!" and immediately his smile fell.

Dada?

But he didn't have time to think any further, because Anabel was running toward him, seemingly at Mach one speed, and hurtling herself against his legs with enough force to send him toppling backward. He landed with a heartfelt "Oof" on his fanny, then went flailing onto his back when his niece climbed on top of him.

"Dada!" she shouted again. Then she began to emit a sound at the top of her lungs that was unlike anything Ramsey had ever heard before, though it did sort of resemble fingernails being dragged over a blackboard. *Long* fingernails. Over a *wet* blackboard. Horizontally. Oh, man, did that hurt his ears. And then she followed up with another sincere and, amazingly, even louder, "DADA!"

But Ramsey was too busy trying to wrestle a toddler off of his neck to voice his concerns. Wow. He never would have thought a little kid could have so much strength. What had Claire been feeding her? And why couldn't he breathe . . . ?

"Dadadadadadadadadadadadadadadadadadada!" Anabel squealed as Ramsey struggled to get free.

With great care, he finally managed to disengage himself and return to a sitting position—sort of—wherein his niece scrambled into his lap and sat down, settling herself in nicely. She rested her pudgy arms on his thighs and leaned back against his chest, as if she were Queen Anabel I of Toddlerland and he was her own personal throne.

"Dada," she then decreed quite happily.

"She thinks I'm her father?" Ramsey asked Claire. "How did that happen?"

"That's not what she thinks," Claire said mildly. " 'Dada' is a multipurpose word to her. She uses it a lot. If it makes you feel better, she calls the bathtub drain 'dada,' too."

Oh, and that was supposed to make him feel better?

"She also used it once to refer to a dried-up worm she saw on the sidewalk."

Oh, and *that* was supposed to make him feel better?

Claire crossed her arms over her midsection, gazing down at Ramsey with thinly disguised amusement at how he had been turned into a piece of furniture by a one-year-old child. "I do think she only uses it for things she likes, however," she tried to assure him. "It took me ten minutes to get that worm out of her mouth."

Oh, and she thought *she* was better equipped to raise the kid?

"So by calling you Dada," Claire concluded, "Anabel is only telling you how much she likes you." She hesitated a moment, her mouth open as if she wanted to say more. Then, finally, "She's never called me that," she confided.

And damned if she didn't seem to be bothered by that. Funny, Ramsey thought. But in spite of Claire's reluctance to turn Anabel over to him, he hadn't gotten the feeling from her during their last visit that she had relished taking care of the kid herself. And Edison had pretty much said flat out that Claire Willoughby wasn't exactly a child-friendly institution. And she still didn't seem comfortable with Anabel, even having hosted her in her home for a week. So why did she sound disappointed that the child who had been forced upon her didn't seem to like her?

"I'm sure she's thought of you as 'Dada' lots of times," Ramsey said, even though he couldn't possibly be sure of such a thing.

Her expression changed at his assertion, looking almost hopeful. "You think so?"

He nodded. "Hey, even after knowing you a short time, I can tell that you're *much* more likable than a dead worm."

Her expression fell again at that. "Mm," she replied.

Evidently tired of sitting, even in a human throne, Anabel jumped up and spun around to look at Ramsey. Up close, she wasn't quite the dead ringer for his sister that he'd originally thought her. Her eyes were blue, where Eleanor's had been green, her nose was rounder, and her hair was lighter. But she was definitely his sister's daughter. He wondered briefly about the little girl's father, but decided that if Eleanor hadn't thought the man important enough to include in Anabel's life, then Ramsey probably shouldn't think of him that way, either.

Maybe, like him, his sister had had trouble falling in love. Maybe, like him, she hadn't thought it was important. Still, the girl's father deserved to know he had a daughter out in the world. Once Ramsey was more accustomed to his new role as her guardian—and once he was sure he'd be able to keep that role—he'd see if he could find Anabel's father. Surely the guy would want to know about his next generation.

"Dada," that next generation said now, pointing at Ramsey's ear.

Automatically, he lifted a hand and felt the gold hoop there. He glanced at Anabel again. "What?" he asked.

Claire, however, must have been one up on him, because she was making her way hastily toward them, and saying, "No, no, Anabel. *No.*"

Anabel, however, ignored Claire and began to reach toward Ramsey's ear. Ramsey, thinking it pretty cute that his niece would be so fascinated by his earring, turned his head to facilitate her exploration.

Only to have Claire accelerate her pace, and say, "No, no, Ramsey. *No.*"

Before Ramsey had a chance to say another word, little Anabel was grabbing his earring, jerking it hard, to the point where it pretty much threatened to rip right out of his earlobe. Wow. She really was strong. What *was* Claire feeding her? And then he couldn't think at all because he was too busy gasping for breath, thanks to the pain that shot through his ear.

The next thing he knew, Claire was shouting, "No, Anabel, NO! Let him GO!" and pulling the toddler off of his lap, tugging her chubby little hand free of his earring. And then, just like that, he was breathing again, and the pain had lessened, and Anabel was making that fingernails-across-the-blackboard sound again, and Claire was looking like she wanted to cry.

"I am so sorry," she said, though it sounded like her voice was bouncing off a tin wall. A tin wall that was exploding, thanks to Anabel's continued ruckus. "I should have warned you about the earring thing."

Ramsey gave his head one good, final shake, then struggled to standing. By now, Claire had relinquished little Anabel—probably because Ramsey had seen little Anabel bite her—and the girl went scampering back over to where she had been before, to pick up a toy that looked like . . . like . . . Hmmm. Well, actually, it looked a lot like a disemboweled bunny rabbit. And surely that wasn't a bloodstain on it . . .

"How's she been this week?" Ramsey asked Claire, even though he continued to look at his niece. When his question received no reply, though, he turned to his hostess, to find she was also studying Anabel. Thinking she must not have heard him, he prodded, "Claire?"

Her entire body jerked at the sound of her name, and she

turned abruptly, her expression looking guilty for some reason. "I'm sorry, what did you say?"

"I asked how Anabel's been this wee—"

"Fine," Claire said quickly. A little *too* quickly, seeing as how she said it before Ramsey even finished asking the question.

He eyed her with much suspicion. "Do you really think you're better equipped to take care of her than—?"

She nodded vigorously. A little *too* vigorously, seeing as how she started doing it before Ramsey even finished asking the question.

"Because I get the feeling you may have a few doubts about—"

"Don't be silly," she told him, her eyes widening in something akin to panic. "Anabel's only a baby. What could possibly go wrong?"

Gee, besides ripped earlobes? Ramsey wanted to ask. Instead, he told Claire, "Look, all I want is a little time with Anabel, to get to know her, and a little time with you, to show you that I'm perfectly capable of taking care of her. All I need is a chance to prove to you that I'm not the kind of man you think I am."

Claire's expression revealed nothing of what she might be feeling. "And what kind of man do I think you are, Mr. Sage?"

"You think I'm uncivilized, uneducated, unmanageable, and uncouth," he said. "Don't you?"

"And you're not all of those things?" she asked.

"I'm educated," he assured her, opting not to ponder those other qualities for now.

Her eyebrows shot up in astonishment, but he told himself not to blame her for being surprised. Hell, he'd surprised himself by even getting accepted, let alone graduating. "And, given time, I can be civilized. And, um, couth. I can be that, too."

Claire did smile at that. "How about manageable?" she asked. "Can you be manageable?"

Well, now, Claire, he thought, *that just depends on how you want to manage me.* But he pushed the thought away, knowing he was getting ahead of himself. "Hell, yeah," he told her. Not that he actually believed it.

"Watch your language in front of the baby, Mr. Sage."

"It's Ramsey," he told her. "Please. Call me Ramsey."

He wasn't sure, but he thought he saw two faint circles of pink bloom on her cheeks in response. He couldn't imagine why she would blush at a request to call a man by his first name. That was barely a familiarity, let alone an actual intimacy. But that was exactly what she was doing—blushing because he'd asked her to call him Ramsey. And once he realized that, all he could do was wonder how she'd react to a real intimacy. Like, say, to a physical touch. To a part of her person. A part of her person she normally didn't allow people to touch. Better yet, a part of her person she rarely touched herself.

Oh, yeah. He was definitely getting ahead of himself. But, man, was it interesting to think about.

Maybe it hadn't been such a good idea to ask Claire if he could spend more time with her, he thought. Because spending time with her would lead to thinking about her in ways he probably shouldn't think about her. Not when there was a minor present. He was about to backpedal and retract what he'd said about the whole time-spending thing, thinking there must be some other way for him to visit his niece and make a good impression on Claire without Claire having to actually be present. But before he had a chance to do so, she spoke again, and what she said made him totally rethink all the stuff that he had been rethinking.

"All right . . . Ramsey."

Because hearing his given name spoken by her the way he had asked her to speak it made him want to hear her say it again. And again. And again. Only in a different way next time. One, say, where she was breathless and insensate with passion, and also writhing naked beneath him, where he was also naked and writhing, not to mention gasping her name in response.

Oops. Once again, way ahead of himself. He was really going to have to be more careful with that stuff now that he would be spending more time with Claire.

"You can visit Anabel whenever you want," she continued. "Provided I'm, or Olive is, with you when you're here. And if you can prove to me—and then to a judge—that you're able to take care of her . . ."

But her voice trailed off at that, as if she couldn't quite bring herself to make even a verbal, conditional commitment to relinquish Anabel's guardianship to him.

He supposed it was the most he was going to get from her for the time being. Now all he had to do was prove to her that he was a decent guy, one who was capable of giving all the affection and care needed to sustain another individual. And Ramsey could do that. He knew he could. Because he'd done it before, once, when he was in college.

It was just too bad his care and affection then hadn't been enough.

Seven

$\mathcal{T}$he moment she made the promise to Ramsey Sage that he could call on Anabel whenever he wanted, Claire knew it would come back to haunt her. She just hadn't planned on it being less than twenty-four hours before she was visited again by the Ghost of Legal Guardian Yet-to-Come. But Sunday morning, at the ungodly hour of ten o'clock, who should appear at her front door—again—than Anabel's uncle, all bright-eyed and bushy-tailed and salient-bicepsed. Damn him.

Even though Claire had awoken earlier with Anabel—at five-thirty, to be precise, the little cherub—Olive, another early riser, bless her, had arrived promptly at eight to take the little girl to the park, or the zoo, or some such place. The only destination Claire would have recognized at that hour would have been Starbucks, and she was reasonably certain Olive hadn't taken Anabel there. All that had mattered was that Olive had come to the rescue, because she knew of Claire's Sunday morning ritual and had hoped to help her friend preserve what she could of it. Because Sunday really was the holiest of days to Claire. Every Sunday, without fail, she religiously slept late, since that was the only day she could anoint for such a ritual. She was nothing if not devout in practicing her faith, too. Everyone knew not to call Claire or come to her house before, say, noon, on Sunday. *Everyone* knew that.

Everyone except Ramsey Sage.

Claire supposed, as she stifled a yawn and made her way down the stairs to answer the summons of her doorbell, that she should have been more specific in outlining some parameters for Ramsey's visitation schedule. Like, for instance, she should have told him that no matter what, he should never ever ever ever . . . Never ever ever . . . Never ever . . . Never . . . Well, shoot. The thought had completely gotten away from her. Where was she? She could never think straight until she'd had her second cup of coffee. Oh, yeah. Now she remembered. She should have told Ramsey that no matter what, he should never ever call her or come to her house before, say, noon, on Sunday. Or any other time before she'd had her second cup of coffee.

Gee, hindsight really was twenty-twenty.

So now, bleary-eyed and incoherent—so bleary-eyed and incoherent, in fact, that she didn't even care that she was still wearing her shorty pajamas with the cartoon terriers on them, over which she had tossed an equally short matching robe—she opened her front door and found Ramsey Sage standing on the other side. But she quickly decided she must still be asleep and dreaming, because he just looked *that good.* And also because, in addition to Ramsey, she saw the vehicle sitting at her curb that must have accompanied him, not a Harley hog on its last legs, but . . .

Maybe she just still had sleep in her eyes, she told herself, knuckling her eyes softly to rectify the condition. But no. When she opened her eyes again, the vehicle was still there. She was definitely awake. And Ramsey Sage had definitely driven to her house in . . .

A station wagon. A *Volvo* station wagon. Oh, dear. She hoped he hadn't stolen it.

She turned her attention back to him again and discovered that, oddly, his manliness seemed to have remained completely unaffected by his choice of vehicle, because he was every bit as virile as he had been before—damn him—in his blue jeans and heather gray T-shirt, with the barbed-wire tattoo peeking out from beneath his sleeve. Even with his hair tied back in a ponytail and the gold hoop in his ear, he was more dynamic and robust than any man she'd ever met. Damn him.

"Not a morning person, huh?" he said cheerfully by way of a greeting. Damn him.

She stifled another yawn as best she could—which actually wound up being not very well at all—and said, "Wow, you must be psychic."

"Not really," he said. "You just look like hell."

She narrowed her eyes at him. "And *you* said you could be couth."

"Given time," he qualified. "I said given time, I could be couth." He almost smiled then, and his eyes shone with something that might have been merriment in a lesser man. And suddenly, Claire felt as if she'd just consumed three cups of coffee. "But I'll try to step on it," he said graciously. "My apologies for being a boor."

Oh, he wasn't boring at all, Claire thought. Unless he meant that other kind of boar. But he was being much too hard on himself. He wasn't a big wild pig, either. Oh, wait. Now she got it. Bore, boar, *boor*. That was what he meant. So much for the three-cups-of-coffee sensation. Clearly, she'd just been dreaming that.

"Good morning," he tried again.

"Morning," she replied. Because that much she would concede.

And then they just sort of stared at each other. Probably because neither knew quite what to say. In Claire's case, that was because of the coffee situation—or lack thereof. She had no idea what Ramsey's excuse was, since he was so chipper. So damned chipper. So damned, damned chipper. Finally, though, he did break the silence, but it was by asking a question Claire didn't exactly hear everyday.

"Did you know there's a chicken in your front yard?" he asked.

She closed her eyes and expelled a long sigh of frustration. Oh, no. Not again. Although Francesca the emancipated chicken had lived on the set of *Simple Pleasures* for a week with fairly little incident—and without Claire's being able to find her a home—Claire had felt obliged to rescue her once and for all when Ginny Lymon had come into her office one day and assured Claire she knew "just the right place" for the bird. Somehow, Claire had known that by *just right place*, Ginny had meant, *the left side of my dinner plate*, and for some reason, Claire simply hadn't been able to tolerate the knowledge of the animal coming to such an ignoble end. She'd figured that until she could find a good home for her, Francesca would be comfortable enough—and safe enough from Ginny's appetite—tucked into a little corner of the backyard.

But Francesca, Claire had discovered over the last couple

of weeks, had a real penchant for jailbreaks. It was the berry patch that did it. The chicken seemed to have a weakness for the plump fruit that grew within smelling distance of her new home. Of course, since Francesca had no nose, Claire wouldn't have thought the bird would be able to smell. Except awful. What was worse, though, was what Francesca did with the berries when she was finished with them. No amount of hosing off the garden path seemed to work. There always seemed to be one little pile of chicken doo Claire missed. Until Anabel found it. Usually with the sort of results one only read about in the "It Happened to Me" feature in *Parents* magazine.

"That's Francesca," Claire said as she lifted a hand to rub at a headache that seemed to come out of nowhere.

Ramsey eyed her warily. "What's Francesca?"

"The chicken," Claire said.

Now Ramsey eyed her with something she decided she'd best not try to identify. "You have a chicken named Francesca?"

She nodded, but decided not to explain. When she'd tried to explain to Chandler, he hadn't understood, either, and had in fact told Claire that if she insisted on giving the chicken an Italian name, it should have been Cacciatore.

That was the thing about men. They didn't understand chickens any better than they did cats.

"Anabel's not home," she told Ramsey instead, hoping to divert the conversation.

And divert it, she did. Because he looked faintly alarmed at the announcement. "Where is she?"

"I have no idea."

He looked *very* alarmed at that announcement. "What do you mean you have no idea?"

Claire held up what she hoped was a calming hand when she realized she was making a mess of things in her coffee-less state. "I meant she's out with Olive," she said placatingly.

He relaxed visibly at that, so she continued.

"I usually sleep late on Sundays, and Olive's an early riser, like Anabel, so the two of them enjoy an early-morning outing together. Frankly, I'm barely human until I've had my coffee."

Ramsey studied her in silence for a moment, then nodded slowly, but he seemed to be thinking deeply about something else. "Can I come in and wait for her?" he asked.

Claire had really been hoping he would just go away and come back later—say, after noon—but something in his expression prohibited her from telling him to go away. Well, something in his expression did that, and also the fact that telling a man who longed to reunite his family to "Go away" probably wasn't very polite. Or nice. She'd know for sure after her second cup of coffee.

"Fine," she told him. "Would you like some coffee?"

"Oh, no thanks," he told her. "I've already had two cups."

Yeah, well, just rub it in, why don't you? she thought. "Then you'll understand when I tell you that I *have* to have coffee, and I hope you won't mind waiting while I brew some."

"Of course I understand and don't mind."

She stood aside in a silent bid for him to enter, then found herself inhaling again as he passed, hoping to relive that masculine machinery aroma of him. But today, Ramsey smelled like Ivory Soap, and she was overcome with an odd sort of poignancy for having experienced some strange, elemental loss. Not that she had anything against Ivory Soap, mind you, but if there was one thing Ramsey Sage wasn't, it was ninety-nine and forty-four one-hundredths percent pure.

They made their way to her kitchen in silence, and as her guest seated himself on a wide pine bench at the wide pine table nestled in the corner of the pine-paneled kitchen, Claire padded barefoot across the pine floor to the pine pantry, reverently retrieved the sacred French roast and bore it to the altar of the holy Mr. Coffee. There, she went about performing the sacrament of the brew, and yea, the holy Mr. Coffee began to sputtereth and wheezeth, and, lo, the heavens parted and the aroma of fresh coffee filled the air, and then the coffee did appear in the carafe, and it was good.

And Claire rejoiceth.

Ramsey seemed to understand the sanctity of the ritual, because he spoke not a word until Claire's cup runneth over—literally, so she had to grab a paper towel to wipe up the holy mess. Only when she had seated herself across the table from him and enjoyed a few sips—oh, yea, it *was* good—did he finally break his vow of silence.

"So how did you get started in the Simple Pleasures business, anyway?" he asked as Claire savored a second sacred sip.

His question surprised her, though she wasn't sure why. Although she was a public figure, they hadn't talked about her job. And Ramsey didn't seem the type of person to take an interest in lifestyle shows and magazines. "You know what I do for a living?" she asked.

He shrugged. "Well, let's just say I've done some research since that first time I was here."

She couldn't help wondering how he'd gone about his research and just how thorough he'd been. Not that she was a difficult person to learn about, naturally, but he had been out of the country for some time. Did he have access to the Internet? Had he gone to the library? Hired a private investigator?

It occurred to Claire for the first time how very little she knew about the man who wanted to be Anabel's guardian. He'd been in no way forthcoming about how he made his living, something that still bothered her a great deal. He claimed to be educated, and he bandied about Latin as if he knew what he was talking about, so he couldn't be *too* much of a deadbeat. But he seemed to have no visible means of support. Nor did he go out of his way to try and impress people. He really was a bundle of enigmas, Ramsey Sage. And she really did wish she could figure out just exactly who—and what—he was. And not just because he wanted to win custody of Anabel.

"I picked up the latest issue of your magazine," he told her, "and I caught your show a few times this week." He eyed the coffeemaker significantly. "I thought you did everything the old-fashioned way."

"Well, one can only take the concept of simple pleasures so far," she said. "And there were some simple pleasures way back when that were really very complicated and annoying. But—just a shot in the dark here—probably not many people would watch a show or buy a magazine called *Complicated Annoyances*."

"Good point."

"Besides, Rebecca Boone had a coffeemaker just like that."

Ramsey didn't look anywhere near convinced.

"Look," she said, "yes, the slogan of *Simple Pleasures* is 'Back to Basics,' and yes, we do try to do as many things as possible the old-fashioned way, because a lot of times, those ways really are simpler. But we also strive to combine modern practices with more traditional customs, to update the old-fashioned and refine the newfangled."

Wow, Claire thought when she finished speaking. Sometimes she surprised herself with her ability to make sense in the morning. That had actually sounded pretty good. Lifting her cup for another sip, "Besides," she added, "it doesn't matter what I do in my private life, since Olive's really the driving force behind the whole business, and comes up with all the ideas and everything, and I'm just a front for all of it."

Until she said that. Then the cup stopped halfway to her mouth, sloshing coffee over the brim and onto the table, and all Claire could think about was that she really, really, *really* shouldn't try to make conversation before having her second cuppa. Panicked, ignoring the hot coffee that had just baptized her hand, she looked at Ramsey and said, "Tell me I didn't just say what I just said."

But he remained silent, something that didn't exactly reassure her. Worse, he seemed to be very interested in what she had just said—whatever it was. Worst of all, he seemed to be looking at her in that thoughtful way again.

"Ramsey?" she spurred him.

"What?" he asked. Still looking interested and thoughtful. Uh-oh.

"Did I just tell you something I shouldn't have?"

"You just told me you're a front for the business, and Olive does all the work. Were you not supposed to tell me that?"

Claire closed her eyes in horror, but all that did was bring everything crashing into focus. "Please tell me you won't tell anyone else what I just said."

"Why would I do that?"

Why indeed? she wondered. Maybe because, oh . . .

Claire didn't know . . . it could ruin her? "Just forget you heard me say that," she instructed him as blandly as she could. "It's really not a big deal," she added, hoping he believed her. "Lots of companies are run that way."

"I'm sure they are."

"It doesn't change anything."

"I'm sure it doesn't."

He *sounded* like he believed her, and his expression hadn't changed at all as they'd spoken. Maybe the enormity of what she had just revealed hadn't registered on him. Maybe he hadn't been paying attention. Maybe he didn't even care. Or maybe he was waiting for a break in the conversation, so he could jump up and call every tabloid he could find in the book to tell them, "Claire Willoughby is a fraud! She's just a front for Simple Pleasures! Pass it on!"

No, she decided as she finally completed her sip of coffee, he wasn't going to do that. He really did look like he had no idea of the relevance of her revelation. Probably, she was worrying for nothing. Maybe if she didn't belabor the topic, he'd forget all about it.

Ramsey wasn't sure when he had started tallying up all the things about Claire Willoughby that might be used against her in a court of law, but as he sat there in her kitchen—a kitchen boasting enough pine to make even Rebecca Boone think twice about claiming it, he realized he was doing exactly that. Making a mental note of everything Claire said that an attorney—like, say, Ramsey's attorney, the one he still hadn't ruled out hiring—might misconstrue in someone else's favor—like, say, Ramsey's favor. Chronologically speaking:

She slept late whenever she got the chance and left Anabel in the care of someone else, suggesting she was irresponsible. Never mind that Anabel was with someone Claire trusted implicitly, someone she had known for years, someone who was perfectly good with the little girl.

She was incoherent without coffee, suggesting a chemical dependency. Never mind that it was a dependency the majority of the country also shared and was pretty much harmless.

She entertained strange men in her home while wearing her pajamas, something that suggested the potential for promiscuity and sexual misconduct. Never mind that her pajamas were the kind that would repel most thinking men, and that the man she was currently entertaining had come over without an invitation.

She misled millions of people by preaching a lifestyle someone else dictated to her, suggesting she was a hypocrite and a liar. Never mind that her hypocrisy was mild by even the strictest standards, and neither her practices nor her preaching hurt anyone.

He hadn't been lying when he'd said he'd done some research this week. He had read the latest issue of her magazine, and he had watched her show several times. And, truthfully, he'd had a hard time reconciling the ice princess businesswoman who had met him at the door that first day with the gracious, gregarious family woman who personified *Simple Pleasures*. He had an even harder time reconciling those women—both organized and capable—with the one who sat before him now, all sleep-rumpled and caffeine-deprived. The magazine's theme this month had been "Family Ties" and had featured stories about knitting and crocheting gifts for family members. Claire's column had sung the praises of "homemade love." On her show, she smiled often, laughed frequently, and came across as a warm, welcoming homemaker who lived her life simply, pleasurably, perfectly. Yet this morning, she seemed like still another person, less organized and less reserved than the other two. This version of Claire seemed more human, more attainable.

And she was infinitely more appealing.

It was no wonder she had so many avid fans, Ramsey thought. And it was no wonder his sister Eleanor had adopted her as a substitute family member worthy of raising her child. Not only was the public Claire a symbol for the sort of life everyone wanted to lead, but she gave off the kind of vibes that made a person want to pull up a chair, pour a cup of coffee, and chat for hours and hours about quilting and stenciling and churning butter. Even Ramsey wasn't immune.

During his meetings with the private Claire, though, she had been, at varying times, icy and tense and uncertain. And she had no family whatever that he could see. No one to take care of, no one to do things for, even though doing things like that was an integral part of her lifestyle business. Of course, now he realized she was only a front for that business. Still, who did she knit, crochet, and cook for? he wondered. Provided she could even do any of those things, which it was looking like wasn't the case at all anyway.

Hypocrite? Ramsey didn't think so. Shrewd businesswoman was probably a more accurate description. But damned if he didn't find himself thinking he might like to tell someone something else entirely. Because if Claire's business was compromised by ugly rumors that she didn't really know how to do any of those things she claimed to do, she'd be way too embroiled in other activities—activities like salvaging Simple Pleasures, Inc. and public relations nightmares—to have any time for a young child. If she were exposed as a potential phony in the newspapers, then the aura of the perfect homemaker would be more than a little tarnished. She wouldn't be nearly as economically sound. The big house might have to go up for sale. The ties to the community would be broken.

In other words, in the eyes of a courtroom, she would appear to be no better fit to take care of a child than Ramsey appeared to be. They'd be on much more equal footing should he be required to take her to court to sue for custody of Anabel.

But could he actually do something like that? he asked himself. Could he intentionally ferret out more information about Claire Willoughby—from Claire Willoughby—with the express purpose of twisting and turning and manipulating what he learned to paint her in a bad light in the eyes of the law? And could he do it knowing that the result would be the deliberate destruction of another person's entire life? Was he the kind of man who could do all that?

The only thing worse than the question itself was the answer Ramsey got in return.

Because honestly, he just didn't know.

When *Simple Pleasures* went into hiatus in mid-August— the broadcasting world's polite way of saying it went into reruns in mid-August so that its host could have a much-needed break, for God's sake, have some pity on the poor woman—Claire breathed a long, lusty sigh of relief. Because by mid-August, it was becoming evident that she was being stretched way too thin, in way too many directions.

Pulling her one way was Anabel, who could pull surprisingly hard for such a little thing, usually breaking something of significant value in the process. Because even after a month in residence, Claire still had no idea what to do about the girl. She continued to tell herself—every day, in fact, until it be-

came a veritable mantra to her—that the arrangement with Anabel Sage was a temporary one. But it was seeming less and
less temporary with every passing day. Because although
Ramsey Sage continued to visit his niece three or four times a
week, Claire hadn't come any closer to believing he was the
most appropriate person to raise the child. Probably because
she still didn't know him from Adam. Whatever the hell that
meant. Though, to be fair, her inability to know him wasn't
just because he was so reluctant to reveal anything about himself. Too, it was because Claire had been so busy trying to
wrap up the show, she honestly hadn't seen that much of him.

Oh, all right, that wasn't just because she had been so
busy trying to wrap up the show. It was also because she had
been making a conscious effort to avoid him and his barbed-
wire tattoo and salient biceps.

But it wasn't just Anabel and Ramsey stretching Claire too
thin. Olive was yanking her in yet another direction, because
Olive was acting very strangely lately. Not only was she
showing signs of wanting to keep little Anabel around for a
while—like maybe forever, since no one had bonded with the
little girl the way Olive had—but she was also extraordinarily
jumpy. What was really odd was that she seemed to be jumpi-
est whenever Davis Webster was around. Which, okay, maybe
wasn't so strange, because some of Davis Webster's wardrobe
selections made Claire a little twitchy, too. Still, Olive's behavior of late had Claire a tad preoccupied.

And then there was Chandler jerking Claire in still another
direction—*jerk* being the operative word, since scarcely a day
went by when he wasn't badgering her about turning Anabel
over to her uncle. Or over to the courts. Or over to the state of
Tennessee. Or over to the state of North Carolina. Or over to

anywhere else the child might find a roof to put over her head that didn't have Claire's name on the mortgage. Because the process, Chandler said, could be potentially time-consuming, ergo he should get started on it right away.

Surprisingly, it wasn't her attorney's suggestion that Anabel be turned over to the courts or various states that bothered Claire the most. Nor was it his urging that she give Ramsey Sage a chance with the girl, even as he made obvious his distaste for and disapproval of Ramsey Sage. It wasn't even Chandler's use of the word *ergo*. It was that Claire just couldn't shake the sensation, however ridiculous, that there was something less than benevolent in Chandler's motives.

As obvious as he made his disapproval of Ramsey, he *really* made obvious his distaste for Anabel. Which Claire supposed she could understand—kind of—since Chandler just wasn't the sort of man to tolerate baby shenanigans. He tolerated even less baby doody. But where Claire had warmed to Anabel over the passage of a month, Chandler's attitude toward the girl grew colder and colder with every visit, and his recommendations that Claire relinquish her *temporary*— he kept stressing that word—guardianship of Anabel grew hotter and hotter.

But of all the things that had Claire hopping by mid-August—speaking of hotter and hotter—there was one that made her jump higher than all the others combined. And that was Ramsey Sage, who always seemed to be underfoot. Though, come to think of it, Claire supposed it was better to have him under her foot than under . . . well, never mind. But every time she turned around those first few weeks after Anabel entered her life, Ramsey seemed to be there. Always, he was handsome. Always, he was smoldering. Always, he watched Claire very closely for some reason. Always, he seemed to be thinking about something she couldn't begin to interpret.

But always, he came to see Anabel.

So it was unusual to find him at the studio that last day of production, just as they were wrapping up the show for a few months. What was even stranger was that when she strode over to greet him, he told her he'd been there since the show had begun to air that morning.

"You've been here since we went on the air?" she asked, surprised.

He nodded.

"I'm sorry," she apologized. "Once I go into *Simple Pleasures* mode, I'm so focused on the show, I don't notice much else."

The comment seemed to capture his attention more than it should. "Really?" he asked.

She nodded. "It's like entering a zone of some kind," she said. "It's like everything else ceases to exist."

"Everything?" Again, his voice carried an odd note of concern.

"Ye-es," she said, "everything."

"Even things like, oh . . . I don't know . . . Anabel?"

Oh, now she got it. He was fishing. Fishing for excuses to make her seem unfit as a mother. Claire's back went up fast at the realization, and any warm, fuzzy feelings she might have been entertaining about Ramsey Sage—not that she'd been entertaining any feelings of the sort, mind you—dried right up.

"No, not Anabel," she denied.

"But you just said—"

"Never mind what I said," she snapped. "Why are you here, instead of at the house? Olive's with Anabel today."

"As she so frequently seems to be," he said. His voice was edged with something akin to disapproval as he spoke, and Claire knew he was once again trying to cast her into the role of negligent guardian.

"I have to work," she reminded him evenly. "Not just for myself, but for the hundreds of other people whose livelihoods depend on the success of *Simple Pleasures*. And also," she added, knowing she had no reason to feel defensive, but feeling defensive nonetheless, "I *like* my work, and I wouldn't be happy if I couldn't do it."

"Even though you're just a front for the business?" he asked spitefully.

"Ssshhh," she shushed him vehemently, gritting her teeth. She glanced quickly over one shoulder, then the other, hoping no one else heard what he had said. Thankfully, the sound stage was empty, save the two of them. "What's the matter with you?" she demanded. "How could you say such a thing?"

"Hey, nothing's the matter with me," Ramsey said. "I'm not the one who's misleading millions of viewers. And *you're* the one who said—"

"*Ssshhh*," she hushed him again. So much for him not having been paying attention to what she'd revealed before her regular injection of caffeine three weeks ago. So much for him not fully realizing the enormity of her revelation. So much for him being an ignoramus. She really had convinced herself that he hadn't been listening to her that day. She should have known better.

Because that was the thing about men. They only heard the things you *didn't* want them to hear. The important stuff—stuff like, "Just forget you heard me say that" and "It's really no big deal" and "Lots of businesses are run that way"—went in one ear and out the other. But mumble a little negligible something about being a fraud, and boy, they were all over that.

"It makes me a better person to do my job," she continued evenly, pretending he hadn't spoken. "So there are going to be times, Ramsey, when Anabel has to be in Olive's care. Not that it bothers Anabel," she felt it necessary to add. "She and Olive have grown very close over the past month. So it's not a problem for me to have to work." Then, to drive the point home, she added, "Just like millions of mothers do."

But in response to her impassioned expression, all Ramsey offered in reply was a flat, "You're not Anabel's mother, Claire."

"And you're not her father," she retorted.

"But I *am* her family."

Claire glared at him. "*Family* is a relative term," she said.

"And just what's that supposed to mean?"

She expelled a growl of discontent. "I don't know. I don't know what it means. Just that . . . that . . . that it takes more to make a family than people swimming in the same gene pool, that's all."

He opened his mouth, presumably to argue with her some more, then closed it again. He studied her for a long time before speaking, as if he were thinking very hard about what he wanted to say. So, deciding maybe she should give him some time to decide—or cool off, or go away, or whatever—Claire spun around on her heel and started to make her way to her office.

But Ramsey stopped her before she was even able to complete three steps in that direction. And he did it by covering the distance between them in one long stride and circling her wrist with loose fingers.

And then by very, very softly petitioning her, "Claire, wait."

She really wasn't sure what surprised her the most. The gentleness of his hand on her skin when he touched her or the tenderness in his voice when he spoke her name. Or maybe it was the tiny ripple of radiant warmth that seeped through her when she registered both. Probably, she decided, it was a combination of all three that caused her to halt abruptly, then spin around to meet his gaze . . . and nearly catch fire at the way he was looking at her.

"What?" she asked, her voice sounding as if it were coming from a great distance.

He hesitated a moment, then, "I didn't come to see Anabel today," he said. Still softly. Still gently. Still tenderly. "I came to see you."

And that was when the tiny ripple of radiant warmth seeping through Claire suddenly metamorphosed into a great shuddering curtain of heat that threatened to swamp her completely.

Somehow, she managed to keep her voice steady when she said, "Why would you come to see me?"

"I was hoping you could take the rest of the day off," he told her.

"Well, I was kind of hoping to go home and change into something a little more comfortable," she replied.

And immediately regretted the words. Because Ramsey clearly didn't take her admission in the way she had intended it. She had been thinking it would be nice to go home and change into a loose T-shirt and some big ol' khaki shorts, then spend the rest of the afternoon working out in the garden. That was her idea of "more comfortable." Ramsey, though . . .

Still grasping her wrist loosely in his hand, he followed her example and enjoyed a long, leisurely inspection of her, dragging his gaze *verrry* slowly from her face, over her dove gray suit jacket and skirt, then to her legs, then to her feet, and then *verrry* slowly back up again. Okay, so maybe she'd set herself up for that, Claire conceded reluctantly as he concluded his blatant inspection of her person. She told herself she should feel insulted by it, but strangely, she discovered that what she actually felt was . . . aroused? Oh, surely not. Nevertheless, by the time Ramsey's gaze reconnected with hers, heat had crept up from her belly to her breasts, then into her face, and she knew that he knew she was blushing. Ferociously. When he smiled this time, the gesture was sincere—and more than a little sensual—and this time, in response, Claire's heart revved and gunned and squealed right out of the bank parking lot burning rubber, with the law from three states right on its heels, sirens blazing.

"Is Olive available to watch Anabel for the rest of the day?" he asked, seeming to have forgotten all about how he'd taken exception to Olive's baby-sitting only moments ago. His voice was a little ragged for some reason when he spoke, and he watched Claire intently, as if he were very, *very* interested in her reply.

But his interest this time clearly didn't stem from the fact that he wanted to catch her out and impugn her fitness as Anabel's guardian. No, his interest now obviously had nothing to do with his niece and everything to do with Claire. She knew that unequivocally, because his voice was low and dark and silky when he spoke, and his gaze was fixed on hers, a gaze that was smoky and turbulent and vaguely ominous, a gaze that spoke volumes. And what it said was—

Well. Suffice it to say Claire's mouth just went dry

when Ramsey looked at her the way he did. How strange that her mouth should go dry when other parts of her were feeling so—

"Ah, yeah. Yeah," she said quickly, doing her best not to stumble over the words. Such as they were. As unobtrusively as she could, she tugged her wrist free of Ramsey's fingers and thrust both hands behind her back. Whether that was because she didn't want him to touch her again, or because she was afraid she might reach out to him, she decided not to ponder. Instead, she hurried on, striving to be a bit more articulate this time. "Yes, as a matter of fact, she is. Available, I mean. Olive, I mean. Olive is always available." *And I'm always an idiot, she thought further.* So much for being articulate. Then she stopped herself. It wasn't that she was *always* an idiot. Only when Ramsey Sage was around was she reduced to incoherent babbling. "Why do you ask?"

He smiled that lascivious smile again, and Claire's entire midsection began to shudder and purr in response.

"Because I thought maybe you and I could spend some time together today," he said softly.

"You and I?" she echoed stupidly. "I and you? Us? We? Together?"

He nodded. "Is that a problem? I mean, you said you were finished shooting for today, and that the show's going into hiatus now. Is there any reason why we *can't* spend the rest of the day together?" He hesitated a telling moment before adding uncertainly, "And maybe, you know, a few other days, too?"

Claire started to respond, then realized she had so many responses crashing into each other in her head at the moment, few of them in any way intelligible, that she had no idea which one to pick. So instead of answering his question, she asked him one of her own. "Why?"

He relaxed his stance some, but she could tell the gesture was forced, as if he were trying to make her think he didn't care what he was saying, when in fact, he cared a lot. "Because I get the feeling that even after a month, you still don't approve of me."

She started to deny it. Wanted to deny it. But deep down, she knew she couldn't. As good as he'd been to Anabel, Claire still couldn't shake the feeling that there was something about Ramsey that just wasn't quite . . . right. There was more than an air of secrecy about him. There was a great, hulking wall of secrecy about him. He'd offered so little of himself. He never talked about his past or discussed his present or voiced plans for his future. She just couldn't bring herself to trust him yet. Maybe not ever. Not unless he opened up to her. Which, maybe, was a good reason to agree to his proposition. Proposal. Idea.

Whatever.

"It's not that I don't approve of you," she hedged.

He hooked his hands loosely on his hips, shifted his weight to one foot, and studied her with much expectation. "I hear a 'but' coming."

"But," she confirmed. And then she decided to just spell it out for him. "I can't quite bring myself to trust you," she said honestly.

His mouth, which had been curled into such a nice smile—such a nice, heart-revving, rubber-burning smile—only moments ago, went flat.

"I'm sorry," she quickly apologized. "But you haven't exactly given me any reason to."

His expression went incredulous. "How can you say that?" he demanded. "I've come to visit Anabel three, four times a week," he reminded her. "I'd come more often, but I was afraid you'd think I was overstepping my bounds, and hell, I don't even know what those bounds are." Claire opened her mouth to protest, but he hastily continued, cutting her off. "Plus, I've had a few things I've had to take care of." Unfortunately, she didn't even want to hazard a guess as to what those things were, mostly because she feared they were illegal in nature. After all, she still didn't know where he'd gotten that Volvo station wagon. "I've been great with Anabel," he continued. "She likes me. And I'm crazy about her. I'm her family," he reiterated emphatically. "How can you not trust me?"

"Because even after a month," she said, "I don't know anything about you."

He gaped at her in silence, as if he couldn't understand why she would say such a thing.

"Well, you never talk about yourself," she said.

"That's because there's nothing for me to say," he replied. But there was something in his voice that made him sound uncertain. She hesitated to call it a deliberate attempt to mislead. Even if that was what it felt like it was.

"I don't know anything about your past," she added.

"That's because it was totally uneventful," he said. Still dodging, she suspected.

"I don't know anything about what you do for a living," she continued. "I don't even know what it is you *do* do for a living."

"It's kind of hard to describe," he said. Definitely dodging.

"I don't know what you do in your spare time," she charged. "I don't know the things you like, or the things you don't like."

"I'm totally average in every way." Oh, yeah. Like she was going to believe *that*.

"I don't know where you got that Volvo station wagon," she blurted.

"Well, I didn't steal it, if that's what you're thinking."

She said nothing.

He gaped again. "You *do* think I stole it."

"No . . ." she began. But her voice trailed off, and for the life of her, she could think of nothing else to say.

"I found it in the classifieds," he told her. "And I paid for it. With my own money. Money I *earned*."

Instead of asking him *how* he earned it, Claire continued, "Well, I don't know how you plan to take care of Anabel when . . . I mean, *if*," she hastily corrected herself, "you take custody of her." There. *Take* that, *Ramsey Sage, Volvo owner*.

"We'll be just fine," he assured her.

"Oh, come on, Ramsey. You haven't even looked for a job," she reminded him.

"That's because I'm planning to take Anabel back to North Carolina with me, once you give the okay. It would be unfair to any employer here for me to go to work when I know I'll be quitting."

"You've sidestepped every question I've asked you about your background and your job," she said, returning to her original objections. "You've told me nothing of a personal nature. How can I turn Anabel over to you when after a month of seeing you, *I don't even know you*?"

She stopped short—just barely—of shouting that last, but her frustration was obvious. She told herself she was frustrated on Anabel's behalf. But she knew she was frustrated for herself, too. There were reasons besides her concern for Anabel that made Claire so curious about Ramsey on a personal level. She just didn't want to explore those reasons in any depth. Mostly because whenever she started to do that, her body parts started to tingle again, parts she'd rather not have tingling, thankyouverymuch, mixed company or no, mostly because it forced her to realize just how little body-tingling she'd had lately, dammit, and realizing that made her very irritable indeed, and feeling irritable about something like that in turn made her feel frustrated as hell. Or maybe that wasn't what made her feel frustrated as hell. Maybe it was something else. But thinking about that only started the cycle again, so she tried not to think about Ramsey at all.

Um, what was the question?

"But don't you see?" Ramsey said.

No, that wasn't the question. It was something else, she was sure.

"That's why I want the two of us to spend some time together," he told her. "So you *can* get to know me."

Oh, that's right. She'd been wondering how he expected her to turn over Anabel when she didn't even know him. Now it looked like he was going to give her the opportunity to rectify that. Somehow, though, that made her start feeling frustrated again.

Fortunately, Ramsey continued, thereby diverting her attention. Sort of. "And I can get to know you, too," he said. "Because if you do end up being the one to raise Anabel . . . *if,*" he reiterated emphatically—*Take* that, *Claire Willoughby, workaholic*—"I want to make sure you'll be all right for the job."

Only then did it occur to Claire that Ramsey might not approve of her any more than she did him. And only then did she begin to realize how worried he was about Anabel's future. His concession that she might end up being Anabel's keeper had been pulled from him with much unwillingness, she knew. But he had been forced to keep that option open.

It probably would be a good idea for the two of them to spend more time together, she thought. If they spent the day together, for example, not only could she finally maybe get some answers from him for all the questions that had been plaguing her, but she could reassure him, too, that she wasn't a bad option for Anabel. Even if, she had to admit, she'd told herself that very thing over and over again. So, really, she told herself as she considered his petition, there was no reason why she shouldn't spend the day with Ramsey today.

Except for the fact that it was probably a very bad idea.

Finally, though, she reached a compromise. "I can't today," she said. And that was the truth. She did still have a few things to do at the studio before she could get away. More to the point, she felt like she needed some time to prepare before she exposed herself to Ramsey Sage for any length of time.

And, oh, she really wished she'd come up with a word other than *exposed*.

He expelled a sound of frustration, and his entire body went lax.

"Tomorrow," she told him before he had a chance to erupt again. "I can give you tomorrow. How will that be?"

He straightened, and she could tell he wasn't any too happy about having his plans changed. Especially by someone other than himself. Finally, though, "I'll take it," he replied.

And Claire did her best to reassure herself that was the *only* thing he took.

Eight

*D*avis Webster watched Olive Tully very closely as she interacted with Anabel Sage in the big, lush garden behind the Willoughby home. But where Anabel, in her bright yellow romper, was a front-and-center splash of color amid a riot of other brilliant hues in the form of roses and daisies and a host of flowers he couldn't possibly begin to identify, Olive was a drab little side note in gray, following behind her.

A month had passed since he'd first brought the girl here to live, and little seemed to have changed. The August air was as hot and heavy with summer as the July air had been. He still dressed in his usual work uniform of baggy khakis and ugly Hawaiian shirt—today it was an orange number spattered with turquoise surfboards and fuchsia flamingos. Anabel Sage still seemed to be powered by energy that was nothing short of atomic. Olive Tully was still trying to make herself invisible to the naked eye.

And Davis was still fascinated by Olive.

But his fascination didn't result from the fact that he was

a case worker, following up on a child's care. This was his eighth visit with Anabel, and on each occasion, he'd been satisfied with what he'd seen and heard, in spite of the stream of continually gutted and filleted toys he encountered. Nevertheless, Davis had a court order to oblige by coming to the Willoughby home once a week or more to check on Anabel Sage for the first six months of her residence, so naturally, he would comply. It wasn't his fault if he'd ended up visiting not "once a week," but "or more." Anabel's was a demanding case, that was all.

But even the court order wasn't the real reason he had come today. In fact, nothing about his job had inspired this particular visit. Today, Davis hadn't come to see Anabel. He had come to see Olive. Because he couldn't stop thinking about Olive. And not just because of her haunting whiskey-colored eyes or her puzzling—and totally ineffective, as far as he was concerned—attempts to make herself invisible, either.

It was because Olive Tully didn't exist.

As a matter of course—and also to assuage his rampant curiosity—Davis had run a check on her and Claire Willoughby, which was standard operating procedure for anyone assigned by the courts to take on the care of a child not their own. It was also standard operating procedure for anyone who was naturally suspicious of everyone in the world, as Davis was.

What he had discovered about Claire had been unexpected—that she'd been raised almost entirely as a ward of the state of Tennessee, and had then been booted out of a government-sponsored home at the age of eighteen to make her own way in the world. Her parents had both been killed when she was quite young, and although she'd been available for adoption, she'd been repeatedly passed over, probably because of her age. Davis had, of course, seen that happen often enough. But Claire had built herself into what would have been considered a spectacular success even if she'd had an easy time of it. Knowing she had overcome obstacles that would have stymied many had reluctantly notched up his admiration for her.

Olive Tully, however, had been another matter. Not because he didn't admire her—au contraire, though his admiration for her differed considerably from the admiration he entertained for her employer—but because Olive Tully had no discernible origins whatsoever.

None.

Of course, it was possible that Tully wasn't her birth name, Davis had realized when he'd been unable to locate anything of significance about her, including a record of her birth. But there had been no marriage record for a newly minted by matrimony Olive Tully anywhere, either. Nor an adoption record. And no application for a legal name change. Not in Tennessee, not in New Jersey, where she had claimed to be born, and not in any other state in the union.

The only records of an Olive Tully that Davis had found that might be her—and only after he'd completed some serious searching—had been for school enrollments. Oddly, there had been plenty of those. The Olive Tully whose records Davis had followed had started kindergarten in the middle of November in Tupelo, Mississippi, and had moved some months later to a kindergarten in Jackson. Then she'd started elementary school in yet another location, Dothan, Alabama, and had changed schools a half dozen times, across three different states, before entering middle school in yet another state, South Carolina. She'd attended several more schools before finally graduating from a high school in Florida. Eventually, she'd landed at Vanderbilt University when she was eighteen, and she'd been living in Tennessee ever since.

But there had been no records for her anywhere prior to kindergarten. It was as if she had simply been dropped onto the planet when she was five years old, to receive her education from as many schools as possible. And from what Davis could tell, she'd arrived here through parthenogenesis, because she'd evidently never had a father. Certainly he'd found no reference to one in his investigation. Her mother was the only person listed as a parent on Olive's school forms, and she had died not long after Olive graduated from college.

But therein lay yet another mystery. Olive's mother had no discernible origins, either. No birth certificate, no marriage certificate, no legal name changes, nothing. What made that especially odd was that Olive had said her mother was in the military, which, if nothing else, might have accounted for the numerous transitions she had made between schools. *If* Davis had actually found a record of a mother in the military, and there had been none for that, either. The armed forces kept excellent records of who its people were and where its people went and why its people went there. If Olive's mother had been in the service, Davis, or one of his numerous government contacts, would have located her records. Obviously, Olive had lied about that. But why?

And why hadn't he been able to find any records of her birth? Or of her adoption, if that were the case? Why had she suddenly just materialized out of thin air as a kindergarten student? Why had her mother suddenly just appeared at the same time? And why the constant moving around for both of them?

Surprisingly, Davis had been able to come up with a couple of answers for those questions, but only because, by the time he formed them, it was way past his bedtime, and he'd downed a couple of Bourbons straight. The first explanation featured an alternate universe and little silver creatures with almond-shaped eyes with names like XQ7 and Z14 zinging around the solar system in light-speed UFOs. The second explanation had been even more far-fetched, one that defied credence by even conspiracy theorists, and was more suited to bad movies of the week. That explanation involved WIT-SEC. More officially known as the Witness Security Program, and more familiarly known as the Witness Protection Program. Davis didn't have to be a government employee to have some nodding acquaintance with that. No, he need only have viewed a few bad movies of the week to know that when people went into the program, they received new identities, identities that totally erased whatever—whoever—they had been before.

But how could a woman like Olive Tully be involved in something like that? Especially since, if that were the case, she had entered the program when she was a young child. Her parents, of course, could have been involved in something they shouldn't have been, but even at that, the idea simply seemed too ridiculous to consider.

But that was the idea Davis kept coming back to. There was no other explanation for her strange lack of origin. Except for that one with XQ7 and Z14, and even with a couple of Bourbons in him, that one just hadn't seemed likely.

What was she hiding from? he wondered again. *Had* she gone into WITSEC? And after all these years, could she still be afraid that someone would find her? Surely after all these years, she was safe, he told himself, if indeed she had ever been in any danger to begin with. Especially with both of her parents now gone. Surely there was a statute of limitations on being terrified.

But then Davis remembered what line of work he was in, recalled some of the things he'd seen people do to their own children. Hell, he knew better than most people that there wasn't a statute of limitations on being terrified. He'd been a social worker for more than ten years, long enough that some of his early cases had grown to adulthood—well, those who had lived long enough to grow to adulthood, at any rate. And, as adults, many of them hadn't fared particularly well, thanks to their experiences as children. Many of them still lived in fear. Many would never escape it.

He studied Olive again in the late-afternoon sunlight. She hadn't been happy about his arrival today. He'd been able to tell that the moment she opened the front door to him—after opening the little window in the front door that served as a peephole, and then unlocking what had sounded like two or three hundred dead bolts. Of course, Davis hadn't called first to let anyone know he was coming. But he wasn't required to do that. Besides, he had done that the last several times he'd come by, and Olive hadn't been home, even though she had been the one to answer the phone a couple of times when Davis called to announce his visit.

By the time he'd arrived at the house, though, Claire Willoughby had been the one watching Anabel, and she'd always assured him she had been with the little girl all day. But Claire hadn't always been dressed as if she were the one watching Anabel—sometimes she had been dressed as if she'd just come home from work. In a hurry. And Davis hadn't quite been able to squash the idea that Olive had called Claire home from wherever she was so that Olive could perform her disappearing act and not be there when he arrived.

So today, Davis hadn't given her the chance to disappear. And today, he was being rewarded for that. Because although Olive was dressed as she had been on those few occasions when he'd seen her before, in muted shades reminiscent of absolutely nothing, today she wore them in the form of a gauzy, loose-fitting dress that draped lovingly over her curves. Better than that, though, whenever she stood in the sunlight just so the garment was virtually translucent.

And she was standing in the sunlight *just so* right now, he couldn't help noticing, bending over to look at a mangled daisy Anabel was holding up for her inspection. Olive tucked a strand of her short brown hair behind one ear as she did, her fingers lingering there as if that were her only hope of anchoring the unruly locks in place. Her other hand was pressed against one thigh, pushing her dress against her in a way that made the curve of her breasts more visible. Davis could just make out the silhouette of her legs through the fabric, surprisingly long for such a petite woman.

Behind her, massive cascades of clematis wound up an arbor in an uproar of purple, their fragrance oppressive and sweet in the ponderous August heat. The whole garden was redolent with washes of cloying perfume, an aroma so luscious Davis almost couldn't tolerate it, because it reminded him too much of another such garden he had once loved. Somehow, though, Olive Tully seemed to belong here, as if she were some ethereal fairy-tale nymph, the product of an afternoon daydream that had gotten completely beyond his control.

"So, Olive," he said, taking a perverse sort of pleasure in the way she flinched at the sound of his voice. Hey, at least he moved her. Just because it was literally instead of emotionally didn't mean he couldn't treasure it. "You don't mind if I call you Olive, do you?" he asked belatedly. And only as a formality, since he had no intention of calling her *Ms. Tully* anymore. Once he started having sexual fantasies about a woman—which usually occurred, oh, about fifteen minutes after meeting one—he couldn't possibly think of her as *Ms. Anything* anymore.

"Actually," she said, her attention fixed not on Davis, but on Anabel, "I'd prefer it if you'd call me—"

"Terrific," he interjected. "And you should call me Davis."

"Actually, I'd prefer to call you—"

"So what happened when you were a kid that caused you to end up in WITSEC?" he asked conversationally, cutting her off before she could finish her statement—and bringing her attention snapping around to him faster than a bullet tearing through the jack of spades.

For one split second, Davis knew he had hit exactly on why there was no record of her origin. She *was* in the program. He could tell because of the absolute panic and terror that came over her face in that one split second. But she recovered almost immediately, blanking out her features so that she only looked mildly confused.

"What are you talking about?" she asked.

"WITSEC," he repeated. "The Witness Protection Program. Why are you in it?"

Although he was bluffing, he wasn't bluffing. He didn't have any evidence to back up his assertion, but he knew without question that his assertion was true.

Olive eyed him thoughtfully for a moment, then smiled.

"Mr. Webster, have you been drinking?" she asked, her voice oozing a courtesy that was belied by the fire of combat glittering in her eyes.

Unable to help himself, Davis smiled back. "Not today, no," he told her, his voice the very picture of politeness, just as hers had been. "Today I haven't had any reason to drink. But it's still early, and I still have a couple of cases to visit after Anabel. Why do you ask?"

She took a minute to digest all that he had said—and really, he thought, he had said way more than he'd intended to say for some reason—her smile falling when she seemed to get the gist of it. But instead of inquiring further about his comments, she rallied her smile—only it wasn't quite as bright this time—and told him, "Because the only reason I can think of why you would ask me such a ridiculous question is that your brain is soggy with whiskey."

Davis took a few idle steps forward, ignoring the sweetness of the nearby roses that assailed him as he went. Thrusting his hands into his trouser pockets with feigned indifference, he countered easily, "Or maybe it's because I know what I'm talking about."

She expelled a sound of almost convincing skepticism. "No, I don't believe that you do."

"Was it your mother or your father who got into trouble?" he asked, unperturbed by her unwillingness to confide in him. "I mean, it couldn't have been you—you must have been, what? Five years old at the time? It was more than twenty-five years ago, after all."

She didn't answer right away, and in fact stayed silent so long that he figured she wasn't going to answer him at all. He was about to press her again when, as she silently directed Anabel's attention to a peony so round and heavy it was drooping nearly to the cobbled walkway, she said, "The only thing that happened when I was five years old, Mr. Webster, was that my father disappeared one day without a trace. He went out to buy groceries, and he never came back. When I was older, Mama told me it was because he had a girlfriend in St. Louis, and he went to live with her." She turned to look at Davis now and shrugged. "We never heard from him again. But that was the only notable thing that happened to me when I was five."

He supposed she had been trying to sidestep his question by responding the way she had. Instead, Davis learned quite a bit from what she told him. He learned even more from what she didn't tell him.

"What brought you from Newark, where you said you were born, to Tupelo, Mississippi, where you went to kindergarten?"

He wasn't sure, but he thought she paled a bit at the question. "How do you know where I went to kindergarten?" she asked.

He shrugged, hoping he pulled off one that at least looked unconcerned. "It's SOP in my job to run checks on people if they're going to be caring for someone else's child," he said. "I ran one on your employer, too."

"I see," she said coolly.

Well, she might have seen, Davis thought, but she sure didn't like what she saw. "Why did you move around so much when you were a child?" he asked further, deciding she probably wasn't going to answer his question about her move from Newark to Tupelo, anyway.

She crossed her arms over her chest in what was clearly a defensive gesture. Davis tried not to notice how it pushed the wispy fabric of her dress against her breasts to the point where he could just detect a hint of delicate lace beneath. Really, he tried. But unfortunately—or maybe not so unfortunately—he failed in his efforts.

"My mother wasn't skilled at very many things," Olive said. Though she deflected her gaze from his as she spoke. "We went wherever she could find work."

"You said she was in the service," he reminded her.

"At one point, she was," Olive said. "She was in the Navy."

"Why did she leave it if she was so unskilled?" he asked.

But again, Olive hesitated before responding, "Why are you asking me these things? I mean, what business is it of yours?"

"It's none of my business," he conceded readily. Then, shamelessly, he played the state care card, even though none of this was any of the state's business, either. "But the state of Tennessee deserves to know what kind of person will be taking care of Anabel."

"Well, then, the state of Tennessee will have to ask me."

"The state of Tennessee is asking you."

"No, it isn't."

Damn. He was going to have to stop underestimating her. "All right," he said. "Then let's just talk for a minute, man to woman."

She looked at him full on, her eyes going wide behind her glasses. "Oh, I don't *think* so," she said. "What I do think, Mr. Webster, is that it's time for your visit to end."

"But I just got here twenty minutes ago," he objected. "I'm supposed to stay for an hour."

"No, you arrived a long time ago," she told him. "And you've been here a lot longer than an hour. In fact, you've completely overstayed your welcome."

Davis didn't have time to wonder what she meant by her

comment, because she reached for Anabel's hand then, clearly intending for both of them to make their departure. Without hesitation, and with complete trust, the little girl tucked her fingers into Olive's and allowed herself to be led away, back toward the house.

Not for the first time, it occurred to Davis that Olive was the only one who seemed to have any sort of control over the child. Anabel, he had learned immediately upon meeting her, was a spirited little thing, which was a polite way of saying she was trouble. Not that she wasn't charming and sweet sometimes, but even at her best, she wanted to get into *everything*. Really, that was a good sign, Davis knew. It meant she hadn't been hindered or oppressed. Her curiosity about whatever she encountered meant that her curiosity had been encouraged. But it also meant she would be a challenge for anyone to raise, especially strangers to whom she felt no obligation to behave.

With Olive, though, Anabel behaved very well. He wondered why the little girl related so completely to the woman, in a way she didn't with anyone else. Later, Davis would wonder about that some more. Right now, he had some damage control to see to. Because as quickly as Olive Tully had entered his life, she was exiting it again. And she was making it clear—mostly by the way she was hastening her step the nearer she drew to the house—that she wasn't coming back if she could help it.

So Davis hastened his step, too, following the retreating woman and child up the cobbled walkway. He caught up with them both just as Olive's foot hit the first of the wide, wooden porch steps. Without thinking, he reached forward and circled her wrist with loose fingers, tugging gently on her arm in an effort to halt her forward motion.

Big mistake, he immediately realized. Because touching Olive, even in so innocuous a way, set off all kinds of thoughts he really shouldn't have. But he couldn't bring himself to release her. Her skin was warm and soft and alive beneath his fingertips, and for some reason, he just wanted to let his hand linger there for a little while longer.

Olive, not surprisingly, had other ideas. Because she jerked her wrist free from his grasp and spun around quickly enough to make herself stumble. Davis reached both arms out this time, to steady her, but she leapt backward, landing with surprising grace on the next step up. Anabel, evidently thinking they were playing a game, jumped up onto that step, too, clapping her hands and laughing when she completed the action as well as Olive had.

"Don't touch me," Olive said crisply as she came to a stop, lifting one hand, index finger extended, in warning. "Do not . . . touch me," she repeated more adamantly. "Ever."

"I'm sorry," Davis immediately apologized. Hoping to show her he was no threat to her, he stepped back down to the ground and extended his hands, palm out, to his sides. "I didn't mean anything by it," he told her. "I was just trying to get you to slow down."

"Why?" she demanded.

He expelled a soft sound of exasperation. "Because I want to talk to you, that's why."

"I'll talk to you about Anabel," she said. "But I *won't* talk to you about myself."

"Oh, come on, Olive," he said, some of his exasperation creeping into his voice. "I just want to know what happened to you, that's all."

"No," she said eloquently. "There's nothing to talk about. Nothing happened to me. Ever. Do you understand? Nothing . . . ever . . . happened. I had a totally normal, totally un-eventful life. I'm just like everyone else. Understand?" Her amber eyes were fierce as she spoke, so fierce that Davis knew she was lying about all of it. "And don't call me Olive, Mr. Webster," she said further. "I never said that you could."

"Olive," he tried again, ignoring her admonition, "if you'd just—"

She glared at him as she cut him off. "I'll be calling your office this afternoon, Mr. Webster, and lodging a sexual ha-rassment complaint against you. And I'll be demanding they assign another social worker to Anabel's case."

He gaped at her, incredulous. "Whoa, whoa, whoa," he said, holding up both hands in the *Don't overreact* gesture. "Sexual harassment?" he echoed. "Are you serious? I didn't say anything sexual to you. Hell, lady, I didn't even ask you to go out with me yet."

Only when that last statement was out of his mouth did Davis realize how much he'd revealed in his objection. And not just to Olive, either. But to himself, as well. He hadn't known until that moment that he wanted to ask her out. But now that he knew, and now that he'd voiced his intention, he also knew he didn't want to take it back. Probably. Not un-less she laughed in his face.

But judging by her expression, Olive had no intention of laughing. On the contrary, for some reason, she looked like she wanted to cry. Jeez, he knew he wasn't the greatest catch in town. And he hadn't exactly given her any reason to think he was interested in her. But he would have liked to think he wasn't so monstrous that he'd drive a woman to tears.

For a moment, he didn't think she was going to respond. And even when she finally did, her voice was quiet and sub-dued. "Were you planning to ask me to go out with you?"

"Maybe," he said, still surprised to realize it. "Would you go out with me if I asked?"

She shook her head slowly, but he detected some reluctance in the gesture. "No."

"Then I wasn't planning to ask," he retorted through gritted teeth. "But I sure as hell wasn't planning to harass you sexually, either."

"You just planned to harass me in the usual old way, is that it?"

"Of course not."

"Then what were you planning to do?"

Davis shoved a hand into his hair, restlessly pushing a handful back from his face. "I just want to know what you're afraid of, Olive. That's all."

Once again, the words were out of his mouth before he could stop them. But this time, he immediately regretted voicing them. Not just because the statement itself was so personal and inappropriate, but because the irritation that edged his voice indicated he had lost control. And he couldn't remember the last time he had done such a thing.

Oh, hang on a minute. Yes, he could. And he'd felt like a creep then, too.

For a long moment, Olive only stared at him, her amber eyes huge behind the frames of her little glasses. Then, very softly, she said, "I'm not afraid of anything, Mr. Webster. Not even you."

Davis told himself to just drop it, to get going and finish up the last two cases he had waiting for him, and forget that Olive Tully even existed. But instead of saying something that might end the conversation as quickly and as painlessly as possible, he said, very quietly, "Then if you're not afraid of me . . . will you go out with me?"

And he was stunned to realize that his heart was hammering hard as he concluded the question. Maybe Olive wasn't afraid of him, he thought. But he sure as hell was terrified of her.

She gazed at him so solemnly and so intently, that, for a moment, he began to think she had ducked out without his seeing her, and left one of those life-sized, easel-back cardboard Olive Tullys in her wake. But then she nodded slowly once.

And damned if his heart didn't beat even harder then. Man, he'd forgotten how good that could feel.

Still not quite able to believe his luck, but wanting to seal the deal as quickly as he could, he said, "Saturday night?"

For another long moment, Olive only gazed at him in that cardboard silence way. And then she nodded slowly one more time.

"I'll pick you up at seven," he told her.

Another heavy silence, another slow nod.

"On the dot."

More silence. Another nod.

"I promise."

One last silence. One last nod.

Davis couldn't quite believe that Olive had said yes, and he was afraid if he pushed his luck, asked even one more question or made one more specification, she would turn tail and flee. So while things were running in his favor, before either of them had a chance to change their minds—and not entirely certain he hadn't completely lost his—he turned tail and fled. And he didn't stop fleeing until he reached his car, threw it into gear, and fled even faster that way.

Nine

*R*amsey didn't think he could remember a single day in his entire life that he enjoyed more than the one he spent with Claire. Then again, seeing as how his life had consisted almost entirely of days that left a lot to be desired, maybe that wasn't saying much. Although, seeing as how he enjoyed himself so much when he was used to days that left a lot to be desired, maybe it was saying *a lot*. Especially since he and Claire had done nothing out of the ordinary, and he'd *still* had the best time of his life.

Wow, he thought when he realized that. His life really *had* sucked up until today.

But he wouldn't think about that because it would ruin an otherwise enjoyable day, starting with the way Claire had opened her front door to him looking like something from a watercolor painting. Her loose, sleeveless dress was the color of butter and spattered with pale blue flowers, its neck scooping slightly down toward her breasts, its filmy hem swirling around her calves with every step she took. Toes painted pearl pink peeked out from plain flat sandals, and a strip of yellow satin ribbon was wound around the base of a loosely woven braid that spilled to the middle of her back—he hadn't realized until then just how long her hair was. And here he'd thought he was getting all dressed up by donning a blue chambray shirt with buttons—and sleeves—over his jeans.

She was the very picture of delicate femininity, but Ramsey had seen for himself over the past month that there was nothing delicate about her. No, Claire Willoughby, he knew, was strong, tough, and focused, by both nature and by necessity. And seeing her like this, an intriguing combination of warm woman and steel spine, did something funny to his insides. All day long, his heart had been meting out a peculiar rhythm, and something hot and manic had been splashing around in his belly.

She just wasn't like any woman he'd ever been with, that was all. She was so cultured and refined and elegant, so cautious and precise and out of reach. So filled with a quiet sort of beauty he'd never really been attracted to before. Every time he'd glanced at her through the course of the day, hoping he wasn't being obvious, fearful that he was, she'd looked prettier than the last time he'd sneaked a look. And every time he'd stolen a look at her, he'd wanted to steal more. And soon, it wasn't just looks he'd wanted to take.

Conversation had been awkward at first. Ramsey had been so hyperaware of everything. He'd felt like he had to watch every word he said, worried she might misconstrue something. Then he'd scrutinized every comment she made in case it might hold some hidden meaning as to her intentions regarding Anabel. He'd noticed her slip yesterday at the studio, when she'd used the word *when* instead of *if* in discussing his potential guardianship. Oh, she'd corrected herself, naturally, but clearly, she must at least have it at the back of her mind that she would eventually relinquish Anabel into his care.

Because Ramsey *did* want to care for Anabel. Now more than ever. She was a great kid, and she reminded him so much of the sister he had abandoned when she was still too young to fend for herself. He wanted to do right by Eleanor's daughter, wanted to make sure Anabel never questioned her origins or felt as if she had been unwanted and left behind. And as Ramsey and Claire returned to her house at the end of their day together, he thought that maybe, just maybe, he was a couple of steps closer to taking his niece home.

Because by the end of the day, he and Claire felt much more relaxed together, probably thanks to the very mundanity of their excursion. They'd started off having brunch at a café Claire had recommended not far from her home, where they had sipped lattes and listened to guitar music and talked about Anabel. Then they'd strolled leisurely through a neighboring park, where they'd fed the ducks, watched people flying kites, and talked about Anabel. Then they had enjoyed dinner together at a marina Ramsey had discovered during his exploration of the area, where they had watched the boats gliding along the Cumberland River and speared plump pink shrimp from the rim of a bowl and talked about Anabel. And all the while Ramsey had marveled at how much he had forgotten what it was like just to have a nice, simple day with a beautiful woman whose company he enjoyed.

And then he'd realized that it wasn't that he had forgotten any of that. It was that he'd never had the chance to know what it was like in the first place.

But now he did. Better still, now he knew what it was like
to finish that day by sitting on a porch swing in the evening, as
the sun burned low and red over the trees, staining the western
sky with a riot of orange and purple and pink. He knew what
it was like to hear the rapid warble of a whippoorwill vying
with the leisurely *creak . . . creak . . . creak . . .* of the porch
swing, as it swayed back . . . and forth . . . and back . . . and
forth . . . the sporadic jangle of its chain a poignant side note.
He knew what it was like to feel a soft summer breeze ruf-
fling his hair and enjoy the last rolling warmth of the day on
his face. He knew what it was like to sit next to Claire
Willoughby, who looked like a dream, and smelled like honeysuckle, and probably tasted just as sweet.

He might as well have tumbled into a Norman Rockwell
painting. Or worse, a Hayley Mills movie. But damned if he
didn't actually like it here. More than he probably should.
Because this wasn't his world by a long shot. It was Claire's.
And he no more belonged in this fairy-tale land than a dragon
or ogre or troll would. Of course, he reminded himself, ogres
and dragons and trolls appeared with some regularity in fairy
tales, didn't they? But they never, ever got the girl.

"You know, something just occurred to me," Claire said
from beside him, her voice purling through the balmy twilight like languid circles on tranquil waters.

"What's that?" he asked, feeling as mellow and benign as
he would had he just consumed half a bottle of fine wine.
But the only spirits he'd enjoyed today had been Claire's.
Then again, she was pretty intoxicating.

She turned to look at him, her expression dreamy, her
skin seeming to radiate in the last lingering bit of light. "The
reason we spent the day together was to learn more about

each other," she reminded him. "But all we talked about was Anabel."

Ramsey smiled. Hell, he knew that. Had she thought that was an accident? "Okay, then," he said. "Tell me about yourself."

She shook her head. "No, you already know about me. If you've watched the show and read the magazine like you say you have, then you know everything about me that's worth knowing."

Oh, he sincerely doubted that. For one thing, he wanted to know why she would think her work self was all there was worth knowing.

"I'd rather hear about you," she said before he had a chance to sidetrack her again.

And that, of course, was what he'd been afraid of. In spite of his earlier assurances to her that he wanted the two of them to get to know each other, what he'd really meant was that he wanted to know more about her. The last thing Claire needed to know was anything about Ramsey. Because it went without saying that everything she'd learn about him was bad. Which, of course, was why it would go without saying. He'd intended to show her he was a good guy by his actions, not his words. So now he would act by not saying a word about himself.

"I told you. I'm an average guy," he lied. See there? He was a liar, for one thing. "I'm totally unremarkable in every way."

She smiled, obviously intending to ignore his objections. "What's your favorite color?" she asked.

Fine, he thought. If she just wanted surface stuff, he could supply that. Maybe if he answered enough harmless questions like that one, she'd be satisfied. He doubted it, but it was worth a shot. So he replied, "Blue, I guess."

She smiled, clearly delighted to have even that much information about him. Man, she was easy.

"And what's your favorite food?" she asked further.

He didn't have to think about that at all. "Barbecued ribs."

"Favorite music?"

"Pure rock 'n' roll."

She thought for a minute. Already running out of questions? Ramsey wondered. This was going to be easier than he thought.

Finally, though, she asked, "If you could be any animal in the world, what would you be?"

This time Ramsey was the one to smile, but he gave the question some serious thought before replying. Finally, he said, "A coyote. They're survivors."

That response clearly piqued her interest. Damn.

"Hmm . . . that's a revealing response," she said.

Uh-oh. "Is it? How?"

"Yes, it is," she replied to the first question. Then ignored the second by hurrying on, "If you could be any vegetable in the world, what would you be?"

Wow. That was a toughie. Ramsey didn't like too many vegetables. What he ultimately decided on was, "A leek."

Oh, that *really* piqued her interest, he could see. "A leek?" she asked skeptically.

He nodded. "Sure. Why not?" It was kinda phallic. Not that he'd point that out to her.

"Okay," she conceded without further comment. "If you could be any musical instrument in the world, what would you be?"

That was an easy one. "An acoustic guitar." Not phallic, but a nice shape all the same.

"If you had to be stranded on a deserted island with only one other person, who would you want that person to be?"

Oh, trick question, he thought. This one, he was sure, was worth a lot of points. "I should probably say someone like Gandhi or da Vinci, shouldn't I?"

She grinned, and his heart kicked up that peculiar rhythm again, and this time, what splashed through his belly was less hot and manic and more mild and tender. But it was still unlike anything he had ever felt before.

"Well, yes," she said, "if you want to impress me."

"But you'd know I was lying, wouldn't you?" he asked.

"Probably."

"And that wouldn't be very impressive, would it?"

"No, not really."

"Then I'll just tell you the truth. I'd have to go with Lauren Bacall."

Claire studied him in silence for a moment, a moment he used to drink in her loveliness and fill himself to near overflowing with it. Damn, she was beautiful.

She nodded slowly as she said, "I can see that."

Ramsey wondered what his score was up to by now. And he wondered why he was even playing this game. "So, what?" he asked. "You're going to play twenty questions to find out more about me? Is that the plan?"

She shook her head, the gesture sending a few stray strands of pale gold flying around her face, circling her features like an errant halo. "No," she said, her voice tinged with laughter, "it'll probably end up being more like fifty questions since you keep dodging them."

"I'm not dodging," he dodged. "I answered every question you asked me."

"Oh, sure, the superficial ones that really don't tell me that much."

"You don't think the fact I want to be a leek isn't telling?"

"See, you're doing it again," she charged. "You're dodging."

"I'm *not* dodging."

"You are, too, dodging."

"I am not."

"You are, too."

"Am not.'

"Are, too."

"Not."

"Are."

"Claire . . ."

"Ramsey . . ."

And just like that, the day they had shared so agreeably and comfortably ended in a deadlock. And just when things had begun to look up, too. Well, there was only one thing to do now, Ramsey thought. The thing he'd been wanting to do since he'd arrived at her house this morning. Hell, if he were honest with himself, he'd admit it was the thing he'd been wanting to do since he arrived at her house that first day.

As the porch swing continued its languorous, melodious to and fro, Claire sat quietly beside him, as motionless as he, almost as if they'd both fallen under a singular sort of spell that had made time halt completely. Her brilliant blue gaze was bound to his, her ripe, lush mouth was opened just barely, and her slender thigh, draped in frothy yellow, was almost, *almost*, touching his. The warm wind swirled around them again, nudging the honeysuckle scent of her closer to him, deluging him, very nearly overwhelming him. And suddenly Ramsey wanted . . .

Well, he just plain wanted.

So, without thinking about what he was doing, he dipped his head toward Claire's. And after only a second's hesitation—long enough for her to stop him, but she made no move to do so—he kissed her. Slow. And sweet. And tender.

In spite of Ramsey's nearness and the way he inched his head closer to hers, Claire was caught off guard by the touch of his mouth on her own. And she was totally unprepared for the wild ricochet of heat that launched through her upon contact, searing her to the core as it rocketed through. All she knew was that one minute, she was caught up in a playful feud with Ramsey Sage, and the next . . .

Oh, the *next*.

The next minute, she was very nearly overcome by the most wondrous sensations she had ever experienced in her life, astonishing, arousing, almost otherworldly sensations that made her entire body sizzle with a keen awareness of the man who sat beside her. She never saw that kiss coming. And she told herself it was only her lack of preparation that allowed it to go on for so long.

And it did go on. For so long.

Ramsey claimed her mouth cautiously at first, a soft brush of his lips across hers, once, twice, three times, four. Then, slowly, almost lethargically, as if he had to battle some weird, resistive force to do it, he lifted a hand to her face, curving his palm tenderly under her jaw, tracing his fingertips along her cheekbone, skimming the pad of his thumb under her chin. He pressed his mouth more eagerly to hers as he did, keeping it there this time, his soft lips finessing hers with great care, again and again and again. Instinctively, Claire lifted her hand to his face, too, touching tentative fingers to his jaw, now rough with a day's growth of beard. She savored the impression, so exotic did it seem to someone who'd had scant experience with the male anatomy of late. But that lone, limited touch of him, and that single, succulent taste of him made Claire want to experience so much more.

The sun had dipped low enough in the sky by now that the swing was cast entirely in shadow. Lilac bushes grew thick and imperious at this corner of the porch, and lavish morning glory vines hung a sweet-scented drape between Claire and Ramsey and the front walk. She knew no one could see them from the street, that there would be nothing to inhibit her exploration of him, should she indeed endeavor to discover more. So, almost shyly, she lifted her other hand, too, laying it against his chest, splaying her fingers open wide over the soft chambray of his shirt. She felt the steady thump-thump-thump of his heart buffeting her palm when she did, noting how it jumped and danced and accelerated the moment she pressed her hand over him. How encouraging, she thought, that she would set him off-kilter the same way he did her.

She pushed the hand on his chest higher, toward his shoulder, marveling at the solid ridges of muscle that spanned beneath her fingers as she went, loving the way the heat of his body seeped through the fabric of his shirt and into her own skin. She curled her fingers briefly over his shoulder, then urged her hand inward, dragging it along the strong column of his throat. Then she scooted it back, cupping her hand over his warm nape for a moment before driving her fingers higher, threading them into the silky, inky locks that coiled around them.

He murmured a soft sound of approval against her mouth as she tangled her fingers in his hair, then brought his other hand up to her face, sketching the line of her jaw before reaching behind her to seize her braid possessively in his hand and pull it forward, over her shoulder. He turned the back of his hand against her neck, then skimmed his fingers slowly down the length of her braid, over her collarbone and lightly—oh, too lightly—over her breasts, until he reached the yellow ribbon that bound her hair at the end. Deftly, he liberated the length of satin, then separated her long, loose tresses until he could sift them through his fingers. Claire started to whimper an objection, but Ramsey silenced her by deepening the kiss, and then she had no desire to object at all. Because as he bunched a fistful of her hair in one hand, he cupped the back of her head in his other and tilted his own head to the side, pushing her body closer to his. And then he thoroughly, unapologetically, thrust his tongue into her mouth.

Claire very nearly cried out at the explosion of wanting that erupted inside her then. Her hand fell from his jaw to his shirtfront, and she clutched the fabric roughly, as if doing so might somehow steady her outrageous desires. But her action only made her aware of the beating of his heart again, and how it thundered against her fingers now, completely out of control. His breathing had become as ragged as hers had, but she couldn't bring herself to tear her mouth from his, because what he was doing just felt so good, so perfect, so right. All she could do was clench tighter the fingers she had wound in his hair, as if she had every intention of holding him there forever. Because suddenly, she wanted very much to hold Ramsey forever.

Cupping her jaw more ardently in his hand, he spurred her mouth open wider and tasted her more deeply. Claire's head pitched backward under his assault, but Ramsey followed, roping one arm around her back to hold her steady. For long moments, they both vied for possession of the kiss, then, willingly, Claire yielded. He gentled the kiss then, a little, and gradually her heart rate steadied. But it began to hammer erratically again when he closed his hand loosely over the column of her throat, and began strumming his thumb and fingers along her sensitive flesh.

Something unfamiliar and irrepressible stirred deep inside her at the touch, something that was utterly in tune with Ramsey. Then he turned his hand backward again, so that his knuckles were grazing her skin, skimming lower and lower, over the divot at the base of her throat, along first one collarbone and then the other, then dipping lower still, to the scooped neckline of her dress, and turning once again. His fingertips ducked deftly beneath the fabric, but only just, dragging a long, slow line across her chest, from one side to the other and back again. Her pulse leapt higher at the caress, dizzying her. Then he withdrew his fingers and turned his hand once more, drawing the back of it down the front of her dress, gliding it between her breasts without touching either of them, then back up over the garment again in exactly the same way. Then he repeated the gesture again. And again. And again.

Never once did he touch her inappropriately, yet never in her life had Claire felt more aroused. "Ramsey," she whispered on a ragged rush of air. But she had no idea what she wanted to tell him. She'd just needed to say his name, to make sure he was really there, that this was really happening, that she really did feel the way she felt.

He seemed to know she required no answer, because in response, he only pulled his mouth from hers to drag soft, butterfly kisses along her throat and the part of her shoulder that lay bare. And then she felt his hand moving again, from the center of her chest toward her breast, his fingers slowly uncurling as he crept closer, his palm scooting toward the lower curve, his fingers curling closed again, cradling her sensitive flesh, until—

A shock of ugly yellow light exploded above them, and Ramsey and Claire both jerked away from each other, recoiling to the far sides of the swing as if they'd just been burned. But in a way, she had been. Because Ramsey had scorched her to her very essence. And it would be a long time before the embers began to cool.

She squinted in the direction of the sudden burst of light, then realized it was emanating from the yellow bug lamps that hung on each side of her front door. Another rectangle of white light spilled from the open doorway, and it was into that light that Chandler Edison stepped.

"Claire," he said tersely, his voice tinged with the same sort of disapproval one might hear from one's father, had one been in the eighth grade and just caught necking on the porch swing with the bad boy from the local high school.

"Chandler," she replied automatically, confused by his presence in her home when she wasn't, her voice sounding thick and startled, her brain feeling much the same way—as if she were in the eighth grade and had just been caught necking on the porch swing with the bad boy from the local high school.

Then Claire remembered that she had been necking on the

porch swing with the adult equivalent of the bad boy from the local high school. So, hastily, she moved her hands to her hair, doing her best to gather the wildly disarrayed tresses and twist them into a makeshift knot at her nape. But after what she had experienced with Ramsey, she doubted she would ever be able to pull herself together again.

"Wh-what are you doing here?" she asked Chandler, pushing thoughts of Ramsey to the side for now, because the last thing she wanted to do was share them with her attorney. Olive had eagerly consented to baby-sit Anabel while Claire was out with Ramsey, and she had obviously let Chandler in to wait for Claire. But that didn't explain why Chandler had come in the first place.

And Chandler didn't explain that either, at least not right away. In fact, he didn't answer her question at all. Instead, he only continued to glare at her, until Claire honestly did start to feel like that hormonally surging eighth-grader facing her angry father. Which was bizarre—not to mention disturbing—on a number of levels, not the least of which was that Chandler was by no means her father, and Claire had never experienced any situation in her life that she might hold up for comparison anyway.

"Chandler, what's wrong?" she asked further.

But much to her dismay, Chandler only shook his head in censure. And as he did, the explosive sensations Claire had just discovered with Ramsey fizzled into a spiral of smoke.

As Chandler stood framed by Claire's front door with one hand settled on the porch light switch and his other hand loosely fisted on his hip, he told himself he was *not* behaving like an overprotective father making sure his daughter wasn't up to no good with the bad boy from the local high school. No, he was behaving as a cautious investor keeping an eye on his financial interests. He'd devoted too much of his professional time to Simple Pleasures, Inc. over the years—and too much of his personal time cultivating Claire's trust—to let some worthless little nobody from nowhere like Ramsey Sage come in and cull the benefits for himself. Even if Ramsey Sage was actually a great hulking nobody from nowhere who topped Chandler by a good half foot. Chandler wasn't intimidated by the other man. Well, except for physically. Because he had every intention of making Claire his own someday. More to the point, he had every intention of making her millions his own someday. And he wasn't about to let Ramsey Sage interfere with that.

Oh, he liked Claire well enough, he supposed. In a cordial, tolerant sort of way. But her fortune, ah . . . now *that* made his libido rush, and wedding bells ring.

Which was why he found himself now on her front porch, wanting to scold her as if she were a child. To his perspective, she was a child in many ways. She had no idea of the value of her weekly allowance, and she often wasted it on things like ice cream and toys. Okay, so the ice cream— among other grocery items—went to the local food bank and the toys were for the children's hospital. Frivolous expenses were frivolous expenses as far as Chandler was concerned, even if they were charitable contributions. *Especially* if they were charitable contributions, because one received *nothing* in return for those, save a meager tax break that paled in comparison to what she might make if the money had been properly invested. And Claire was letting too much of her vast wealth go to unworthy causes. Bad enough she split everything fifty-fifty with Olive. *His* bank account would be a much better beneficiary.

"Claire?" he said mildly, pretending he hadn't seen her

throwing herself shamelessly at Ramsey Sage. "Is everything all right out here?"

It wasn't Claire who answered the question, however. It was that upstart Ramsey Sage.

"We're fine, Dad," he replied with an obvious edge to his voice. "Go back inside and enjoy the game. Tell Mom we'll be in soon."

Game? Chandler echoed to himself, puzzled. Mom? What on earth was he talking about? Oh, he got it now. Ramsey Sage was making a joke. Ha ha ha. He was such a clever boy. Certainly clever enough to make Claire think he had something to offer her. Which was all the more reason to get rid of him. And to make sure he had that dreadful little urchin with him when he went. Claire was becoming far too attached to the beastly little creature. There had been days when Chandler had been overcome by horrific visions of Claire succumbing to Ramsey and marrying the blackguard, then adopting little Anabel as her own child and rightful heir. He wished he could find some way to make them both disappear. The sooner Chandler had the guttersnipe and her uncle out from underfoot, the sooner he could go back to courting Claire's millions.

Looking back, Chandler wished now that he had kept on the investigator he had initially hired to find Ramsey Sage. Maybe the former could have dug further into the latter's background and found some cold, hard evidence to prove what Chandler suspected—that Ramsey Sage was a cold, hard criminal. Maybe it would be worth a few dollars more to call the investigator back in. Because the more Chandler thought about it, the more certain he became that Ramsey Sage possessed a past that was as checkered as a bad necktie. And he had to show Claire, once and for all, what a mistake it would be for her to have anything to do with the man beyond turning his niece over to him and telling him to go. Of course, learning that Ramsey Sage had an ugly past would only make Claire cling to the little brat more tightly, he thought. And that wouldn't do, either.

Such a dilemma.

"I think it's time you came in, Claire," Chandler said now. "It's getting late. And I have some papers for you to look over and sign."

"It's only eight-thirty," Ramsey pointed out. "That's hardly Claire's bedtime."

"I don't believe I was addressing you, Mr. Sage," Chandler said, still looking at Claire. "And knowing Claire as well as I do, which is infinitely better than you do, I know she can speak for herself. I also know that eighty-thirty is indeed her bedtime."

He found immeasurable satisfaction in turning toward Ramsey Sage in time to see his eyes go wide in disbelief and to see him turn to Claire for verification. What was even better was the blush of embarrassment darkening Claire's cheeks and the way she looked away from Ramsey and focused on Chandler instead.

That's my girl, he thought. *Remember whom it is you trust.*

"Well, only when the show's live," she said.

"And the show's on hiatus now," Ramsey reminded her.

"Still, I probably should go in," she said, standing. Making Chandler's smile grow even broader and more smug. "Especially if Chandler has some business that needs seeing to."

"I'll come with you," Ramsey offered.

She turned to him and shook her head. "No, that's okay.

I've already taken up your whole day. I'm sure you need to be getting ho . . . ah, back to your hotel."

That's right, Claire, Chandler silently reminded her. *Remember how rootless the man is. He has no home. No origins. Absolutely nothing to offer a woman like you.*

He could see that Ramsey Sage wanted to object, but Claire hastily told him, "Good night. Come to see Anabel whenever you want. I'm sure she missed you today."

And that was when Chandler realized he was worrying needlessly. Claire understood. She might have found Ramsey Sage attractive—God alone knew why—but she was smart enough to realize that the man was beneath her. Then again, Claire was beneath Chandler, and that hadn't stopped him from pursuing her, had it? But Claire had redeemed herself and risen above her poverty-stricken, state-sponsored origins by having the decency to become a cash cow. Ramsey, on the other hand, although Chandler supposed he could see where the man might be compared to a stallion—damn him—had nothing to offer a woman except for an enormous, full-throttled, inflamed . . . gallop, most likely alone into the sunset.

"Yes, do come in," Chandler told Claire, stepping onto the porch to allow her entry into the house, knowing he was assuming the role of host as he did. But that was because someday he would be the host—and master—of this house. And he would be the master of its owner. And its owner's millions. "I'm sure Mr. Sage can find his way to his car." The car he had no doubt stolen, Chandler added uncharitably to himself.

Claire turned away from Ramsey then and took a few steps toward Chandler. He was about to grin even more smugly than before when she spun around again to face

Ramsey and offered him a brief and rather pretty smile, something that made Chandler frown instead. Worse, it made Ramsey Sage smile, and if Chandler wasn't mistaken, there was more than an ounce of smugness in *his* expression. The parvenu.

"Claire?" Chandler said again. "Are you coming?"

But instead of replying to his question, she spoke to Ramsey, in an intimate sort of voice that Chandler found most disconcerting. "Thank you for today," she said. "For the meals and the walks and the chats and . . . Well. Thanks for everything, Ramsey."

Ramsey stood, too, and took a step forward, and, ignoring Chandler, cupped both of his hands gently over Claire's shoulders. Then, shamelessly, he leaned forward and covered her mouth with his again, a quick, chaste kiss that Chandler couldn't help noticing still left Claire panting for breath.

"You're welcome," he said as he dropped his hands back to his sides and took a step away from her. "I'll see you tomorrow."

So stunned was Claire, Chandler noted, that she only nodded in response. Then with another one of those longing looks that, honestly, anyone could see was manufactured, Ramsey Sage descended the porch steps and strode toward his car—or whoever's car it was—parked at the curb. When Claire turned to Chandler, she looked like someone who had just inhaled a bottle of fine champagne. She even stumbled when she took a step toward him and sighed with much poetic yearning as she strode past him into the house without even sparing him a glance.

Definitely, Chandler thought, he would recall his investigator in the morning, and he would charge the man with the task of uncovering every sordid, nasty little secret he could find about Ramsey Sage. Starting with where the man had been most recently and ending with what rotting pile of vegetation had spawned him to begin with.

Of course, proving Ramsey was a criminal sort would only convince Claire not to turn his atrocious niece over to his care, Chandler realized. But that was all right. He had plans for Anabel, too, should she threaten to become a permanent fixture in Claire's life.

Oh, yes. He knew exactly what to do with the child. Once and for all. And if everything worked out the way Chandler intended for it to, Anabel Sage would never be heard from again.

Ramsey sat in the driver's seat of his station wagon—*his* station wagon, dammit, the one he'd paid for with his own hard-earned money, by God—and watched Claire's house until the front door closed behind Edison, and the porch lights went out. Then he sat there some more. For the next half hour, in fact, Ramsey simply sat in his car, swatting the mosquitoes that were brave enough to get close to him in his foul mood, gazing at Claire's house, and feeling like a randy seventeen-year-old kid whose hormones were about to explode.

Jesus, what had happened tonight? he wondered. And *how* had it happened? He'd intended for this day to be one where she might learn to trust him and see him as a decent guy. Then he'd ended it by pawing all over her in the most indecent way possible and trying to consume her in one big, voracious bite. Of course, Claire had done some pawing of her own, hadn't she? And she hadn't exactly tried to stop him from pawing her, had she? She'd been as turned on by what was happening between them as Ramsey had been, had participated in that kiss as eagerly as he had. And had it not been for Edison's untimely appearance . . .

Damn Edison anyway.

Had it not been for the attorney's appearance, Ramsey would have ended his evening, he was confident, writhing naked and sweaty and gasping for breath in Claire's bed—with Claire, incidentally—saying and doing things to her he would probably regret in the morning, but feeling not one iota of contrition until then. Because that was just how well things had been going between the two of them, and just how explosive their reaction to each other had been.

Whatever it was burning up the air between him and Claire, it was potent and incendiary and relentless. Sooner or later, he knew, they were going to wind up in bed. Hers, his, it didn't matter. Hell, it might not even be a bed when the two of them finally got around to it, which, now that he thought about it, could be pretty damned interesting. Like maybe it would happen on that flowered loveseat in her sitting room. Or the pine table in her pioneer kitchen. Or that creaky porch swing. Or the back of the Volvo that he had *not* stolen. Or it could happen in *all* those places, what the hell.

Anyway, he was reasonably certain that wherever it happened, it would be sooner rather than later. What he didn't know was what would happen afterward.

He was in no way averse, however, to finding out.

Obviously Claire and her attorney weren't an item after all, romantically speaking. Although Edison had certainly acted outraged by what he had caught them doing, he hadn't reacted as a jealous lover would. He had acted—Ramsey fought off a major wiggins—like a possessive father. Which was really, really weird, because the guy couldn't be much older than Ramsey was; nor did he seem paternal in any way. Except maybe in the way of those animals who ate their offspring so that they wouldn't have to vie with those offspring for the attentions of their mother.

Oh, gross. Ramsey really wished he hadn't thought about that.

So he thought about Claire instead. And thinking about Claire made him want to see her again. Want to be with her again. To touch her again. Kiss her again. Unfortunately, there would be no more of that this evening, he knew, not with Chandler Edison barring the gate. Unless . . .

Pulling himself out of his ruminations, Ramsey discovered that the sun had finally dissolved into the horizon—damn these long summer days, anyway—and that the sky was now smudged inky blue. A slice of sterling moon and a generous spattering of stars provided the only light visible in the heavens. Maybe he couldn't touch or hold or kiss Claire again this evening, but if he played his cards right and let darkness be his cover, then maybe, just maybe, he could see her one last time.

He turned the key in the car's ignition and thrust the gearshift into drive, then steered the station wagon down the street and around the corner, parking it again in a dense shadow of oaks two blocks from her house. Then he exited the vehicle and retraced his steps on foot, until he located an alley overgrown with lush greenery that separated the backyards of the houses on both sides of Claire's block. Just as he ducked into it, he saw Edison's black Mercedes slither down the street, and he smiled. If the attorney was leaving this soon after telling Ramsey to vacate the premises, it was for sure he and Claire had nothing of a romantic nature going on. Well, nothing of a romantic nature that wasn't gross, anyway.

And now Claire would, for all intents and purposes—or, at the very least, for Ramsey's intents and purposes—be home alone. Sure, Anabel and Olive were there, too, but there wouldn't be anyone who could compromise Claire's time, or Claire, with more masculine pursuits. Not that there would be anything masculine about Edison's pursuit, of that Ramsey was certain. Because there was nothing much masculine about Edison himself. The bogus candyass jerk.

Even though it was full dark by the time Ramsey made his way through the alley, he found Claire's house with no problem, thanks to the abundantly growing flowers he recalled from earlier visits with Anabel in the garden, not to mention the white picket fence that enclosed said garden. A white picket fence, he noted now with mixed feelings, that had no gate at this end of the yard. No matter. In one fluid, effortless gesture, he cleared the fence and landed capably in the backyard. Then he deftly made his way through vines and stalks and timber, until he unearthed the treasure he sought.

Claire's bedroom window was open, and her light was on.

Better still, Claire was on the other side of that window.

Best of all, she was undressing.

Or, rather, dressing—dammit—because after that one heart-stopping moment, Ramsey noted that she was buttoning a garment she hadn't been wearing before instead of unbuttoning one she had been wearing. Evidently Edison had been telling the truth about that eight-thirty bedtime, because she had changed into a nightgown of some snowy fabric that flowed over her body, held in place by little more than two ribbons tied at each shoulder.

Ramsey's fingers twitched at his sides as he thought about how easy it would be to tug those ties free had he been in the room with her at that moment. Then he could have watched the supple fabric pool gracefully at her ankles, leaving her naked for his eyes only. And it was all he could do not to make a run for the rose trellis clinging to the side of the house, so that he could scale it and swing himself into her boudoir window, like an outlaw highwayman in a nineteenth-century novel, with the intention of ravishing her until dawn.

Instead, he moved backward, into the shadow of a wide waterfall of something heavy and sweet-smelling, and he watched.

Claire couldn't have been more than fifty feet away from him, so he could see much of her face, but little of her expression. Maybe it was just his imagination—or maybe it was just wishful thinking—but she seemed at that moment to be lost in thought. Ramsey wondered what she was thinking about, wondered if she was recalling what had happened on the porch swing earlier, and if she was, was it with the same clarity and agitation with which he kept recalling it himself. Was she thinking about the feel of his fingers tracing over her skin, the way he thought about her tentative touches on his? Was she relishing the taste of him the way he still savored the sensation of her mouth under his? And did she remember how close he had been to covering her breast with his hand and how that might just have incited both of them into a fury of wanting that neither would have been able to ignore?

Next time, he thought as he watched Claire move toward the window, they would be alone when they touched. Next time, there would be no one to turn on a light and dissuade them from doing what they both wanted to do. Next time, for sure, he and Claire would make love. Ramsey knew that. He *knew* it. And he knew that she knew it, too.

From his stealthy stance in the garden, he watched as

Claire stopped at her window between lacy curtains and gazed out into the night, up at the moon, and the stars, and the sooty black sky. And his heart hammered triple time as he drank in the sight of her, because he knew she was thinking about exactly what he was thinking about himself. About how it had felt so good to touch each other. To hold each other. To be together.

And he knew she was thinking about something else he was thinking about, too. That the next time they were together, there would be no stopping them.

Oh, yeah, he thought as he slunk further into the shadows and Claire tugged the curtains together over her window. The next time they were together, sparks were really going to fly.

Ten

*O*h, God, what had she been thinking?

As Olive gazed at herself in the mirror over her bedroom dresser, she berated herself yet again for ever agreeing to go out with Davis Webster. He was too intense, too brash, too bold, too flamboyant, too . . . *everything*. And even if he weren't any of those things, even if he were the most average, unremarkable man in the world, she still shouldn't be going out with him. He suspected things about her she simply could not have anyone suspecting. And he made her feel things she simply could not have herself feeling. And he made her feel way too fiercely. Why did she respond to him that way? she wondered. She'd met handsome, compelling men on occasion—at least twice—and she hadn't responded to them that way at all. With Davis, though . . .

She just hadn't been able to resist him. The minute he'd walked into Anabel's room that first day, Olive had known she was in trouble. Those blue eyes, those tousled curls, that full mouth . . . She'd done her best—honest, she had—to avoid seeing him since then, but he'd tricked her earlier this week by showing up unannounced. And he'd *meant* to trick her, too. Somehow, she knew that he had shown up unannounced precisely because he'd wanted to see Olive alone. Or, at least, alone with Anabel, which was as close as he was going to get. Until tonight, she meant. But when she'd been alone with him and Anabel in the garden, the longer Olive had stayed with him, the more aware of him she'd become. And the more aware of him she'd become, the more dangerous he had been to her.

The way he'd watched her, she recalled now, her entire body humming with heat at the memory. She had been able to *feel* him watching her, almost as if he had reached out a hand to drag the backs of his bent knuckles down her spine. And then, when he had actually touched her, when he'd circled his fingers around her wrist as she'd tried to flee up the porch steps, she'd felt as if someone had jabbed her in the chest with a live wire. By the time he'd asked her if she would go out with him, Olive had been too frazzled to react the way she had known she should. When his sexy mouth had formed the words *Will you go out with me?*, even though her brain had been screaming *No, no, no, no, no!*, her heart had cried out, even louder, *You bet I will!*

So now here she was, trying to look nice for Davis Webster instead of invisible to the human race. But she'd had to go shopping for that, since she had absolutely nothing in her wardrobe that was suitable for a date. Not that she had a clue how to dress for a date, since she'd never been on one in her life. And not that she even knew what this date would be, since Davis had only said he'd be by to pick her up at seven and had made no mention of where they would be going.

Regardless of the occasion, however, Olive had nothing to

wear, since she'd spent her life cultivating a wardrobe that would make her look drab and insignificant. Tonight, though, for the first time in her life, she wanted to look significant. She wanted to *be* significant. And she wanted to be pretty, too. She wanted to be noticed, at least by Davis. So even though it meant she would have to battle fear and paranoia for the entirety of the evening, she had chosen a dress with color. Because pale lavender *was* a color. Kind of.

Okay, so maybe Olive wasn't ready to be as flamboyant as Davis Webster was. She could look pretty. She could. She just hoped no one besides Davis noticed her when she did.

She eyed herself again in the mirror, in her new dress. Despite the color, it was still a fairly plain garment, sleeveless and scoop-necked and unadorned. But its color was lovely, and its hourglass cut flattered Olive's curvaceous figure. Funny, but she'd never noticed how curvy she was, thanks to the baggy clothes she generally preferred to wear. An uncharacteristic sense of feminine pride washed over her at the realization. So much so that she impulsively swept a band of pearly eye shadow over her lids and brushed on a little mascara, more newly purchased items she'd never owned before. Then, in a fit of profligacy, she left her glasses on the dresser. She didn't really need them all the time. She was only slightly nearsighted. But she wore them all the time because they made her less attractive, and therefore less noticeable. Would Davis think she looked pretty? she wondered. Or would he even notice a difference?

And how had he known she was in the program?

The question roared up out of nowhere, as it had so many times over the past several days, and it hit Olive like a ton of beige, nondescript clothing. No one—*no one*—knew about that, not even Claire. Olive was excellent at keeping secrets, having lived her life clinging to them. There was no way Davis Webster could have known she and her parents had entered the Witness Security Program when she was five years old. No way. He had been bluffing. He must have been. He had been speaking from suspicion, not knowledge, because he couldn't possibly have found any evidence to support what he assumed. She only hoped she had effectively masked her alarm and astonishment when she had responded to his assertions with her own bluffing. And she hoped that, from here on out, he would just let sleeping dogs lie. Because if he didn't, those dogs would turn rabid. And then they'd turn on Olive, and any small chance at happiness she might find.

Probably, these days, she was safe enough from harm. Her parents were both gone, and so were the people who'd wanted them all dead. Her father had fallen off the face of the earth two decades ago, and the path her mother had chosen for the two of them after his disappearance was convoluted and chaotic and cold. Even if there were still a few people up in New Jersey with long memories, they would probably never associate Olive Tully of Nashville with Cynthia and Raymond Tolliver of Newark. But *probably* wasn't enough to make Olive risk everything. It wasn't enough to make her risk anything.

She closed her eyes when the image in the mirror began to waver, counted slowly to ten, then blinked back the tears that hadn't quite been stifled. She wouldn't think about any of that, she told herself. And in not thinking about it, she could pretend it never happened. And if she pretended long enough, and hard enough, then maybe, just maybe, eventually the memories would go away. Just because they were still so fresh, and so painful, after all these years, that didn't mean anything.

A quick glance at the clock told Olive she had precisely fourteen minutes left to finish getting ready if Davis arrived at seven o'clock on the dot, as he had promised he would. And she wondered if he *would* arrive at seven o'clock on the dot, as he had promised he would.

For most of her life—before she'd met Claire, anyway— Olive had heard hundreds of promises made that had been broken one after the other. Every time she and her mother had settled somewhere, her mother had promised it would be the last time they moved. She'd promised Olive wouldn't have to change schools again, and yes, she could join Brownies this time—or the art club, or the swim team, or enroll in ceramics classes, or whatever else took her fancy. Her mother had always *promised* Olive could do those things. Then, invariably, she'd come home from work early one day—or home from the grocery store, or home from the park, or home from the fast-food place where she'd bought dinner—and she'd tell Olive they had to pack. That they had to leave immediately. That she'd seen someone—or heard someone, or something else had happened—that made her think they were in danger again. And just like that, Olive would be uprooted and dragged across the state—or the country—to someplace new, where the cycle would begin again.

No Brownies. No art club. No swim team. No ceramics classes. Nothing that ever took her fancy. Promises made. Promises broken. They'd always been the same thing to Olive.

She wondered again if Davis Webster would show up at seven o'clock on the dot, as he had promised. And if he did, she wondered if that would make her fall in love him even faster than she already was.

Dammit, she thought when she realized the avenue her

brain had wandered down. Again with the memories. And what was with the falling in love with Davis Webster stuff? she asked herself. She barely knew the man. She had no idea what he was really like. She couldn't possibly be falling in love with him yet. She couldn't possibly fall in love with him at all. It was a date, nothing more. After tonight, she'd probably never see him again, if for no other reason than he would doubtless find her insignificant and in no way pretty. She wasn't falling in love with him. She couldn't be.

But she did wonder if he would keep his promise.

Davis sat across the table from Olive Tully in what was supposed to be a nonthreatening, non-idea-giving environment, since it was a restaurant he knew well and where he ate dinner a couple of times a week. But tonight, with Olive, he felt utterly threatened. And tonight, with Olive, he was entertaining all sorts of ideas. So much for giving himself the upper hand.

Because she looked amazing.

He'd had no idea.

With just an added hint of color in the form of what should have been a very plain dress but somehow wasn't plain at all on her, Olive Tully had blossomed into quite the flower. Where before Davis had thought her glasses complimented her eyes, making them appear larger than they actually were, he saw now that he had been mistaken. Because now that she had removed her spectacles, he saw that her eyes actually were very large, not to mention beautiful, even without them. And where before he had considered their color to be similar to that of his favorite brand of Bourbon, he now saw that they were an even richer shade of amber. And they were infinitely more intoxicating, too.

The restaurant he had chosen for dinner was a casual one, known mostly for its surprisingly sophisticated wine list. Not that Davis drank much wine—a good shot of Bourbon, after all, worked so much more quickly. But the food was good, and the place was only three blocks from his apartment. Oh, and it was near plenty of clubs, too, should he and Olive want to hear a good local band—of which there were many in Nashville—afterward. Instead of going to his apartment only three blocks away, he meant, of course.

Of course.

And since it was an establishment Davis frequented, he had been certain he would feel comfortable for this, their first date. Somehow, though, the place didn't feel comfortable tonight. No, tonight, with Olive sitting on the other side of the table, it felt totally new and unfamiliar. It even felt . . . special. Yet he'd chosen it specifically because he hadn't wanted this to feel like a special occasion. Because he hadn't wanted Olive to feel like a special person. He'd assured himself and reassured himself over the course of the last few days that he must be romanticizing her, idealizing her, that she couldn't possibly be as fresh or as fascinating or as fine as he'd found her to be.

He was such an idiot.

And he should have realized just how big an idiot when he'd found himself dressing for the evening in clothing that was entirely socially acceptable—or, at least, more socially acceptable than what he was accustomed to wearing: khakis that weren't battered and faded, and a pale blue bowling shirt that didn't boast any obnoxious logos or annoying nicknames. He'd dressed in a way that wouldn't embarrass Olive. Because he'd known she cared about that sort of thing. He had dressed not to please himself, but to please her. And he could have been doing that only because he cared about her.

And he really didn't want to care about her.

So then why did you ask her out, Einstein? he demanded of himself. And it bothered him a lot to realize he didn't have an answer to the question. It bothered him even more to realize he might indeed have an answer, but just didn't want to tell himself what it was.

"So . . . do you come here often?" Olive asked now, glancing around at their surroundings and seeming even more uncomfortable amid them than Davis was. She sat with her arms crossed over her chest, her hands cupped over her opposite upper arms, as if she were cold. But Davis found the restaurant almost uncomfortably warm and crowded.

He let his own gaze wander in the wake of hers, absorbing the restaurant's decor, seeing it, in many ways, for the very first time. He usually didn't pay much attention to his surroundings, unless he was working—and then he paid too much attention to them. Bare brick walls festooned with framed posters of fabulous forties films rose up to a fifteen-foot-high ceiling overhead. From it, wrought-iron chandeliers dangled low, loaded with glass-enclosed candles that provided mellow, but generous enough, illumination. Candles in small hurricanes on the tables added more light, and not a little ambiance, enhanced by a sweet aroma that drifted from fresh pink flowers in a cobalt blue vase. Soft, sexy saxophone music added to the atmosphere, making Davis notice then that the place was a lot more romantic than he'd realized. Funny, but it had never seemed especially romantic when he was here alone.

"I do come here often, actually," he told Olive, trying not to sound as if he was just now noticing the place.

"It's nice," she said. "Comfortable." But her actions belied her words, because she skimmed her hands up and down her arms again as if an arctic wind had just swept in from the north, and she spoke the words not to Davis, but over her shoulder, as if she were trying to keep an eye on the door.

Well, it always had been comfortable enough before, Davis agreed. Now, though . . . "Yeah, it's all right, I guess," he said with profound understatement. Because it was all right with Olive there. More than all right. Too right. Even if she didn't seem as if she really wanted to be there. "Look," he added, "if you don't feel comfortable here, we can—"

Jerking her head around to meet Davis's gaze with what he could only liken to alarm, she snapped, "Didn't I just say I was comfortable?"

He blinked at the vehemence in her voice. "Yeah, but you sure as hell don't act it," he retorted before he could stop himself. Immediately, he softened his voice and apologized. "I'm sorry. I just meant that if you'd rather go somewhere else, we could—"

"I'm fine," she said crisply. Then, she, too, seemed to realize she had overreacted. Dipping her head forward, she sighed, then gentled her tone. "I'm sorry, too. I'm just not used to being out in a crowd."

And why is that? he wondered.

Davis came very close to asking the question aloud, but their server arrived to take their orders, prohibiting him from venturing into the personal just yet. He started to order his usual, a shot of Bourbon with a Bourbon chaser to take the edge off the day—among other things—then realized that just sitting at a table with Olive Tully had already done that. So he arched an eyebrow at her in silent question, to indicate she should order first, and figured he'd just follow her lead.

But she ordered iced tea, sweet please, and he couldn't help feeling just a tad disappointed about where she planned on leading him. Then, strangely, he discovered he didn't care where she led him. As long as she held his hand when they went.

"I'll have the same," he told the server. And he wondered if maybe, later, he might have Olive, too.

Oh, hell. He was presuming things he had no right to presume. Again. Especially since the beverage of choice tonight was going to be—dammit—sweet tea. Then again, tea had caffeine in it, right? And caffeine was a stimulant, right? And stimulants were stimulating, right? And another word for stimulating was arousing, right? So maybe the path Olive had chosen for the rest of the evening wouldn't be such a bad one after all. Provided, of course, Davis could continue with his convoluted reasoning for the rest of the evening.

Then he glanced over at Olive again, noticed again just how beautiful she looked, and figured it was going to be a long time before he felt anything *but* convoluted. Gee, maybe he should have ordered that shot of Bourbon with a Bourbon chaser after all.

Their server left, and Davis realized he had no idea what to say next. Which wasn't like him at all. Normally, he experienced no shortage of words whatsoever. Normally, he knew exactly what to say in any given situation. Of course, most of the situations he found himself in were pretty awful ones, and most of what he said at such times was sarcastic at best and barbaric at worst. Nevertheless, he shouldn't be suffering from a heinous condition like reticence. Especially in the presence of a beautiful, desirable woman. Then, suddenly, he no longer felt reticent. Suddenly, he realized he knew exactly what to say next—or, at least, what he wanted to say next. But it turned out to be "Hey, Olive, how about we split this joint and go to my place instead?" and somehow, he just didn't think that would go over too well with Olive.

Until he heard her say, "Look, Davis, would you mind if we left and went somewhere else instead? You said you don't live too far from here. Maybe we could go to your place?"

Wherein a chorus of angels erupted in song, the sun shone down in a golden covenant, and the heavens wept with joy.

"Um. Yeah. Okay," he said, hoping none of the quaking turmoil that squalled through him at her response was evident in his comment. "We could do that. Sure."

She rubbed her arms anxiously again, looking even more panicked than she had before. "I just . . . I feel so . . . so *exposed* here," she added timorously.

Which meant she'd probably object to him exposing her even more at his place, Davis concluded morosely. Then he shook off the rampant—and altogether inappropriate—thought. "That's all right," he reassured her. "We don't have to stay."

"I thought I could do this," she continued, sounding as if she were battling something akin to hysteria. "I thought I could go out with you, in a public place, and be okay with it. But I can't. I'm just . . . I'm not okay. I get a little uneasy in crowds. I'm sorry. Can we go?"

Their server hadn't yet returned with their tea, so Davis stood and tugged his wallet from his back pocket, opened it to discover that he didn't have any small bills, then tossed down what amounted to the cost of the beverages and a five hundred percent tip. At the moment, he really wasn't all that

interested in change. Not unless it was Olive changing into
something more comfortable, or something like that.

But then he glanced at her and saw that she was standing,
too, and that she didn't look comfortable about anything. He
started to extend his hand toward the door to indicate he
would follow her out, but she started heading that way before he even completed the gesture, so he followed as
quickly as he could. She threaded her way gracefully
enough through the crowded clutter of tables, but faltered
when she hit a wall of people waiting outside the restaurant.
Davis came up behind her just as she was completing a few
steps in retreat, and when she backed into him, the collision
was nothing short of momentous. Because the second her
back came into contact with his front, even though the impact wasn't what you'd call staggering, Davis saw stars. And
then he saw hearts. And then he saw annoying little cupids in
diapers that couldn't possibly be a sign of anything good.

Thanks to those damned, distracting cupids, when Olive
pitched against him, Davis automatically lifted his hands to
steady her, and inescapably landed them on her bare upper
arms. And even as he noted the way her skin warmed beneath his fingers, and how that warmth traveled up his arms
and into his chest to pool around his heart, he braced himself
for her recoil, which he knew would be forthcoming. But
this time, when he touched her, Olive didn't recoil. Instead,
she folded herself into him, curling her arms between their
bodies and tucking her head into his chest, as if she were a
terrified child.

Davis had often dealt with terrified children. There was no
shortage of them in his line of work, unfortunately. But none
of them had ever roused the wave of protectiveness that

surged through him in that moment. Without even thinking about what he was doing, he wrapped an arm around Olive's shoulder and gently urged her forward, steering her through the writhing wall of people and out into the warm night. Even when they were clear of the crowd, though, he continued to hold her, guiding her down the street until the parade of pedestrians thinned to a mere trickle. But when he tried to disengage himself from her, thinking she would balk if he didn't, Olive continued to cling to him, looping both arms around his waist, pressing her face to his chest, cobbling her stride to his.

"Don't let go," she murmured against him, so quietly he almost didn't hear her. "Please, Davis, don't let go of me."

Well, hell. He could certainly accommodate that request. Command. Plea. Whatever. Looping one arm across her shoulders again and folding the other across her middle, he pulled her as close to himself as he dared, trying not to notice how she fit so perfectly against him, trying even harder not to notice how he fit so perfectly against her, too. Instead, he slowed his pace and told himself it was so they could walk as easily as possible together. But he knew it was really because he just wanted to hold her this way for as long as he could.

They continued walking, their silence evidently agreed upon mutually. What was also silently but mutually agreed upon—at least, Davis was pretty sure they'd both agreed to it before leaving the restaurant—was the direction in which they headed. Even though Olive didn't know which way it was to his apartment, she didn't dissuade him from going whatever way he chose. Nor did she inquire about their destination. So when they arrived at an old brownstone, and Davis guided her up the stairs, she didn't utter a word of objection. Nor did she protest when they entered the building, and he led her up three flights of stairs. Nor did she say a word when he reluctantly released her to unlock a door on the third floor and push it open, tilting his head toward the interior in tacit invitation.

What was really weird was that Davis didn't say anything during all those circumstances, either, even though there were a million words swirling around in his head that wanted to be said.

He waited for a cue—pick a cue, any cue—from Olive, then finally got one when she entered his apartment ahead of him. Still, Davis wasn't quite sure what to make of the cue, so he didn't press his luck. He just closed the door behind himself and, recalling that Olive didn't like to have the exits blocked, he left the door unlocked and crossed to the other side of the room to switch on a lamp.

But no sooner had the light splashed across the floor than he wished he hadn't turned it on at all. Not because darkness would have been more conducive to a seduction attempt— and in spite of everything, thoughts of making love to Olive tonight still lingered in his brain—but because the decor of his apartment left a lot to be desired. In fact, mostly what it desired was a decor.

Since Davis spent so little time at home, he'd never really bothered to make his apartment feel homey. There were no personal touches to speak of, no family photos, no plants, no rugs, no pictures on the plain white walls. There were lots of books, to be sure, but they were crammed haphazardly into mismatched cases and/or stacked unevenly and without organization on the hardwood floor. The furniture—what little there was of it—was serviceable and ordinary, mostly cast-off pieces from family members and friends who had moved to new digs and wanted to upgrade. Davis never cared much about upgrading. So he didn't mind taking the downgrades that came his way.

At least, he hadn't until now. Because Olive Tully was an upgrade in every sense of the word, and he didn't want her to look around at the way he lived and think he was beneath her. Even if that was exactly where he wanted to be, at least in the literal, sexual, sense. It wasn't where he wanted to be in the figurative, nonsexual sense. Unfortunately, he knew that was where he was all the same.

"Sorry, maid's day off," he quipped when he saw her absorbing the ascetic surroundings.

"Mm," Olive said as she returned her attention to him. "Looks like she took everything to the cleaner's yesterday."

He smiled, but there was nothing happy in the gesture. "Yeah, well, I'm not much one for material possessions," he said, wondering how that would go over. Although Olive's house was small, he had seen when he picked her up earlier, it was as abundantly and luxuriously decorated as Claire Willoughby's had been. Olive obviously enjoyed an environment—enjoyed a life—that was overflowing with grace and style and beauty. And she wasn't going to find any of those things here. Not in Davis's environment, and certainly not in his life.

He didn't stand a chance.

"So I see," she said softly. And she sounded a little sad when she added, "But there's a lot to be said for keeping things simple. Not collecting any moss. That sort of thing."

"You sound like maybe you're talking from experience," he said.

She arched her brows philosophically and hooked her fingers together behind her back. "Maybe I am."

"Didn't have a lot of stuff growing up, huh?"

"Not really," she said. "We moved around so much, we couldn't afford to saddle ourselves with a lot of stuff we'd have to move."

"And why was that?" Davis asked. "The moving around a lot, I mean? I can totally understand not wanting to saddle yourselves with a lot of stuff."

"Now you sound like you're talking from experience."

"Maybe I am," he replied readily.

She didn't respond right away, only met his gaze unflinchingly and appeared to be thinking very, very hard about something. After a moment, though, she did reply, but it was only to change the subject.

"Anabel had a very good day today," she said.

Davis tried not to sound too disappointed by her diversionary tactic when he replied blandly, "Did she now?"

Not that he was disappointed about Anabel's having a good day. On the contrary, he was glad the little girl seemed to be adapting so well to her new situation. Hers was one of the few cases he'd ever been assigned that looked as if it would actually have a genuinely happy ending. But he was disappointed that Olive was so unwilling to talk about herself. That was why people went out on dates, wasn't it? To learn more about each other? And to steam up the sheets, too, of course, but there would be time enough for that after the learning about each other stuff. Provided the learning about each other stuff didn't last for more than, say, half an hour. With Olive, though, it looked as if the learning about each other phase was going to take half a century instead. By the time they got to the sheet-steaming phase, Davis was going to need Viagra.

He sighed with something akin to frustration and resigned

himself to a long night. A long night of no sheet-steaming. And a long night of not learning more about Olive.

Until she said, "It's really been kind of funny, because Anabel reminds me of myself in a lot of ways."

And then Davis thought maybe there would be a very good chance to learn more about Olive Tully indeed. Better still, maybe he could do it without her even realizing she was revealing anything about herself.

"Like what ways?" he asked.

They were both still standing, he noticed then, and on opposite sides of the room at that. Olive, not surprisingly, remained poised for flight near the front door, and Davis was standing in front of a bricked-up fireplace that hadn't been used, probably, for a century. The building was old, and not in the best of shape, but it was safe enough, and close to his work, and within walking distance of just about anything he could want. Except Olive Tully, but he hadn't known about her when he signed the lease, had he? His apartment, he realized now, was much like him. Functional. Basic. No frills. Just enough to get by. He wondered if Olive realized that, too.

She seemed not to, he thought as he observed her. Because she was looking at him as if she found him . . . interesting. As if she were sizing him up for . . . something. As if she were trying to decide if he was worthy of . . . some important job. He just couldn't tell what.

"Anabel is curious about everything she comes into contact with," she said.

"That's not unusual," Davis told her. "Most children that age are extremely curious." And whether or not they stayed that way, he thought further, depended on how that curiosity was met.

"She also destroys everything she comes into contact with," Olive said.

Davis couldn't help smiling. Mostly because he'd seen for himself how the little girl could pretty much annihilate everything that entered her path. What he'd also seen, though, was how Claire and Olive faced that annihilation with staunch acceptance. Well, okay, maybe Claire was a little less staunch, bursting into tears as she was wont to do in the face of that annihilation, but all in all, both women knew Anabel's destruction wasn't malicious, and they'd carried on valiantly, rebuilding the wreckage without tearing down the girl responsible for it.

"But she doesn't destroy things out of anger," Davis said.

"No, that's true," Olive agreed.

But her voice trailed off as she spoke, as if she were thinking about something—or perhaps some*one* else. Like maybe herself as a child. She'd said Anabel reminded her of herself. Then she'd pointed out that Anabel was destructive. So could Davis conclude that Olive had been destructive when she was a child, too? And had she been destructive because she was angry? And what had she been angry about? Had her own curiosity been met with something other than encouragement? And just what kind of questions had she felt the need to ask as a child?

"How else does Anabel remind you of you?" he said. "Aside from her being curious and destructive, I mean?" he added, smiling because he wanted Olive to think he was taking this conversation lightly, when in fact nothing could be further from the truth.

"She doesn't talk a lot," Olive said. "I mean, I know she's too young to have a very large vocabulary, but she doesn't babble much, either."

"Maybe she doesn't feel the need to communicate verbally," Davis offered. "Maybe she doesn't have to ask questions because you and Claire are doing such a good job of making her understand things."

"Or maybe she doesn't ask questions because she's afraid of what she'll find out," Olive said.

That was a revealing statement, Davis thought. "And what would Anabel find out, if she asked more questions?"

He was afraid he'd pushed too hard, because Olive didn't answer right away. He was beginning to think she wouldn't answer at all when she responded in a way he hadn't anticipated.

She took a step forward, toward Davis. And then she took another. And another. And another. But she halted in front of the sofa and primly sat down. And she perched on the very edge of the cushion, he noted, still poised for flight, should it become necessary. He decided to stay where he was for the moment. Because he didn't want to do anything that might make her feel threatened. He didn't want her to flee.

"She would find out," Olive said softly, "that the world isn't what she thought it would be. What she hoped it would be."

He was surprised to find that his heart was hammering hard in his chest as he said, even more softly than she had, "And what do you think she hopes the world will be?"

Olive swallowed with some difficulty, her eyes never leaving his. "Safe," she said quietly. "She wants the world to be safe."

Davis wished he could tell her the world *was* safe. But he knew better. So he didn't even try to lie. "Maybe if you promise her you'll do everything you can to keep her safe, she'll feel better," he said.

Very slowly, Olive shook her head. "Promises aren't good enough," she told him.

"Why not?" he asked.

She glanced down at the hands she had twisted together in her lap as she spoke. "Because . . . because promises always get broken."

Another revealing statement, Davis thought. "Always?"

She nodded. "Always." But then she glanced up again, and her lips parted fractionally, as if she were surprised by something that occurred to her. "Except for—" she began. But she cut herself off without finishing the statement.

"Except for what?" he asked.

Her gaze flew to his and held there. "Except for . . . to-night."

He narrowed his eyes in confusion. "Tonight?"

She nodded. "You promised me you'd pick me up at seven o'clock on the dot," she said. "And you did. You arrived exactly at seven. Just like you promised you would."

He lifted a shoulder and let it drop, not seeing the significance at all. "What can I say? I'm a punctual guy."

"You're more than that," she told him. "Way more."

And something about the way she said it made Davis go all warm and gooey and sticky-sweet inside. "What am I?" he asked her.

But she only smiled, just a little, and shook her head in silence. Somehow, though, Davis didn't need a spoken answer to the question. Just the way she was looking at him told him a lot.

"I don't have any iced tea," he told her, "but I can put on a pot of coffee if you want."

"I'd like that," she said.

"And we could order a pizza or something."

"That would be nice."

And it would be, too, Davis realized. Even if all they did was stay on opposite sides of the room, drinking coffee and eating pizza, even if they didn't go near any sheets, steamy or otherwise, just being with Olive would be nice. And *nice* would be enough with Olive.

Weird. It had been a long time since Davis had felt like that. When all he'd wanted from a woman was to spend a little time with her. Talking. He wasn't big on relationships. He wasn't the kind of man to attach himself to a woman for very long. Oh, he liked women well enough. He'd just found it difficult to care deeply for them. Usually, his feelings never did more than scratch the surface—both his own and the woman's involved. The liaisons he'd enjoyed with women—though maybe *enjoyed* wasn't the best word to use, really—had been almost entirely physical. Agreeable, certainly. But never quite satisfying. And never meaningful, either.

With Olive, though, he was surprised to find that he actually wanted something more than the physical. He wanted more than the surface. He wanted depth. He wanted emotion. He wanted . . . Well. He wanted what he probably shouldn't be wanting, what he almost certainly didn't deserve. Because when he got something like that, he didn't take care of it. Not the way it needed to be cared for.

He still wanted it with Olive, though. He just wished he knew what to do with it, should he by some wild miracle get it.

It was nearly three o'clock in the morning when Olive arrived home and turned in the passenger seat of Davis's car to tell him good night. But before she could even open her mouth, he smiled tenderly, and said quietly, "I'll walk you to your door," and a delicious sort of heat purled through her unlike anything she had ever felt.

No one had ever walked Olive to her door before. There had been no dating when she was a teenager, not just because she'd never stayed in one place long enough to form a relationship with a boy, but because growing up in the shadow of her mother's suspicion and worry and anxiety, Olive had learned to trust no one and fear everyone.

She had trusted no one when she was a child. She had trusted no one when she was an adolescent. She had trusted no one when she was a young woman headed off to college. Even now, when she knew better, when she understood why her mother had felt the way she had, Olive simply couldn't trust anyone. Even with Claire, it had taken living with her for a year before Olive had become comfortable enough even to start sharing bits of herself with her friend.

But now, she found herself trusting Davis Webster. And she couldn't quite quell the thrill of excitement that hastened through her when she realized that, for the first time in her life, a boy was walking her to her door. It was another miraculous first to celebrate. Because tonight, with Davis, had been full of them.

She smiled as she watched him circle the front of his car and come to her side to open the door for her. She couldn't remember the last time she'd even been awake at three o'clock in the morning, let alone out doing something. Out doing something with a man, no less. And not feeling a bit uncomfortable while doing it. In fact, she didn't think she could remember an evening she'd enjoyed more. Not that that was saying much, really, since before tonight, her evenings had consisted mostly of books, A&E mysteries, and chamomile tea.

Nevertheless, she had enjoyed herself. Maybe more than she should have. Unless Davis had enjoyed himself, too. In which case . . .

Well, she wouldn't even allow herself to think that far ahead. Right now, she only wanted to enjoy the present. Or better still, the immediate past. Because at present, she was coming to the end of her date with Davis. And she didn't want to think about that yet, either. So she took a moment to dwell on the evening behind her instead.

Usually, men scared Olive. A lot. Usually, she didn't know how to act around them, didn't know what to say. And although the evening had started off awkwardly enough, with her feeling scared and uncertain and tense, now she felt anything but. Davis didn't scare her at all anymore. On the contrary, she'd never felt safer in her life than she had this evening. Ever since he'd come to her aid in the restaurant, ever since he'd wrapped his arms so protectively around her to shield her from the crowd she had feared would swallow her, ever since he'd guided her so carefully to his home. And then later, at his apartment, when he'd stayed on one side of the room and hadn't pressed her for anything more than conversation. He'd just made her feel . . . safe. Protected. Secure. And although she had craved safety and protection and security all her life, she'd never felt any of those things before.

They'd spent the entire evening talking. Talking about nothing. Talking about everything. They'd talked about An-abel, but it had felt like they were talking about Olive. And still she hadn't felt threatened by him in any way. She'd told herself over the course of the evening at his apartment that she'd only felt safe there because she'd had a straight, un-hampered path to his front door, should she feel the need to escape. But she hadn't wanted to escape. Even when it was way past time for her to go home, she hadn't wanted to leave. She'd been surprised to discover that she wanted to stay all night at Davis's apartment. But she'd been afraid if she told him that, he would have taken it the wrong way. He would have thought she meant that she wanted to make love with him, not simply be in the same room where he was, be-cause he made her feel good inside.

But being in the same room with him had been almost as exhilarating as making love with him. Or, at least, she thought it was. Having never made love with anyone, Olive couldn't be sure just how exhilarating that was. But it couldn't possibly be that much nicer than just being with Davis, talking. She couldn't imagine anything more thrilling than that.

"Thank you," she told him now, as they paused at the front door, and she turned around to say good night to him. "Thank you for a really wonderful evening."

He smiled again, that tender smile she had seen so fre-quently this evening, the one that made her feel as if she were melting inside. "But we didn't do anything except talk," he pointed out.

"And it was wonderful," she told him earnestly. More wonderful than anything she had ever done before.

"You're a cheap date, Olive Tully," he said with a grin.

She shook her head, but she was grinning, too. "No, to-night cost a lot, trust me. More than you know. But it was worth every penny."

She could see that he was puzzled by her remark, but she wasn't about to explain when she wasn't entirely sure she understood herself. He had shoved his hands into his pockets as they'd strode up the front walk, but now he removed one and, after only a small hesitation, he lifted it to her face. She was surprised when she didn't flinch at the mere prospect of being touched by him. She was even more surprised to discover she wanted him to touch her. Hoped that he would. But even though he went so far as to curl his fingers and position his hand to frame her face, he halted before he actually touched her. Then he dropped his hand back to his side and took a step back.

Surprised at how disappointed she was by his withdrawal, and without really thinking about what she was doing, Olive followed his retreat, closing the distance between them with a small, nervous step of her own. Then she lifted her hand to his face, hesitating not at all before cupping her hand tentatively over his jaw. His skin was warm and rough against her palm, and she smiled at how different his physique was from hers. Bigger, rougher, harder. She should have been frightened by all of that, she told herself. Instead, it only reinforced how very good he would be at the whole protectiveness thing.

"Good night, Davis," she said. Then she pushed herself on tiptoe and pressed her lips to the cheek she wasn't framing in her hand.

But he turned his head a split second before she made contact, though she couldn't tell if his action was intentional or intuitive. In any event, her lips landed on his mouth instead of his cheek, and an electric shudder of need fired through her on impact.

Alarmed by the intensity of her response to such a small gesture, Olive immediately jerked her head back, amazed to find herself gasping for breath and her heart pounding behind her ribs. For one strange, interminable moment, she and Davis only stared at each other, her hand still curled over his jaw, their faces separated by no more than a scant inch of feverish heat. A frenetic energy arced between them, fusing them in way that was primal, immutable, and fierce. And then slowly, so slowly, Davis lowered his head to hers.

Olive told herself to pull away, to whisper *Good night* and escape into the house as quickly as she could. It was what she would have done before. But now, instead, she stood firmly in place and waited to see what would happen next. And what happened next was . . .

Oh. So exquisite. So excellent. So extraordinary. It was perfect in every way. Davis kissed her as sweetly as a promise, as tenderly as a pledge. There was little more to it than the warm, soft caress of his mouth against hers, but it swamped her with an eager longing for something she couldn't even identify. Then he pulled back, and he smiled the sort of smile Olive wished she could see every single day for the rest of her life.

"Good night," he told her quietly. He cupped his hand over the one she still pressed to his face, pulled it away, and pressed one final kiss into the center of her palm. "I'll call you," he added as he gently let her fingers go.

"You'd better," she told him, her voice sounding shaky and uncertain, even to her own ears.

"I will," he told her. "I promise."

Olive smiled again. That was good enough for her.

Eleven

On Sunday, as Claire pulled her car to a stop in the parking lot of the marina where she had enjoyed dinner with Ramsey only a week earlier, she did her best to quell the tumble of nerves that were cartwheeling through her midsection. Telling herself she was *not* putting off the inevitable, but just wanted to enjoy the lovely view for a moment, she gazed through the open driver's side window at the forest of sailboat masts, trying to focus on the leisurely *ping . . . ping . . . ping-ping . . . ping* of sail lines as they clinked against their aluminum columns in the wake of the afternoon breeze. Beyond the grove of masts, she could just make out the thick green ripples of the Cumberland River as it wandered on its way, and beyond the river, the rolling green hills that rose and fell into the distance. The sun hung high and bright and yellow in a faultless azure sky, and really, it was the kind of day that would normally have made Claire feel as if nothing in the world could go wrong.

Today, though, everything felt wrong. Because today, like

every other day since she had last seen Ramsey, she couldn't stop thinking about him, or about the way he had kissed her the last time they were together. Involuntarily, her fingers convulsed on the steering wheel, and she bent forward, pressing her forehead to the backs of her hands. In spite of the eighty-plus-degree temperature, her flesh felt cold. She was cold in places she hadn't known could even feel that way.

She still couldn't understand what had happened that night on the porch swing, as often as she had replayed the episode in her mind. And she had replayed the episode in her mind *a lot* over the past week. So often, in fact, that she had been forced to avoid Ramsey whenever he came to the house because she just didn't know what to say to him. Nevertheless, when he had come to visit Anabel, he had sought out Claire, too, clearly wanting to include her in his visits with his niece. But, alas, her schedule just hadn't permitted much of that. Her sense of self-preservation hadn't permitted it, either, seeing as how every time Ramsey came within fifteen feet of her, she'd felt as if she were going to go up in flames, and her instincts had commanded she flee. Fast. Preferably to the nearest nunnery.

So she'd always made sure she only spent a few minutes with him—only long enough for her body to do a little smoldering, which was bad enough, even if it felt really, really good—then had manufactured some excuse to leave him with Anabel while she saw to something in her office two rooms down, even if that "something" ended up being two hours of spider solitaire on the computer. That was as close to a nunnery as she could get in her situation.

But as successful as she had been in avoiding Ramsey in person, Claire hadn't been able to avoid him in thought. Because as often as she had replayed the swing episode in her mind, she had replayed it even more often in her dreams.

And usually, in her dreams, the outcome was entirely different from what it had been in reality. Because in her dreams, Chandler wasn't there to interrupt things. In her dreams, always, it was only Claire and Ramsey. Usually naked. Often horizontal. And occasionally with a can of whipped cream.

Oh, yes, it was all coming back to her now. And so were the sweaty palms she always seemed to wake up with when those nighttime fantasies finally ended, usually after a long, leisurely bout of dreamy—in more ways than one—lovemaking.

Banishing the thought as well as she could, Claire sat up straight and released the steering wheel, then rubbed her hands fiercely on the skirt of her pale blue cotton dress. That took care of the sweaty palms, but she could do nothing about the tingly sensations that also accompanied the dreams. And also the memories of those dreams. And not just her hands got tingly, either. No, other places got tingly, too, places she'd just as soon not have tingling, thank you very much, especially now, when she was about to have lunch with the person responsible for the tingles.

Because as hard as she'd worked to avoid Ramsey this week, last night he'd ambushed her by calling later than his usual time, long past Anabel's bedtime. Claire had already gone to bed, too, in fact, but she had still been awake, reading, and she'd been so caught up in her book that she'd automatically reached for the telephone on the nightstand before thinking about who it might be. And the minute she'd heard Ramsey's dark, velvety voice speak her name, she'd known she wouldn't be able to say no to anything he wanted, even if it was down-and-dirty phone sex, with or without whipped cream.

But he hadn't wanted phone sex. Alas. All he'd wanted, in

fact, was to ask her if she would meet him for lunch the following day, so that they could talk. About what had happened. The week before. On the porch swing. And just hearing him mention that kiss in such vague terms, Claire had felt as feverish and not-quite-satisfied as she would have had she just had down-and-dirty phone sex. *With* whipped cream. And a cherry on top.

Now she exited her car and scanned the parking lot for Ramsey's, finally locating it in a numbered slot. So it hadn't been impounded yet by the Nashville PD, she thought. Gee, maybe it really did belong to him. But where was he?

No sooner had the question formed in her head than Claire heard him call out her name. She spun around to face the boats again and saw him heading toward her down one of the piers, his hand lifted in greeting, smiling at her as if she had an oversize check from Publishers Clearing House tucked under her arm. In fact, he was practically jogging toward her, so eager did he seem to get to her. What was really strange was that Claire, who had a deep-seated aversion to physical fitness—unless it was someone else doing the physical fitting, in which case she had no objection, even if she couldn't imagine what the person was thinking—wanted to start jogging toward him, too.

Ramsey was barely winded when he came to a halt in front of her. As was generally the case, he was dressed in blue jeans and a T-shirt—this one a white V-neck that offered her a tantalizing glimpse of the dark hair scattered across his chest beneath. But his scuffed motorcycle boots, she noted, had been replaced with brand-spanking-new Top-Siders, and she almost smiled at the incongruity of the preppy footwear with regard to his attire. His hair, though, was its usual undisciplined self, the silky jet locks tumultuous and wild because of wind whipping off the river.

And likewise as usual, a thrill of excitement shuddered through Claire when she caught a glimpse of his barbed-wire tattoo beneath the taut sleeve of his T-shirt. She marveled that she could still find the decoration so fascinating. Especially since, coupled with the gold hoop that winked in his earlobe, she was reminded again of his rebellious—perhaps unreliable?—nature. But she forgot all about that when she noted how his eyes seemed even more vivid than usual, his smile more enchanting. He was just more handsome and compelling today than she had ever seen him. Yet she couldn't imagine what had changed in the past week that might wreak such an alteration in him.

Oh, wait, yes she could. A mind-numbing, libido-scrambling kiss that had preoccupied her every waking moment. Yep, that could potentially change the way she saw the guy.

"I want to show you something," he said before even telling her hello. "Something I think you'll approve of."

Well, if it involved a can of whipped cream, he was probably right . . .

Giving herself a good mental slap upside the head, Claire cleared her throat delicately, and replied, "Well, hello to you, too, Mr. Sage."

Instead of being put off, Ramsey only smiled even more. "You can still call me that with a straight face, after that exchange of bodily fluids we shared last week?"

Goodness, nothing like cutting to the chase, Claire thought. And he made it sound so romantic, too. The charmer. "Oh, was *that* what that was?" she asked. And she did her best to ignore the dryness in her mouth when she recalled it, not to mention the dampness in her—Ah, never mind. She probably shouldn't mention it.

"And then some," he replied.

"I've scarcely thought about it all week," she assured him in her best Scarlett O'Hara, fiddle-dee-dee voice.

"Liar," he replied eloquently.

She had no idea how to respond to that charge. Mostly because it was true. So she arched her brows in a silent request to hear more about this allegedly approvable whatever it was he was talking about.

But instead of talking about that, what he said was, "I like your hair better when it's down."

Automatically, her hand flew to the tidy chignon she had fixed at her nape. And also automatically, heat surged through her midsection, because she was reminded so acutely of the way Ramsey had freed her hair the week before, and how he had sifted it so reverently through his fingers, and that made her remember how silky his own hair had felt to her, and—

"This way is easier to manage," she said. And she wasn't just talking about her hair when she said it, either.

He nodded, and she knew he comprehended the double meaning, because he didn't belabor the point. Instead, "This way," he said, cocking his head back toward the marina.

Claire followed as he made his way back down the pier, past slips that housed boats running the gamut of nautical quality. Tiny, bare-bones day-sailers bobbed in the water next to larger, sleeker, state-of-the-art vessels. A handful of powerboats mingled with the sailboats, and at the farthest end of the pier floated a very handsome yacht. For one delirious moment, Claire honestly thought it was that last toward which Ramsey was headed, and she wondered if he had stolen it from the same place he'd scored the Volvo. Thankfully, he halted several slips before reaching the massive vessel and, without asking permission of anyone, climbed aboard the sailboat moored there.

A modest size, maybe thirty-five feet to Claire's admittedly untrained eye, it still stood out amid all the fiberglass and aluminum boats. Not just because of its gleaming wooden hull and deck and mast, but because it was absolutely beautiful, with nary a nick to mar its perfection. She wondered if it had ever even been out in deep water, so clean and well kept was it. And she also wondered what on earth Ramsey thought he was doing, trespassing on someone else's property—someone else's pretty valuable property— the way he was.

"It's mine," he announced, obviously reading her thoughts from her worried expression. "I paid for it, Claire. With my money. In full. This boat belongs to me."

"But . . . how?" she said, the two words all she was able to manage in her state of amazement.

He lifted one shoulder and let it drop, but there was something in his expression that belied the casualness of the gesture. "Like I said. I paid for it. In full," he also reiterated, seeming to think that part of his declaration very important, too.

And, of course, it was very important, since the boat had been no cheap purchase, Claire was sure. If Ramsey had enough money to buy it outright, then just how much money did he have overall? Even more important than that, how had he come by it? Most wealthy men didn't favor barbed-wire tattoos or earrings or motorcycle boots. Not unless they'd come by that wealth, oh, say . . . illegally.

"But . . . how?" she repeated, still not sure what to make of this new development.

"With my money," he said again.

"But . . . how?" she repeated. "You don't have a job."

"I'm on sabbatical," he reminded her. "I do have a job. And even if I weren't on sabbatical, even if I were currently unemployed, which I'm *not*," he added, "being jobless now wouldn't mean I didn't save a good part of my salary from my last one."

"But . . . how?"

"Claire," he began calmly, taking a few steps across the deck and extending his hand toward her in obvious invitation. "As I've said, many times, in fact, I'm currently on sabbatical from my job. But it's been a fairly well paying job, and I have modest needs. Most of the money I've made, I've saved. And although it doesn't add up to a fortune like Bill Gates has, it ain't bad. I'm a fiscally responsible person, in spite of the conclusions you've drawn about me."

"Oh, I haven't drawn any conclusions," she lied smoothly.

"The hell you haven't."

"Well, okay, maybe one or two," she lied a little less smoothly. "But they're not carved in stone." That part of her statement, at least, was truthful. Because she'd actually only carved her conclusions about him in really stiff, hard sand that was way far away from the ocean's ebb and flow, so there was little chance of them being erased. Still, it's not like they were carved in stone.

When she remained standing on the pier, showing no intention of joining him on the boat—she just wanted to so badly, she didn't think it was a good idea—Ramsey waggled his hand at her in another silent indication that he was waiting for her to take it and let him help her aboard. With no small reluctance, Claire extended her own hand, and he gingerly took it. Then he caught her elbow in his other hand as she carefully stepped over the lines to settle her sandal-clad foot firmly on the deck. He didn't even grimace at her inappropriate footwear, she noted, which told her that, as much as he appreciated fine things like this boat, he appreciated human presence on it even more.

That realization was made more evident when, even after she landed safely, Ramsey continued to curl his palm gently over her elbow and entwine his fingers with the hand he still held. And when he did, Claire couldn't quite bring herself to shrug him off. Maybe because it felt so good to be held by him, even in so modest a way. He wasn't the only one who appreciated human presence, she thought. And she had enjoyed precious little of that in her life. Oh, certainly there had been humans around her while she was growing up—too many of them, in fact. But few had ever tried to get close to her, emotionally *or* physically. And none had shown any displays of affection. Even the men with whom Claire had been romantically involved had all been reluctant to be overly affectionate—which, now that she thought about it, was probably pretty telling. So even this tiny physical gesture on Ramsey's part felt far too pleasant to put an end to.

"So why did you save all that money?" she asked him. "Why didn't you spend it?"

He managed another one of those not-so-casual shrugs. "At the time, I never really thought about it," he told her. "I only knew I had no need—or any desire—to spend it. But over the last couple of weeks, while I was trying to decide if I wanted to buy the boat, I think maybe I started to understand."

"What?" she asked.

He hesitated a moment before revealing, "I think somehow, even without realizing it, I was always saving for the future. I just never knew what kind of future I'd have, you know? Hell, half the time, I'm not sure I even knew if I had a future." He met her gaze levelly when he said, very decisively, "But I do have a future now. And I realize now that that's what I've been saving for all along."

"Because of Anabel?" Claire asked, even though she was sure that would be his answer.

"Among other things," he replied.

And something in her heart caught fire at the way he looked at her when he said it. "What other things?" she asked, the words seeming to appear from thin air, since, suddenly, she could scarcely breathe.

He studied her in silence for several moments, as if he either didn't know how to answer, or he did know how but didn't want to tell her what his answer would be. Finally, "Just . . . things," he said enigmatically. "Things I never really thought I'd have. Things I didn't even realize I wanted. Not until—"

Again, something in his expression put something inside her on a slow simmer. A slow simmer she knew could turn boiling hot with just the right word, just the right look, just the right touch. And the things Ramsey was saying right now, the way he was looking at her, the way he was touching her . . .

Oh, boy . . .

"Not until what?" she asked, her breath still snared in her lungs. She began to feel a little dizzy, though she wasn't sure if it was because she'd forgotten how to breathe, or if it was because of the way Ramsey continued to gaze at her as if he wanted to . . .

Oh, boy . . .

"What?" he said instead of answering her question. "Why are you looking at me like that?"

Claire shook her head helplessly, utterly and completely confounded by him. By him, and by her feelings for him. Her reactions to him. Part of her still didn't trust him. Part of her trusted him way too much. Part of her felt apprehensive around him. Part of her wanted to curl up in his lap. Part of her thought he was the worst possible candidate to care for Anabel. Part of her thought Anabel didn't belong with anyone but him. Part of her wanted to turn around right now and leave this boat and never see Ramsey again. And part of her . . .

Oh, *boy*.

Well. Part of her wanted to weave her fingers through the dark hair the breeze blew over his forehead, then loop an arm around his neck and pull him down to kiss his mouth and lead him belowdecks to where she knew there must be a bed, a soft, inviting bed, just big enough for the two of them, where they could spend the rest of the afternoon. Alone. Together. Doing all the things they'd done in her dreams. Again and again and again. Whether he had any whipped cream or not.

There were so many pieces to the puzzle that was Ramsey Sage. And even more to the puzzle that was her feelings for him. And Claire couldn't begin to put any of those pieces in their proper places. She wasn't even sure if all the pieces were there.

"I just don't know who you are," she finally told him. "First you're this dangerous-looking guy with ripped jeans who roars up on a ratty motorcycle. Then you're driving a Volvo station wagon and drinking lattes and feeding ducks in the park. Now you're the captain of a sailboat you bought with money you've saved from some job you won't even identify."

She searched his face for some clue, even the tiniest indication of what kind of man he might truly be. But she found nothing to aid her in her examination. Only brilliant green eyes whose depths seemed to go on to infinity, and the strong, blunt jaw of a man who didn't compromise, and the full, delicious mouth she wanted so badly to kiss.

"Just who are you, Ramsey Sage?" she finally said. "And why can't I figure you out?"

He studied her in silence for so long this time that Claire thought he wasn't going to answer. Finally, though, his gaze never leaving hers, he replied quietly, "That's just the problem, Claire. Lately, I'm not really sure I know who I am."

And only when he spoke the words aloud did Ramsey realize they were true. He really didn't know who he was anymore. He wasn't sure he'd ever known himself in the first place. He'd grown up living by other people's rules, then he'd had to live by other people's instructions, then by other people's commands. He honestly couldn't say where—or even *if*—he'd ever put anything of himself into his life. It had only been since leaving his life behind to see about Anabel's that he'd begun to realize just how little life he'd had to leave behind.

When was the last time he'd stopped a moment to do something for *himself*? he wondered. And it bothered him a lot to realize he wasn't sure. It bothered him even more to realize that he didn't know if he'd *ever* done anything for himself. Oh, sure, he'd chosen his occupation, but really, his job had more come looking for him than he had looked for it. And within that occupation, who did he really claim as anything more than a coworker? Good God, he couldn't buddy up with the people he'd found himself surrounded by over the past few years. They were animals.

But even beyond his small circle of fiends, out in that nether region where a few decent souls actually did dwell, who did he call a friend? No one. Not really. Oh, there were the guys he could share a beer—or shot of bad tequila—with on occasion. And there were women to warm his bed, among other things, sometimes for weeks at a time. But when was the last time Ramsey had actually had a *relation-ship* with anyone, of either gender? Not for a long, long time. In fact, he could think of only one real relationship that he'd had in his entire life. And it had ended abruptly, before he'd really realized its significance. Doubtless because, even though Ramsey had finally learned how to love someone, he hadn't been able to love her enough. And she, understand-ably, had wanted more. More than he had been able to give.

But that had been years ago, and Ramsey wasn't that guy anymore. And that guy hadn't been the remote child who'd grown up the way he had with the elder Sages. He had changed a lot, a number of times, over his life, he knew, and he supposed all of his identities over the years had left a lit-tle bit of themselves behind. But just who was he *now*? he asked himself. Who was he *really*? It troubled him to realize he just didn't know. He didn't know who he was or what he wanted. Except for Anabel, of course.

And except for Claire, too.

Because Ramsey did want Claire. He'd wanted her, he guessed, since the moment he first saw her. He just hadn't been sure what to do with her then. Hell, he wasn't sure what to do with her now. Assuming he had a chance with her in the first place, which was a pretty damned big assump-tion. Then again, judging by the way she was looking at him at the moment . . .

"But I'm not dangerous, Claire," he said, knowing that

THE THING ABOUT MEN

much, at least, was true. He wished he could tell her he *was* harmless, but he didn't think that would be truthful. Not when he remembered some of the things he'd fantasized doing to her. Not that he wanted to harm her, no way. But he wasn't a forever-after kind of guy, either, not with women. And after doing with him what he found himself wanting to do with her, Claire would want him to be around forever. She wasn't the kind of woman who would tolerate a one-night stand. One night would mean many more nights to her—a happily-ever-after of nights. And Ramsey just didn't think he could be that. Not for her. Not for anyone.

Except, of course, Anabel. He would always be there for her. But that was different. Anabel was family.

"Come on inside," he said, before his thoughts could wander any farther into realms he didn't want to explore right now. Because for the time being, he only wanted to talk to Claire, to show her he was a good guy, to explain why it was so important to him that he be the one to raise Anabel. In all the time they had spent together over the past month—which, granted, wasn't as much as he would have liked—he hadn't petitioned her again for Anabel's guardianship the way he had that first day. Surely, after the kiss they had shared last week, she trusted him more. Maybe she hadn't admitted it in so many words, but a woman didn't kiss a man the way Claire had kissed him unless she was warming to him. Okay, so maybe he wanted Claire to warm to him in more ways than one, but he was pretty sure that was the case, too.

Once he talked to Claire about Anabel again, he was confident she would realize his niece belonged with him, and she would turn Anabel over without a fight. He knew Claire and Olive both had grown attached to the little girl over the past five weeks, and he had no desire to expel them from An-abel's life. But it was time for Ramsey to move on with his own life—wherever that life might lead—and that meant it was time for him to assume responsibility for his niece. It was time for him to take Anabel home. And he needed for Claire to see that, too.

"Come on," he said again, "I made us some lunch."

"*You* made lunch?" she said, obviously astonished by his culinary accomplishment.

He grinned. "Yes, I made lunch," he repeated proudly. "And I got the recipes from a Simple Pleasures cookbook."

She grinned back. "Then I'm sure it will be delicious."

And lunch was delicious, Ramsey had to admit once they were finally seated in the cabin belowdecks enjoying it. And not just delicious, but good-looking, too, dammit. Though he wouldn't have exactly called the recipe for "Chilled Pesto Tuna Pasta" *simple*, even though the front cover of the Sim-ple Pleasures cookbook had claimed it would be. Thirty minutes at the blender feeding in fresh basil and thyme—not to mention what had seemed like hours trying to find fresh herbs in the first place, hell, he probably could have grown his own faster—and all that garlic peeling and crushing, and having to read all those damned olive oil labels until he fig-ured out the difference between virgin and extra virgin when that seemed like an either/or sort of situation to him, like be-ing pregnant or extra pregnant or something, and then *more* time looking for fresh parmesan, which, like the fresh herbs, the recipe had *demanded* he find, and then . . .

Where was he? Oh, yeah. The *simple* pesto recipe that had taken hours from his life and made him drive to three differ-ent supermarkets to find all the necessary ingredients. Oh, well. He really had impressed himself with how successful he'd been in making it—and the rest of the fare, too—such a pleasure. Funny, but he never would have thought himself an especially capable cook. Then again, he'd never tried cooking before, so how could he have known whether or not he'd be good at it? He couldn't help wondering what other talents he might possess, too.

As he and Claire finished their meal, he leaned back in his seat and pondered his new home. He was still kind of surprised he'd bought the boat, but when he'd seen it for sale on his first visit to the marina, he'd fallen in love with it, and an idea had taken root in his head. Now that he had Anabel to raise, he knew he needed a place to call home, but the thought of owning a piece of land and being confined to it for the rest of his life had frankly scared the hell out of him. He'd been on the move for twenty years, and the thought of settling down, even though he knew he had to do that with Anabel, was just too terrifying to consider. A boat, he'd decided, would be a nice compromise. He and his niece would be comfortable enough here for a while, and he'd never have to feel as if he were pinned down. By the time she was old enough to go to school, he'd be ready, he was sure, to commit to a landlocked dwelling. For now, though, the boat was as close as Ramsey was willing to get to a roof over his head.

He hesitated to call its cabin *crowded*, preferring instead to think of it as *intimate*. But that word didn't quite seem right, either—well, it seemed *right*, it just didn't seem *appropriate* under the circumstances, not yet—so he decided not to dwell on the size of the cabin and focused on Claire instead. She looked, as always, beautiful. Her hair had been faultlessly swept back into one of those seemingly simple 'dos earlier, but as they'd stood on deck talking, the breeze had knocked a few of the pale blond tresses free. Now a handful of soft, errant tendrils fell around her face in a way that made him want to reach across the table and tuck them back behind her ears. Or, better yet, to reach behind her and free the rest of her hair and watch it cascade over her shoulders and breasts, preferably her *naked* shoulders and breasts, and then—

"Dessert!" he said suddenly, reminding himself that he had brought Claire here to talk to her—at least, first. "We, ah, we need to have something for dessert." But then, hadn't he just been thinking about what—or, rather, who—he'd like to have for dessert? he asked himself. "Something sweet, I mean," he hastily specified. But then, hadn't he just been thinking about something—or, rather, someone—sweet? "Something edible, I mean," he specified even more specifically. But then hadn't he just been thinking about—Ah, hell. "Food, I mean," he specified most specifically of all. "And as luck would have it, I just so happen to have some food, some sweet, edible food, that would be perfect for dessert."

Wherein Ramsey jumped up and wedged himself into the tiny galley—a generous way to put it, since "the galley" was really just "the corner of the cabin nearest Claire that had a sink and refrigerator and stuff." Once there, he foraged around in the tiny cabinets for the bag of Oreos he always kept handy, since the simple pleasure of lunch had taken up so much time, it hadn't allowed any extra for anything like dessert. Well, for sweet dessert, anyway. For edible dessert, anyway. For *food* dessert, anyway.

Oh, hell.

"That's okay," Claire said, holding up a hand. "I really don't want dessert."

Damn.

"Maybe we could just talk," she added.

Double damn.

"Sure," he agreed amiably, since that was what he wanted, too, right? At least, he hoped he sounded amiable. It was hard to do that when you felt, um, deserted.

Oh, he really wished he hadn't thought that.

"What do you want to talk about?" he asked, shoving aside all thoughts of dessert, and being deserted, and anything else that might even remotely resemble those two words.

"Tell me more about Eleanor," Claire said.

Instead of returning to his seat, Ramsey began clearing their lunch dishes from the table. That gave him something to do besides look at Claire, because it would be too difficult to talk about personal things if he had to do that. "I really don't remember that much about her," he confessed as he reached for a plate. "Eleanor was only four when I left home."

"And why exactly did you leave home again?" Claire asked.

He hesitated, but still didn't look at her. "I thought we were going to talk about Eleanor."

"So we were."

He went back to collecting dishes from the tiny table and avoiding Claire's gaze. "I left home because I couldn't stand living there anymore," he told her. So much for talking about Eleanor. "Because my parents made our *home*," he tried not to choke on that last word, but couldn't quite avoid the bitterness that crept into his voice when he uttered it, "anything but hospitable."

"They mistreated you?"

He shrugged off the suggestion. "Not really. But they didn't treat us much, either. They just weren't warm, loving, nurturing people, the way parents are supposed to be, you know?"

He did finally look at Claire as he concluded the statement, and he saw something in her face that told him she did indeed understand. Which was kind of strange, really. He would have thought that a woman who made her living telling others how to create the perfect family environment would have come from a perfect family environment herself. But she really did seem to have no one to call family. Maybe the reason she did what she did for a living—creating an ideal home life and a perfect all-American family atmosphere—was because she *hadn't* had that kind of upbringing and had wanted it so badly.

"Yeah, I do know," she said softly, bringing Ramsey back to the matter at hand and confirming his suspicions.

"Your parents were lousy at the parenting thing, too?" he asked.

"Actually, I never really had any parents," she told him. "They died when I was three."

"I'm sorry," he said, not sure what else to say.

"I was probably better off," she told him with obviously feigned indifference. "From what I've gathered of my home life before then, my parents weren't exactly Ward and June Cleaver."

Ramsey nodded. He understood that, too. "What I remember of Eleanor," he said, returning to the lesser of two evil topics, "is that she looked a lot like Anabel. But she wasn't as happy as Anabel is. She didn't laugh as much. Didn't smile as much. But then, I don't guess Eleanor had much to be happy about, being raised by our parents. Not like Anabel does with you." *And, hopefully*, he added to himself, *with me. Someday. Soon.*

"Anabel was happy with her mother, too," Claire told him in a tone of voice that was soft and certain and surprisingly reassuring. "Your sister was very loving toward her daughter, Ramsey."

"How do you know?" he asked, even though he was grateful for the information and told himself he shouldn't question it.

"Because she wrote to me a lot, and her letters were always filled with stories about Anabel, and she always sent me pictures, and in those pictures, Anabel was always smiling. Always."

When Ramsey glanced up at Claire again, she was smiling, too. But it was a melancholy sort of smile that said she wished things could have turned out differently for the little girl.

"Which makes me think," she continued, "that Eleanor must have been happy, too. She always sounded happy in her letters. And I know Anabel brought her great joy."

Hearing that his sister had found happiness as an adult—that she had found a family as an adult, at least with little Anabel—made Ramsey feel better. He hoped Claire was right, hoped Eleanor hadn't just been putting on a front—for Claire *or* for herself. He wished he could have known his sister as an adult woman, wished he hadn't spent so much time away, wished he could have been there for her when—

Well. He just wished a lot of things, that was all. A lot of things that were never going to come true. So he made himself think of Anabel instead, and of all the wishes he had for her. Those wishes, he vowed now, *would* come true. He'd make them come true. Somehow. If only he could make Claire understand how important it was that he do that. Not just for Anabel. And not just for Eleanor, either.

"Thanks, Claire," he said softly.

"For what?" she asked, surprised.

"For telling me my sister was happy as an adult. For telling me she turned out okay. It means more than you realize."

Claire hesitated a moment before asking, very tentatively at that, "But what about Eleanor's brother? Did he turn out okay? Is he happy as an adult, too?"

A couple of months ago, Ramsey would have known how to answer those last two questions. He would have responded, "Relatively." Meaning he was more okay than he'd been as a kid, and that he had found more happiness as an adult than he had known as a boy. But seeing as how he'd known so little happiness as a child, achieving even some meager amount as an adult didn't seem like much of an accomplishment.

Over the past couple of months, though, that *relatively* had changed again, had become even more relative. He was better and happier than he had been when Gordon Stantler found him drunk and disorderly down in Central America. Quite a bit better and happier, really, now that he thought about it. And not all of that okayness and happiness had come about because of Anabel. More than a little had come about because of Claire. Just being with her over the last several weeks, talking to her, sharing Anabel with her, then kissing her on her front porch swing as the heavy scent of lilacs overwhelmed him . . .

"Well, Eleanor's brother is more okay and happier now than he was a few months ago," he finally said. Then he further confessed, "But he could stand to be a little happier, I guess."

"And what would it take to make him happier?" Claire asked softly.

Anabel, Ramsey thought, thinking her question the perfect opening to discuss what he told himself he really wanted to discuss. He'd thought since coming back to the States that winning custody of his niece was his primary goal, was the one thing he really wanted. Now, though, he was beginning to see that Anabel was only part of what he wanted. And maybe not even the biggest part. Because there was something else he wanted now, too. Wanted very badly.

So when he opened his mouth to tell Claire that Anabel was the key to his happiness, what he actually heard himself say was, "You."

It was clearly not what she had expected to hear, because her cheeks flushed pink, and her lips parted in surprise, and her pupils expanded suddenly, nearly eclipsing the blue of her irises. And all Ramsey could think was how very much he wanted to touch her. Hold her. Kiss her. Love her.

"Me?" she whispered.

He nodded slowly. "Yeah, you."

And before she could say another word, before he had a chance to question what he was doing, Ramsey reached down to circle her wrist with sure fingers, and tugged her gently to standing. No sooner was she on her feet, however, than he pulled her into his arms. And before she had a chance to object, he covered her mouth with his.

Twelve

*C*laire told herself she should have been prepared for his kiss this time, that ever since they'd sat down to lunch, the air had fairly crackled with their awareness of each other. But she wasn't prepared. Because his kiss this time wasn't tentative or exploratory. No, his kiss this time was filled with passion and possession and purpose. He knew what he was doing this time, knew what he wanted. More than that, she could tell, he knew Claire wanted it, too.

So without questioning her reactions, without thinking about what she was doing, knowing only that she wanted to do it, and had wanted to for some time, she lifted both arms to bend them around his neck, then wove the fingers of one hand into the dark silk of his hair and returned his kiss with equal fire.

A hungry growl rumbled up from inside him at her response, and he deepened the kiss, driving his tongue into her mouth to taste her more completely. As he did, he cupped his hand over the crown of her head, then pushed his fingers lower, searching for—and finding—every pin that held her chignon in place. One by one, he plucked them free, until her hair cascaded down over his hand and her shoulders. He uttered another wild little sound as he bunched a fistful of the tresses in his hand, tangling his fingers in her hair until she wasn't sure where she ended and Ramsey began. He curved his palm over her nape and urged her head back a bit more, then opened his mouth wider and fairly consumed her.

Claire's heart thundered in her chest at the utter absoluteness of his possession. She felt bewitched, enchanted, completely in his thrall. Never had she reacted to a man with such unconditional surrender. But then, she didn't feel as if she were surrendering to him. On the contrary, she felt as if she were winning a battle she'd fought for too long, and Ramsey was the prize she could plunder at will. She splayed her hand open over the taut fabric of his shirt, pressing her fingertips into the firm, warm flesh beneath it. He was hard where she was soft, solid where she was yielding. Their bodies were so different from each other. Yet they fitted together perfectly.

Ramsey seemed to think so, too, because he dropped a hand to the small of her back and pushed her body more intimately against his. She felt him swell to life against her belly, and gasped at the realization of how ready he was for what was happening. But then, her body seemed to be ready for him, too, because heat was spiraling through her, and places that would welcome him had begun to dampen in anticipation. That heat and dampness only multiplied when he urged his hand lower, bending his fingers over the soft curves of her derriere and molding her to himself. Again, Claire gasped, and Ramsey took advantage of her action by deepening their kiss even more.

And then she realized they were moving, that he was slowly walking her backward, toward the front of the boat, where she'd noticed a tiny cabin that was overcome by a bunk just large enough for two people—provided the two people slept *very* closely together. Or provided the two people were joined as one. And she knew that she and Ramsey would fall into that bed together, and that they would do whatever it took to assuage the desire that had been building since perhaps the moment they had met. What she didn't know was what would happen after that. At the moment, though, she couldn't think that far ahead. Because her brain—and her heart—were too full of what was happening.

Step by leisurely step, she and Ramsey completed a slow, sensuous dance that brought them closer to that tiny cabin with its tiny bed. And all along the way, they continued to kiss, to touch, to explore. He was so big, and so hard, all of him, all over. And he was so adamant, so resolute about what he wanted. There wasn't a scrap of uncertainty in him, something she envied. He seemed to have no misgivings, no second thoughts, no fear about what was going to happen. But Claire . . .

Claire feared nothing would ever be the same again after today.

She tore her mouth away from his long enough to inhale a frantic breath, but he immediately reclaimed it, kissing her hungrily, again and again and again. By now, they had almost made it to the cabin. Just another step . . . But as if he just couldn't wait any longer, Ramsey pressed Claire back against a clear, crowded space on the wall, flattening a forearm against it on each side of her head, insinuating one of his legs between both of hers. Her own legs went weak when he did, and she sank down far enough that his thigh rested at the juncture of hers. He moved his leg then, deliberately raising his thigh to rub it insolently against her, a delicious friction that sent a shock of heat scurrying through her.

Claire groaned aloud at the sensation, and in response, Ramsey urged his leg higher still, pushing it more wantonly, more skillfully, against her. She moaned once more against his mouth, clinging to his shirt, twisting her fingers until she worried she would tear it. So she flattened her palms against his broad chest instead, savoring the heat and life that permeated the soft fabric beneath her fingertips. His heart pounded ferociously against her palm, and it heartened her to know she was responsible for his reaction.

He did finally pull his mouth free of hers, breathing raggedly as he touched his forehead to hers. Claire curled her fingers over his shoulders, and her gaze fell on his barbed-wire tattoo, the tattoo that had so fascinated her since that first day. Softly, she drew her index finger down over his shoulder and upper arm, until her fingertips met the hem of his shirtsleeve. She hesitated for a moment, as if what she wanted to do were somehow forbidden, then quickly pushed her hand lower to skim the pads of her fingertips over the dark ink. The decoration was warm and smooth beneath her touch, and she pushed her fingers around his arm in a perfect circle, to trace the band completely.

Her own breathing frayed and unsteady, she struggled to collect her thoughts. But her thoughts were so jumbled, she gave up on thinking, and instead just let herself feel. And what she felt, she realized, was an odd sort of calmness about what was happening, even as her body and her senses seemed ready to explode.

Ramsey's gaze found hers and held it, but he said not a word as he dipped his hand between their bodies, toward the row of tidy buttons that marched all the way down the front of her dress. For a moment, he only skimmed the pad of his index finger over the ones he could reach, as if he were trying to decide what to do with them. Then, one by one, he began to unfasten them, starting at the scooped neck and moving down past her waist, to her thighs, until the pale blue cotton opened over the froth of pink lace bra and panties beneath. But instead of tucking a hand inside her dress, as Claire had anticipated he would do, he moved his hand sideways, to press his palm over the outside of her thigh.

From there, he bunched the fabric of her dress in his fist and began to lift it, urging the hem higher and higher, until Claire felt the warm, damp kiss of the afternoon air on her legs and knees. And as he pulled her dress up, he dipped his head low, to drag a long line of openmouthed kisses along her throat and across her collarbone. Then, finally, he did move his free hand to where her dress fell open, nudging the fabric aside until he had bared her shoulder. And then she felt the whisper of his damp breath warming her there, too, and still she clung to him, not sure what she should do, because it had been so long since she had felt like this, so long since her body had reacted to a man the way hers was reacting to Ramsey. In fact, she couldn't remember ever reacting like this to anyone, and that only left her more confused.

"Ramsey," she gasped as he nipped lightly the tender skin at the base of her throat. Then she cried out softly as he laved with his tongue the place he had just tasted. "Ramsey, please," she tried again, her voice a tattered whisper.

"Please what?" he whispered back before dipping his mouth to her throat once again.

But all Claire could manage in response was another weakly offered, "Please . . ."

He seemed to sense her distress, because he pulled away, far enough that he could gaze down at her face. But his expression was inscrutable, offering not a clue what might be going on inside him. His breathing was labored and uneven, though, and his fingers convulsed on the delicate flesh of her thigh. The hand that had pushed her dress from her shoulder now drew a careful line across the sensitive skin above her bra, his middle fingertip dipping down briefly to touch the soft swells of her breasts as it passed. Claire closed her eyes and tilted her head back until the hard plane of the wall prohibited further movement, then bit back another soft sound of need.

"Please what?" Ramsey asked again.

His voice was soft and hypnotic when he spoke, and still he traced his fingertips along her skin, with an aching slowness that enabled her to feel every pulse in his fingertips, back and forth and back again, each new course tracing a bit lower, toward the top of her bra. She hesitated to think about what he would do when he reached it. Because somehow she knew he wouldn't let a little scrap of lace stop him. And she knew she wouldn't be able to resist him once he breached it.

She inhaled a deep breath and released it slowly, then brought her head forward again. "This is going so fast, Ramsey," she said. But she laced her fingers through his hair again as she spoke, her actions belying her words. It was going fast, she thought, but somehow, the pace felt right.

He said nothing for a moment, only continued to watch the languid back and forth movement of his hand as it moved across her skin. Then, finally, "Is it?" he asked without looking up.

"Yes."

He brought his gaze up to meet hers. "But I've been wanting to do this for a long, long time. To me, it feels like it's taken forever."

She told herself not to ask him what she wanted to ask him, because she wasn't sure she wanted to know the answer. In spite of that, and almost as if she hadn't made the decision consciously, she heard herself say, "Because, usually, you don't have any trouble getting women into bed, do you?"

He didn't respond right away, as if he were being very careful to choose the right words for his reply. Finally, he lifted his hand to her hair, to stroke back a single strand before cupping her jaw tenderly in his palm. "I never told you I was a saint, Claire. I've been with other women. Just like you, I'm sure, have been with other men."

She nodded. "It's just that . . ."

"What?" he asked when she didn't finish.

"I guess I just want to be sure, before we go through with this, that you don't think I'm like the rest of them."

He turned his hand to skim the backs of his knuckles over her cheekbone, along her jaw, down her throat, and back to her chest, then turned it again to trail his fingertips along her skin again, this time with maddening slowness. His hand was low enough now that, after one slow caress, he was able to dip three fingers into the lace of her bra. Claire's heart thundered harder, but he halted his hand when only the pads of his fingers pressed against her, and she curled her hands over his shoulders again, trying, she supposed, to keep herself from falling. But falling where, she decided not to think about.

"Do you think I'm like the other men you've been with?" he asked, his voice low and level. But he wasn't looking at her face, and instead kept his gaze fixed on the fingers pressing into her breast.

Without hesitating, Claire shook her head. Ramsey wasn't

like any of the men she had been with. They couldn't come close to being the kind of man he was. "No," she said. "You're nothing like them."

"Those men were dignified and refined, and cultivated and educated, I bet."

"Yes," Claire told him. "They were."

Unless she compared them to Ramsey Sage, in which case they were sober and dull, and unfinished and untrained. At least in all the things that were important. But she didn't tell Ramsey that. He was obviously feeling confident enough at the moment.

"And they probably liked their sex orderly and conservative and traditional," he added.

More like methodical and boring and typical, she thought. But she only repeated, "Yes. They did."

When Ramsey moved his hand this time, it was to drive it completely beneath the lace of her bra, and cover her breast thoroughly with confident fingers. "Then you're right," he told her as he curved an impudent hand over her tender flesh and brought his gaze up to meet hers unapologetically. "I'm nothing like them."

With deft, capable movements, he brought his other hand into the action, shoving the straps of her bra over her shoulders and down her arms, baring her breasts completely. Claire uttered a soft sound of surrender as he dipped his head to pull the peak of one deep, deep into his mouth. After one long, leisurely suck that left her skin wet and hot and tingling, he lifted his head again, meeting her gaze even more fiercely than before. "Because I like my sex hot and uncivilized and indecent."

Oh, my . . .

"You're not like the women I've been with, either, Claire,"

he said, his voice softening some. But he continued to cradle her breast possessively in his hand, rolling the pad of his thumb idly over the damp, burgeoning nipple. "You're nothing like them at all."

She swallowed hard, trying to reclaim her composure in light of the way he was touching her, but her breath got caught in her throat. The fingers she had curled over his shoulders tightened, but she might as well have been trying to grasp solid rock, so hard and unyielding was he beneath her hands. "Is that because . . ." she began. But her throat felt thick, and her mouth was dry, so she licked her lips before speaking again. "Is it because you think I like my sex orderly and conservative and traditional, too?" she asked.

He shook his head, smiling a devilish smile. "No," he said. "I don't think you like it like that. You're too alive, too passionate."

"Then you think I like it . . . the way you like it," she guessed.

He cupped his other hand over her other breast, closing the fingers of both hands intently over her. "I don't know," he said, catching the peaks of both in the deep Vs of index and middle fingers. "Do you?"

"I . . . I don't know, either," she said breathlessly, honestly. "I've never had it like that before."

He moved a hand to her hip, scooping it under her dress, then pushed it back and shoved it beneath the fabric of her panties to splay his fingers wide over the lower curve of her bare bottom. "Then you'll have to let me know what you think when it's over," he murmured. "Hours and hours and hours from now."

If I live that long, Claire thought, her entire body on fire now.

"Because that's how I know you're different from the other women I've been with," he said, his voice gritty, his breath hot against her neck. "They never made me feel the way you make me feel."

"And how do I make you feel?" she asked.

He gave both her breast and her bottom a firm but gentle squeeze, and a flash of need seared her belly. "Wild and reckless and out of control," he said. "I want to bury myself in you and never come up for air." And then, as if to illustrate that, he bent his head to hers again, covered her mouth with his, and did his best to devour her.

And that was when Claire stopped thinking and just allowed herself to feel what was happening between them. By now, the skirt of her dress was wrapped around her waist, and Ramsey's hand was firmly planted beneath her panties. Instead of pushing them down, however, he kneaded her sensitive buttock before pushing it away from its twin and tracing a long finger down the elegant line that bisected them. He paused long enough to briefly insert the tip of his finger inside her, and Claire gasped at the shocking, unfamiliar foray . . . until she realized how oddly arousing it had been. As quickly as he had penetrated her, however, he was moving his hand lower again, toward her damp center. He pushed his fingers forward until he could just barely stroke her from behind, and instinctively, Claire arched her body forward into his.

She really felt him then, his shaft hard and long as it pressed into her torso. Instinctively, she rubbed herself against him, dropping her hands to his hips, gripping him deliberately to push him closer still. For long moments, they only touched that way, rubbing against each other with a delicious sort of friction, until the fingers between Claire's legs left her whimpering with pleasure. At the soft sound, Ramsey retreated again, and Claire was about to protest when she felt him tugging at her panties, pulling them down to bare her bottom completely. She lifted her dress to help him as he moved his body downward, dragging her panties as he went, over her knees and calves, helping her to lift one foot, then the other, until he could discard the scrap of pink lace completely.

And then he was kneeling before her, his thumbs pressing against the insides of her thighs, his fingers fanning toward the outside. Claire continued to grasp her dress in her hands until he rose again, then was surprised when Ramsey didn't rise. Instead, still gripping her thighs, he pushed to spread them wider, and, unable to resist him, Claire obediently opened her legs. Then he leaned forward and opened his mouth over the hot, wet core of her, tonguing her, mouthing her, shocking her. She cried out at first contact, and impulsively thrust her hand down to stop him. No man had ever . . . Oh, *Ramsey*. But he easily brushed her hand away, and tasted her again, feasting on her as if she were the sweetest delicacy he had ever encountered.

"Ramsey," she gasped. Though she honestly wasn't sure if she was trying to tell him to stop or urging him to go further still.

He opted for the latter, because he pushed himself even closer to her and tilted back his head, burying his face between her legs. Claire felt as if she were turning into a hot, flowing river as he savored her, his tongue delving and licking, his mouth opening and closing, until she was nearly insensate with wanting. Then, without warning, a fast-spiraling orgasm bolted through her, exploding from deep within, sending flame and fury to every cell she possessed, and she cried out helplessly in response.

Only then did he move away from her and rise unsteadily

to his feet, burying his face this time in the tender flesh where her neck joined her shoulders. He held her for a moment as she trembled in the aftermath, rubbing his open mouth lightly over her shoulder and neck and jaw. Then he lifted his hands to frame her face gently, and kissed first one cheek, then the other, before scooping her up into his arms.

"Ramsey," she said, her voice sounding weak and uncertain.

"Shh," he told her. "No more words, Claire. Just actions. Just responses. Feel what I do to you, the way I feel what you do to me."

When he set her on her feet beside the tiny bed in his tiny cabin, he silenced her with a slow, thorough kiss she felt all the way to her soul, a kiss that seemed to go on forever. He cupped his hands over her shoulders and pushed her dress down over her arms, and in another quick move had removed her bra. She returned the favor in kind, undressing him, but her fingers shook as they tugged his shirt free of his waistband and over his head, and he had to help her with the buttons on the fly of his jeans. It was Claire alone, though, who pulled his jeans down his strong, muscular legs, and Claire alone who marveled at the exquisiteness of the body beneath them and the briefs that joined them. And it was Claire by herself who stroked her fingers along the long, firm length of him, tracing the plump head of his shaft before touching her lips to it.

"Claire," he said roughly as she flicked the tip of her tongue over him. "You don't have to—"

But his words halted, to be replaced by a stout, lengthy sigh as she took him more completely into her mouth. Never had she done such a thing before, but something about Ramsey made her want to. He tasted hot and wild and bold, and he made her feel that way, too. So she took her time to explore him with her mouth and tongue, loving the way he threaded his fingers through her hair and murmured soft sounds of pleasure in response.

And when she rose again, he pulled her forward, brushing his hands along her arms, down over her hands, to hook his fingers through hers. He kissed her again, once, softly, then turned her around, looping their arms in such a way that she ended up pulled against him, her back flush with his front. For a moment, he only held her that way, letting them both enjoy the simple nearness of each others' bodies. Then he released her hands and moved his to her belly, splaying them open over her heated skin to push her back even more.

"I need to put on a condom, Claire," he said softly. "Unless you've already taken some precautions."

She shook her head. "It's been so long since I've—" She didn't finish, knowing it wasn't necessary, knowing he already realized that.

She had hoped he would tell her it had been a long time for him, too, but he said nothing. And the fact that he simply pulled open a drawer beneath the bunk and lifted out a condom from a box inside only reinforced her certainty that it hadn't been nearly as long for him as it had been for her. She battled a twist of jealousy that knifed through her, knowing it was irrational. And she told herself it didn't matter that he was far more experienced than she.

But then he was pulling her back against his naked body again, and he felt so good there that she stopped thinking about anything other than the way they fit so well together. She felt him nestled against her fanny, hard and hot and ready for her, and she reached behind herself to run her fingers through his hair. Ramsey kissed the side of her neck and cupped one of her breasts in each hand, palming them, pushing them together and apart, capturing her nipples beneath his fingers, then releasing them again. Then he bent her forward over the bed, nudging her legs apart with one strong thigh.

Claire started to object, wanted to face him when they joined, but he began skimming his open hands across her back and over her bottom, and the sensation was just too exquisite for her to ask him to end it just yet. He moved his hands lower, over her hips and beneath her bent body, then up again, over her torso and breasts. He opened his hand flat and ran his palms lightly over her nipples, then down again, to the ache between her legs. As he threaded his fingers through the damp folds of flesh there, he entered her from behind, slowly, insistently, deeply, thoroughly.

Never had Claire felt so full, so vital, so alive, as she did when Ramsey was inside of her. He gripped her hips in his hands and held her still while he withdrew himself, then he slipped easily into her again. Over and over he pushed and pulled her against him, until she mimicked the rhythm he set. Then he moved one hand forward again, pushing it between her legs to finger her sensitive flesh. He splayed his other hand open over her buttocks, his thumb venturing between them for a scant, more intimate, penetration.

Never, ever, in her life had Claire experienced such an onslaught of stimulation. Ramsey seemed to be everywhere, inside her and out, touching her in ways she had never been touched before. And then he was pulling out of her completely, and turning her around to face him, and urging her back onto the bed. He joined her as she felt the cool kiss of the sheets beneath her back, entering her again, and she wrapped her legs around his waist to hold him close. As he began to pump harder inside her, heat began to coil tight in her belly, tighter, tighter, and tighter still, until it sprang open again in one vital rush, spilling pleasure throughout her body. She cried out at the absolute perfection of her response, Ramsey's cry of completion echoing her own. For a moment, their bodies stilled, their voices went silent, and they succumbed to the waves of ecstasy that overtook them. Then, as the rush slowly ebbed, Ramsey pulled Claire into his arms and held her close, and kissed her as if the two of them were united as one forever.

More moments passed as they clung to each other, listening to the gradually slowing thunder of their hearts. And later, as Claire snuggled into Ramsey, she said, "You know, that wasn't so indecent."

She heard his chuckle beneath her ear before it even left his mouth, and she smiled. "No?" he asked. "I must be losing my touch."

"Oh, believe me—there was nothing wrong with your touch. Now that I think about it, I suppose it *was* rather hot and uncivilized."

"*Rather* hot and uncivilized?" he echoed incredulously. "You *suppose*?"

"Mm," she told him.

"Then I guess I'll just have to try harder next time, won't I?"

Claire's heart raced at hearing that, though she wasn't sure whether it was because of the idea of Ramsey trying harder, or the fact that he wanted there to be a next time. Because she wanted there to be a next time, too. And not just because she wanted to see what it would be like when Ramsey tried harder. No, there was another reason for it, one she told herself she shouldn't even think about. Because if she started thinking about it . . .

Well, she wouldn't think about it, that was all. She just wouldn't think about how she might very well be falling in love with Ramsey Sage.

* * *

Nothing in Ramsey's entire life had felt better than holding Claire. Nothing. It was like a dream, lying here with her, a misty, mellow, late-afternoon dream from which he hoped he would never awaken. A reddish bronze shaft of end-of-the-day sunlight splashed through the open companionway to flow over their naked bodies, and a heavy summer breeze poured down to skim across their dewy flesh. Through the open porthole beside them, he saw an early moon peeking out from behind a gold-tipped cloud, and he reasoned that he *must* be sleeping, and this *must* be a dream. This shimmering moment of perfection couldn't possibly be anything but a desperate invention of his imagination. Because it was what he had wanted so much for so long.

But her skin was so silky everywhere it touched his, and her hair smelled so sweet as it spilled across his chest, and her breath was so soft against his neck every time she exhaled. She felt real. Warm. Alive. So maybe this wasn't a dream after all.

She stirred some, murmuring a quiet, contented sound, then launched herself into a languid full-body stretch. Ramsey stirred, too, but in a different way, and he curled his arm more possessively around her waist, pulling her completely atop him. She landed in a cozy heap with a lazy smile, her hands splayed open on his chest. Her hair fell into her eyes for a moment before she shoved it behind one ear, then the long tresses fell forward again. The gesture was sexy as hell.

"Hi," she murmured.

"Hi," he replied, just as softly.

"I must have fallen asleep," she said.

"We both did, I think."

"What time is it?"

It's too late for regrets, he thought. Not that he had any. Well, not many. Aloud, though, he said, "Does it matter?"

She soughed another sighing sound and smiled another dreamy smile. "I don't want to get home too late," she told him. "Olive will wonder what happened to me."

"You can call her and tell her you got sidetracked," Ramsey said.

Claire chuckled. "Is that what that was? Sidetracked? I could have sworn it was something else. I've gotten sidetracked before, but it was never like that."

He sobered some as he lifted a hand to her hair, draping a long strand over one finger before pushing it back behind her ear as she had tried to do a moment ago. Wow. That was an even sexier gesture. "It was never like that for me, either," he told her. And he hoped she knew he wasn't talking about being sidetracked when he said it.

"What happens now?" she asked. "Is this the part where we bare our souls to each other? I mean, we've already bared everything else."

"Depends on whether or not you feel like baring your soul to me," he said. And he hoped she didn't detect how very interested he was in her response to the statement.

"Do you feel like baring your soul to me?" she asked.

"Not really."

"Then I think we probably should."

Yeah, he'd been afraid she would say that. "You first," he said.

She looked surprised. "Me? Why me?"

"Because it was your idea."

She opened her mouth to object, but obviously had no idea how to do that—hey, it *was* her idea, after all—so closed it again.

"C'mon, Claire," he cajoled in his best cajoling voice. "I answered your twenty questions the other day."

"I don't think there were actually twenty," she said.

"You're stalling."

"Then ask me a question."

"All right," he said. But he extended the same courtesy to her that she had given him the other day, and started with something easy. "What's your sign?"

She grinned, then sat up a little and wound what she could of the sheet around herself, toga-style. That gesture, too, was sexy as hell. There was just something about a woman in a man's bed, wrapping herself up in the sheets he had been sleeping in, that made him want to keep her there forever. Add to it the fact that she was all sleep-rumpled and sex-tossed, and she became wholly enchanting.

"I'm a Virgo," she said.

"Not anymore, you're not," he quipped.

She smiled. "What else do you want to know?"

Everything, he thought. He wanted to learn every inch of her, inside and out. The outside inches, though, he figured he knew pretty well by now. But the inside ones . . . Well, okay, he knew some of those, too. But not the best ones. Not yet.

"Let's start with the basics," he said. "Are you a Nashville native?"

"Yes," she told him readily enough. "That's one question."

Oh, so she was going to keep tally, was she? Still, twenty questions was an awful lot. Probably. "You said you lost your folks when you weren't much older than Anabel," he continued. "Do you have any other family here?"

"Yes. I think so. That's two questions."

He waited for her to elaborate, should have realized she wouldn't, so repeated, "You *think* so?"

"Well, I assume so," she amended. "I really don't know for sure."

"Why not? Don't you ever see them?" Ramsey had no idea why he was harping so much on the family thing. Probably, it was significant. But he really didn't want to think about how.

"No, I never see them," she said. "Because I don't know any of them. After my parents died, I went to live in a state home. Which, I guess, is a polite word for 'orphanage.' That's where I grew up. They booted me out when I was eighteen, and the rest, as they say, is history." She smiled at Ramsey again, but there was something kind of sad in her expression. "Recorded history, too. You can read all about it in the March 2003 issue of *People* magazine."

To say he was surprised by the revelation that Claire had grown up in a state home would have been a bit of an understatement. He wasn't sure what he *had* thought her upbringing might have been, even after hearing she'd lost her parents so young, but he certainly hadn't thought she would have grown up like that.

"Why didn't you go to live with family members?" he asked.

She shrugged lightly, the action making the sheet dip low over her breasts. Not that he noticed. Not much. Well, okay, maybe a little. But only enough to make him want to topple her onto her back and make love to her again. Before he had the chance to do that, though, she tugged the sheet back up and began to talk, and he thought it would probably be impolite to interrupt her that way.

"At the risk of sounding like a maudlin cliché," she said wearily, "nobody wanted me. Nobody cared."

Ramsey didn't know what to say to that, so he remained silent. There had been nothing mawkish or pitiful in her voice, only a straightforward, matter-of-fact tone. If no one had wanted her or cared about her, Claire had dealt with it just fine. He guessed.

"I'll have to look for some back issues of *People*," was all he said.

And when she smiled this time, there was clearly some gratitude there. Though he suspected that was more because he hadn't insisted on prying any deeper into her background than because he'd expressed an interest in reading about her.

"I just wish I *could* have grown up with a family," she said. "Any family. That would have been nice. Not that the group home was terrible, or anything, but . . . It wasn't like having a family."

"Hey, family's not necessarily a great gig," Ramsey was quick to respond. Too quick, dammit. He really hadn't wanted to say anything more about himself or that time in his life, and he still had a boatload of questions left that he wanted to ask Claire. But that remark, he knew, was going to invite comment from her. Comment that would inescapably turn the conversation back to his own upbringing.

And, inescapably, it did. "Your parents really did a number on you, huh?" she asked.

Hoping he sounded as matter-of-fact about his own upbringing as Claire had about hers, he said, "My parents were cold, unloving, selfish people. And that was when they were sober," he qualified. "Which wasn't often. And when they weren't sober . . ." He let his voice trail off, not just because he didn't want to say any more, but because he figured Claire was smart enough to put two and two together. "Eleanor and I both had to pull our own weight around there and grow up way faster than we should have had to."

"Sounds more like a work camp than a family life," Claire said with remarkable insight.

"Yeah, except without all the great benefits," he said wryly.

"So you wish you'd grown up with a family, too, huh?"

"I did grow up with a family," he said, not quite able to keep the tartness out of the retort.

"That's not family," Claire said. "You all may have shared the same blood and lived in the same house, but that's not what makes a family."

Ramsey wasn't sure what to say in response to that, so he left the past where it belonged and moved back into the present. "My one regret," he said—okay, so maybe he hadn't quite left the past behind—"is that I didn't hang around for Eleanor. Looking back, I realize I shouldn't have left home when I did. I should have stayed close to her, to keep an eye on her. I should have tried to give her the things our parents couldn't. Or wouldn't. I just . . ." He sighed heavily. "At the time, I just didn't think I could. I honestly don't think I had it in me to care for her the way she needed to be cared for."

"You were just a kid when you left, Ramsey," Claire reminded him. "Don't be so hard on yourself."

"I wasn't a kid," he countered, decisively enough, evidently, that she didn't argue with him. "But Eleanor was. And she deserved better than what she got."

"So did you," Claire said softly.

Yeah, he guessed maybe that was true. "Still, she was so little when I left. And if I'd stayed, maybe I could have made things easier for her. Had I known then what I know now, had I learned then what I learned afterward . . ." But he let his voice trail off because he really didn't want to revisit that part of his life, either.

He should have known, though, that Claire would pick up on the omission and run with it.

"And what did you learn afterward?" she said. "What did you discover once you were out there in the big, wide world that you never found at home?"

"Love," Ramsey heard himself say before he could stop himself, before he even realized he intended to say it. And the second the word was out of his mouth, he regretted putting voice to it. Because the look that came over Claire's face when he did . . .

Oh, man . . .

She thought he was talking about her! And she was panicking now, because he'd used the word people were *never* supposed to use after the first time. But it hadn't been Claire he was talking about when he'd used it. It wasn't the here and now he had meant. It was the there and then. And figuring he should make that absolutely, positively clear, because he didn't want to scare Claire off, thinking he'd fallen in love with her—which was preposterous, because love had nothing to do with what had just happened between them, right?—he hurried on, "Her name was Miranda, and I met her in a bar in Raleigh. She was a bartender."

"Oh. And you . . . um . . . you loved her?" Claire asked, her tone of voice revealing nothing of what she might be thinking, though the fact that she stumbled over the word *loved* was enlightening. If only Ramsey could figure out how . . .

"As much as I ever loved anyone," he said. "I just didn't figure it out until it was too late."

He tried to gauge Claire's level of alarm at the way the conversation was going and was relieved to see that she was looking at him in the same way she had been when they first started talking. So he'd obviously been successful in making her realize it wasn't her he'd been talking about when he said he'd found love after leaving home. Clearly, she hadn't assigned any more significance to their afternoon assignation than that it had been a pleasant way to spend some time. Clearly, she wasn't thinking in terms of endearment with him any more than he was thinking in terms of endearment with her.

He exhaled a mental sigh of relief that everything was exactly as it was supposed to be, and nobody loved anybody else. Then he wondered why he didn't really feel relieved about that at all.

Later, he told himself. He could think about all that later. Right now, he owed Claire an explanation.

So he continued, "By the time I met Miranda, I had pretty much fossilized into an unfeeling rock. But she was a really warm, wonderful person, the kind of person who could break through all that, you know?"

"I'm not sure," Claire said, her voice still reflecting nothing of what she might actually be feeling. "I don't think I've ever really known anyone like that."

The hell she hadn't, Ramsey thought. Claire was more like Miranda than she knew. She was even more like Miranda than Miranda had been. He knew that, because she made him feel even more—

Later, he told himself again. He could think about that later. When he didn't feel so exposed and confused.

"So what happened?" Claire asked. "How come you and she didn't . . . Or did you . . . ?"

"What?" Ramsey asked, perplexed.

"Get married?" Claire asked. And even though she'd voiced the two words distinctly, he still somehow got the impression that she'd stumbled over them.

"Married?" he echoed incredulously. "The thought never entered my mind. Or Miranda's mind, for that matter."

"Are you sure?"

"Of course, I'm sure. It never occurred to me."

"What about to her?"

"No, never," he reiterated with all confidence. Because Miranda hadn't been the marrying type any more than he had been. She'd been two tons of fun, had taught Ramsey how to laugh, and how to live, and how to *feel*, but she hadn't wanted a forever-after any more than he had. She'd seen him as a challenge, as a closed fist she needed to open. She'd been a student, too, majoring in social work, after all. And she'd been successful in helping Ramsey fight his way out from behind the walls he'd spent his life erecting. But once he was free, Miranda had liberated him. She'd moved on to something—someone—else. And Ramsey, surprisingly, hadn't really minded that much.

"How do you know she didn't want to marry you?" Claire asked.

He shrugged, his voice now very matter-of-fact, because very matter-of-fact was the way he felt. "She's the one who left, Claire."

"Oh."

And why did that little word sound like it had been wrenched from her so painfully? He studied her face again, and was again left with absolutely no impression of what she might have been feeling. In spite of that, she didn't seem to be feeling particularly good.

"It was a long time ago," he said, thinking that was what she wanted to hear.

"But she was important to you."

Ramsey nodded, not wanting to be dishonest. "She and I were together for a couple of years. A couple of years that were pretty notable for me. Because she was the first person who showed me any measure of real affection," he said. "And she was the first person I was ever able to feel any real affection for in return. If it hadn't been for her, I don't know that I ever would have amounted to anything."

Then he remembered that Claire already thought he hadn't amounted to anything. And maybe, in a way, he hadn't. Not until now. Yeah, after Miranda left, he went on to better things, better things than he would have found had he never met her. But those good things didn't feel nearly as good as the good things he'd found more recently. Miranda might have been the one to knock holes in the walls Ramsey had erected around himself, and she'd been the one to let in the light. She'd paved the way for him to have feelings, to care about other people, and to care about himself, too. Because of her, he hadn't given up on the world. Or himself.

But it was Claire, he was beginning to see, who had really made him feel things. It was Claire who'd made him understand what he really wanted from life. Weirdly, it was because of Miranda that Ramsey was able to have feelings for Claire. But it was Claire for whom he felt—

Later, he told himself. He could think about that later.

"Miranda made it possible for me to learn to care," he told Claire, hoping she would understand just how significant that was. "Had that been a lesson I learned at home, I think I could have been more beneficial to Eleanor. I could have helped her through the rough spots and made her see that what we got from our parents wasn't all that was out there in the big wide world. That there was a better way to live, and better people to live with. Does that make sense?"

Claire's expression softened some, and he saw that she was more comfortable with Eleanor as the subject matter again, instead of Miranda. And really, he thought, when he considered the big picture, Miranda was just a little part of it. And really, so was Eleanor. And even Anabel, to a lesser extent. Because it was Claire who dominated that picture, he realized, more than a little surprised by his awareness of that. And it was Claire who he most wanted to make understand.

Evidently, she didn't quite get that part of it though, because she said, "Eleanor seemed to have done all right, Ramsey. Not that I knew her well, but as I said, she *was* happy. And there aren't a whole lot of people who can claim that. Not really."

"I still should have stayed around for her," he said.

Claire looked thoughtful for a moment, then reached over to cover the hand Ramsey had settled on his chest. Carefully, she wove her fingers with his, and quietly, she said, "That's why you want to raise Anabel, isn't it? Because you think you let Eleanor down, and you want to make it up to her."

He nodded, folding his fingers over hers. "I know I let her down."

"I think you're wrong."

He shook his head slowly, still disagreeing with her, but unwilling to argue. "I just want Anabel to know that there are people in the world who love her," he said. "People who care about what happens to her. I don't want her to go through her life not wanting to look back because everything back there is so bleak and cold, and not wanting to look ahead, because she's afraid everything will stay bleak and cold. I want her to have happy memories to sustain her through the rough times, and I want her to have hope that the future will be good to her. I don't want her to spend her life alone. I want her to be able to form loving relationships with other people. Relationships that last more than a couple of years. Relationships that will last forever."

God, he was babbling, he thought distastefully. How the hell had that happened? But all the things he'd mentioned were things that, until he'd uttered them, he had never really thought about before. And then he realized something else, something that rattled him to his core. He hadn't just been talking about Anabel when he'd said all those things. He'd been talking about himself, too.

"Anabel will know all that," Claire promised him from what sounded like a million miles away. "Regardless of what happens, Ramsey, she'll know."

He wasn't sure he liked that *regardless of what happens* tag on her comment. But he was so befuddled, trying to work so many things out in his head, that he couldn't devote much time to figuring it all out right now. Especially since Claire was looking at him in a way that made him feel even more befuddled, and his heart was pounding in his chest, and his blood was racing through his body at a dizzying pace, and all he wanted was to lose himself the way he had lost himself before, alone with Claire in that cloistered, secret place that they had only just discovered together.

Without questioning any of it, he leaned over and kissed her. Kissed her until all she could do was kiss him back. As he tangled his fingers in her hair and urged her body back down to the bed, he realized that Claire would indeed be getting home late tonight. Judging by the way she melted into him, though, he didn't think she minded too much.

Thirteen

Olive sat beside Davis on the back stoop of his apartment building, gazing at a star and making a wish. She hoped Claire didn't mind that she hadn't been available to watch Anabel tonight. That wasn't what she wished, of course, but she did hope Claire didn't mind. Then again, Claire had gone out a lot more this week than Olive had. And Ramsey Sage had been looking more than a little fatigued on his visits to see Anabel. Not that Olive minded either development. On the contrary, she wondered what had taken the two of them so long.

No, what she was wishing tonight was that Davis would kiss her again. And she was pretty much terrified of what would happen if he did.

He had cooked for her this evening, lasagna and salad that had turned out surprisingly well. He'd apologized for its not being quite up to the standards of Simple Pleasures, especially since he'd had to rely on the store-brand pasta—you know, the stuff that looked like it would still be around after a nuclear holocaust—but Olive hadn't minded. She'd just been touched that he went to any trouble at all for her. Usually she was the one doing things for other people—not that she had ever minded. But she'd had no idea until tonight how pleasant it could be to let someone take care of her instead. And from the moment she'd arrived at Davis's front door, he'd taken care of her. He'd poured her a glass of Chianti, had settled her at the two-seater table in his minuscule kitchen, popped a Three Tenors CD into the player atop his fridge, and gone about making dinner for the two of them.

And all the while, they had talked, through the preparation of dinner, and then dinner itself, and then dessert and coffee, and then the cleanup, which Olive had insisted on helping him with, even when he'd balked. Now, though, they were running out of talk. And she was afraid to think about what that meant, about what happened when people ran out of things to say. She and Davis had come out to the back stoop half an hour ago, and since sitting down—with a respectable six inches between their bodies—they'd scarcely said a word to each other.

Davis, dressed tonight in a Hawaiian shirt spattered with tropical drinks and hula dancers, along with his standard-issue baggy khaki trousers, leaned back against the rough wooden spindles of the stair rail, his body turned to face Olive, just as he had faced her all night, his gaze fixed—she could feel it—intently on her. Olive, though, less bold than he, sat facing the yard, staring up at the sky. She had tugged her pale yellow, sleeveless jumper down over her knees so that the hem reached nearly to her ankles, then had folded her arms over her shins to hug herself tight. She did that because something about the fine, sultry evening made her want to be hugged, but she was too afraid to ask Davis to be the one to do it.

It wasn't that she didn't trust him. It was that she didn't trust herself.

In so many ways, this yard, and this building, were like ones she had known as a child. Yet sitting here with Davis, Olive felt totally different. Before, she had always been afraid to be outside. On those few occasions when she had ventured into the yard, her mother had come running outside to grab her and tug her back into the house. There had been days growing up, honestly, when Olive had scarcely seen the sun. Cathy Tully had always made sure that the curtains were drawn and the shades were down. If someone came to the door, she never answered it, and forbade Olive to. The phone was left to ring and ring and ring. Her mother would only answer if she was expecting someone to call. They never had guests, and Olive was never encouraged to invite her friends home. Not that she'd had any friends to invite home. They never stayed anywhere long enough for her to make any.

Would Davis kiss her again tonight? she wondered. As he had kissed her last weekend when they'd gone out? And what would she do if he did?

"What are you thinking about?"

His voice was quiet as it sliced through the late-evening heat, and when she turned to look at him, she could barely make him out in the darkness. The only light available spilled from a spastic streetlamp half a block down the alley, its eerie bluish light moored in a hazy circle on the pavement below. All Olive could make out of Davis was his mop of tawny curls, silvered now in the moonlight, and the angular planes of his face. His pose was casual, as his question had been, but she couldn't help thinking there was something momentous in the air around them. It was so still, so quiet, in the city tonight. She and Davis might very well be the last two people on earth. Or maybe it wasn't that the city was quiet. Maybe it was just that she had ceased to notice anything but him.

She couldn't very well tell him she'd been thinking about what it would be like to have him kiss her again, so she told him the other thing she'd been thinking about instead. "I was just remembering how we used to live in an apartment building almost just like this when I was a kid. Several apartment buildings like this, actually."

Davis drove his gaze around the backyard, which looked better in the darkness than it had in twilight. Darkness had buffed its rough edges and hidden the clutter. But even though it looked okay from Olive's point of view, she knew it really wasn't okay. Like so many other things, she couldn't help thinking.

"So then you must have lived in some pretty crappy neighborhoods," Davis said when his gaze found her face again.

She nodded, but couldn't help smiling at his light tone. "Yeah. Though some were crappier than others."

"It was always just you and your mom?"

"Pretty much," she said. "I don't remember my father very well. And after he left, my mother was . . . reluctant to remarry."

"Why?"

Because she was terrified of every human being she met, Olive thought. "Because she had . . . trust issues," she said aloud.

"Must be genetic."

Olive snapped her head around to look at him, her back going ramrod straight. How could he have made such a comment? They'd been getting along so well. "Excuse me?" she said tersely.

Even in the darkness, she could tell he was smiling. "I said, 'Must be genetic,'" he repeated, enunciating each word more clearly. "The trust thing, I meant," he elaborated, in case she hadn't understood. And then, as if he didn't mind belaboring the point, he added, "You have trust issues, too."

"No, I don't."

He had the temerity to laugh out loud at that. And when Olive realized what a stupid thing she'd just said, she had no choice but to laugh with him. "Okay, so maybe I have a— tiny—problem with trusting people, too."

"Tiny," he echoed derisively, still smiling. "Yeah, right."

"Okay," she relented. "More than tiny. A little more."

"Colossal," he supplied for her. "What you have, Olive, is a colossal problem with trusting people. But considering the way you grew up," he conceded, "I guess I can see where it comes from."

"You have no idea how I grew up," she said. But her objection sounded halfhearted, even to her own ears.

Nevertheless, it was true. For all the time she and Davis had spent together, they'd never talked about their past experiences. They'd covered music, movies, books, and TV. They'd talked politics, religion, and philosophy. They'd discussed individual hopes and dreams for the future. They'd discovered much in common in just about every area, and enough differences of opinion to make conversation interesting. But neither had mentioned the past in anything but very vague terms.

Until now.

"I know better than you think how you grew up, Olive," Davis said. "And as bad as it was, believe me, it could have been worse. A helluva lot worse."

That, too, put Olive's back up, and she snapped, "Oh, what do you know about it?"

"I know you and your mom ran scared for most of your life," he said without a trace of pity to color the words. "And I know why. Maybe not the particulars, but I know you were in a government-run program designed to protect people from other people who are dangerous. Deny it all you want," he said when she opened her mouth to do just that, "but I know something happened when you were a kid that made your family have to go into hiding. New names, new jobs, new school, new social security numbers, new everything. And as scary as that would be for an adult, I'm sure it was terrifying for a little kid."

Olive didn't say anything at first, mostly because she didn't know what to say. She could barely remember a time in her life when she hadn't been Olive Tully, and when she hadn't been running scared. But there were memories, a handful of them, that had never left her. Memories of a tidy brick bungalow in Newark, New Jersey, and a father who went to work every day wearing a hard hat, and a mother who baked the absolute best chocolate chip cookies in the neighborhood, good enough that all the kids liked coming to Olive's house most of all. But her name hadn't been Olive then. It had been—

"Melanie," she said aloud. "Melanie Tolliver."

When Davis said nothing in response to her cryptic offering, she turned to look at him again, and found him gazing at her with much interest. But his smile was gone, and his eyes were intent, and she knew he was just waiting for her to say more. So, feeling helpless not to do so, she continued. "That used to be my name. Melanie Tolliver. My mother was Cynthia Tolliver. Before she married my dad, she was a nurse in the U.S. Navy. I didn't lie to you about that," she added, wanting him to know that she had tried to be as honest as she could. "But by the time I was born, she was a homemaker. And then she was my mother. My father was Raymond Tolliver. He was a construction worker."

"Sounds like the Tollivers were the picture of middle-class America," Davis said quietly.

"We were," Olive told him. "For a time."

"So what happened?"

She shook her head. "To this day, I don't know all the details. My mother never told me, even when I was old enough to understand. I think, somehow, she thought I was better off not knowing. But really, *not* knowing has always been a lot scarier."

"What *do* you know?" Davis asked.

"Just that my father overheard something at work one day that made him think he was working for a crooked outfit. He told my mother he was going to look for another job, but before he found one, he . . ." She hesitated, honestly unclear about what exactly had happened, because her mother had never mentioned specific details. "Evidently," she tried again, "one night when he stayed late at work, he saw his boss get . . . killed." She looked at Davis again. "Murdered. It was a professional hit, and he knew one of the guys who did it, from his union."

"And then he did what any good middle-class American dad would do," Davis surmised. "He told the cops what he'd seen."

Olive nodded. "I remember one day really well. I always have. And when I finally asked my mother about it, when I was in high school, she told me that the day before he testified at the trial was the day the marshals came to our house to get us. After they escorted us out, we never went back. I remember not understanding what was going on. My mom packed one suitcase each for us, and that was all we could take. I remember I wanted to take some more of my toys, and they wouldn't let me. And I remember riding in the back of a car, my mom and me squeezed between two men I'd never seen before. I remember staying in a motel in . . ." She shook her head. "I don't remember where it was. On the coast. Ocean City, maybe? We vacationed there once."

"So how did you end up in Mississippi?"

Olive would ask him later how he found out about where she had ended up, but for now, she replied, "Originally, they settled us in Ohio. In Cleveland. But a few months after we got there, my dad really did go to the store one day, and he really did never come back. My mom always told me he left us to go live with a girlfriend. But I think she was lying about that to keep me from getting scared. I think she really thought he was . . ." She swallowed with some difficulty, not wanting to even think about it. "We never heard from him again, and he didn't take anything with him. If he were leaving us for another woman, don't you think he would have at least taken something with him? Some clothes? His car? And don't you think he would have at least called us at some point, to let us know he was okay?"

"I'd think so, yeah."

"But he didn't do any of those things," Olive said, fear thickening in her throat, even more than two decades and a thousand miles after the fact. "So I guess she could have been right. I guess it's possible that he was . . ."

"Murdered?" Davis supplied helpfully. Kind of.

Olive nodded. "My mom just freaked when he didn't

come back. I think she thought we were next. Hey, if they'd found him, they could find us, too. And if they'd . . . killed him, they'd kill us, too. So she packed a couple of bags for us again, and we took off."

"You left the program?" Davis asked incredulously.

"My mother didn't trust it to keep us safe," Olive said. "Not if they couldn't keep my father safe. And we had to keep moving around because every time we found a new place, something would happen to spook my mom and make her think they found us. She'd see someone who looked familiar, or she'd think she was followed home from work one night. Once, it was because she answered the phone and it was a wrong number. It took nothing to scare her into moving again."

"So you spent the next, what . . . ten years? Fifteen? . . . running. Hiding. Never trusting anyone."

"Until Claire," Olive said. "Not that that happened overnight. It took a long time for me to feel comfortable enough to confide in her. And even then, I never told her about my past. I've never told her what I just told you." Very quietly, she added, "So I guess . . . I guess I must trust you, too, Davis. What's weird is that it didn't take me a long time to do it."

For a moment, he said nothing, and she wished she could tell what he was thinking. Finally, though, "And why is that?" he asked.

She shook her head, wishing she could give him an answer that made sense. But the only one she had was, "I don't know. There's just something about you. Something protective. You're like a guardian, like a . . . a . . . a champion. I know that sounds silly," she hurried on when she saw the way his entire body seemed to go slack with disbelief, "but you just . . . I mean, look at what you do for a living. You're a defender of children. Children you've never even met before. You make sure they don't get hurt. You take care of them. That's such an honorable, decent thing to do. How could I not trust someone like you?"

Again, her response from him was silence, and it went on long enough that Olive began to wonder if he even understood what she was trying to tell him. But then, she wasn't sure she understood, either. Still, she'd told him flat out that she considered him to be an honorable, decent person. And how hard could it be to comprehend compassion?

When Davis finally replied, it was in a voice she'd never heard from him before, one that spewed words rather than saying them.

"Honorable," he spat. "Decent," he hissed.

Olive nodded nervously, but all she managed in reply was, "Yeah."

"A *defender* of children," he mimicked in an acid tone.

She recoiled at the bitterness in his tone. He sounded so angry all of a sudden, so harsh. What had she said to cause such a change in him? Why was he so furious?

"What's wrong?" she asked tentatively. "What did I say?"

Davis gazed at Olive through the darkness, battling feelings he hadn't allowed himself to acknowledge for years. He didn't mean to attack her. She wasn't responsible for what was going on inside him. But what she'd said about him just now had only hammered home how very much he *wasn't* those things. On the contrary, he was the most *dis*honorable, most *in*decent human being he knew. Defender of children? Hah. No one had let children down more than he had. He, who was allegedly in the best situation to help them.

Oh, he hadn't always been that way. Fresh out of college,

with two newly minted degrees in social work, he'd been confident he could change the world—or at the very least, the state child welfare system—single-handedly. Confident, nothing. He'd been cocky as hell.

God, that felt like it was so long ago. A lifetime ago. Since then, he'd seen so many things that had defeated and demoralized him. Nobody could change the world single-handedly. Hell, nobody could change the state child welfare system. Not unless they were able to complete an overhaul of human nature. Not unless they were able to wipe out the blackness that lurked in every person's soul.

He wished he could find the words to tell Olive all the things he'd seen in his line of work, the ways people—for lack of a better word—were capable of behaving. But adequate words didn't exist for much of what he'd witnessed. Because he'd witnessed the absolute underbelly of civilization, and the ugly, putrid flesh that grew there. He'd seen people who felt not a single qualm about hurting the most innocent of creatures. He'd seen what adults could do to children. Often their own children. And there simply were no words in his vocabulary that could describe the way that made him feel.

So all he could say to Olive was, "I'm not honorable. And I'm not decent, either. And when it comes to protecting children, Olive, I suck."

She gaped at him. "How can you say that? You're wonderful with Anabel. That first day I saw you with her, I couldn't believe how gentle you were with her, and how you seemed so intent on keeping her safe until you knew for sure that Claire was going to be okay with her. You can't tell me Anabel's an exception."

"Actually, she is," he said. He grumbled restlessly as he thrust a hand through his hair. "Because she ended up in a pretty good place. You can't imagine how rarely that happens to the children I see. It's even rarer for it to happen with their mothers, with whom I *really* suck in the protection thing."

And, *dammit*, why had he said that? he wondered the moment the words were out of his mouth. Probably because it was something Olive needed to know about him. She was talking like she was about to entrust herself to him—hell, she'd already entrusted herself to him—and she needed to know he wasn't worthy of that. She had turned her body to face him at some point—probably when she was telling him she trusted him—and now he had her complete attention. Oh, sure, *now* he did. Now that he was about to tell her what a fraud and a phony he was.

"What are you talking about?" she asked uncertainly.

He sighed roughly. "I'm talking about how you shouldn't put too much faith in me," he told her. "Because I haven't earned it, and I sure as hell don't deserve it."

"Of course you—"

"There was a woman once," he interrupted her. "A woman who had a son. She also had a husband. They were a family, such as it was. A family I had been assigned to work with after a teacher reported seeing some suspicious bruises on the boy. Turned out the father was mean as hell, and the boy and his mother were both scared to death of him.

"I liked that kid a lot, Olive," Davis told her. "More than any other kid I ever met. And by then, I'd met a lot of them. But," he confessed, "I liked his mother even more."

"You fell in love with her," Olive guessed.

Davis shook his head. "I don't know. I'm not sure if it was love. But I did care for her when I shouldn't have. She was married and in trouble, and I was the case worker assigned to her case. Her husband was a very prominent person in

Nashville—and no, I won't name names," he told her. "But they lived in a big, beautiful house, with a big, beautiful garden out back that she absolutely loved. We spent a lot of hours there, talking. That's all it ever was, though, talking. Still, it was wrong—not to mention crazy—for me to feel anything for her at all."

"It was human of you, Davis," Olive said.

"It was wrong," he repeated.

"So what happened?"

There wasn't a single thing in Olive's voice to make Davis think she felt anything other than genuinely interested in where he was going with this story. No injury, no judgment, no abhorrence, nothing. Whatever she was feeling, she kept it to herself. Or else she was waiting to feel anything until she heard what he had to say. Damn. It would be just like her to be fair.

"What happened was a very long story," he said. "But the way it ended was that I went to check on them one night, on my way home from work. It wasn't a scheduled stop—I wasn't supposed to meet with them until the following week. But I just wanted to be sure they were okay. And all right, maybe I wanted to see her, too. Nothing happened," he assured Olive again. "Nothing ever happened. But her husband came home while I was there, and . . ."

"And he blew up," Olive guessed when he didn't elaborate.

"Just the opposite, actually," Davis told her. "He was frighteningly calm about the discovery."

"Well, you said nothing happened."

"No, but I think he knew how I felt about his wife. And I think she knew it, too."

"So if he didn't blow up," Olive spurred him to continue, "then that was good, right?"

Davis shook his head again, slowly this time, not wanting to remember that night, or the days that followed it. "I didn't think it was good. And I didn't want to leave," he said. "Not without her and her son. I asked her to come with me. She assured me everything would be fine and escorted me to the front door. I had no choice but to leave. But I hung around outside the front of their house for almost an hour, waiting to see if he started yelling, or if he tried to hurt her. They did argue, but things seemed to quiet down after a while. Then cops patrolling the neighborhood saw me hanging around and told me I had to go. I apprised them of the situation, and they assured me they'd keep an eye on things. I thought she'd be okay, and I promised myself I'd check on her the next day, on my way home from work again."

"And did you?"

"I did," he said. "I went by her house, and I rang the bell, and she opened the door, and . . ." He bit back a vicious oath when he remembered how she had looked that night. "He'd beat her up real bad, Olive. And her son, too, when he tried to intervene. Christ, the kid was only seven years old. I did make her leave that night, before her husband came home, her and her son both. And I got them into a shelter, and I kept tabs and pulled some strings to make sure they didn't have to go back to the guy. Last I heard, she'd divorced him and was living in Florida. But I never saw either of them again. I couldn't. I'd let them both down. I hadn't been there when they needed me. I wasn't able to protect them."

"You did what you could, Davis."

"I didn't do enough."

"What else could you have done? Picked her up and thrown her over your shoulder, then thrown her son over your other shoulder, and forced them both to leave?"

"If that was what it took, yeah."

"Do you realize how ridiculous that sounds?"

"The point is, Olive, I didn't protect *them*."

"No, the point is, Davis, you *couldn't* protect them. And there will doubtless be a lot of others you won't be able to protect, either. But you know what?" she asked.

He didn't respond. Couldn't. Wouldn't. Didn't want to.

That didn't deter Olive. "There have been others that you *did* protect. Others who are in better places because of you."

"Name one."

He figured she'd say Anabel. But she surprised him by saying, "Me." And then she said, "And Anabel. There, I named two. And hey, you're still young. You've got a lot of years in you. Who's to say there won't be more? And how do you know there haven't been others? Have you checked up on every case you ever had?"

"Of course not. I barely have time to keep up with the ones that are current."

"So how do you know there aren't more people out there who are in better places now than they were before you entered their lives? And even if there's not, Davis, you've changed two lives, just in the past month. For the better. How many people can say that?"

"Don't try to make me feel better," he said.

"Why not?" she asked.

But for the life of him, he had no idea how to reply.

And when he didn't, Olive ventured a very small smile. "You know," she said, "it sounds to me like you and I both have what's known in novels as 'a lot of emotional baggage.'"

Davis muttered a quiet sound of vaguely amused consent. "Yeah. Sounds like." Then he, too, smiled a little. "It's kinda bulky and unmanageable, huh?"

She nodded. "Seems like every time I turn around, I trip over it."

"Yeah."

"But hey," she added, "I'll help you haul around yours if you'll help me haul around mine."

"I have a better idea," he said. "Maybe we can look for a locker somewhere to stow it for a while."

Olive chuckled at that. "And maybe, someday, we can lose the key to the locker. Or better yet, forget where the locker is."

This time Davis nodded. Halfheartedly, but at least he agreed. "Might take a while," he told her.

"Yeah, it might," she concurred. "But if there's two of us traveling together, maybe we can leave a little bit behind every time we stop someplace, and eventually we won't have so much to cart around."

Davis scooted over a little on the stoop, until he'd cut the distance between them in half. "And then what we did have left," he said, "we could maybe pack it together into one bag. Then it'd be easier to stow."

Olive scooted over a little on the stoop, too, until her hip and thigh were flush against his. Then she smiled. "It'd be easier to leave behind somewhere, too."

Davis smiled back, and for the first time that he could remember, the gesture didn't feel sarcastic or forced. He wasn't sure if he'd helped put Olive in a better place. But she sure as hell had put him in one. "So . . . whattaya say?" he asked. "You wanna hop the next train together? See where it takes us?"

Olive nodded. "I'd like that a lot," she said. " 'Cause you know, Davis, I'm really getting tired of traveling alone."

Fourteen

*I*f summer vacations were essays, Claire's that year would have been titled "Dog Days and Love Muffins." Because the long, languid days of August were drawing to a close the week following her afternoon idyll with Ramsey on his boat, and she spent nearly every one of them with him. And each of those days was better than the one that preceded it. More enriching. More enchanting. More exhilarating. More exhausting.

But it was a good kind of exhaustion, the kind that came with knowing you were living life as fully as it could be lived, packing the days, and making every minute count. Okay, okay, so it was actually the kind of exhaustion that came with making love *a lot*. But she defied anyone to come up with one thing that made a minute count more than being with someone you loved in the most intimate way there was to be together.

Because she realized that week that, at some point, she had fallen in love with Ramsey. She couldn't identify the exact moment it had happened, though it could have been as he was licking whipped cream off of her fingertip—oh, please, at the ice-cream parlor, where else?—or it might have been when he smiled at her from his side of the bed when they'd slept late one morning. Or maybe it had been while he was pushing Anabel in a swing at the park, the soft summer breeze lifting his dark hair from his forehead, the crisp azure sky behind him making his eyes seem even greener somehow. It might have even been the first day she opened her front door to him, when she first caught a glimpse of him looking like a refugee intent on finding a better life.

Or maybe it had been a moment just like this one, she thought as she watched him sip his postdinner coffee at her kitchen table. A moment that was utterly normal and unremarkable, save the fact that she was in love with him. A streak of something purplish smudged the collar of his blue chambray work shirt—strained beets, if Claire wasn't mistaken, being more than a little familiar with the color herself—and a smear of dark brown—prunes, to be sure—tinted the corner of his shirt pocket. A spray of squash was stuck to one cheek, and a clump of something sort of greenish hung limply from his hair. And still she considered him the most handsome man alive.

Dinner with Anabel, she thought as she reached over to flick away both the squash and greenish clump, was like an aviation show: full of color and noise and spectacle, and things flying through the air in every direction.

Ramsey lifted his hand to where Claire had placed hers, doing his best to tidy himself without being able to see what he was doing. "What? Did Anabel nail me again?" he asked, smiling.

"Only six or seven times," Claire replied, unable to help her own grin. "Gee, her aim is improving."

Ramsey laughed. "I just hope she gets as much *in* herself as she gets *on* us."

And Claire just hoped the little tike wore herself out in the garden, where she had retreated with their dinner guests: Olive and—would wonders never cease?—Olive's new beau, Davis Webster. It would be nice if the little darling went to sleep at a decent hour tonight. Decent being anything before 1 A.M. Because Claire had other things she needed to see to tonight. Like Ramsey, for instance. Because it wasn't just the days they were living to their fullest.

Just thinking about the evening ahead made her want to touch him, so she pushed her hand across the table to cup it over his. But he anticipated her and turned his own hand upside down before she got there, so that their palms lay against each other and he could curl his fingers between hers, effectively lacing their hands together.

Claire wouldn't have minded if time just stopped right there. Because when all was said and done, it was simply being close to Ramsey, touching him, gazing at him, talking to him, being with him, that really brought her the most pleasure. How had she managed this long without him? she wondered. How could she have thought her life was full and rewarding? Because now she understood what it truly was that made life complete. It wasn't the high-profile job or the big house she'd re-created, or the projects that filled her weekends. It was just being with someone you cared for—lots of someones you cared for—and knowing they cared for you, too. Claire could live without her job, or her house, or all the things that went into Simple Pleasures. But she couldn't live without her loved ones. What was weird was that, a few months ago, her loved ones would have numbered only one—Olive. Now, though, she had Anabel and Ramsey, too. She'd even found a pet, of sorts, in Francesca. It seemed like such a cliché to say it, but . . .

Life is good, she thought. And simple pleasures really were the best.

She was opening her mouth to tell Ramsey that—that and so much more—but was halted when Chandler came striding into the kitchen with a big, fat file folder tucked under one arm. He had been there for dinner, too, but a courier had arrived just as they were all sitting down, with a package Chandler said he'd been expecting, so he had excused himself to see to whatever it was. Since Claire and Olive were gearing up for some new plans to expand Simple Pleasures, Inc. yet again, Chandler had been at the house frequently this week, often conducting business from Claire's office. She assumed that was where he had been for the last half hour or so, but he'd obviously concluded his business, whatever it was. And it must have gone really, really well, because he was smiling the kind of smile he only used when huge sums of cash were involved.

Hmm, Claire thought. She hadn't been expecting any significant financial windfalls. But she couldn't think of anything else that might have made Chandler that happy.

"Claire, darling," he said, his voice dripping with sweetness.

Wow, she thought, that was the voice he only used when there were seven figures involved. This must be really good. Whatever it was. She and Ramsey both turned to face the attorney, but where Claire arched her brows with light inquiry, Ramsey, she noted, scowled darkly.

"Can I talk to you?" Chandler asked.

"Of course," she said.

"Alone," Chandler told her.

Claire and Ramsey exchanged looks, hers confused, his wary. Then she turned back to Chandler. "Ramsey can hear anything you have to tell me."

"Oh, he'll definitely be hearing about this," Chandler assured her. "But I think it's something you'll want to hear first."

"What are you talking about?" Claire asked, confused. "If he'll be hearing about it anyway, then just tell me what it is."

Chandler's grin grew even broader at that, and somehow she knew he'd been hoping she would reply the way she had, because in spite of what he'd just said, he really did want to talk to her in Ramsey's presence. And knowing what Claire did of Chandler's feelings for Ramsey—he loathed him—that could only be because he wanted to talk about something that would make Ramsey uncomfortable in some way. She started to rise and tell Chandler fine, they could talk in the parlor, when he whipped the file folder out from under his arm and opened it.

"Ah, well, if you insist," he said agreeably. "What I have to tell you actually does have something to do with Mr. Sage. In fact, it's entirely about Mr. Sage. More to the point, it's about one of Mr. Sage's possessions."

The car, Claire thought. Oh, God, he really did steal it. Then she gave herself a good, mental shake. He didn't steal the car, she reminded herself. Or the boat. Or anything else. He wasn't a thief, for goodness sake. He was the man she loved.

"One of my possessions?" Ramsey echoed, clearly as bewildered by this turn of events as Claire was.

Chandler nodded. "Yes, one of your possessions," he reiterated. "Your criminal record to be precise."

Claire spared a quick glance at Ramsey before returning

her attention to Chandler, certain she must have misunderstood what the latter had just revealed about the former. "I beg your pardon?" she said. "Ramsey's what? His what kind of record?"

She wasn't sure what bothered her more—the fact that what Chandler had just revealed about Ramsey having a criminal record might be true, or the fact that Chandler was smiling so damned cheerfully about his revelation.

And his smile broadened even more as he began, "I said your Mr. Sage—"

"He's not my Mr. Sage," Claire interjected automatically, before she could stop herself. Because she knew that was true. Despite her growing feelings for him, she knew he didn't belong to her and probably never would. It was nothing personal, she was certain. He would never belong to anyone. He couldn't. It wasn't in his nature. The man had bought a sailboat to live on—how rootless was that? No way would he ever allow anyone to have any kind of ownership of him. Not that Claire wanted to own him. But she wouldn't have minded if he wanted to give himself to her in some ways. In ways other than the sexual, she meant. But she knew he wouldn't do that, either. Oh, sure, he'd opened up to her over the past several weeks. But he'd never spoken in terms of a future with her. And he'd gone out of his way, with his story of the late, lamented Miranda, to make clear she had been the only woman he'd ever loved.

He'd never be hers, she told herself again. Mostly because she figured she needed reminding of that. And no amount of wanting him would change that.

She wouldn't have thought Chandler could look any happier than he already did, but her hastily offered objection about Ramsey not belonging to her made him positively beam. "Well, then," he said. "If that's the case, it won't be as difficult for you to hear all this, will it?"

"Hear what?"

The question came not from Claire this time, but from Ramsey, who had also stood and turned to face Chandler. He moved out from behind the table to circumvent it, stopping only when he stood clear of all furnishings. Claire couldn't help thinking it was because he didn't want anything standing between him and Chandler when he attacked. But he only hooked his hands loosely on his denim-clad hips and gazed at the attorney expectantly, his thunderous expression at odds with Chandler's beatific one.

Something inside Claire urged her to mover closer to him, because now he stood on the other side of the kitchen from her. Something told her to reach out to him, to pull him close and hold him there, to protect him from what was to come, whatever it was. But something else just as powerful made her hesitate. The last thing a man like Ramsey needed was protecting. So all she could do was stand between him and Chandler, and wonder which of them was really more of a threat.

"Come on, Edison," Ramsey jeered when the attorney wasn't forthcoming with information. "What've ya got?"

But Chandler didn't rise to the bait. Very calmly, he replied, "What I've got, Mr. Sage, is a copy of your arrest record. It appears that you've been convicted on a number of drug-related charges."

"*What?*" This time the exclamation did come from Claire.

But Chandler ignored her outburst. "And what I've also got," he continued gleefully, "are reports that you've done time in federal prisons for possession and trafficking in narcotics. And that you're suspected of smuggling illegal substances into the United States, though, alas, they've not been able to prove any of that. Yet." His smile fell some, and he almost pouted as he added, "Unfortunately, they couldn't make those murder charges stick, either."

"Murder charg*es*?" Claire repeated with a gasp. "As in, more than one?" As if one murder charge wouldn't have been shocking enough. As if all those other charges hadn't been shocking enough. Something cold and slick and nasty slithered through her belly, and she turned to look at Ramsey pleadingly. "Is it true?" she asked, telling herself it couldn't possibly be. Chandler was making some sick joke, making it all up because he was resentful of how Claire had fallen in lo— Because he was resentful of how much Claire liked Ramsey, she hastily amended. So Chandler was trying every lame trick he could think up to make her reconsider her feelings. Ramsey couldn't possibly have been guilty of any of those things.

But his expression had gone hard and icy as Chandler had spoken, and his eyes, the eyes she'd always thought so dazzling and enchanting, were as flinty and as cruel as a gravestone. Suddenly, he did indeed look like a man who could commit murder. Especially if his intended victim was Chandler.

"Ramsey?" she said, her voice sounding weak, even to her own ears. "It *isn't* true, is it?"

"Of course it's true," Chandler said, flipping open the thick file. "I have all the documentation right here."

He strode over to the kitchen table, putting it between himself and Ramsey, Claire couldn't help noting, then fanned some pages across the surface. But she wasn't looking at them—couldn't look at them. She could only gaze in silence at Ramsey, who also stood silent, staring back at her. And when he offered not a single word in his defense, not one little shred of testimony that might exonerate him and prove Chandler a liar, something inside Claire went numb.

"Here we go," Chandler said happily, selecting one sheet of paper to hold it up in front of Claire's face, effectively blocking Ramsey from her view. "This first charge came almost twenty years ago, just after his eighteenth birthday, and was for trafficking in marijuana. In our nation's capital, no less. And shame on you, Mr. Sage," he added haughtily, "sullying the very cradle of our American way of life that way." Chandler's next words, though, were again intended for Claire. "He only served a year at Lorton for that—God knows why they let him off so lightly—but it wasn't long before . . ." He jerked down the first piece of paper and held up a second in its place, "he was arrested again. This time for possession with intent to sell. Back to Lorton for another year. And then back out again and quickly arrested again," he said, displaying a third sheet of paper, "for trafficking in cocaine. Near a school yard in Arlington.

"There are several other charges like that," he went on, sorting through the pages he held in one hand, "Mr. Sage was in and out of prison for the next twelve years. But this," he continued, holding up a fourth piece of paper, "is the really good one. Five years ago, Mr. Sage apparently killed a man. Granted, the man was a filthy drug dealer just like Mr. Sage, but it's still against the law to take a life, even a lowlife. Unfortunately, they didn't have enough evidence to convict on that one. Or for the woman he killed a year and a half later," Chandler continued deliciously. "She *wasn't* a filthy drug dealer like him, however, but a good, decent, law-abiding woman who was trying to rid her urban neighborhood of filthy drug dealers like him. Claire, you're fortunate to have escaped with your life."

Chandler had held up yet another sheet of paper for her inspection as he mentioned that last charge against Ramsey, but the writing on this one, she noted, was blurry, and she couldn't quite make out what it said. Then she realized it wasn't that the writing on the paper was blurry, making it illegible. It was that she was trying to read it through a sheen of tears.

Oh, Ramsey . . .

Without even realizing she was doing it, she took the sheet of paper from Chandler's grasp with one hand, swiped at her eyes with the other, and quickly scanned the information written there. It wasn't an official document, but appeared to be a brief narrative prepared for Chandler by a private investigator. She recognized the name Gordon Stantler at the bottom and remembered he was the same man Chandler had hired to find Ramsey in the first place. As Claire read over the account, Chandler pressed the other pages prepared by the investigator into her free hand, and she, without wanting to, but knowing she must, reluctantly perused them all.

As she read, she waited for some kind of objection from Ramsey, some kind of outcry or outrage or outpouring of excuses. But he uttered not one word of explanation or defense. She wasn't sure if that was good or bad, so she decided not to think about it, and instead continued to read, and prayed that she would soon wake up from what was, without question, the worst nightmare she had ever had.

If what the PI said in his report was true—and he had backed up every assertion with references to documents and depositions and affidavits that she was certain Chandler also had in his possession—then Ramsey did indeed have a long, and brutal, criminal record. But how? she wondered. How could that possibly be? He was so sweet. So kind. So gentle. So attentive. He had always been so wonderful with Anabel. And he had been so tender with Claire. He couldn't have faked any of that.

But then, from all accounts, Ted Bundy had been charming, too . . .

No, Claire immediately countered herself. No way was Ramsey Sage anything like Ted Bundy. But how could she contradict the evidence in front of her face? Unless Chandler really had made it all up, which she wouldn't put past him. Maybe he didn't really have any documents or depositions or affidavits in his possession. Maybe he was just bluff—

"I have copies of all the documents, depositions, and affidavits in the folder," Chandler said as he withdrew another collection of papers and handed them to Claire. Again not wanting to, but again knowing she must, she thumbed quickly through them, and saw that they contained photocopies of exactly what Chandler had said, along with copies of arrest records and detectives' notes and mug shots of Ramsey. In each and every one of those photos, he looked dirty and dangerous, menacing and mean. He looked nothing like the Ramsey Sage she had come to know and lo— Nothing like the Ramsey Sage she had come to like very much. The man in those photos was a total stranger to her. Or maybe, she thought, looking up at him again, it was the man standing in her kitchen who was the total stranger.

Oh, Ramsey . . .

"This is why you bought the boat, isn't it?" she said as understanding began to dawn. Dawn like a two-by-four upside the head, granted, but dawn nonetheless. "So you'll be able to move around freely. So you'll be able to escape at a moment's notice without leaving anything behind. So you can just pack up Anabel and go wherever the authorities aren't looking for you, and just disappear without a—"

Oh, God, *Anabel*. Claire's assumptions halted there, unable to move any further. If she turned over custody of Anabel to Ramsey, she might never see the girl again. Ramsey would have a boat, a means of taking off whenever he needed or wanted to, not to mention the kind of past that made a man hesitant to stay in one place for very long. He really would take Anabel and disappear without a trace. She really would never see her again. And when she realized that, she also began to understand how very much Anabel had come to mean to her.

"That's not why I bought the boat," Ramsey said, his voice slicing through the tension that had erupted between them.

"Then why did you buy it?" she demanded.

He blew out an exasperated sound, but his demeanor gentled some. "I bought it because I liked it," he said earnestly. "Because I needed a place to live, but the thought of putting down roots literally by buying a house scared the hell out of me. But that doesn't mean I won't stay in one place," he added when she opened her mouth to comment. "When I saw the boat for sale at the marina, it was like a little light went on in my head. It seemed like the perfect compromise to owning a home, so I bought it to take back to North Carolina. I figured Anabel and I could live on it until it's time for her to go to school, and by then I'd be ready to start looking for a house. But that's all there was to it, Claire, I swear."

She shook her head slowly, but she wasn't sure if she was

doing it to express her disbelief in what he was saying, or her disbelief that this whole episode was even happening.

"Claire, what Edison is telling you, what he's trying to make you believe . . . It's not what you're thinking," Ramsey said more softly, in the same gentle voice he had always spoken in whenever they were lying side by side in bed, stroking each other's naked bodies, luxuriating in each other's heat, listening to the contented beating of each other's heart.

Of course it wasn't what she was thinking, she thought. It couldn't possibly be *that* bad. Still, it was pretty terrible. So terrible that Ramsey's voice seemed to be coming to her now from a million miles away. And he seemed physically to be farther away even than that.

"No, I don't suppose it is what I'm thinking," she said.

His expression turned puzzled. "Then what *are* you thinking?"

She was thinking too many things ever to be able to articulate them in any way that made verbal sense, she knew. Not when she couldn't even make psychological or emotional sense of them. So she only said the one thing of which she was absolutely certain. "There's no way Anabel can live with you. She'll stay with me. I'll raise her myself."

And only when she said it out loud that way did Claire realize how steadfast she was in her convictions. She would raise Anabel. She *could* raise her. The last several weeks might not have been the most harmonic, but in many ways, they'd been extremely rewarding. She'd grown attached to little Anabel, in spite of her chaotic ways. No, more than attached. She felt a deep and abiding affection for the little girl. No, more than affection, she realized then. In many ways, she'd grown to love her new charge. Oh, she knew she had a long way to go in the parenting department, but then, even biological parents didn't learn their trade overnight, did they? She'd read enough issues of *Parents* and *Parenting* magazines in recent weeks to understand that no matter when or how one became a parent, one had no idea what one was getting oneself into until it was too late. And she'd learned, too, that no matter how chaotic and challenging the child, parents grew to love them unconditionally.

It wasn't too late for Claire and Anabel. Even if it was too late for Claire and Anabel's uncle. And strangely, when she realized how much she wanted to keep her newly inherited charge, a swell of contentment radiated through her. All she could do now was hope that someday, that contentment might somehow begin to fill and warm all the cold, empty places Ramsey's betrayal would leave behind.

"No, Claire, wait," he pleaded now. "Don't say that about keeping Anabel with you. I can explain."

Oh, sure, *now* he could explain. Now that he'd had a chance to think about what he should say. Now that he'd had time to come up with all sorts of sweet words that would sway Claire around to his way of thinking. Several precious minutes had ticked by as she'd read over Gordon Stantler's reports, certainly enough time for Ramsey to contrive all kinds of reasons for why he'd been charged with so many crimes. He would say he was innocent, she was sure. That it was a case of mistaken identity, perhaps. Or maybe he'd been framed. Whatever excuse he came up with, it was sure to be convincing, even if it wasn't true.

That was probably why he'd always been able to be so charming, she thought now. Because he'd always had time to prepare before their meetings and come up with just the right things to say. But try as she might, Claire couldn't make herself believe that, either. Nobody could fake the sort of sincerity that had come from Ramsey. But how could he have been sincerely sweet on one day and a cold-hearted criminal on another? Maybe he had an evil doppelgänger somewhere . . .

Oh, stop it, Claire, she told herself. *You're embarrassing yourself, truly you are.*

She simply had to accept the fact that she'd been hoodwinked by someone who had made it his life's work to con and cheat and hurt people. Chandler was right. She really should count herself lucky to have gotten away with nothing more than a broken heart. And, gosh, that shouldn't take very long to heal, should it? No more than a lifetime or two, surely. And when one considered the age of the universe, a lifetime was barely a blip on the screen. It was all relative.

"I don't doubt you can explain," she conceded. "Unfortunately, I do doubt that your explanation would be in any way truthful."

"Claire . . ."

"I think you should go," she told him, proud of the fact that her voice was level and her eyes were dry when she offered the observation. Then she wondered if maybe he was currently wanted by the police for something, and if she should call them to tell them he was here. It really hit her then, just how very little she still knew about him. She had made love with him, but she barely knew who he was at all.

But how could that be? she asked herself. Because, in so many ways, she felt like she knew Ramsey better than she knew herself.

"Claire, I—" he tried again.

"Ramsey, I—" she intercepted him.

But he persevered. "Claire, I'm a cop."

Since he interrupted her midsentence, she hadn't yet closed her mouth, and hearing his rushed words did nothing to change that. She gaped at him in confusion for a moment, then, very softly, "You're what?" she said. "You're a what?"

"I'm a cop," he reiterated more forcefully.

"But you can't be a policeman," Chandler interjected, sounding every bit as confused as Claire. "You killed people. You dealt drugs. Even in this day and age, even in Washington, DC, I'm sure the constabulary frown on that sort of thing."

Ramsey continued to gaze at Claire, even though he was obviously replying to the attorney, when he said, "Are you bad-mouthing the cradle of our American way of life, Edison? Because if you are, then shame on you."

"But—" Chandler began.

Thankfully, he said nothing more after that. Which was good, because Claire suddenly had plenty to say.

"If you're a cop, then why didn't you just tell me that the first time I asked you what you do for a living?" she demanded. "It's completely respectable work."

"Not the work I do," he told her.

She narrowed her eyes at him. "What do you mean?"

Instead of answering her second question, he backpedaled to the first. "I didn't tell you I was a cop because the work I do is covert, and I've been undercover for a long time. Just talking about it, even to you, could compromise an operation that is years old and still ongoing. And I couldn't let it be compromised."

"You're talking about it now," she pointed out. "Isn't that going to compromise it?"

"Yeah, it is," he agreed ruefully, braving a few steps in her direction, enough to put him within touching distance. But he didn't touch her. And she couldn't quite bring herself to touch him, either. Not just yet. "In fact, after what I'm about to tell you," he continued, "there's going to be very little chance I'll be able to go back to the work I was doing."

"Then why are you telling me?"

He sighed softly, his gaze never leaving hers. "Because compromising things with you, Claire, would be a helluva lot worse."

More confused now than ever, she started to object, "But maybe you shouldn't say any—"

"I work for the DEA," he interrupted before she could stop him. "I'm a narcotics investigator. I've been deep undercover in Central America for almost three years now. Everything Chandler found out about me during his investigation was fabricated. I was given a phony background to make me more credible to the guys I was sent in to investigate. It was a profile the DEA created for me, so that if any of the guys I was investigating tried to check into my background, they'd find out I was just like them."

"Fabricated?" she echoed.

Ramsey nodded. "All those records, right down to the mug shots, were falsified. None of it ever happened."

"So you've never killed anyone?" Claire asked inanely.

He shook his head and chuckled ruefully. "The people I was accused of killing didn't even exist, so how could I have murdered them?"

"The drug dealing?"

"Totally made up."

"Now hold on there," Chandler interjected. "Just who do you think you're fooling with all this—"

"Shut up, Edison."

It wasn't Ramsey who muttered the warning, however. It

was Claire. Still looking at Ramsey, still not understanding, she said, "I still don't understand."

He expelled another frustrated sound. "Yeah, I was afraid of that."

"Maybe you should start at the beginning," she told him.

He nodded disconsolately. "Yeah, maybe I should."

By the time Claire made coffee, Ramsey had managed to gather his thoughts and collect his wits, and was thinking a little more clearly. Unfortunately, the thing he was thinking most was *How the hell did I get myself into this?* And the thing he was thinking second most was *How the hell do I get myself out of this?*

Man, was he in it now. Deep. He should *not* have told Claire about working for the DEA. He should *not* have mentioned his undercover work in Central America. And he should *really* not have mentioned that the work was still ongoing.

But what else was he supposed to do? Lose her because she thought he was a murderer and a drug dealer? Let her keep Anabel from him because she thought he was a murderer and a drug dealer? And how could she think he was a murderer and a drug dealer, after everything they'd shared together? Everything they'd *done* together? Just because Edison had ironclad proof of Ramsey's wrongdoing, right down to the mug shots? Pshaw. If someone had come to Ramsey with mug shots of Claire, he wouldn't have believed them when they said she'd killed people and dealt drugs.

Of course, Claire hadn't come striding up to his house that first day dressed in ragged clothes and riding a Harley hog, had she? She wasn't all rough and coarse and pierced and tattooed, was she? But even if she had been, Ramsey thought—stealing just a quick moment to think about Claire all rough and coarse and tattooed and pierced, and getting a little aroused at the idea, truth be told, but then, thinking about Claire dressed in a duck suit got him aroused, too—he still wouldn't have believed her capable of murder and dope dealing. Probably.

All right, all right, so he could see where maybe her initial reaction to Edison's ironclad proof might have been to believe the things the attorney told her. If given more time, he was certain, she would have come around and realized how ridiculous the charges were. People were always a little emotionally raw and ready to jump to conclusions after having sex with someone for such a short time. Especially if they'd fallen in love with the person they just had sex wi—

Whoa. Hold on thar. Rewind.

Fallen in love? Ramsey echoed to himself. Nobody had mentioned falling in love, had they? Claire had never told him she loved him. And he sure as hell hadn't told Claire he loved her. Yeah, they'd generated some pretty amazing fireworks together, and yeah, they'd both reacted with great fervor to those fireworks. But that hadn't been love. That had been . . . something else. Something spontaneous and explosive and hot. Love was . . . something else. Something quiet and calm and affectionate. And okay, so maybe there had been more to his and Claire's fireworks than a hot, spontaneous explosion, he conceded when he remembered how the two of them had lain so quietly and calmly and affectionately together after the bombs finished bursting in air. That had just been afterglow. It hadn't been love.

Had it?

Nah. Couldn't be.

Where was he? Ramsey wondered, feeling more confused

now than ever. Oh, yeah. He'd been telling himself what an idiot he was to have told Claire about his job. And he'd been trying to figure out a way to undo the damage of having made that revelation. But too much damage had been done, and too much more would be done if he tried to backpedal.

Ah, hell, he thought in frustration as Claire placed a cup of coffee on the table in front of him. Edison had taken a seat at the table, too, opposite Ramsey. Now Claire folded herself onto a chair between the two men, but her attention was focused entirely on Ramsey. He tried not to feel superior to Edison when he realized that. But then, feeling superior to Edison was just so damned easy, no matter what the circumstances, he decided there would be no harm done if he continued.

"So," Claire said, breaking the silence, "you were going to start at the beginning."

But the beginning seemed way too far away to start there. And it was a place Ramsey would just as soon not visit again. Especially since he'd already told Claire about his unhappy childhood and adolescence. So he picked up the story where he'd left off with her. He didn't care if he lost Edison somewhere along the line. That would actually be preferable.

"You know how I left home when I was eighteen," he said.

Claire nodded. "According to Chandler's investigation, it was shortly after that that you became a drug dealer."

"No, that's according to the history the DEA made up for me when I went undercover," Ramsey corrected her. "What really happened after I left home was that I went to college. Duke University, to be exact."

"Duke?" Edison said incredulously.

"Yeah, Duke," Ramsey countered. "You got a problem with that?"

"Duke is Chandler's alma mater," Claire said.

And although there wasn't a smile on her face when she said it, there was one in her voice. Edison, however, was frowning even worse than he had been before.

"How'd you finish, Edison?" Ramsey asked him.

"Magna cum laude," Edison replied with a sniff, his back straightening with pride.

Ramsey grinned. "I was summa cum laude myself."

Edison slumped a bit and gazed back into his coffee.

"My degree's in public policy," Ramsey continued, talking once more to Claire. "I had planned to go to law school," he continued, thinking how ironic it was that he might have ended up just like Edison, and fighting off a major wiggins at the realization, "but I got recruited into government service right after I got my BA."

"Recruited?" Claire asked.

He nodded. "A lot of government law enforcement agencies actively recruit from college campuses. I evidently fit the profile. I had good grades in a preferred major, had worked hard to get them, was kind of a loner, and was estranged from my family. I wasn't relishing another three years of law school, so when opportunity knocked, I answered the door. Found myself working for the DEA. Long story short, eventually, they put me out in the field. I'd taken Spanish all through high school and college, so was fairly fluent, and when things started heating up in Central and South America, I was one of the guys they sent down there to try and infiltrate some of the more active—and more dangerous—groups. That's when they created a criminal history for me, in case anyone checked me out. And that's where I'd been working for three years when Edison's PI found me and told me about Eleanor's death and Anabel."

"You said you're on sabbatical now," Claire reminded him.

"Yeah, well, it's been sort of a self-inflicted sabbatical. The boys at the home office weren't all that thrilled about my taking it. But they let me when they realized I had a legitimate family crisis. And I was at a good stopping point by then, having just wrapped up one leg of the assignment and getting ready to embark on another one. They okayed it that I could put that second leg on hold for a few months, so that I could see to my family situation."

"And just what did this *work* in Central America involve?" Claire asked. Her voice was nonchalant, but he could see she felt anything but. Her gaze was fixed intently on his face, and she was searching, he knew, for even the tiniest hint of deception.

Ramsey had really been hoping she wouldn't ask for details about his work. He really didn't want to tell her just how deep undercover he had been. Because where he had been working by the time they found him was an ugly, violent, hateful place, a place totally unsuited to children. Hell, totally unsuited to any decent human being, regardless of age. Nevertheless, he said, "I was posing as a smuggler and a dealer and a bastard, and I helped the guys down south smuggle a shitload of illegal substances into this country."

"You pretended to, you mean," Claire said.

He shook his head. "No, I helped them do it. All with the government's blessing, of course, and all with the government watching. But I acted as a smuggler and dealer, Claire. I hung out with the people who make the drugs, and deliver the drugs, and smuggle the drugs, and sell the drugs. And some of them, a lot of them, are real animals. They steal, they rape, they kill."

She swallowed with some difficulty. "And did you ever see them do any of these things?"

Ramsey shook his head. "No," he said truthfully. "I was never actively involved in anything like that. I was good at steering clear of everything except the movement of the stuff. But I learned about a lot of pretty terrible things after the fact."

"And what did you do?"

"Made a mental note of it."

"And then you arrested them," she said.

"No, I didn't. That was up to someone else, down the line. I was, for all intents and purposes, one of the bad guys. I looked the other way, even if what they did was illegal and terrible."

Her expression was impassive, but something in her eyes went despondent when she said, "You were still able to work with those people, knowing the things they did."

"I had to, Claire," he told her. "I'm not proud of it, but that was my job. Believe me, they all got what was coming to them, eventually. But it wasn't my job to make that happen. My job was to work with them, cooperate with them, and be just like them."

"And were you just like them?" she asked softly.

"No," he told her. Then, because he didn't want to deceive her, he felt compelled to add, "But there were times when I wondered."

"Sounds like your job is pretty dangerous," she said. But her voice was flat, and her expression was unreadable, and God help him, he couldn't tell what she was thinking.

"My job is extremely dangerous," he admitted reluctantly. "If any of those guys ever find out I really work for the DEA, they'll torture me and kill me and leave my body for the scorpions."

"You talk as if you're intending to go back," Claire said, her voice still lifeless, her face still expressionless.

"I'm supposed to," he told her.

"You can't be thinking that you'll take Anabel to Central America with you."

"No, I'm not thinking that," he assured her.

"Then what are you thinking you'll do with her?"

He expelled that sound of frustration again. "I guess I haven't really thought that far ahead."

Claire, in turn, expelled a sound of disbelief. "Then think that far ahead now."

So Ramsey did. And he wasn't too crazy about the thoughts that occurred to him. Because he realized then that he actually *had* been thinking further ahead on some subconscious level. He already knew what he was going to have to do. And he'd already come to terms with it. Pretty much. "I guess I'm going to have to make some . . . adjustments," he said, "in how I do my work."

He had thought she would be happy to hear him say that. Instead, she told him, "That's not good enough."

"What do you mean, it's not good enough?" he demanded, a little more harshly than he'd intended. "I'm willing to rearrange my whole life for Anabel."

"But you speak as if you'll still stay in the same line of work."

"Claire, it's the only work I know. How can I do something different now?"

"But it makes you dangerous," she said.

"I'm a *cop*, Claire," he repeated unnecessarily. "How can I be dangerous?"

"What if one of those cutthroats finds out they've been working with a DEA agent? Or what if one of them gets suspicious when you don't come back to work down there? What if one of them comes looking for you?"

Her expression grew frantic as she spoke, and Ramsey realized her concern wasn't entirely for Anabel's safety. She was worried about him, too. Had the situation not been so strained, he would have been happy about that.

"There's very little chance that something like that would ever happen," he tried to reassure her.

"But what if it does?" she insisted. "Either way, they might want to find you again. If they think you're a criminal, they might look you up to help them commit some crime, and that would throw Anabel into their path. And if they find out you're a cop . . ." It didn't bear thinking about, Ramsey knew. But Claire was obviously thinking about it anyway, because she demanded, "What would happen then?"

"They'd probably kill me," he told her truthfully.

"And they'd find Anabel there when they came to do it."

Ramsey battled the urge to reach across the table and take her hand in his. Somehow, he didn't think she'd welcome the gesture. Still, he had to make her realize how serious he was about Anabel. Softly, adamantly, he told her, "I'd never let any harm come to her."

Something fearful and painful flashed in Claire's eyes. "I know that," she said. "But what if you didn't have any say in the matter? I can't allow Anabel to be put in the line of fire that way."

"I'll take a desk job when Anabel comes to live with me," he said. "I won't do field work anymore."

"But what if some of that field work comes back to haunt

you?" Claire said, her voice edged with desperation. "What if someone comes looking for you?"

"And what if someone breaks into *your* home while *you're* asleep, putting *you* and Anabel in danger?" Ramsey charged angrily, turning the tables. "Hell, that's just as likely to happen as the scenario you've painted for me."

"No, it isn't," she countered calmly. "I haven't put myself in the way of danger like you have."

"Well, what if you slip in the bathtub and break your neck?" he asked. "What if you get electrocuted on that damned Rebecca Boone coffeemaker of yours? Jesus, Claire, if you want to talk risk factor, then every human being on the planet is put in a position of risk every time they open their eyes in the morning."

"Not the way you've put yourself at risk," she insisted. "It's not the same at all."

And it wasn't, Ramsey had to admit. His job was a dangerous one that put him in contact with all kinds of dangerous people. Yeah, maybe Claire could be the victim of an accident someday, but that was a whole different situation— it wouldn't put Anabel at risk. And if something happened to Claire, then Olive could step in to take care of Anabel, he knew. What would happen to his niece if Ramsey were the victim of something horrible, something fatal? There wouldn't be anyone to step in for him. Not that it would probably be necessary, because if anyone came looking for Ramsey, they'd find Anabel, too. And they'd have no qualms about taking the life of a child along with his.

"Anabel will stay with me," Claire said again, even more decisively than before. "Eleanor wanted me to be the one to raise her," she added. Not to be spiteful, Ramsey was sure, but to simply state a fact. "So I'll be the one to raise her. I'm sorry, Ramsey, but I just can't let her live with you. I'm better suited to care for her."

"Claire, you can't just—"

"Yes, I can," she told him. "I already have. According to her mother's wishes, and according to the courts, I'll keep her. She'll be safe with me. You can visit her whenever you want. But after you go back to your life, Anabel will stay here with me."

And Ramsey wasn't sure what bothered him more about that comment. Whether it was her insistence that Anabel would stay with her, or that with that *after you go back to your life* remark, she was dismissing him once and for all.

"I'll challenge you," he said, surprising himself with both his utter calmness in saying it, and his absolute conviction in his feelings. "I'll do whatever I have to do, Claire, to make sure I win custody of my niece. I *will* reunite my family. And I'll make sure it stays together this time."

"You won't win," she told him simply.

Hell, she didn't have to tell him that, Ramsey thought morosely. He knew he didn't stand a chance. The thing was, it wasn't just Anabel he feared losing.

Chandler narrowed his eyes as he listened to the caustic exchange that bulleted back and forth before him. So wrapped up in that exchange were they that Claire and Ramsey Sage seemed to have forgotten he even existed. Worse, Claire was telling Ramsey how she would keep his odious niece and raise the little spawn of Satan as her own. Chandler simply couldn't allow that. Not just because Claire's business was on the verge of exploding in a way that would ultimately net her billions, so he couldn't afford to have her distracted but because, when he married her, he didn't want that abominable little heathen underfoot.

Anabel Sage would have to go. But it was clear she wouldn't be going with her uncle. Even if he wasn't a common criminal, the courts, Chandler knew, wouldn't side with a man who'd been spending so much time with drug dealers. And with her wealth, Claire was far more suitable. She would be the one to whom Anabel was awarded.

Hmpf. Some award.

No, Chandler simply could not have the little cretin living with Claire, regardless of how misguided she was in wanting to care for the urchin. Fortunately, he knew exactly the place for Anabel. A number of his colleagues dealt in private adoptions. There were legions of deluded couples out there looking for a child to adopt, couples who had money to burn for the luxury of a family. A little blond hellion like Anabel would bring in tens of thousands of dollars from such a couple. And Chandler's colleagues knew all sorts of ways to make the sale of a child look like a perfectly legal adoption—even to the purchasers of said child. Now all he had to do was figure out a way to ensure Anabel's disappearance, without drawing attention to himself.

But then that shouldn't be such a difficult task for a man like him. He had, after all, graduated magna cum laude. And nobody would suspect *Chandler* of having anything to do with Anabel's disappearance. Of course, Anabel's *uncle* had just said he would do whatever he had to do to keep his family together, hadn't he? And kidnapping certainly wouldn't be outside the realm of possibility for a man who had spent the last three years of his life surrounded by criminals.

Oh, yes, Chandler thought as he sipped his coffee and

watched the antagonism build between Claire and the detestable Mr. Sage. Goodness, they were even beginning to raise their voices at each other now. How delightful. He could manage this quite well. He'd be rid of Anabel and he'd line his pockets in the process. Better yet, he'd see to it that Ramsey Sage was harassed by the law until the cows came home. All Chandler had to do was find the highest bidder in his quest to sell the child. He savored his coffee again and smiled when Claire stood with enough force to topple her chair.

Was this an excellent country, or what?

$\mathcal{F}$*ifteen*

$\mathcal{W}$hat happened the next day was nothing short of catastrophic. And Claire's ultimate reaction to it was nothing short of catatonic.

Oh, the day started off pleasantly enough. Well, except for the chilling hopelessness that overcame her whenever she thought about how Ramsey was out of her life forever. Because after the way the argument over Anabel had escalated yesterday—they'd barely been able to be civil to each other by the time he left—she knew that *if* he ever came to her house again, he'd be armed with an attorney and court injunctions.

Not that Claire thought for a moment that a court injunction regarding Anabel's custody would materialize. Well, not for *too* many moments, anyway. She supposed there might be *one* judge out there who would hold the family unit sacred enough to see that Anabel Sage was turned over to her blood kin instead of being raised by someone who had been a total stranger before, even if that blood kin had been a total stranger, too. And Ramsey did work in law enforcement, she was forced to remind herself. He might even know a judge or two who owed him a favor, and finagle a court order that way.

But not in Tennessee, she would then remind herself. He was from North Carolina originally and had lived in Washington, DC after that. And he hadn't even been in the country for the past three years. There was little chance he'd had the opportunity to cultivate too many connections in law enforcement. And even if he had, Claire could insist on a jury trial, Chandler had told her, and should a case for Anabel's custody go before a jury, she was confident she would come out the winner. In spite of Ramsey's blood tie, she was more fit to raise Anabel. And possession was nine-tenths of the law, right?

But none of Claire's rationalizations or reassurances comforted her much. Because even if she hadn't lost Anabel, she'd lost something else that was just as important to her—Ramsey. She simply could not see how they were going to be able to mend the rift that Anabel's situation had created in their relationship.

Not that they really even *had* a relationship, Claire had to be honest with herself. They'd had some good times, some intimate conversations, and some extraordinary sex. Certainly all those things connected them in ways that went beyond the casual. But it didn't mean they had a relationship. In spite of the time they had spent together, neither of them had talked about the future—unless it was about Anabel's future. And neither of them had really talked about each other—or themselves—in ways that didn't include Anabel. Claire wasn't sure how the two of them would relate to each other *without* Anabel. Of course, now they wouldn't even have the chance to find out, because the relationship they'd never generated in the first place sure wouldn't be materializing now.

Then Claire remembered that day on the boat. Anabel hadn't been with them that day, not really. Not in conversation, not in thought, and certainly not in action. That day, it had been only about Ramsey and Claire, almost as if they'd had a silent agreement not to mention Anabel. And they'd related to each other pretty well that day.

Oh, sure, in the physical sense, she reminded herself brutally. They'd connected *really* well there.

But deep down, she knew that wasn't the only way they'd connected that day. Because afterward, as they'd lain in each others arms, they'd connected in a way that was even more intimate. They'd shared their pasts with each other, as painful as those pasts had been. They'd shared their fears, their dreams, their hopes. They'd shared themselves. But it still hadn't been enough to unite them completely.

Claire shoved such thoughts out of her brain whenever they formed that day, and did her best to focus on other matters. She donned her stay-at-home-with-Anabel clothes, baggy khaki shorts and an even baggier sleeveless shirt, and proceeded to focus her time entirely on the little girl. And she discovered—not exactly to her surprise, funnily enough—that she enjoyed the child's company enormously. She also discovered that when she gave Anabel her undivided attention, and didn't reserve so much of herself, the little girl acted in ways that were much less chaotic. Oh, she still managed to crush an expanse of gladiolas in the garden, and an expensive antique brooch disappeared from Claire's bedside table, and that Lalique paperweight was beyond repair, but still. Anabel's destruction was cut by at least 50 percent once Claire made up her mind to interact more fully with her charge.

But she was going to have to think of some way to refer to her charge besides *her charge*, she thought when she caught herself thinking that way again. Hmmm . . . Just how should she introduce Anabel to others as her own, now that she'd be introducing Anabel to others as her own? Claire was still mulling over the question late in the afternoon—and marveling at the complete evaporation of the panic that had once accompanied the prospect of Anabel being her own—when her entire world suddenly blew up in her face without warning.

She hated it when that happened.

She had put down Anabel for a much-needed nap—though Claire was probably the one who needed it most—and was heading back down the stairs when she heard the telephone in the kitchen begin to ring. But just as she turned in that direction to answer it, the front doorbell began to *bong-bong-bong* quite frantically. She decided to answer the latter, since it was closer and the machine could take care of the incoming call, but then someone began to knock furiously at the back door, as well.

Strange, she thought, that all three things should happen at once, especially on a day when she wasn't even working. Still opting for the nearest distraction of the front door, Claire was startled to hear a loud *thump thump* come from overhead, as if someone were tromping around in one of the rooms upstairs, even though she and Anabel were the only ones home. Clearly, Anabel wasn't napping after all, and in not doing so, she became Claire's number one priority. So, ignoring the phone and both the front and back doors, Claire spun around and took the stairs two at a time up to the second floor.

Halfway down the hall, though, she heard the sound of a

window being thrust down hard, and her heart leapt into her throat. Someone else was in the house. No way could Anabel have done that, in spite of her propensity for wreaking havoc. But then Claire heard Olive's voice coming from the same direction as the *thump thump*/thrusting, shouting, "Oh, yeah? Well, I said, 'No comment' and I meant it, you big ape!" and she felt a little better.

For a whole nanosecond.

Then she remembered that Olive didn't shout. Ever. And she really didn't ever call anyone names. Even more to the point, Olive didn't climb through windows. She always came to the front door. Just what on earth was going on?

Just as Claire's foot hit the second floor, the door to her office came crashing open, and Olive came scrambling through it. It was yet another indication that there was something very wrong, because Olive didn't scramble. Ever. And she really didn't ever *look* as if she'd been scrambling. But she did now. Or maybe she just looked scrambl*ed*. In any event, she did *not* look like herself. Her pale blue dress was rumpled and smudged with dirt, one sleeve hanging from the torn shoulder seam. Her glasses were gone, and her face, like her dress, was streaked with dirt.

"Olive, what the . . . ?" Claire began eloquently.

Olive stopped dead in her tracks when she saw her. "Don't panic," she said by way of a greeting. "I'm sure it's been all blown out of proportion. We should be able to handle it. We just need to figure out what kind of spin to put on it, that's all."

"Spin?" Claire asked inanely. "What are you talking about? And why do you look like you just scaled the rose trellis and climbed through the window?"

Still swiping at her dress, Olive muttered, "Because I did.

I had to get away from the hordes of reporters that are camped out on your front and back lawns."

It wasn't exactly the reply Claire had expected to hear. "Why are there hordes of reporters camped out on my front and back lawns?" she asked, thinking it an even better question than the other ones had been. "We're not doing that new gardening piece until fall," she pointed out. "And even at that, it's hardly such a revolutionary piece that it would warrant hordes of reporters. A handful from the main networks and maybe a correspondent or two for *House Beautiful* and *House & Garden* would be more than enough, I should think, and even that's a little more exposure than we really need."

Olive glanced up at that, her expression going slack. "You don't know?" she asked. "No one's called you?"

Now Claire was really baffled. "Know what? The phone was ringing when you . . . ah . . . came in, but I didn't get a chance to answer it."

She noticed then that the phone was ringing again—or maybe it was still ringing from that first time—and that the front doorbell was also still *bong-bong-bong*ing, and that the pounding at the back door had increased to the violent stage.

Yet Anabel managed to sleep through it all. But of course she would. It was daytime, after all. The time traditionally reserved for being awake. And Anabel had all night to be that.

"Olive?" Claire asked. "What's going on?"

Olive stopped batting at her dress and straightened, meeting Claire's gaze. "Um, the hordes of reporters aren't here to cover the gardening piece," she said.

"Then why are they here?" Claire asked.

"They came to cover . . ." Olive hesitated, then seemed resolved to what she had to say. "The jig is up, Claire. They know it wasn't your idea to make clever and festive wall stencils from a grocery bag or use a garlic press to make unique and festive holiday ornaments. Word has gotten out somehow that you're not the one who comes up with all those great ideas on *Simple Pleasures*, and that you are, in fact, a fraud."

Uh-oh.

"Every network and cable station that has an entertainment feature has a correspondent out there wanting to talk to you," Olive continued. "They're saying you've been encouraging people to live a lifestyle that you don't embrace yourself."

Even though she knew it was pointless to try to defend herself, and even though she knew Olive wasn't the one she had to defend herself to, Claire said halfheartedly, "Well, I've never told anyone I actually live the way I tell them to, have I?"

Because, really, she hadn't. She'd never gone on camera and said, "When I get home tonight, I'm going to pick some grapes and put them in the pressure cooker with lots of cane sugar and make jam." She just told other people how to do that, if they wanted to. And then she went to Winn-Dixie for a jar of Welch's. Was that such a crime?

"That's beside the point, Claire," Olive said. "Your public has viewed you as being a certain kind of person for years. And now they're being told you aren't that person at all. It's making them kinda testy. Inquiring minds wanna know if you're actually the fraud you're being rumored to be."

"And who started the rumors?" Claire asked, afraid to even think about the answer to that question. "How did the press find out? No one knows except for a handful of people, and they're all people I trust. Who would do something like this? And why?"

I'll do whatever I have to do, Claire, to make sure I win custody of my niece.

Ramsey's words of the day before swamped her just as she concluded her question. No, Claire immediately told herself. Surely, he wouldn't do something like this. Even wanting custody of Anabel as badly as he did, Ramsey couldn't be that vicious. He wouldn't do something like this to Claire.

Oh, come on, she chastised herself. Who was she kidding? Of course he'd do something like this. After the way they'd parted yesterday, after telling her flat out that he'd do whatever he had to do to win Anabel? What better way to compromise Claire than to thrust her into a messy, public, professionally damaging media circus? Not only did it discredit her, but it meant she'd be so wrapped up in salvaging her career and her business that she'd have little time to devote to a legal battle coming at her from another front.

Oh, well done, Ramsey, she saluted him morosely. She had to hand it to him. It was going to be a damned effective strategy.

She turned to Olive pleadingly. "What do we do?" she asked. Because Olive always knew what to do and what to say, and Olive always knew how to fix everything. "What do we say?" she further pleaded. "How do we fix this?"

Olive exhaled a long sigh of something that sounded dangerously like bewilderment. And then she said something Claire had never heard her say before, something that was frankly terrifying: "I have no idea." Claire was about to start hyperventilating—it wasn't like she had anything better to do at the moment—but Olive rallied herself with a sturdy rolling of her shoulders. "But we'll think of something, Claire," she promised as she sat up straighter. "We always do. Hey, we managed the alien Elvis love child, didn't we?"

That was true enough, Claire thought. But the things they'd always thought up before had been resolutions that were simple and pleasurable. This . . .

This was going to be neither of those things. Not by a long shot.

She was going to think he did it.

That was the thought that shot through Ramsey's brain when he turned on the morning news two days after he parted ways with Claire in a less-than-tidy fashion.

The first thing he saw on the screen was Claire's big house in Belmont, but instead of the peaceful, picturesque abode he had glimpsed on all his visits there, it was flanked by media vans on all sides and overrun with what appeared to be dozens of newspeople. This image was followed by another, one of Claire leaving her television studio and being set upon by more reporters, who all thrust microphones into her face. One angrily demanded to know if it was true that the fun and festive children's musical instruments she'd created out of gourds and rubber bands *hadn't* been her idea, because there were millions of Americans who deserved to know the truth. Then Ramsey listened in stupefaction as the reporter offered a long list of other ideas that hadn't been Claire's, including, but not limited to, darling and festive Halloween costumes from bedsheets, fragrant and festive potpourri from melon rinds, bright and festive hamster houses from tomato juice cans, and charming and festive soap holders from seashells.

But what was most shocking of all—besides the fact that this was the stupidest thing Ramsey had ever seen covered on television news—was that he realized he was watching not local coverage, but national.

God, was this actually *news?* he wondered, flipping the channel to find a similar report running on one of the other networks at the same time. Jeez, it wasn't like Claire had been caught insider trading or something. The way the news anchors were frothing at the mouth, he might have thought she'd killed someone.

Still damp from his shower and wearing nothing but a towel knotted loosely around his waist, Ramsey fell back onto the settee in the galley of his sailboat and watched the action playing out on the tiny TV that sat on the counter. There were more shots of Claire trying to escape reporters, some clips from her show, and then—*Unbelievable*, he thought—a close-up of an egg carton that Claire had "allegedly" turned into an elegant and festive jewelry box, but which, it was rumored, had actually been created by someone on her staff. Exhibit A. Murder by arts and crafts—of a career, at any rate.

That was when he remembered Claire telling him, in her half-asleep state, that she was just a front for the business, and that it was really Olive who ran the show, and if the press got hold of that bit of knowledge, it could spell an end to her career. At the time, Ramsey had thought she was being just a tad unrealistic. Now he saw that it was actually the *media* who were unrealistic. And more than just a tad. He shook his head in disbelief that anyone could possibly get so caught up in the drama of—gasp—handicraft abuse.

What was really bad, though, was that he realized Claire was going to think *he* was the one who had ratted her out. And, hell, why shouldn't she think that, after the way they'd parted last time? He'd practically threatened her when he'd told her he'd do whatever he had to do to ensure he won custody of Anabel. But he hadn't meant he'd attack her professionally. He'd only meant he'd hire an attorney who was more tenacious than a pit bull, that was all. In spite of that, he told himself to ignore how all this was going to affect Claire, and to instead focus on how it was good news for him. Because having her wrapped up in a media frenzy like this one would definitely increase his chances of reuniting what little family he had left.

But Ramsey didn't want it to happen this way. He didn't want there to be antagonism. Or at least, no more than they could avoid. And he certainly didn't want Claire to be hurt. Hell, he'd even wanted her to stay a part of Anabel's life, because he knew his niece was crazy about her. And he knew Claire was crazy about his niece, too. Yeah, he'd planned to go back to North Carolina with Anabel, but he'd still thought Claire could be a part of their lives. Or, rather, be a part of Anabel's life. Somehow.

Ah, dammit. He didn't know what he'd been thinking. He'd been thinking so many things since meeting Claire that he wasn't sure what the hell he wanted anymore. Except for Anabel.

And except for Claire.

Because he realized then, not much to his surprise, really, that he wanted her, too. That he needed her, too. Somehow, somewhere along the way, Claire had begun to be as much a part of his future, his happiness, his life, as his niece was. But how could that be? he asked himself. With Anabel, it was because she was his family. The only family he had left. But Claire was . . .

Just what *was* Claire to him, anyway? he asked himself. And only when he finally allowed himself to think about that did he begin to really understand. Because the more he thought about it, the more he realized that what he wanted Claire to be was . . . Well. He wanted Claire to be family, too. And not because he wanted to adopt her and raise her as his own, either. But because he wanted to—

Oh, no, he thought, backpedaling in the face of his epiphany. No, no, no, no, no. He did *not* want to marry Claire. He didn't want to marry anybody. He couldn't marry anybody. He wasn't the marrying kind. He wasn't good at that kind of thing. He'd never had any good examples to follow. His family life had always been a shambles. He'd never learned how to care for someone else for any length of time. He'd be terrible at the whole family thing. He wasn't the settling-down type. He'd lived his life on the edge for so long, he wasn't sure he could rein himself in. He was a lone wolf. He was a solitary man. He was an island. He—

He stopped when he realized how many excuses he was making for himself. Lame excuses at that. Who was he trying to kid? Well, besides himself, obviously. Because even though he'd told himself all these things for years—over and over again, in fact, ad nauseum, in fact, world without end, amen, amen, in fact—hadn't he proved just the opposite to himself over the past month and a half? Yeah, his family life growing up had pretty much sucked, but his family life now—what little there was of it—wasn't going too badly. He'd hit it off with Anabel really well, and he cared very much for his niece. And he'd hit it off with Claire, too, and cared very much for her.

No, not cared very much for them, Ramsey made himself admit. He loved them. He'd loved them practically since meeting them. He just hadn't been able to acknowledge it because . . . because . . . Well, because he didn't want to marry anybody. He couldn't marry anybody. He wasn't the marrying kind. He wasn't good at that kind of thing. He'd never had any good examples to follow. His family life had always been a shambles. He'd never learned how to care for someone else for any length of time. He'd be terrible at that. He wasn't the settling-down type. He'd lived his life on the edge for so long, he wasn't sure he could rein himself in. He was a lone wolf. He was a solitary man. He was an island. He—

He was an idiot.

Oh, man . . .

He loved Claire, he realized now. And he loved Anabel. And he wanted to be with both of them. Forever. He wanted them to be a family—*his* family. He wanted to show people how family ought to be done. Because he could do it. *They* could do it. He just had to make Claire realize that, too. But how?

He looked at the TV again, but the newspeople had finally moved on to another story. Still, Claire's face lingered in his mind, looking the way it had when she'd been set upon by reporters outside her studio. She'd looked startled and frightened, pale and sad. And he couldn't help wondering how much of that was a result of the media flare-up in which she'd found herself embroiled, and how much was a result of something else entirely. Because for the past couple of days, Ramsey had been looking pretty startled and frightened, pale and sad, too, when he'd stared back at himself from the mirror. And he hadn't been anywhere near a media flare-up.

He stood then, and switched off the TV. On automatic pilot, he shaved and dressed and fixed himself some breakfast. On automatic pilot, he brushed his teeth and made his bunk. On automatic pilot, he debarked, strode down the pier, and climbed into his car. But it was with his complete and utter attention that he started the engine. He had some things to do. Some people to call. Some arrangements to make. And then . . . Well. Then he would go see Claire. He just hoped he could get through to her when he got to her house. And not because a media fiasco and a sea of news correspondents stood between them, either.

But because so much more than that did.

The last person Claire expected to find at her front door a week after the creative and festive crafts hit the fan was Ramsey Sage. What was even more surprising was that he seemed less her adversary when he showed up this time, and more her knight in shining armor. Because there he stood, between her and the huddled masses of newspeople on her front lawn, in his faded jeans and black T-shirt, his diamond winking in his earlobe again, his barbed-wire tattoo and salient biceps looking sturdy enough to ward off even the most obnoxious cable lifestyle correspondents.

Then she remembered that the reason all those newspeople were huddling in masses out on her front lawn was because Ramsey Sage had ratted her out. Some Knight in Shining Armor he'd turned out to be.

"I don't think it's a good idea for you to be here," she told him without preamble.

"I need to talk to you."

"Oh, I think you've said more than enough."

"It wasn't me," he said, obviously knowing she suspected him of that ratting out business. Probably because he was the one who'd ratted her out. The rat. But he continued, quite adamantly, "I didn't say a word to anyone, Claire. I swear it. It wasn't me. And I need to talk to you."

The newspeople on her lawn had started filming, she noted, even though the only thing they had to film at the moment was two people grumbling at each other. And one of those people was still in her pajamas, Claire remembered then, pajamas consisting of baggy bottoms emblazoned with a bold motif of bacon and eggs, and a T-shirt that read "My friend went to Dollywood, and all I got was this lousy T-shirt." Well, since her lifestyle empire was crumbling around her, she didn't see any reason why she had to live with style anymore. If she wanted to dress like a deposed lifestyle empress then, dammit, she would.

Still, there was no reason why anyone who owned a television set had to know that.

Grabbing Ramsey by the front of his shirt, she jerked him into the house and closed the door behind him. Tersely, she said, "You need to talk? So talk."

He did, but it wasn't what she expected him to say. She'd expected him to start groveling and apologizing and making lame excuses. What she hadn't expected him to say was, "You look wonderful."

Especially since she knew she didn't look wonderful. In addition to her mismatched sleepwear, she had her hair pulled high on her head and stuffed into a ponytail that looked as if she'd slept in it. Because she *had* slept in it. She was barefoot and wore no makeup, and she couldn't remember if she'd wiped the Pop-Tart crumbs off her face after she'd finished breakfast. Quickly, and as unobtrusively as possible, she swiped a hand across her mouth. But Ramsey only smiled as she completed the action.

"I don't look wonderful, I look awful," she countered. "But what do you expect? For the last week, I've watched my business take a hit from every angle. The value of my stock has plummeted. Almost all of my advertisers have pulled their spots from my show and their ads from my magazine. News reporters have been following me around wherever I go, asking me the dumbest questions. I swear to God, if I hear the word *festive* one more time, someone's going to pay for it with their teeth." She thrust a hand against her forehead and pushed back a strand of hair that had fallen free of its bonds. "I don't think I've slept more than a few hours since everything fell apart, Ramsey. I know I look awful."

"You don't look awful," he told her. "You look like a woman who's fighting for her life. I love women like that."

Well, since he put it *that* way . . .

Then it hit her, what he had actually said, and she snapped her head around to look at him, narrowing her eyes suspiciously. "What was that?" she asked.

"I said, 'I love women like that,'" he repeated matter-of-factly. "Women who are willing to fight for what's really important to them. Their business, say. Or their good reputation. Or a kid somebody's asked them to raise as their own."

Claire straightened a bit at that. She supposed she had been doing a lot of fighting this week. Unfortunately, what she hadn't been doing a lot of was winning.

"Women like that are good examples," Ramsey continued. "They make me want to fight for what's really important to me, too."

Claire said nothing in response to his remark at first, because she was too afraid to think it meant what he was sort of making it sound like he meant. Was he saying he was going to fight for her? Or that he was going to fight for Anabel? Just why was he here, anyway?

"Just why are you here, anyway?" she said.

"I missed you," he told her.

She hadn't expected him to say something like that, either. Especially since it sounded so much like something she could have said to him. She really had missed Ramsey. A lot. She'd missed talking to him, touching him, being with him, making love with him. The house had felt empty without him. Anabel had been moping, too. And really, when she thought about it, it had been Ramsey's absence even more than the hit to her business that had made her feel so miserable all week.

"I've missed you, too," she said. Because, hey, if he could admit such a thing, then so could she. Especially if he really had missed her. And judging by the way he lit up when she told him that, he'd been telling her the truth.

"I also came because I need to ask you something," he said. "I need to ask you a lot of things, actually," he then corrected himself.

"Like what?" she said, still a little suspicious. Still a little hopeful.

"Like if there's a way you and I can work out something with Anabel," he said.

"That's not a question," she told him, knowing she was stalling, but not sure she wanted to have this dialogue played out. "You didn't phrase it as a question, and you didn't punctuate it with a question mark. Therefore, it can't be a question."

"You're trying to avoid the issue," he said.

"No, I'm not," she said. "I'm just a big proponent of good grammar, that's all. In fact, I employ a grammarian full-time at the magazine, just to be sure we never overstep the bounds of good gram—"

"Claire."

"What?"

"You're avoiding."

"No, I'm not," she denied. "I was just listing the merits of good grammar, of which there are many."

"Fine," he said. "I think we're all in agreement that good grammar is a good thing. Now then. Let's move on."

But still Claire hedged. "Actually, we can't *move on*, since we haven't addressed this first thing, this first question that you never asked. Grammatically speaking, I mean."

To his credit, Ramsey didn't offer a single sign that he was getting irritated with her. Which was saying something, because Claire was getting plenty irritated with herself. She was acting like an idiot. All because she was afraid to hear what Ramsey was going to say.

"Okay," he began. "Question number one. Do you think it's possible for you and me to come to agreeable terms with regard to Anabel's care and feeding?"

She decided not to be put out with the fact that he was speaking to her in slow, simple terms, as if he were speaking to a child. She wasn't exactly behaving like a big girl, was she? "I think it's possible," she said. "But I don't think it's likely," she added honestly. "Not with things the way they stand between us right now. I mean, even if it wasn't you who ratted me out—"

"It wasn't," he told her emphatically.

"I believe you," she said. And she was surprised to realize that she did. Ramsey didn't have it in him to rat her out any more than he had it in him to murder people and deal drugs. He was a good guy. She knew that. He was just a good guy who'd never be *her* guy, that was all.

"Even if it wasn't you who ratted me out," she tried again, "we're just not on the same page, you and I. About a lot of things."

Ramsey nodded once, but she wasn't sure if he was agreeing with her, or just making a note of her response. It didn't help when he continued, "Question number two. Would you object to things being different between the two of us? The two of us finding a way to *be* on the same page?"

Well, that could certainly be interpreted in about a billion different ways, Claire thought. Nevertheless, she answered, "No, I wouldn't object to that. As long as they got different by being better."

He nodded again, once, and again, she didn't know how to interpret the action. He offered nothing to help her figure it out, either, when he said, "Question number three. What would you think about the two of us sharing custody of Anabel equally?"

Okay, now she knew what he was up to. He was going to try and finagle some kind of joint custody thing that would never work out if he was planning to live on a boat he would be taking to North Carolina. "I don't see how we could do that, if we're living in two different cities."

"But what would you think about it, if we could figure out a way to do it?" he persisted.

She sighed heavily. "I guess it would be okay," she said carefully, "*if* we could figure out a way to do it that was agreeable to us *both*."

He did that single nod thing again, and again, it told Claire nothing. But what he said next confused her more than ever. "Question number four." He paused significantly. "How do you feel about nontraditional gender roles?"

Okay, now they were really getting into weird waters, Claire thought. Nevertheless, she answered, "I don't believe in traditional and nontraditional gender roles."

That seemed to worry him for some reason. "Oh?"

So she clarified, "I think people should do whatever they want to do, regardless of their gender or society's expectations of their gender."

That seemed to make him feel better. "Oh."

"Ramsey, where is all this leading?" Claire finally asked, hopelessly befuddled now.

He smiled, but there was something in his expression that was more than a little anxious. "Where it's leading, where it's *all* leading, Claire," he said, "is to question number five."

"And that is?"

He inhaled deeply, as if he needed to fortify himself, then let the air out of his lungs in a long, silent breath. He licked his lips, swallowed with some difficulty, and said, "Question number five." He hesitated for a moment, then, "Will you marry me?" he asked.

Claire was certain she misheard that last question. Surely he hadn't asked her to marry him. Surely what he'd said was *Will you bury me?* because he was still scared she suspected him of being the one who ratted her out. Or maybe he'd said *Will you carry me?* because he was feeling tired. *Or Will you ferry me?* because he needed a ride somewhere—maybe the police had finally repossessed what was in fact his stolen station wagon. She couldn't remember if it was parked outside or not, there'd been so many news vans around.

Yeah, that had to be it. He needed a lift somewhere.

"Claire?" he said when she didn't respond. "Did you hear me?"

She nodded. "I heard you. I'm just not sure I understood what you said."

He eyed her a little nervously. "What's not to understand? I punctuated it correctly."

"I'm still working out the verb," she told him.

He smiled at that, albeit a bit nervously. "You need a minute to make a phone call to your grammarian?"

She shook her head. "No, I need to know if you just asked me to marry you."

He reached over and took her hand, but held it loosely, just in case maybe she wanted to let go. Or, she couldn't help thinking, in case she wanted to hold it tighter. "Yeah," he said. "I asked you to marry me."

This time Claire was the one to nod once, but she didn't tighten her hold on his hand. Nor did she let go. Instead, she said, "Okay. Now I need to know *why* you asked me to marry you." She met his gaze and held it. "Is it because of Anabel? Because you think it would be the best thing for her?"

Without a single hesitation, Ramsey said, "No. It's because I think it would be the best thing for us. You and me, Claire. I love Anabel, too, but this . . . this is just between you and me."

"You still haven't told me *why* you want me to marry you," she said. "Not really."

He smiled at that. "Because I love you," he said. "And because I've never felt more alive, more complete, than I am when I'm with you. And because you make me feel things I never felt before, things I never thought I'd feel, good things, things that I want to feel forever. And because I can't imagine a future without you. That's why I want you to marry me, Claire. And that's why I want to marry you."

As reasons went, she thought, those were all pretty good ones. Better yet, they pretty much mirrored the reasons she wanted to say yes to his proposal. Because she felt all those things for him, too. She hesitated, though, before accepting.

"Are you sure you want me?" she asked. "My business may be going under any minute, and I'm a total fraud when it comes to the whole lifestyle thing. I can't cook. I can't keep house. And I'm really not much on the parenting thing, either," she confessed.

"You don't have to worry about any of that," Ramsey told her.

"Oh, I think I do," she said. "Because I think I'm going to end up with nothing, Ramsey, when this all finally plays out."

He shook his head. "No, you won't."

"How can you say that? Haven't you seen the news?"

"Yeah, I have. But trust me, Claire, I know what it is to have nothing. And you and I won't end up with that. What you and I will end up with, as long as we're together . . ." He smiled again. "Sweetheart, we'll have everything."

She smiled, too, and laced her fingers snugly with his. Well, since he put it *that* way . . .

"At least we'll have a roof over our heads," she told him. "The house is paid for. If I have to go back to odd jobs and such, we'll still have that. Unless . . ." She battled a fear that poked at her with cold fingers. "Unless you're still planning to go back to your old job."

"I'm not going back to my old job," he said. "I have something else in mind. I've made a few calls, and I've pulled some favors, and I took care of all my obligations with the DEA. But I do have another job in mind. It's demanding and has long hours, but I can do it here. Will that be okay?" he asked her.

"Is it dangerous?" she asked.

He made a little face and shrugged. "Maybe a little. But I won't be surrounded by dangerous guys."

"What if they come back to haunt you?" she asked.

"You're still worried about that?"

"Some," she admitted. Then she grinned a wicked grin.

"But I wouldn't be if you changed your name when we get married."

"Ramsey Willoughby?" he asked. "Ah . . . I don't think so."

She reached for his other hand, then, weaving the fingers of those snugly together, too. With one step forward, she brought her body flush with his and dropped their hands down to their sides. Then she pushed herself up on tiptoe and brushed her lips lightly along the line of his jaw. "Then I guess," she said between kisses, "that we'll just have to put everything in my name so that no one will be able to find you."

Ramsey grasped her hands in his and pushed their arms behind her back, effectively pinning her to him. "I think I'm comfortable enough in my masculinity to go for that," he said.

"I'm comfortable in your masculinity, too," Claire told him as she snuggled closer. "And if we go upstairs, we could slip into something even *more* comfortable."

"Your femininity?" he asked.

"Well, *you* could slip into that," she said. "I thought I might slip into some whipped cream or something."

"I'll do your back."

"I was hoping you would."

"After I do your front."

"That goes without saying."

"And then I'll do all the other parts of you, too."

"I knew that you would."

Yeah, that was the thing about men, Claire thought as Ramsey bent his head and covered her mouth with his. They were *so* predictable.

Epilogue

*S*ummer turned to fall, turned to winter, turned to spring, turned to summer again, and after the passage of a year, Claire was amazed to find that very little in her life had changed. Well, except for Chandler's having been disbarred and run out of town when it was discovered he was trying to sell a child to the highest bidder and call it adoption. Last Claire had heard, he was selling shoes at a Walmart in Branson, Missouri. And except for Nina Ritchie having been blacklisted from the entire entertainment community for ratting out her employer in an effort to pump up the ratings of said employer's show amid controversy. Last Claire had heard, she was working as the cigarette girl for a men's club in Poughkeepsie. And except for Olive having eloped with a social worker in Las Vegas. Last Claire had heard—which was just a few minutes ago, seeing as how Olive and Davis were joining her and Ramsey and Anabel for dinner tonight—she and her new husband were closing on a new house next week.

And except for Francesca having taken up with a stray rooster up the street—who knew chickens were such popular pets?—and leaving little chicks all over the backyard for a change. Last Claire had heard—which was this morning—little Luigi and Sergio were learning to crow just like their papa. And doing much too fine a job of it, as Claire had been awake since daybreak.

Okay, so maybe a lot had changed, she amended as she came home from work one evening in late August. What was really important hadn't changed a bit. She loved Ramsey. He loved her. Olive wasn't the only one who'd eloped. Claire and Ramsey had just done it in Acapulco, that was all. Anabel had been the flower girl. Except that she'd eaten all of the flowers just before the ceremony. Then she'd broken the basket that was supposed to hold them. Then she'd knocked over the floral arrangements in the back of the church.

So, see? A lot hadn't changed.

Now Claire breezed into the kitchen of the big house in Belmont she shared with her family, and found her husband rattling around amid bubbling saucepans and a steaming pot and what smelled very much like fresh-baked bread. He'd fallen into the role of homemaker beautifully. And he had such an affinity for it. He was a wonderful husband and father, and she didn't know where she—or Anabel—would be without him.

"What's for supper?" she asked as she tossed her briefcase onto a kitchen chair and unbuttoned the top two buttons of her blouse.

She and Olive hadn't launched their new business yet, but Claire still donned the traditional attire of businesswoman, since she was making frequent calls on potential advertisers and such. Simple Pleasures, Inc. had never quite recovered from the media fallout of the previous summer, quite possibly because Claire and Olive had decided that maybe it was time to move on to something else, something that wouldn't put either of them in a position of potentially being compromised, and one where they could be completely forthcoming with their audience.

So before the year was out, they hoped to sell their new syndicated show, *Time Savers,* and were putting the final touches on a *Time Savers* cookbook and decorating manual. Claire and Olive both planned to appear in the show—at least, that was the plan, though Olive was still working on the whole stage fright thing, Claire knew, and was making great strides in overcoming it—and both their names would be present on the books they'd authored together, since they had authored those books *together*. Both of them.

Because they both had lives now. Lives that were full with family and friends and everything else that made life worth living. Simple things. Pleasant things. And they'd both hit upon a number of original ways to save time for those things. So they were building a business to teach others how to save time for simple pleasures, too.

Ramsey glanced up from his dinner preparations with a smile and reached for an open bottle of wine, to pour a glass for Claire. "We're having coq au vin," he told her as he handed her wine to her.

Claire paled when she remembered what Ramsey had promised to do to Francesca the next time she ruined a pair of his sneakers by using them for pecking practice. "Oh, my God," she gasped. "Where's Francesca?"

Ramsey laughed. "Relax, she's outside." He glanced out

the window over the sink, then back at Claire. "Eating the gladiolas you planned to use in the pilot for *Time Savers*, as a matter of fact."

Claire sighed. "Oh, well. I guess we'll just do the begonias for that segment instead."

"Don't count on it," he told her. "They were the appetizers. And the peonies are dessert. And she also ate a full square yard of blackberries today." He turned back to stir one of the pots simmering on the stove. "So you might want to watch your step if you go out in the garden later."

"No problem. I'm getting really good at tiptoeing through the chicken doo."

And speaking of tiptoeing, she pushed herself up on tiptoe to look over his shoulder at what he was stirring, then was nearly overcome by the spicy aroma of wild rice. Boy, she was hungry. And Ramsey was a really excellent cook.

"So where'd you find a recipe for coq au vin?" she asked as she toed off first one shoe, then the other. Might as well get comfortable. She knew they were home for the night. And nothing made her happier. "You've really come a long way in this husband-and-father stuff," she added. "It hasn't been that long ago that you were making prefab dinners in the microwave all the time. And you hardly ever got out of your sweats those first few weeks after we got married, because Anabel ran you so ragged," she added as she took in—with much pleasure—the tight, berry-colored T-shirt whose sleeves were stretched taut over his barbed-wire tattoo, and the faded jeans that hugged his nether regions so nicely.

He puffed up his chest proudly. "I found the recipe for tonight's dinner in the manuscript for your and Olive's new cookbook. It's very simple and very time-saving." He smiled. "I did not make it from a box. I did not make it in my socks."

He grinned. "But I guess Anabel and I might have read too much Dr. Seuss today."

Claire chuckled, too. She couldn't help it. This whole scenario was just so . . . weird. Big, burly Ramsey Sage cooking coq au vin and wild rice—And was that sweet potatoes she smelled? She loved his sweet potatoes—for his wife and child. This time last year, he would have been way too busy having his head slammed repeatedly into the tequila-stained floor of a bar in Central America to be able to cook supper for his family.

His family, she marveled again. And her family, too. They were one and the same. A ribbon of warm contentment wound through her at the realization that they had both found exactly what they'd searched so long to find, and they'd found it right here, together.

"Are you sure this is what you want to do with the rest of your life?" she asked now, even though Ramsey had already answered the question a million different times, in a million different ways. "Be a househusband?"

He smiled. "I'm not a househusband," he told her. "I'm a homemaker. I make a home. And I defy you to name one vocation that is more important or prestigious than that."

Well, when he put it *that* way . . .

"I love this job, Claire," he assured her. And something in his voice was just so confident, so resolute. "There are benefits I never could have imagined."

Oh, now that was pushing it, she thought. "Like what?" she asked. "You get no retirement, no pension, no medical, no dental, no 401(K). There's not an expense account or a company car. You don't even get minimum wage."

"What, you call those benefits?" he asked. "Pshaw. Those aren't benefits. I get *great* benefits."

She couldn't wait to hear this. "Oh, like what?"

He smiled again, and there was something positively sublime in his expression. "Like how Anabel's face lights up when she sees a butterfly out in the garden. Like how, even if you leave the clean laundry in the laundry basket for hours after you fold it, it's still warm when you go to put it away. Like how, sometimes, when you take a bite of oatmeal, you get a little piece of brown sugar that didn't quite dissolve, and it gives you that extra, unexpected burst of sweetness when you bite into it. Like how your wife's pillow smells like her hair, even when she's not in bed with you, reinforcing the fact that even when she's not around, she's right there with you always." He leaned forward to kiss Claire on the cheek. "Those," he said as he pulled away, "are truly simple pleasures. And if it weren't for you—and Anabel—I never would have had any of them."

Claire smiled as she tucked her hand into his. "You're right," she agreed. And he was.

Because that was the thing about men. Or, at least, that was the thing about this man. He knew a lot about pleasures. And he knew how to keep them simple. And when all was said and done, that really was the best.

Welcome to
Avon Romance Superleader

CONFIDENTIAL!

He has secrets . . . deep, dark
and mysterious . . . but he can't keep
passions hidden for too long . . .

Each month, learn every intimate detail
in the lives of these men . . .
the heroes of the Avon Romance Superleaders.
What makes them tick? What are the things
they don't want anyone to know?

**Following is a preview of four upcoming
Avon Romance Superleaders
written by three of Avon's brightest stars:**
Elizabeth Bevarly in January,
Rachel Gibson in February,
and, in March and April,
a *super special event—*
back-to-back books by Eloisa James.

*So read ahead . . . and discover the innermost secrets
of four outstanding heroes!*

*A*nd they were going to have a lot more to chat about than Claire had initially thought, too. Like how his arrival had made this temporary arrangement with Anabel suddenly seem much less temporary.

"Is Anabel here?" Mr. Sage asked before making a move to enter.

"Not yet," Claire told him. "It's taken nearly a week to get everything worked out with the authorities in North Carolina. But I spoke with the social worker assigned to the case yesterday, and he said he'd be here with her this afternoon. I'm actually expecting them anytime now. It was rather fortuitous that you were located as quickly as you were."

And also rather amazing, especially since no one seemed to know *why* Ramsey Sage had been drunk in a seedy bar in an obscure village in Central America when they found him. Nor did anyone seem to know how he had gotten there. Even Chandler's private detective still had a lot of pieces missing from the puzzle that was Ramsey Sage, because Ramsey Sage himself had evidently been no help at all providing any answers. It was something Claire decided not to think about, mostly because it didn't bode well for his being named Anabel's permanent guardian.

"Please come in," she invited Ramsey Sage again, stepping aside to offer a physical punctuation mark to the invitation.

But he hesitated for a moment, as if he were reluctant to enter. He surveyed what he could see of the big house from his place on the front porch, and when his gaze returned to hers, Claire could see from his expression that he didn't approve. Why he wouldn't approve, she couldn't imagine. It was certainly a vast improvement over the crowded, spartan institution where she'd grown up, and the tiny, spartan apartment she and Olive had shared in college. She'd made the place as warm and inviting as she could, especially on the inside, and she couldn't imagine why anyone—especially a harsh, raggedy, beat-up man like Ramsey Sage—would disapprove.

Although he smiled at her again as he took a step forward, the naturally breezy grin he had displayed a moment ago was gone, and the one he wore now was decidedly more manufactured. Claire tried not to notice how the air around her seemed to come alive as he passed. She couldn't help noticing, though, how he smelled of heavy machinery and raucous man and endless summer nights, a combination she found strangely appealing since she'd never been drawn to any of those things before. Oh, certainly she enjoyed a summer evening as much as the next person, but she couldn't imagine anything that might make one seem endless.

Then Ramsey Sage looked at her again with his smoldering green gaze, and she suddenly had a very good idea indeed what might make a summer night seem to go on forever, an especially graphic, surprisingly explicit idea, in fact, one that had her squirming on her flowered chintz sofa beneath Ramsey Sage, her blouse gaping open, her skirt hiked up over her hips, her brassiere pushed high, her pearl

necklace clenched in his teeth as he tore it from her neck and
sent the perfect little beads scattering across the Oriental rug
and hardwood floors before dragging his hot mouth across
her collarbone and down between her breasts, moving over
to close his lips over one nipple, tugging her inside, laving
her, licking her, tasting her deeply, and then . . . and then . . .
and then . . .

And, good *heavens*, where had such a thought come
from? Claire wondered as she shook the image out of her
brain. Heat flooded her cheeks, and her lips parted in shock,
and she hoped like hell that Ramsey Sage couldn't tell what
she was thinking about. Because not only did Claire normally not think about such things in such detail, she didn't
think about them in mixed company. And she certainly
didn't think about them with men like Ramsey Sage cast in
the role of seducer.

Seducer nothing, she thought as she closed the door behind him, wishing she could close the door on her rampant
thoughts as easily. Ramsey Sage looked like the kind of man
who would take whatever he wanted, whoever he wanted,
whenever he wanted, the rest of the world be damned. And
the wantee, Claire was certain, would go along quite willingly, and when it was over, be left feeling as if she had just
experienced the highest summit of joy.

She followed Mr. Sage into the living room, but following
him left her gazing, however involuntarily, at his backside—
all right, so maybe it wasn't all *that* involuntary—and she
couldn't help noting, dammit, that his backside was every
bit as noteworthy as his front side had been. Because his
faded jeans hugged his taut hindquarters and strong thighs
with much affection, and his denim work shirt strained
against the muscles of his broad back. His arms were nicely
bulked with sinew without being overblown, his biceps and
forearms curving appreciably with muscle, his skin bronzed
and powerful beneath that oddly erotic, barbed-wire tattoo.

And, strangely, Claire found herself wanting to trace the circumference of that tattoo with her fingertips, and oh, my, but that endless-summer-night thing was starting up again, growing more and more graphic and explicit in her mind—and on her body, too, she had to admit—with every passing moment.

Clink, clink, clink went the chains on his boots as he walked.

And *zing* went the strings of her heart.

"Won't you sit down, Mr. Sage?" she said as he continued across the living room to where Chandler stood to greet him upon his arrival. And also as she continued to ogle his backside. "This is Handler, ah, I mean *Chandler*. Chandler Edison. He's my, um . . . my attorney."

Boy, she was really going to have to be careful. Because in addition to misintroducing Chandler by a moniker that had been what Claire was thinking about doing to Mr. Sage's backside, she had almost called Chandler her "buttorney." That would have really been embarrassing.

"Mr. Edison, good to finally meet you," Ramsey Sage said as he approached Chandler, politely extending his hand again, and surprising Claire once more with his manners.

"Mr. Sage," Chandler replied as he shook the proffered hand, though with none of the easiness Ramsey Sage exhibited, and with all of the reluctance one might expect of Chandler, seeing as how he had a nasty aversion to denim.

"Call me Ramsey," Ramsey told Chandler. Then he turned to Claire and added, "You, too, Miss Willoughby."

Claire told herself to extend the same courtesy to him, but something prohibited her. She wasn't sure she could be responsible for her actions if she heard her given name spoken in that dark, velvety baritone of his. So she only nodded her acknowledgment of his comment and decided to skirt the issue as best she could by calling him nothing at all. The last thing she needed to do anyway was slip up and address him as Mr. Hunka Hunka Burnin' Love.

And just what had gotten into her anyway? she demanded of herself. This was getting silly. Ramsey Sage was a walking, talking warning label for decent women everywhere. He was unkempt, unclean, and uncompromising. Not to mention potentially dangerous. She was probably crazy to even invite him into her home, whether he approved of it or not. And she was even crazier to think there was any chance he would be able to care for Anabel. She bit back the panic that began to rise in her throat and wondered what she was supposed to do. If Ramsey Sage couldn't take on the care and feeding of his niece, then who could? Claire certainly didn't want to be responsible for the little girl any longer than she had to be. She didn't know the first thing about children.

How had she gotten into this mess? And more to the point, what was she going to do to get out of it?

Jack Parrish
CONFIDENTIAL!

in *Daisy's Back in Town*
by Rachel Gibson
Coming February 2004

Name: Jackson Lamott Parrish
Nickname: Jack
Hometown: Lovett, Texas
Car: Red '63 T-Bird with red interior
First Kiss: Daisy Lee Brooks . . . in her cute little cheerleader uniform
Super Secret: Has been known to hang out at The Road Kill bar

---

"*M*y my," his voice drawled in the darkness, "if it isn't Daisy Lee Brooks."

It had been fifteen years, and his voice had changed. It was deeper than the boy she'd known, but she would have recognized that nasty tone anywhere. No one could pack as much derision into his voice as Jack. She'd understood it once. Known what lay behind it. She didn't kid herself that she figured him out anymore.

"Hello, Jack."

"What do you want, Daisy?"

She stared at him through the screen and shadows, at the outline of the man she'd once known so well. The knot in her stomach pulled tighter. "I wanted to . . . I need to talk to you. And I thought . . ." She took a deep breath and forced herself to stop stammering. She was thirty-three. So was he. "I wanted to tell you that I was in town before you heard it from someone else."

"Too late." The rain pounded the rooftop and the silence

that stretched between them. She could feel his gaze on her. It touched her face and the front of her yellow rain slicker, and just when she thought he wasn't going to speak again, he said, "If that's what you came to tell me, you can go now."

There was more. A lot more. She'd promised Steven that she'd give Jack a letter he'd written a few months before his death. The letter was in her purse; now she had to tell Jack the truth about what had happened fifteen years ago, then hand over the letter. "It's important that I talk to you. Please."

He looked at her for several long moments, then he turned and disappeared into the depths of his house. He didn't open the screen for her, but he hadn't slammed the wood door in her face, either. He'd made it clear that he was going to be as difficult as possible. But then, when had he ever made things easy?

Just as it always had, the screen door squeaked when she opened it. She followed him through the living room toward the kitchen. His tall outline disappeared around the corner, but she knew the way.

The inside of the house smelled of new paint. She got an impression of dark furniture and a big-screen television. The outline of Mrs. Parrish's piano pushed against one wall, and she wondered briefly how much had changed since she'd last walked through the house. The light flipped on as she moved into the kitchen, and it was like stepping into a time warp. She half expected to see Mrs. Parrish standing in front by the almond-colored stove, baking bread or Daisy's favorite snicker doodle cookies. The green linoleum had the same worn patch in front of the sink and the countertops were the same speckled blue and turquoise.

Jack stood in front of the refrigerator, his top half hidden behind the open door. His tan fingers curled around the chrome handle, and all she could really see was the curve of his behind and his long legs. One pocket of his snug Levi's had a three-corner tear, and the seams looked like they were almost worn through. Adrenaline rushed through her veins, and she balled her hands into fists to keep them from shaking.

Then he rose to his full height, and everything seemed to slow, as if someone flipped a switch on a movie projector. When he turned and shut the refrigerator door, holding a quart of milk in one hand by his thigh, her attention momentarily centered on the thin line of dark hair rising from the waistband of his jeans and circling his navel. She lifted her gaze past the hair on his flat belly and the defined muscles of his chest. If she'd had any lingering doubts, seeing him like this removed them. This was not the boy she'd once known. This was definitely a man.

She forced herself to look up past his strong chin, the etched bow of his tan lips, and into his eyes. She felt the back of her throat go dry. Jack Parrish had always been a good-looking boy, now he was a lethal man. One lock of his thick hair hung over his forehead and touched his brow. Those light-green eyes and long black lashes that she remembered, that had once looked at her so full of passion and possession, watched her as if he were no more interested in seeing her than a stray dog.

"Did you come here to stare?"

She moved farther into the kitchen and shoved her hands into the pockets of her raincoat. "No, I came to tell you that I'm in town visiting my mother and sister."

He raised the milk and drank from the carton, waiting for her to elaborate.

"I thought you should know."

His gaze met hers over the carton, then he lowered it. Some things hadn't changed after all. Jack Parrish, bad boy and all around hell-raiser, had always been a milk drinker. "What makes you think I give a shit?" he asked and wiped the back of his hand across his mouth.

"I didn't know if you would. I mean, I did wonder what you'd think, but I wasn't sure." This was so much harder than she'd envisioned. And what she'd envisioned had been pretty dang hard.

"Now you don't have to wonder." He pointed with his milk carton toward the other room. "If that's all, there's the door."

"No, that's not all." She looked down at the toes of her boots, the black leather spotted by the rain. "Steven wanted me to tell you something. He wanted me to tell you that he's sorry about . . . everything." She shook her head and corrected herself. "No, . . . was sorry, I mean. He's been gone seven months and it's still hard for me to remember him in the past tense. It seems wrong somehow. Like if I do, he never existed." She looked back at Jack. His expression hadn't changed. "The flowers you sent were really nice."

He shrugged and set the milk on the counter. "Penny sent them."

"Penny?"

"Penny Colten. Married Leon Cribs; she works for me now."

Well, Penny hadn't sent them and signed his name without his knowledge. "Thank Penny for me."

"Don't make it a big deal."

She knew how much Steven had once meant to him. "Don't pretend you don't care that he's gone."

He raised a dark brow. "You forget I tried to kill him."

"You wouldn't have killed him, Jack."

"No, you're right. I guess you just weren't worth it."

The conversation was headed in the wrong direction, and she had to turn it around. "Don't be ugly."

"You call this ugly?" He laughed, but not with pleasure. "This is nothing, buttercup. Stick around and I'll show you how ugly I can get."

She already knew how ugly Jack could get, but while she

might be a coward, she was also as stubborn as ragweed. Just as Jack was not the same boy she'd once known, she was not the same girl he'd once known, either. She'd come to tell him the truth. Finally. Before she could get on with the rest of her life, she had to tell him about Nathan. It had taken her fifteen years to get to this point, and he could get ugly all he wanted, but he was going to listen to her.

A flash of white caught the corner of Daisy's eye a second before a woman entered the kitchen wearing a man's white dress shirt.

"Hey y'all," the woman said as she moved to stand by Jack.

He looked down at her. "I told you to stay in bed."

"I got bored without you."

Heat crept up Daisy's neck to her cheeks, but she seemed to be the only embarrassed person in the room. Jack had a girlfriend. Of course he did. He'd always had a girlfriend or two. There had been a time when that would have hurt.

"Hello, Daisy. I don't know if you remember me. I'm Gina Brown."

It didn't hurt any longer, and Daisy was a bit ashamed to admit to herself that what she mostly felt was an overwhelming relief. She'd come all the way from Seattle to tell him about Nathan, and now all she felt was relief. Like an axe had been lifted from her throat. She guessed she was more of a coward than she thought. Daisy smiled and moved across the kitchen to offer Gina her hand. "Of course I remember you. We were in American Government together our senior year."

"Mr. Simmons."

"That's right."

"Remember when he tripped over an eraser on the floor?" Gina asked, as if she weren't standing there wearing Jack's shirt and, Daisy would bet, nothing else.

"That was so funny. I just about—"

"What the hell is this?" Jack interrupted. "A damn high school reunion?"

Both women looked up at him and Gina said, "I was just being polite to your guest."

"She isn't my guest and she's leaving." He pinned his gaze on Daisy, just as cold and unyielding as when she'd first walked in the door.

"It was nice to see you, Gina," she said.

"Same."

"Good night, Jack."

He shoved his hip into the counter and crossed his arms over his chest.

"See you two around." She walked back through the dark house and out the door. The rain had stopped and she dodged puddles on her way to her mother's Caddie parked on the side of the garage. Next time, she would definitely call first.

Just as she reached for the door, she felt a hand on her arm, whipping her around. She looked up into Jack's face. Security lights shined down on him and the angry set of his jaw. His eyes stared into hers, no longer cold but filled with a burning rage.

"I don't know what you came here looking for, absolution or forgiveness," he said, his drawl more pronounced than before, "but you won't find it." He dropped her arm as if he couldn't stand the touch of her.

"Yes, I know."

"Good. You stay away from me, Daisy Lee," he said. "You stay away or I'll make your life a misery."

She looked up into his dark face, at the passion and anger that had not abated in fifteen years.

"Just stay away," he said one last time, before turning on his bare heels and disappearing into the shadows.

She knew she would be wise to heed his warning. Too bad she didn't have that option.

Although he didn't know it yet, neither did he.

Stephen Fairfax-Lacy
CONFIDENTIAL!

in *A Wild Pursuit*
by Eloisa James
Coming March 2004

Name: Stephen Fairfax-Lacy
Nickname: The Puritan
Hometown: London
Car: A sleek carriage with fine horses
(it is the Regency, after all!)
First kiss: A gentleman does not tell such things
Super secret: Would like to begin a scandalous
affair . . .

$\mathcal{T}$he Puritan had arms like steel. He didn't pay a bit of attention to her wiggling, just picked her up and turned her around and then when she looked up at his face, she suddenly stopped protesting.

He didn't kiss like a Puritan. Or an old man either.

He kissed like a hungry man. Bea's first sensation was triumph. So the Puritan had pretended that he didn't notice her charms. Ha! That was all an act. He was just—he was just like—but then somehow, insidiously, she lost her train of thought.

He was kissing her so sweetly, as if she were the merest babe in arms. He didn't even seem to wish to push his tongue into her mouth. Instead he rubbed his lips against hers, danced on her mouth, his hands cupping her head so sweetly that she almost shivered. She quite liked this.

Oh, she felt his tongue. It sung on her lips, patient and tasting like raspberries. Without thinking her own tongue tangled with his for a second. Then she realized what she was doing and clamped her mouth shut. There was nothing she hated more than a man pushing his great tongue where it didn't belong.

But he didn't. He just nibbled her lips and his mouth drifted across her face and pressed her eyes shut, and then closed back on hers with a ravenous hunger that made her soften, ache deep inside.

He probably thinks I'm a virgin, Bea thought in a foggy sort of way.

His mouth was leaving little trails of fire. He was nibbling her ear and she was tingling all over. In fact, she wanted—she wanted him to try again. Come back, she coaxed silently, turning her face toward his lips. Try to kiss *me*, really kiss *me*. But he didn't. Instead his tongue curled around the delicate whorls of her ear, and Bea made a hoarse sound in her throat. He answered it by nipping her earlobe, which sent another twinge deep between her legs.

He tugged her hair and she obediently tipped her face back, eyes closed, and allowed him to taste her throat, all the time begging silently that he return, return, kiss her again . . . But he seemed to be feasting on her throat and he hadn't even tried to touch her breasts. Men *always* . . .

But that was the thought that woke Bea. She hadn't been thinking of grappling in the field when she dressed in the morning. These particular breasts aren't meant to withstand a man's hand. There was more cotton than flesh.

She opened her mouth to say something but at that moment he apparently decided he had tormented her enough and his mouth closed over hers.

She could no more fight that masculine strength than she could rise to her feet. He didn't coax this time; he took, and she gave. And it wasn't like all the other times, when she tolerated a moment or two of this kind of kissing. The Puritan's kiss was dark and sweet and savage all at once. It sent quivers through her legs and made her strain to be closer. His hands moved down her back, assured, possessive. In a moment he would bring them around to her front, and her breasts were aching for . . .

Except those breasts were covered by wads of cotton.

She tore her mouth away, gasping and stared at him. She didn't even think about giving him a seductive glance. She was too stunned.

"I like you when you're like this," he said, and there was that sweetness to his eyes again. He reached out and rubbed some rain from her cheeks. "You look rain-washed and very young. Also rather startled. It seemed to me that you've been inviting kisses. Was I wrong?"

"No," she said, trying hard to think what to say next. All her practiced seductive lines seems to have fled from her head.

"Alas," he said, even more gently, tucking her hair behind her ear. "I can hardly offer marriage to a woman half my age. So I'm afraid that I shall have to leave your kisses, sweet though they are, to some younger man."

Bea's mouth almost fell open. Marriage? Didn't he know who she was? "I don't want—" she began, but her voice was hoarse. She stopped. "As it happens, I am not interested in marriage either," she said quite sedately. "I find that I am, however, very interested in *you*." She twisted forward and kissed his lips, a promise of pleasure. And she was absolutely honest about that. With him, there would be no boundaries.

But it was he who pulled back. She had been so sure he would lunge at her that she smiled—but the smile faded.

He *was* a Puritan. His eyes had gone cold, dark, condemning. "I thought you played the lusty trollop for fun."

She raised her chin. Her chest had gone icy cold. "Actually, no," she said, and she was very pleased to find her tone utterly calm and with just a hint of sarcasm. "I play myself."

"Yourself? Do you even know who you are, under all that facepaint?"

"I assure you that I do."

"You play a part you needn't," he said, eyes fixed on hers. "You are young and beautiful, Beatrix. You should marry and have children."

"I think not."

"Why?"

"You simply want to make me like everyone else," she said sharply. "I like wearing *macquillage*. I would rather not look like *myself*, as you put it. And I find it incalculably difficult to imagine myself sitting by the fire wearing a lace cap and chattering about my brood of children."

"I think *yourself* is beautiful. All your paints have washed away at the moment. You never needed them."

"I didn't say I needed them. I enjoy them," she retorted, and then added, deliberately, "Just as I occasionally enjoy the company of a man in my bedchamber."

For a moment they just looked at each other, Puritan to trollop. "Am I to take it that you are not interested in taking a mistress?" she asked steadily, meeting his eyes. She was no child to be whipped by his condemnation.

"Actually, I am," he said deliberately. "But I have little interest in one so . . . practiced."

Bea got to her feet, shaking out her skirts. Then she bent over and picked up her mangled spencer, shaking it out and folding it over her arm, taking a moment to make absolutely certain that her face wouldn't reveal even for a second what she felt.

Then she looked him straight in the face. "That was cruel, and quite shabby, Mr. Fairfax-Lacy. I would not have expected it of you."

"I'm sorry."

She nodded and began to turn toward the gate. After all, she'd had much worse things said to her, mostly by women, but then there was her dear father. So when he caught her arm, she turned toward him with a little smile that was almost genuine.

"Don't you think we should take our bedraggled selves home?"

It was rather amusing to see how badly he felt. There was real anguish in his eyes. "I feel like the worst sort of bastard. Kissing you in a field and then insulting you."

At that, she grinned. "I gather you wish I were an innocent, Mr. Fairfax-Lacy. But I am not. I truly enjoyed that kiss." The smile she gave him was as wicked and lazy as any she'd ever bestowed on a man. "And I would very much have enjoyed your company in my bedchamber as well. But I have never forced myself on a man. I fully understand that you are looking for a far more respectable mistress. Perhaps even a possible marriage partner, given your wish for inexperience?"

Men were such dolts! He stared at her as if she were as alien as that hairy goat.

"It was a lovely kiss," she said. Then she turned and made her way across the field, and when the goat rolled his wicked eyes and snapped his lips over a Pomona green satin ribbon, all that remained of her bonnet, she just smiled at him.

Which startled the animal so much that he galloped off to the other end of the field, leaving her hat behind.

Rees, Lord Godwin
CONFIDENTIAL!

in *Your Wicked Ways*
by Eloisa James
Coming April 2004

Name: Rees, Lord Godwin
Nickname: The Sinner
Hometown: London
Conveyance: Anything that he can ride fast
First Kiss: He'd rather think about his *best* kiss
Super secret: He's developed a passion for his own wife . . .

"*I* had no idea that this part of Hyde Park existed," Helene said with fascination, a short time later. The grasses to either side of the little winding path had grown so tall that they touched the slouching limbs of the huge oaks. Daisies poked their heads above the seas of grasses like intrepid soldiers, fighting off nettles and thistles growing breast high.

"I've never met another soul here," Rees said. "All the polite sort prefer raked gravel paths."

Sometimes the oak trees bent down as if they'd been humbled, brushing their branches to the ground, and then suddenly they would fall back, leaving a patch of emerald green grass, or a cascade of daisies. Within twenty minutes, she could no longer hear any din from the city at all, no sound of carriages, bells, or whistles. "It's like being in the country," she said, awed.

They rounded the bend and the trees trailed off again, forming another clearing. "Just look, Rees! Aren't they beautiful?" she cried, running into the middle of a lake of frothy white flowers shaped like stars.

Rees stood on the path, his face unreadable. The sun fell relentlessly on his harsh face, on the lines around his eyes, the scowling eyebrows, the generous lower lip, those two dimples . . .

And Helene realized with a great thump of her heart that she'd never gotten over that first infatuation with him, that first blinding passion that had driven her out of her bed chamber window, and into his carriage, the better to make their way to Gretna Green.

She almost dropped the flowers she held, the realization was so blinding.

When Rees appeared at her side, hamper in hand and sat next to her on the grass, Helene couldn't even bring herself to speak. She'd spent nine years telling herself that the brief infatuation that led to their elopement was a dream, a fribble, a moment's blindness.

But it wasn't. Oh, it wasn't.

Numbly she helped Rees pull a tablecloth from the basket and load it with pieces of chicken, pie, fruit, and a bottle of wine.

She refused a glass of wine. "Hair of the dog," Rees said, "and very nice hair it is." He grinned at her. He had a chicken leg in his hand and was eating it like a savage. And he had that wicked look about him again, the one that made her think about the muscles hidden by his white shirt.

To her surprise, Helene found that she was hungry. She put a plate of chicken on her knee and began struggling to cut it properly.

"Don't bother," Rees said lazily. He was lying on his side, looking twice as comfortable in a bed of flowers as he did in a drawing room. "Just eat it, Helene."

She looked at him with disdain. "I don't eat with my fingers. I discarded that habit in the nursery."

"Who's to see? There's only you and I, and we're nothing more than an old married couple."

Old married couple implied comfort and ease, and she didn't feel any of that with Rees, particularly with the secret prickling awareness she had of his body. He had removed his jacket and rolled up his sleeve and his bronzed arm lay all too close to her. "It seems to me that you are always removing your clothing," she told him, eyeing him with distinct hostility. How dare he be so comfortable, while she was both over-heated and hungry? Her beautiful little blue jacket felt altogether winterish with the sun shining on her back.

In answer, he sat up. Helene edged back. Rees was overpowering at close quarters. "Here," he said simply, holding the chicken leg to her lips.

"I couldn't!" But she hadn't eaten all day. Her stomach gave a little gurgle.

Rees laughed. "Go ahead. There's no one to see."

"You're here," she said mulishly.

"I don't count," he said, giving her an oddly intent look. "That's one of the nicer things about being married, I always thought."

She took a bite. The chicken was delicious, faintly reminiscent of lemon. "It's exquisite," she admitted, taking another bite.

"I pay my cook one hundred guineas a year," Rees said, ripping off a little strip of chicken and bringing it to her lips.

When she didn't open her mouth immediately, he rubbed the chicken on her lip. "Oh my, your lips are greasy," he said, leaning closer.

"Oh!" Helene said, licking her lips.

"Very nice," Rees said, and there was a dark, velvety something in his voice that made the little coil in Helene's stomach grow tighter.

"Give me a real kiss, Rees," she said.

His hand was stroking her neck. It froze for a moment.

"Do you remember how you used to kiss me before we were married?" she asked.

"Aye," he said, "I must have been a beast, always pulling you into a corner. . . ."

"I loved it," Helene admitted.

"You never—"

"Ladies don't."

But Rees had clear memories of his wife refusing to kiss him with an open mouth, telling him he was disgusting to want such a thing. He hesitated. Their newfound friendship was so fragile and (although he didn't really want to think such a thing) important to him. He didn't . . .

So she came to him. The wife who hated kissing opened her mouth and timidly, sweetly, begged for entrance.

Rees had always known he was no gentleman. And he'd known for years that he had no control around his wife either. Nothing seemed to have changed. He plunged into her mouth so violently that she toppled backwards into a bed of flowers and he came with her, his limbs tangling with hers, devouring her mouth.

All the while, some part of him was waiting for her to tear her mouth away, to push him away, to scream that he was depraved, disgusting . . .

But the only thing that happened was that slender arms wound around his neck and a slender body tucked itself into the hard curves of his body with such melting softness that he could barely stop himself from groaning with the pure delight of it.

RITA Award winner and *USA Today* bestselling author of *See Jane Score*

"What a find!" —Jayne Ann Krentz

RACHEL GIBSON

XOXOXOXOXO XOXOXOXOXO

DAISY'S
BACK in Town

Daisy Lee Monroe thought she'd left dusty Lovett, Texas—and bad boy Jackson Lamott Parrish—behind for good. But now she's back, and it seems nothing has changed. Especially Jackson. He's still so sexy it hurts. Daisy would love to avoid him but she's got something to say. As for Jackson, he's determined to keep her quiet any way he can. Yet kissing Daisy had once been his downfall. Now he's got to find out if he's strong enough to resist her—or to make her stay.

Buy and enjoy DAISY'S BACK IN TOWN (available January 27, 2004), then send the coupon below along with your proof of purchase for DAISY'S BACK IN TOWN to Avon Books, and we'll send you a check for $2.00.

- -

Carnival Elation

7 Day Exotic Western Caribbean Itinerary

DAY	PORT	ARRIVE	DEPART
Sun	Galveston		4:00 P.M.
Mon	"Fun Day" at Sea		
Tue	Progreso/Merida	8:00 A.M.	4:00 P.M.
Wed	Cozumel	9:00 A.M.	5:00 P.M.
Thu	Belize	8:00 A.M.	6:00 P.M.
Fri	"Fun Day" at Sea		
Sat	"Fun Day" at Sea		
Sun	Galveston	8:00 A.M.	

TERMS AND CONDITIONS

PAYMENT SCHEDULE:
50% due upon booking
Full and final payment due by July 26, 2004

Acceptable forms of payment are Visa, MasterCard, American Express, Discover and checks. The cardholder must be one of the passengers traveling. A fee of $25 will apply for all returned checks. Check payments must be made payable to **Advantage International, LLC** and sent to: **Advantage International, LLC, 195 North Harbor Drive, Suite 4206, Chicago, IL 60601**

CHANGE/CANCELLATION:
Notice of change/cancellation must be made in writing to Advantage International, LLC.

Change:
Changes in cabin category may be requested and can result in increased rate and penalties. A name change is permitted 60 days or more prior to departure and will incur a penalty of $50 per name change. Deviation from the group schedule and package is a cancellation.

Cancellation:

181 days or more prior to departure	$250 per person
121 - 180 days or more prior to departure	50% of the package price
120 - 61 days prior to departure	75% of the package price
60 days or less prior to departure	100% of the package price (nonrefundable)

US and Canadian citizens are required to present a valid passport or the original birth certificate and state issued photo ID (drivers license). All other nationalities must contact the consulate of the various ports that are visited for verification of documentation.

We strongly recommend trip cancellation insurance!

For further details call 1-877-ADV-NTGE or visit www.GetCaughtReadingatSea.com

- -

For booking form and complete information
go to **www.getcaughtreadingatsea.com** or call **1-877-ADV-NTGE**

Complete coupon and booking form and mail both to:
**Advantage International, LLC,
195 North Harbor Drive, Suite 4206, Chicago, IL 60601**